TEST OF WILLS

Myn Donos, the X-wing squadron commander, looked around in confusion. This wasn't right. He'd been through this already. This mission could only lead to . . .

Death.

The ambush. They were all about to die.

"Talon Leader to squad, break off! Omega Signal!" He rolled up on his port wing and curved in a tight arc. Away from death.

The other Talons did not follow. They sped down their destined path toward annihilation.

"Leader to group! Break off! Follow me!"

A woman's voice: "Can't do it, sir."

"Follow me. That's an order!"

"No sir. What does it matter whether I die down there or on the way out?"

Donos continued his arc until he completed a full circle. He now sped on in the wake of his pilots, heedlessly rushing toward their doom. He felt an unfamiliar weight crushing his chest. It wasn't acceleration; it was the inevitability of those pilots' needless deaths. *"Please."*

"Don't 'please' me, Lieutenant. You don't care enough about yourself to live. So you don't give a damn about us."

"You're wrong. Turn back."

"Swear it."

"I swear it! Turn back!"

The canopy of his X-wing went black and the roar of his engines died. . . .

STAR WARS

X-WING

BOOK FIVE

WRAITH SQUADRON

Aaron Allston

BANTAM BOOKS
New York Toronto London Sydney Auckland

STAR WARS: WRAITH SQUADRON
A Bantam Spectra Book / February 1998

ISBN-0-553-57894-4

Published simultaneously in the United States and Canada

Bantam Books are published by Bantam Books, a division of Bantam
Doubleday Dell Publishing Group, Inc. Its trademark, consisting of
the words "Bantam Books" and the portrayal of a rooster, is
Registered in U.S. Patent and Trademark Office and in other
countries. Marca Registrada. Bantam Books, 1540 Broadway, New
York, New York 10036.

PRINTED IN THE UNITED STATES OF AMERICA

OPM   10 9 8 7 6 5 4 3 2 1

Acknowledgments

Thanks go to:

Tom Dupree, Pat LoBrutto, and Michael A. Stackpole, for the opportunity;

Steven S. Long, Bob Quinlan, and Luray Richmond, my "Eagle-Eyes," who protect me from the worst of my mistakes;

Michael A. Stackpole, Kathy Tyers, Dave Wolverton, and Timothy Zahn, from whose fiction I have been able to draw details and inspiration;

Shane Johnson, Paul Murphy, Peter Schweighofer, Bill Slavicsek, Bill Smith, Curtis Smith, and Dan Wallace, for the invaluable resources they have written;

Sue Rostoni and Lucy Wilson, for making the approval process a pleasure;

Quel Richmond, for being inspirationally big, handsome, and cowardly; and

Denis Loubet, Mark and Luray Richmond, my roommates, for not casting me out into the cold when writer's mania and deadline pressures made it an appropriate option.

The Wraiths

Commander Wedge Antilles (human male from Corellia)

Lieutenant Wes Janson (human male from Taanab)

Lieutenant Myn Donos (human male from Corellia)

Jesmin Ackbar (Mon Calamari female from Mon Calamari)

Hohass "Runt" Ekwesh (Thakwaash male from Thakwaa)

Garik "Face" Loran (human male from Pantolomin)

Ton Phanan (human male from Rudrig)

Falynn Sandskimmer (human female from Tatooine)

Voort "Piggy" saBinring (Gamorrean male from Gamorr)

Tyria Sarkin (human female from Toprawa)

Kell Tainer (human male from Sluis Van)

Eurrsk "Grinder" Thri'ag (Bothan male from Bothuwai)

Rogue Squadron Support Personnel

Cubber Daine (human male from Corellia, squad mechanic)

Chunky (Tyria's R5 unit)

Gadget (Phanan's R2 unit)

Gate (Wedge's R5 unit)

Shiner (Donos's R2 unit)

Squeaky (3PO unit, squadron quartermaster)

Thirteen (Kell's R2 unit)
Vape (Face's R2 unit)

New Republic Military

General Edor Crespin (human male from Corulag)
Captain Choday Hrakness (human male from Agamar)
Lieutenant Atril Tabanne (human female from Coruscant)
Dorset Konnair (human female from Coruscant)
Tetengo Noor (human male from Churba)

Zsinj's Forces

Warlord Zsinj (human male from Fondor)
Admiral Apwar Trigit (human male from Coruscant)
Captain Zurel Darillian (human male from Coruscant)
Lieutenant Gara Petothel (human female from Coruscant)

1

Twelve X-wing snubfighters roared down into the atmosphere.

The world below, Coruscant, former throne world of the Empire, was an unbroken landscape of urban construction, a vast city reaching from pole to pole, blanketed by gray clouds shot through with white and yellow flashes of lightning.

The squadron commander, piloting a black fighter with an incongruously cheerful green and gold checkerboard pattern on the bow, shook his head over the grim vista of the world below. Even after all the time he'd spent here—even after the crucial role he'd played in conquering this world for the New Republic—he still could not get used to the arrogance of Coruscant. It was a world that could only rule or perish, for it produced nothing but soldiers, officers, and bureaucrats, and could not feed its population without importing massive quantities of food from around the galaxy.

He took a visual scan of his immediate surroundings. "Rogue Three, tighten up. We're putting on a show here."

A green X-wing closed in tighter to the formation. "Yes, sir." Though distorted by the comm system, the voice sounded indulgent rather than military.

"That's 'Yes, *Wedge*' until we're formally returned to duty." The commander smiled. "Or perhaps, 'Yes, Exalted One.' Or 'Yes, O envy of all Corellia.' Or—"

A chorus of groans interrupted him. The voice of Nawara Ven, the squadron's Twi'lek executive officer, cut through it: "Stop complaining. He's earned his little vacation from reality."

Then the voice of Tycho Celchu, Wedge's second-in-command, sharp and military: "Sensors register a squadron of fighters rising toward us. Speed is X-wing or better; sensor profiles suggest X-wings."

"Maintain formation," Wedge said, then switched his comm unit over from squadron frequency to New Republic military frequency. "Rogue Squadron to approaching X-wing formation, please identify yourselves."

The voice responding was brisk, amused, and familiar. "Wrong designations, sir. *We're* Rogue Squadron. You're simply a rogue *squadron*. But for the next few minutes we'll do you the courtesy of designating ourselves Red Squadron to avoid confusion. We're your escort."

"Hobbie? Is that you, Lieutenant Klivan?"

"That's *Captain* Klivan . . . again, just for the next few minutes."

The other X-wing unit rose into view, gradually attaining the altitude of Wedge's squadron. Wedge was startled to see that the dozen snubfighters were painted in Rogue Squadron's traditional red stripes and twelve-pointed insignia. "Hobbie, explain this."

"No time, sir. We have a course change for you. High Command has decided to broadcast this entire event across the HoloNet—"

"Oh, no."

"—so set your new course to ninety-three, follow my rate of descent, and we'll get you there in one piece. After that, you're on your own."

Within moments their destination was clear: Imperial Plaza, a ground-level ferrocrete circle so broad that in spite of the surrounding skyscrapers, it could be seen from high in the air at angles other than directly overhead. The plaza was packed with spectators; even at this altitude Wedge could see banners and fluttering haze that looked like chaff but had to be some sort of celebratory confetti.

A speakers platform had been erected on the plaza's west side, with barricaded open areas north and south of it—obvious landing zones for the two squadrons.

As they descended toward the plaza, Wedge flipped his comm system back to the squadron channel. "Once around the park, outbound port, return starboard, at five hundred, Rogues. They're here for a show; let's give them one."

Immediately he heard Hobbie's answer on the same channel: "Same, Reds, but starboard to port return at six hundred meters. Sloppiest flight group buys drinks."

The two squadrons parted, circling the plaza at its perimeter, the wingtips of the X-wings sometimes only meters from the faces of admirers piled up against the skyscraper windows. The squadrons crossed one another's positions on the far side of the plaza and rejoined at their first position, then spiraled down toward the landing zones.

Rogue Squadron angled toward the northern area, Red Squadron toward the southern. At three hundred meters, Wedge said, "Landing gear and repulsorlifts, people," and both squadrons began the safe, vertical descents allowed by the snubfighters' antigravity engines.

Wedge smiled. "Your Red Squadron looks pretty good, Hobbie. A pity you haven't had time to teach them anything about precision flying."

"What?"

"Rogue Squadron, Three Diamonds Parade Formation, execute!"

After a moment's hesitation—it had been some time since the unit had practiced the intricate parade formations—the Rogues split into their three flight groups, each group maneuvering into a diamond-shaped formation—one X-wing forward, one back, the two others side by side in the middle—with Wedge's group forward and the other two side by side behind, making a triangle of diamonds, all facing eastward.

Even over the sound of the repulsorlifts, Wedge could hear the cheers from the crowd.

Hobbie's voice came back immediately: "Red Squadron, same maneuver, but one-eighty to their orientation." He sounded amused rather than angry. And in moments his squadron was in the same Three Diamonds Formation, but his X-wings faced west.

More cheers—the crowd was going wild over the aerial demonstration.

"A little wobbly, Hobbie."

"We haven't been together that long, Wedge, but we still know a few tricks. And *you* started this. Red Group Three, deny Rogue Group One!"

The three-fighter triangle to Hobbie's starboard rear broke away from the Red Squadron formation, sideslipped and reversed orientation while maintaining the same internal order, and came into position a mere ten meters beneath Wedge's group, descending toward the spot where Wedge would have landed.

"Not bad, Hobbie. Rogue Group Two, deny Red Group One!"

Corran Horn, in his green X-wing with the black and white trim, led his group in a similar maneuver and positioned them directly beneath Hobbie Klivan's group.

"You mynock. Red Group Two, deny Rogue Group Three!"

"Rogue Group One, substitute Red Two!"

The two squadrons' flight groups crisscrossed above the speakers platform as they descended, a dazzling display of precision flying, until, when all were a mere ten meters above the ground, Rogue Squadron was reassembled over the southern landing zone, Red Squadron over the northern. The two dozen snubfighters set down within moments of one another.

Their pilots climbed down from their cockpits into a whirlwind of celebration: New Republic diplomats and old friends dragging them up onto the speakers platform, clouds of confetti raining down from the skyscrapers ringing the plaza, roars of appreciation and exuberance from the thousands in the plaza. Wedge managed to get handshakes and backslaps from Hobbie and Red Squadron's second-in-command, Wes Janson, before being dragged into line formation with all the pilots; the crowd's roar was too overwhelming to allow them to hear one another's words.

At the front of the platform, at the speakers lectern, stood the New Republic Provisional Council's best-loved speaker, Princess Leia Organa of Alderaan. Unlike most of the New Republic's representatives present, she was dressed simply, in a belted robe of senatorial white. She caught Wedge's eye and gave him a smile and half shake of the head, acknowledging their mutual dislike of public spectacles such as this, then turned back toward the crowd.

With a few waves of her hand she managed to reduce the crowd's roar to the point her amplified voice could be heard above it. "Citizens of the New Republic, I present to you Rogue Squadron!" Another protracted roar, and then she continued, "Before I bring Commander Antilles up to speak, I think I should put the squadron's recent accomplishments in perspective. With their efforts, we now have, once again, a steady supply of bacta—a supply sufficient to stamp out the last lingering effects of the Krytos Plague. With their efforts—"

Wedge tuned her out. This was all old news to him. Weeks before, he'd led Rogue Squadron—the true Rogue Squadron, the men and women now in civilian dress—on a mission that the New Republic military command could not support. Resigning their commissions, the members of Rogue Squadron and a handful of professional insurgents had mounted a civilian action against the new government of the world of Thyferra, the world where the overwhelming majority of bacta, the miracle medicine, was produced. That new government was headed by the Empire's former espionage leader, Ysanne Isard, and could have become the core of a reunited Empire.

But now Ysanne Isard was dead, and Rogue Squadron's resignations had apparently been creatively misfiled—meaning that they were never civilians—meaning that, with the mission's success, the New Republic was retroactively making the Thyferran mission an officially sanctioned operation.

None of which explained the presence of a new Rogue Squadron flying the unit's traditional colors. Wedge traded places with Tycho, his second-in-command, to stand beside Hobbie Klivan. "So tell me about this ersatz Rogue Squadron."

The pilot with the perpetually mournful face shook his head. "It's not ersatz. Just sort of auxiliary. For morale purposes, the Alliance needed a visible Rogue Squadron while you were off playing pirate. So they brought me and Wes back from training-squad duty to cobble together a temporary Rogue Squadron."

"Temporary."

Hobbie nodded. "We brought in some Rogue Squadron veterans—Riemann, Scotian, Carithlee, several more—and a couple of new pilots each out of Gauntlet and Corsair Squadrons. Now that you're back, they all return to their original units. *Except—*"

"Except what?"

"Except me and Wes. We're back for good. Subject to your approval. That's the reward we were unofficially promised by High Command."

"Well, I'll think about it." At Hobbie's stricken look, Wedge smiled. "I'm kidding you. Welcome home. Is Gauntlet Squadron active? I thought they were still in diapers."

"You're behind the times. Corsair was our first squadron, Gauntlet our second, and our third, Talon, was just commissioned."

"Who's commanding?"

"Lieutenant Myn Donos. A good pilot, smart—"

Lieutenant Wes Janson, still baby-faced despite his years flying for the Alliance and New Republic, leaned in grinning from Hobbie's other side. "Smart, egotistical, self-centered, arrogant, insufferable—you know, a typical Corellian."

"As a fair, broad-minded officer, I should ignore that. But as a Corellian, of course, I'll manage some sort of revenge." Wedge turned back to Hobbie. "Before your Rogues are disbanded, I want to see their personnel files."

"Of course. Why? If I can ask."

"You can. I have an idea for another new X-wing unit

. . . something based on our experiences taking Coruscant and Thyferra."

"You're going to form a new squadron?"

Wedge nodded.

"Just like that? Wave your hand and it appears?"

"Well, I thought I'd tell High Command so they'll know what they need to give me."

Hobbie shook his head. "Wes, you were right. All Corellians are like that. Oh, Wedge, the princess—"

Wedge realized belatedly that Leia had called his name and was beckoning to him. He put on his meet-the-crowd smile and advanced, stopping a pace short of the lectern, taking Leia's outstretched hand.

She gave him her most infectious grin, the private smile she never turned to crowds or official assemblies. She spoke quietly enough that her words would not carry to the amplifiers. "You looked as though you'd been practicing that formation flying for weeks."

"We were," he said, straight-faced. "Liberating Thyferra didn't take up much of our time."

"You're such a liar. Go talk to these people so we can all go home."

Twelve X-wing snubfighters roared down into the atmosphere.

This was a dark world with a polluted sky, its atmosphere formed from gases and smoke hurled from hundreds of active volcanoes. Four kilometers ahead, the TIE interceptor, fastest fighter of the Imperial forces, was distantly visible; it stayed well ahead of the X-wings, though the fact that it was not now outrunning them was a clear indication that its engines were damaged. Further evidence were the sparks and gouts of smoke issuing from its engines, too far away to see except with visual sensors; if the engines failed, the pursuing X-wings could catch the interceptor.

Myn Donos, the X-wing squadron commander, toggled his comm system. "Talon Leader to Talon Eight, any change?"

His communications specialist answered, "No, sir. He's not broadcasting. As far as I can tell, he's not homing in on any sort of a signal. And I'm still not picking up any engine emissions, other than his or ours, on the scanners."

"Very well."

The interceptor's speed suddenly dropped and the vehicle began bobbing as if hit by heavy turbulence. It lost altitude, veering to starboard toward a cleft between two enormous volcanoes. Talon Leader saw glittering orange threads of lava crawling down the near slope of one of the black, fire-capped mountains.

"Leader to squad, it looks like he's losing thrust and going low to lose us with terrain-following flying. Don't give him the opportunity. Get close and force him down." He led his squadron in a lazy arc toward the same gap. He watched the numbers changing on his distance-to-target register: three kilometers, two point five; the interceptor was now emerging from the gap on the far side as the X-wings were entering it.

Talon Eight's voice broke, high-pitched and nervous, over the comm system: "Engines powering up, sir! Directly ahead! I count four, seven, thirteen—"

"S-foils to attack position!" Donos shouted. "Scatter and—"

Shiner, his R2 unit, issued a sharp squeal of alarm. Donos's console echoed it with beeps and indicators showing that someone ahead had a sensor lock on him—two locks— *three* locks—

Donos veered sharply to port—directly toward a volcanic flue and the impenetrable stream of gray-black smoke belching from it. As he hit the cloud he pulled back on the stick, rising straight up the concealing smoke. The sensor locks on him disappeared.

He heard explosions, some near, some far, and the excited comm chatter of his pilots. He added to it: "Talon Two, go skyward in the smoke screen; we'll hit them from above."

No answer.

There was other comm traffic: "Five, Five, he's on your tail!" "Can't get clear, vape him for me, Six—" "Can't, I've got—I've got—" "Nine banked into the volcano wall, she's gone—" Another explosion.

Moments later, at two thousand meters Donos angled to starboard, getting clear of the smoke and emerging directly over the gap between volcanoes.

No one was on his tail. He checked the sensor board—didn't believe what it showed him, checked it again.

He and Talon Twelve were the only New Republic forces remaining on the board. He counted twenty-three, twenty-four, twenty-*five* Imperial blips. A dozen were veering toward Twelve, the remainder toward Donos.

In a matter of seconds, Talon Squadron had been all but destroyed. Glittering pieces of X-wings were still streaming down toward the planet's broken surface. In another few seconds, he and Twelve would be vaped, and the destruction would be complete.

Through the shock of it, he said, "Talon Twelve, dive for the surface. Trench Run Defense. Omega Signal. Acknowledge."

"Omega Signal understood. Diving." The sensor register on Talon Twelve showed decreasing altitude. Donos followed suit, standing his X-wing on its nose and blasting toward the ground.

He hadn't even gotten a shot off at the enemy. Ten pilots dead and he had a full rack of proton torpedoes left, laser batteries charged to full. Time to change that.

The sensors showed an ominous cloud of TIE fighters—eyeballs, in Alliance fighter-jock parlance—pursuing Twelve toward the ground. If she reached the planet's broken surface, which was pocked with craters and crisscrossed with rifts, she might be able to elude them; there, her piloting skill rather than the relative speeds of the fighters could allow her to lose pursuit, and any pilot who tried to follow her from above would quickly lose sight of her—this was the classic Trench Run Defense used against the first Death Star. But for now, Twelve would remain within the enemy's weapons range for long, deadly seconds.

Within moments his sensors indicated that he was coming within range of the weapons of the rising cloud of TIE fighters. He switched his lasers over to dual fire, giving him greater recycling speed, and put the rest of his discretionary power on forward shields, then began firing as quickly as his targeting computer gave him the bracket color changes and pure audible tones of good target locks. He put his X-wing into a corkscrew descent, making it harder for him to hit his enemies, but making it much harder for them to hit him.

Most of his shots hit the ground. One missed his intended target but vaped its wingman. Two more shots hit their intended targets, one shearing off a wing and sending the fighter spinning into the nearest volcanic mountainside, the other having no immediate effect Donos could see— but the TIE fighter ceased all evasive maneuvering, its flight path becoming an easy-to-calculate ballistic curve. Donos almost smiled: It had been a surgical strike, the pilot killed by a beautiful shot straight into the cockpit, leaving the rest of the fighter craft unharmed.

His assault had its desired effect. The oncoming cloud of TIEs spread out and he shot through the gap in the center of their formation. They wheeled, an angry insect cloud, to follow, but now the TIEs pursuing Twelve into the rugged terrain below were in sight. Donos continued firing, vaping one starfighter before the others knew he was upon them; that fighter's wingman, startled by the sudden explosion, reflexively banked rightward, directly into the side of the rift in which they were flying. His fighter also detonated, filling the rift with flame and shrapnel.

Donos dropped into the rift, pulling out of his dive just before he could scrape his keel on the ground. He had stone formations to either side of him—black rock so blurry from his speed that he could make out no details. "Leader to Twelve, report condition," he said.

"Minor damage to lower port strike foil," she answered. "It's giving me a little vibration, which should go away if we can get out of atmosphere. Some starring on the canopy. Pursuit is hanging back— Wait, here comes one! He's trying to get a lock on me!"

Donos put on more speed, increasing the risk that he would not be able to make some difficult turn ahead. He whipped around a bend in the rift and almost slammed into the ion engines of a slow-moving TIE fighter immediately ahead. He snapped off a laser shot out of reflex, saw it lance straight into the starfighter's starboard engine.

The TIE fighter instantly became a glowing fireball of yellow and orange flame and debris. Donos's X-wing rocked as he roared through the fireball; his helmet and hull were barely sufficient to keep the sound of the explosion from deafening him. Then he was through.

One more turn, a tight starboard bank that almost flung him into the rock wall to port, and he had Twelve in sight. Twelve, and the vehicle pursuing her—the interceptor that had led them into this trap. This was the first time Donos had seen it visually, and he fleetingly noted the nonstandard red stripes painted horizontally on the starfighter's wing arrays before something else occurred to him: there were no sparks or smoke plumes emerging from its engines now. With the deception done, all the false signs of the interceptor's weakness had been shut off.

The interceptor had crept up to within meters of Twelve's aft end and was now skillfully matching all of the X-wing pilot's frantic maneuvers. This was a demonstration of superior flying technique, a show of contempt by one pilot for his enemy, and there was no doubt that the interceptor could begin firing on the defenseless Twelve at any second.

Donos fired off a desperate snap-shot. At the same moment, the interceptor took its kill shot.

Donos saw his lasers strike and play across the interceptor's main body, slashing across the engines and burning into the cockpit.

The interceptor's lasers intersected at Twelve's X-wing, hitting her aft shields in spite of her desperate maneuvers . . . and then they penetrated. Both of Twelve's starboard engines flamed out. The starboard strike foils, softened by the lasers' intense heat, began to deform under atmospheric friction.

The interceptor slowed. Sparks and flame, real ones now, issued from the engines. It rose, jumping out of the rocky rift, and was immediately lost to Donos's sight.

Twelve's X-wing began a portward roll. Donos's next command was half a shout: "Twelve, bail out! Twelve, eject!"

"Ejecting now! Leader, get out of here!"

Donos watched helplessly as Twelve's cockpit filled with the fire of an ejection thruster, but the canopy failed to open. The ejector seat smashed Twelve into it. Its transparisteel construction kept the canopy in one piece as the X-wing continued to rotate to port. Under continued pressure from the thrust of the ejection seat, the cockpit finally broke away from the X-wing, but Twelve sat limp in the seat as the ejection seat carried her mere meters from the doomed snubfighter, slamming her into the rift wall to port. In a split second she was gone, lost behind Donos, and her X-wing was nosing over to crash into the rift wall below.

Donos forced himself to look away, to return his mind to mission parameters.

A few minutes of terrain-following flying and he should be able to jump free of these rifts and head for space. But suddenly the prospect of survival didn't appeal much to him.

Donos's R2 shrieked at him. Startled back to attention, he looked around, saw that a pair of TIE fighters had gained on him during his reverie.

He could stay and be killed, or flee and describe his failure to his commanders in cruel, humbling detail.

He'd prefer to die. But the families of eleven good men and women deserved to know how their loved ones had met their fates. With an anguished cry, Donos hit the thrusters again and rounded the next turn.

2

The New Republic guard, his face as emotionless as a ferrocrete bunker, admitted Wedge to the office. Within, the walls were a soothing blue, the furniture smooth and rounded with colors of the sea, the air cool but uncomfortably moist. Still, Wedge was back in New Republic uniform, and that alone made him more comfortable than the office's environment conditioner could have.

Behind the desk, Admiral Ackbar, commander in chief of the New Republic's military operations, returned Wedge's salute. Like other Mon Calamari, with their outsized heads and rubbery skins, he looked to most people like a bipedal and intellectual fish, but Wedge knew him to be far more humane and courageous than many who fought for the New Republic.

Ackbar gestured toward the visitors' chairs. "Commander Antilles. Please, sit. Is it too humid for you? I can make adjustments."

"Not at all." Wedge took the seat indicated. "Thank you for making time in your schedule for me so soon."

"It is not an imposition." Ackbar leaned closer, focusing on Wedge, his two widely separated eyes sometimes moving independently. "I see no signs of hangover on you, Commander. Must I conclude that you did not celebrate adequately?"

Wedge smiled. "Very adequately. Meeting old friends and new, old Rogues and new, and telling stories until we couldn't string two words together. But I left the heavy drinking to the younger pilots."

"Wise of you. Younger pilots. I notice I did not recognize all their names."

"Rogue Squadron is catching up from attrition, sir. At the end of the Thyferran mission we were down a few pilots. Since then, we've brought our numbers up again. We're still one pilot light, but Aril Nunb rejoined us temporarily for yesterday's celebration."

"I'm sure you will employ your customary skill in finding extraordinary replacements. Well, allow me the impatience of office. What brings you to me? Your message hinted at—what was it? 'Recommendations for a new type of unit, particularly well suited to the search for Warlord Zsinj.' "

"That's correct." Warlord Zsinj, a onetime Imperial admiral still in possession of a Super Star Destroyer, an eight-kilometer warship capable of pounding a planetary surface flat, was now the New Republic's most important military objective. His hit-and-run missions against New Republic sites were increasing in bold effectiveness and destructiveness, and the danger that he might assume Ysanne Isard's role as the center of an Imperial resurgence was not an empty one. "I'd like to form a new X-wing group, sir."

Admiral Ackbar's mouth bent in an approximation of a smile. A learned behavior—Mon Calamari did not communicate amusement that way. But Ackbar was well versed in human body language. "Rogue Squadron is no longer good enough for you?"

"Rogue Squadron will *always* be good enough for me, sir. But in the last several years I've bumped repeatedly into a glaring weakness in our military. I've tried to address it before and want to try again."

"Please elaborate."

Wedge leaned back, settling in for a lengthy discussion.

"You'll remember when I reorganized Rogue Squadron a few years back, I took the best pilots I could transfer or steal . . . but when it came down to choosing between pilots of equal skill, I always chose the one who had useful ground-based skills as well."

"Yes. You wanted pilots who could also be commandos."

"I got them. And they got quite a workout as commandos, especially in the liberation of Coruscant from the Empire and then of Thyferra from Ysanne Isard."

Ackbar managed to smile again. "You have certainly justified our faith in your experiment. Rogue Squadron performed magnificently."

"Thank you. Speaking for my men and women, I have to agree. But I'd originally thought that Rogue Squadron would be used opportunistically: a strike mission would reveal a ground-based weakness, and we'd have the training and supplies to go down and perform the necessary ground mission. The way it turned out, we keep landing full-fledged commando missions. So I think we need another commando X-wing squadron, one where we choose pilots so as to have a full range of intrusion and subversion skills. Rogue Squadron was designed as a fighter unit first, commando unit second; this time, I want to go the other way around."

Admiral Ackbar's expression, so far as Wedge could read it, was dubious. "Historically, we've had few problems coordinating the efforts of commandos on the ground and fighter pilots for aerial support."

"I don't agree. Commandos can communicate strike locations to the pilots, but the pilots still won't have the familiarity with these locations that the intrusion team will. Commandos who've had their extraction plans busted might want to seize enemy spacecraft to escape; the way things stand, they can't count on having enough pilots to make that escape, while commando-trained pilots could. Normal pilots follow orders and conform themselves to standard tactics—and should! But a commando X-wing unit might develop new tactics. New ways of mounting even ordinary raids and pursuits. New ways of anticipating assaults and ambushes."

Ackbar abruptly leaned back from him, his eyes half closing; it looked to Wedge like a frown of concentration. "What made you say that?"

"Thinking about the subject on the long flight home, and during the time we were garrisoned on Thyferra before that," Wedge said. "Even though the garrison assignment was cut short from the two months originally planned, it still gave me plenty of time to think."

"You haven't heard any news?"

"No, sir. About what?"

Ackbar shook his head. "Please go on."

"Well, that's actually about it. I can dress it up in a formal report for you. But one other thing I think is important— I can give you a unit like this for free."

Ackbar snorted, the sound emerging as a series of rubbery pops. "Can you, now?"

"Yes, sir. First, the replacement Rogue Squadron is being disbanded, its pilots and X-wings being returned to their original units. Correct?"

"Correct."

"So you'll be issuing a dozen new X-wings to us, won't you? To the original Rogue Squadron."

"Why would we? Your X-wings are in functional shape, are they not?"

"Well, yes, but they're not New Republic property any longer. They were sold to my second-in-command, Tycho Celchu, at the start of our operation against Thyferra. They're his personal property, held in trust for all of us, until and unless he decides to vest ownership in their pilots."

"How uncharitable of you. You could donate their use to the New Republic. I believe one of your pilots has been using his personal X-wing all along."

"Yes, sir. Lieutenant Horn. And Tycho would be glad to loan his snubfighters to the New Republic, for the use of Rogue Squadron, if . . ."

"If the next dozen X-wings out of the factories are assigned to your new commando squadron."

"Yes, sir."

"That's blackmail. It's unbecoming."

"Most unconventional tactics are unbecoming until they succeed, Admiral. I direct your attention to the planet Thyferra . . ."

"Be quiet. There's still the matter of pilots. Fresh out of the Academy, their training costing hundreds of thousands of credits apiece. That is not 'free.' "

"No, sir. I don't want new pilots. I want experienced ones."

"Which is an even more significant expense."

"No, sir, not with these pilots. I want pilots no one else wants. Washouts. Pilots staring court-martials in the face. Troublemakers and screwups."

Ackbar stared as if he couldn't believe his tympanic membranes. "In the name of the Force, Commander, *why*?"

"Well, some of them, of course, will be irredeemable. I'll wash them out, too. Some of them will be good men and women who've screwed up one time too many, who know their careers are dead but would give anything for one more chance . . ."

"You're more likely to get a proton torpedo up your engines than you are to get a functional squadron out of such pilots. The torpedo might be launched accidentally . . . but that's no comfort to a widow."

Wedge spread his hands, palms up, and smiled. "Problem solved. I'm not married."

"I know you're not. You know what I mean."

"Yes, sir."

"What would become of Rogue Squadron?"

"I'd be happy to remain in charge officially, but for all squadron activities, Captain Celchu is more than qualified to lead . . . and now that he's been cleared of the formal charge of Corran Horn's murder and the informal charge of being a brainwashed double agent, there shouldn't be any responsible objection to his full return to duties. I'd return Lieutenant Hobbie Klivan to Rogue Squadron as second-in-command and take Lieutenant Wes Janson as my own second-in-command. Once the new squadron is established, of course, I'd hope to return to direct command of Rogue Squadron."

"You're committed to this idea, aren't you?"

"Yes, sir." Wedge considered what he was about to say. "Since the battle at Endor, the military's public relations groups have represented Rogue Squadron as if we were the lightsaber of the New Republic. A bright, shiny weapon to cut down any dark Imperial holdovers who still stand against us. But, sir, not all battles call for lightsabers. Some of them are fought with vibroblades in back alleys. The New Republic needs those vibroblades too, and doesn't have them."

"I understand." Ackbar nodded agreeably. "Request refused."

Wedge couldn't speak; suddenly all the air seemed to leave his chest. He'd thought he was so close, thought he had convinced the admiral.

"Unless . . ."

Wedge found his voice again. "Unless?"

"I'll make a bet with you, Commander. You get your chance at forming this squadron. If, three months after it goes operational, it has proven its worth—in *my sole estimation*—you can do as you please. Continue with the new squadron, go back to command Rogue Squadron, whichever you choose."

"And if I lose?"

"You accept promotion to the rank of general and join my advisory staff."

Wedge kept his dismay from his face. "I would seem to win either way, sir."

"Stop it. You're not fooling anyone. If you had your way, you'd continue flying snubfighters and commanding fighter squadrons until you were a century old. How many promotions have you turned down? Two? Three?"

"Two."

"Well, if you lose your bet, you accept this one."

Wedge sighed and thought it over. He needed to keep flying; he wouldn't be happy in any other way of life. But the New Republic military needed this new tactic, needed many new ways of doing things, before they became as tactically fossilized as the Empire had been. "I accept, sir."

Ackbar ground out a laugh. "In a sense, you've already

lost, Commander Antilles. You're wagering your career for the good of the New Republic. You're creating new tactics, new weapons for the New Republic, not just for your squadron. You're already a general . . . you just don't know it yet."

"I guess I'll accept that remark in the spirit in which it was intended, sir."

"I have another remark for you, Wedge. News, bad news that you'll have to take to your subordinates. And I don't envy you that task."

Wedge met with the others in the hangar aboard the cruiser *Home One* where the Rogue Squadron X-wings were undergoing repairs and repainting. He watched with a trace of wistfulness as the black and green-and-gold checks of his snubfighter, colors his father had chosen for the family refueling station and never lived to see implemented, were erased and replaced by New Republic grays and the proud but strident Rogue Squadron red stripes.

Tycho frowned, but not at the repainting job. "So how is this going to work?"

"I act as commander for the combined unit—for both Rogue Squadron and the new squadron. I also act as squadron leader for the new squad. Tycho, until I return, you're Rogue Leader, with Hobbie your second-in-command; Nawara, you remain executive officer. Wes, you're my second-in-command. Rogue Squadron is going to be assigned to the hunt for Zsinj; the new squadron will be put together at Folor Base—"

Tycho winced. "Ah, yes, the center of New Republic entertainment and lunar beauty."

"Once it's commissioned, the new X-wing squad will also join, covertly, the hunt for Zsinj, assuming he hasn't been taken out by then. Both squads will fly together when circumstances dictate."

Wes turned to Hobbie, extended his hand. "Sorry to see that you're stuck with the flying fossils, while I stay with Commander Wedge on the cutting edge of—"

Hobbie batted his hand away. "Oh, shut up."

Wedge cleared his throat. "There's something else. Tycho, Nawara, could you excuse us for a moment?"

The two Rogues withdrew, leaving Wedge with Hobbie and Janson. "I have some news for you two," Wedge said. "You're not going to like hearing it. Talon Squad is gone."

Hobbie frowned. "What do you mean, gone?"

"Wiped out. Ambush. Everyone is dead except Lieutenant Donos."

Janson leaned against the near wall. Hobbie looked as shocked as though he'd jammed his hand into a power generator. "How?"

"We don't know all the details yet. Only that they were pursuing an anomaly, a standard TIE interceptor far from any hyperspace-capable ship, into an uninhabited system logged as recently secured by New Republic Intelligence. That secure designation turns out to have been false, sliced into our code at a point yet to be determined. The interceptor led them into a shooting gallery and eleven members of the squadron died. Lieutenant Donos is being debriefed now; I'm having him brought to Folor Base when that's done. Even if he's cleared, a lot of squadron commanders will have no use for him, so I want him evaluated for the new squadron."

Janson's voice was ragged. "Eleven pilots we trained. Wiped out by a simple ambush. What a pair of incompetents we must be."

Wedge shook his head. "It was more than a simple ambush. We'll know how much more soon. In the meantime, don't tear yourselves up. Any one of us could have been lured into something like that—all we'd have to do is base decisions on Intelligence reports that seemed reliable. You understand?"

Both men nodded.

From a flight suit pocket Wedge produced a datapad; this he handed to Janson. "There are a couple of files on this. One is a set of pilot-data criteria. The other is authorization to run it against pilot profiles across records of all New Republic armed forces. Tomorrow, I want you to assemble a list of all pilots matching the criteria, then begin to contact them, find out how many of them are willing to put in for transfer to my new squadron for possible permanent assignment. I'll bet pretty close to one hundred percent will be. Those who answer in the affirmative, send to Folor without informing them of their destination; we'll meet and evaluate them there."

He turned to Hobbie. "As soon as you've had a chance to debrief Donos, I want you to work up a simulator run based on the mission that destroyed Talon Squad. It will be one of the first simulator training sessions the new squad attempts—and the next one Rogue Squad experiences. So it doesn't happen again."

"Understood," Hobbie said.

"After due consideration and review, I think it's a terrible idea," said General Crespin.

It was weeks later, and Wedge Antilles stood before another military leader in another office and prepared to plead his case again. Wedge felt irritation well up within him. Crespin might be his superior, but did not have a grasp of small-unit fighter uses and tactics superior to Wedge's. Few, if any, officers did. But he clamped down on his emotion. It was important to meet Crespin reason for reason, fact for fact; if he let emotion dictate his defense he would lose this argument.

General Crespin, new commander of the fighter training base on the moon called Folor, and personal commander of two training squads of A-wings, paced behind his desk while Wedge remained standing at attention before it. Crespin was a tall, lean man who seemed to know only two expressions, impassive and stern. Since the last time Wedge had seen him, in the briefings before the assault on the second Death Star, Crespin had been promoted from colonel to general, had picked up a limp, and had had his left eye replaced by a glossy black optical; he usually wore a mirrored patch over the mechanical replacement, as the patch was far less ominous than the black, inhuman eye. Wedge suspected the general could see through the patch. Wedge had heard that Crespin had been injured during a bombardment by Zsinj's

Super-class Star Destroyer, *Iron Fist,* against a New Republic military base established near the border to Zsinj-controlled space.

"We don't need misfits representing the New Republic," the general continued. "We need heroes. Men and women with proper character and clean records. Hologenic pilots who'll look good in the broadcasts, good in the archives."

"With all due respect, General, that's equivalent to piloting a course right into the dark side of the Force."

Crespin's head snapped around and he glared at Wedge. "You're insolent. Explain yourself."

Wedge took a deep breath. *Contain your anger. Make him an ally, not an enemy.* "First, since the Alliance was first formed, we've made it a policy to accept Imperial defectors."

"I know that. I'm one of them." Crespin's chin came up, as if he were inviting Wedge to address the question of his loyalty.

"Yes, sir. So, as you know, sometimes these people had just been waiting for the chance to side with us. Like yourself. Sometimes they jumped when our position was stronger than the Empire's. Sometimes they jumped for purely selfish reasons. We never cared, so long as they did their jobs, continued to aid the New Republic, and stayed loyal to our goals."

"So?"

"So all these defectors are retreads, General. Many are men and women with spots on their records. Sometimes more than spots. Here's an example. We pulled Black Sun criminals off Kessel, introduced them onto Coruscant, and kept the faith with them so long as they did with us. You seem to be saying that their contributions should be ignored, kept hidden—the only people whose efforts we acknowledge will be those with spotless records, uniforms, and faces."

"Ridiculous."

"Second, this idea that appearance needs to be a factor in the choice of new pilots so they'll look good on holograms and broadcasts—sir, I understand your reasoning, and I approve"—the lie nearly stuck in Wedge's throat but he accelerated past it—"but it exposes the New Republic, the

Provisional and Inner Councils, to a danger I think you've overlooked."

"Which is what?"

"If all our pilots have to look a specific way, meet or surpass some arbitrary degree of beauty, we're exactly the same as the Empire, which kept hundreds of sapient species under its heel because they weren't human. Because they didn't meet specific human standards of appearance."

"Preposterous!" But Crespin looked a trifle shaken by Wedge's last accusation.

"Of course it is, sir. It's more than preposterous, it's idiotic. Especially in light of all the nonhumans in Rogue Squadron and other units. But put that argument into the hands of Imperial insurgents working within the New Republic and you'll have insurrections, protests from every New Republic signatory race that isn't represented in the cockpit of an X-wing or A-wing somewhere."

Crespin grimaced but didn't answer.

"Third, the new squadron's makeup allows for better, not poorer, public relations. Every pilot who makes it will be a success story, a come-from-behind story, suited to a holodrama or series. Most importantly, they'll be common-being stories. Not everyone can identify with Corran Horn from Corellian Security, or with Bror Jace, millionaire prince of the bacta-producing monopoly on Thyferra. But some tug pilot who joined the Alliance, fumbled his career into the gutter, and then recovered it, repaired the damage he'd done to his life—"

"Yes, yes." Crespin waved for him to be quiet. "Very well, Commander. Your passion for this experiment is obvious. Your reasons are sound. Do it your way for now. Do note that I expect this experiment to be a disaster . . . and I'll be on hand to clean it up when it detonates in your face."

"Yes, sir."

"You'll have to be aware of some changes implemented since the last time you were stationed here. You may have noticed when landing that the base's emissions are much more contained than they used to be; external visual beacons are lit off only when landing craft need them."

"Yes, sir."

"We need the extra security, what with Zsinj's raids increasing in frequency and boldness . . . and with occasional lapses such as your own pilot, Erisi Dlarit, turning out to be a traitor—"

Wedge reined in another flash of anger. "I should point out that she was placed in Rogue Squadron for political reasons, not recruited by me. And so far as we have seen, her controllers kept the information she sent them about Folor Base to themselves, not sharing it with renegades like Zsinj. And now they're dead."

"Whatever. We still need the improved security. So long as this is border territory, we're vulnerable to assaults like the ones Zsinj is so fond of making. All your pilots are being brought in without knowing where they are; the washouts will go out the same way."

"Yes, sir."

"Very well." Suddenly Crespin looked inexpressibly weary. Wedge wondered how many officers regularly brought him arguments and back talk—even when it was as polite and well reasoned as Wedge's. "Dismissed."

3

"You look like you've fought a few rounds with a rancor."

"Thanks, Wes. I'm sure General Crespin will appreciate that comparison." Wedge sat back in his chair with a sigh, put his booted feet up on his desk. His office was a former storeroom with dismal lighting and not even a holoscreen to display a soothing picture of some faraway vista. His chair was a recycled ejection seat mounted on a heavy spring and a cross-brace. His desk was a section of metal bulkhead suspended between two low filing cabinets. It was all typical of the decor in underfunded Folor Base. Janson sat in a similar chair against the wall, and a third ejection seat was situated opposite Wedge's.

"We have pilots today?" Wedge asked.

"We have pilots, possibly the last group, if some late arrivals make it in."

"Let's get started. Who's first?" Since the first day of evaluations, Wedge had followed a simple interview pattern: Janson kept the data on the pilots, allowing Wedge to meet each one without any foreknowledge. It gave him a better opportunity to consult his gut with respect to each candidate.

Janson consulted his datapad. "His name is Kettch, and he's an Ewok."

Wedge came upright. "No."

"Oh, yes. Determined to fight. You should hear him say, 'Yub, yub.' He makes it a battle cry."

"Wes, assuming he could be educated up to Alliance fighter-pilot standards, an Ewok couldn't even reach an X-wing's controls."

"He wears arm and leg extensions, prosthetics built for him by a sympathetic medical droid. And he's anxious to go, Commander."

Wedge slumped and covered his eyes with one hand. "Please tell me you're kidding."

"Of course I'm kidding. Pilot-candidate number one is a human female, from Tatooine, Falynn Sandskimmer."

"I'm going to get you, Janson."

"Yub, yub, Commander."

"Show her in."

Late in the day, Wedge looked over the list of candidates processed so far.

A Tatooine woman with excellent flying marks, already an ace, but a career in the incinerator because of what was listed as "chronic insolence." An inability to keep scorn out of her voice when dealing with superior officers she didn't respect. Failure to maintain military discipline. Wedge wondered how badly this would have affected her record a few years ago, when the New Republic was the Rebel Alliance and the military was a looser, rougher organization where rugged individualism was the norm rather than a common exception.

He wondered, too, whether Falynn Sandskimmer's attitude toward a certain Hero of the New Republic had contributed to the two demotions that had canceled her two promotions. Asked about Luke Skywalker, she'd said, "Can you imagine being compared to him all your adult life just because you're another pilot from Tatooine? No, I've never met Luke Skywalker. In fact, I wish I'd never *heard* of him."

It was an attitude that would not endear her to many of Luke's friends. Wedge, who was among those friends, simply shrugged it off. Her worth was in her performance, not her lack of appreciation of one good man.

The second pilot, a human male from Etti IV, was facing a court-martial for theft. He expressed confidence that he would be cleared and asked for a chance to prove himself to Commander Antilles. A minute after he'd gone, Wedge noticed that the framed holo of his long-dead parents was missing from the tabletop. He sent Janson after the compulsive thief and scrubbed him from the candidate roster.

The third pilot was a Talz, one of the white-furred humanoid inhabitants of Alzoc III. A former Imperial slave, he'd learned to pilot freighters for the Rebel Alliance and had transferred to fighters when the deadly pilot attrition of the year before the Emperor's death had put a premium on good fliers. But his record showed a history of psychosomatic illnesses and the possibility of mental breakdown increasing in the last several years. His mental evaluations suggested that these problems resulted from conflict between the Talz's basically gentle nature and the fighter's mission of destroying enemy targets.

Wedge and Janson put him through a simulator recreation of the fleet action at the battle of Endor—a target-rich environment where the best fighter pilots racked up impressive kill scores. The Talz did well, but Wedge and Janson watched his biomedical readings climb into the red danger zone—a clear sign that even in simulators, stress was eating away at him. They wished the disappointed pilot a good flight home and recommended a transfer back into freighters.

"Number four today," said Janson, "is Lieutenant Myn Donos."

Wedge gave his second-in-command a sympathetic look. "Have you had a chance to talk to him?"

"No, he's just arrived on base. I read Hobbie's report, though. New Republic Military Intelligence has cleared him of error or wrongdoing."

"Good. Show him in."

Janson spoke into his comlink and a moment later a lean man in the standard orange New Republic flight suit entered. He was just over average height, with a round face and a thick mop of black hair. His face betrayed no emotion. He saluted and held it until Wedge returned it.

"Lieutenant Donos, have a seat."

"Thank you, sir." Donos sat, military-straight.

"I understand that Command has reviewed the situation on Gravan Seven and cleared you for continued fighter duty. Congratulations."

"Thank you, sir." Donos's expression did not change.

Wedge glanced at Janson, who wore a puzzled look as he watched Donos.

"You're aware that we're forming a new X-wing squadron."

"Yes, sir."

"Interested in transferring over?"

"Yes, sir." There was no enthusiasm in the pilot's voice, nor was there a trace of the pain he was doubtless still feeling from the destruction of his squadron. Wedge again checked Janson's reaction; Janson was now leaning back in his chair, studying Donos curiously.

"Wes tells me that before joining the Alliance, you belonged to the Corellian armed forces. Sniper for an elite counterinsurgency unit."

"Yes, sir."

"Are you still sharp as a sniper?"

"No, sir. I haven't had a chance to keep up my skills in the last three years."

"Do you think you can train up to your previous standard?"

"Yes, sir." There was no pride, no enthusiasm in his tone.

"Do you have a problem with the role of sniper?"

"No, sir. Whatever my role, my task is the elimination of the enemy."

"Right. I also understand that you were decorated on Corellia for conspicuous gallantry. This entitles you to wear the Corellian Bloodstripes. Yet you don't. Why?"

Donos took a while to answer. "It just seems a bit silly, sir. I could also wear a sign saying 'I'm a wonderful person and I give money to the needy.' What's the point?"

"I see." Wedge tried to discern some hint of anger, pride, regret, *anything* in the pilot's expression or attitude, but he could not. "Well, then, for now, welcome to the squadron of candidate trainees." He shook Donos's hand. An exchange of salutes later, the lieutenant was gone.

"He used to wear the Bloodstripes," Janson said. "I didn't notice until you mentioned it. This isn't the Myn Donos I trained."

"Interesting. How long was it from the time Talon Squad left on its last mission to the time he returned? Was there enough time for him to have been grabbed by the enemy, to have been programmed?"

"No, there's not enough time unaccounted for in his report for him to have stopped into a cantina for a drink. No sign he ever left his cockpit. It's him, but it's not him. He wouldn't even meet my eyes."

"Well, we'll see how he performs. If he shows the slightest sign of cracking up, or of needing a protracted off-duty rest for psychological reasons, I'm going to scrub him."

"Understood."

"Hypercomm signal detected, Admiral!"

Admiral Apwar Trigit looked down from his command chair into the bridge crew pit. His expression was mild. "Its origin?"

"Header code indicates that it's straight from Zsinj at Rancor Base!"

"I'll take it in my private comm chamber." He rose, aware that with his graying black hair and beard, his lean form, and the silver and black uniform he'd designed himself, he was an imposing figure. He kept his walk graceful and casual as he departed the Imperial Star Destroyer's bridge—true, he served the Warlord Zsinj, but his chief officers must understand that he merely hired out his services and those of the *Implacable,* that he was his own master.

In the spherical chamber reserved for his private communications, Trigit hit a switch on the main console. Immediately, a three-dimensional image appeared before him—Zsinj, twice human-sized, sitting in a black command chair, doubtless the one aboard *Iron Fist.* Zsinj wore the crisp white uniform of an Imperial grand admiral, a rank he had never truly attained—yet his current power was such that no one could protest this presumption on his part.

Trigit smiled at the ego Zsinj routinely manifested. "My lord, you're going to twist my neck from staring up at you." He slowly turned a knob and Zsinj's image shrank until it was just over human-sized. He kept from his face the sheer delight the action of shrinking Zsinj brought him; in the Imperial armed forces, it would have been construed as an expression of pure insolence. He would have been lucky merely to have been demoted to garbage scow pilot.

The warlord—a corpulent man, balding and graying, with a florid complexion and drooping mustachios that gave him an exotic look—favored him with a smile. "I've just read the report from your last transmission. I wanted to congratulate you on the destruction of Talon Squadron."

Trigit gave him a sardonic little bow. "Thank you. The code-slicer who planted the false information about the security of the Gravan system later reported that they have decommissioned Talon Squadron entirely."

"The pilot who escaped the ambush—was that by your design? Or an accident? The report doesn't say."

"No, we made every effort to kill him. His reflexes were just good enough to save him. In the final analysis, I consider it to be just as good as a clean sweep. He's doubtless told his tale of woe to his superiors; now they can begin to fret about forces cunning enough to wipe out X-wing squadrons without significant loss or effort. A few more such missions, and they'll begin to develop a supernatural dread about us."

Zsinj smiled. "What about your code-slicer? What if he's caught and broken?"

"Impossible. She has already left her Rebel station. I'm having her brought in and giving her a commission aboard *Implacable.*"

"It would have been cheaper to have eliminated her. Your previous superior would have done it."

"Ysanne Isard kept all her officers and minions in a state of fear," Trigit acknowledged. "And when they failed her, or proved in any way to be a liability, she did eliminate them. So they knew that there were no happy endings in their futures, no rosy retirements. They literally had nothing to look forward to except death or escape. That's not a way to engender loyalty. That's not my way."

"Good."

"But none of this discussion explains why you've contacted me at such considerable expense."

Zsinj's smile grew broader. "I want to hear early results from the Morrt Project."

"Ah. Well, the first few thousand *Morrt*-class parasite-droids have been distributed. I'm getting preliminary reports already. Naturally, there's a concentration of signal hits from known population centers—Imperial, New Republic, and independent. We're also getting a few hits from unknown sites, and sites designated destroyed or abandoned. Once we get reinforcement on them, we can go looking."

"Good. Keep me up-to-date on all your interesting little operations."

"As always, my lord."

Zsinj gave him a gracious little nod and his image faded to nothingness.

Trigit sighed. Zsinj was much easier to deal with than Ysanne Isard, also known as Iceheart, former head of Imperial Intelligence—now dead at the hands of Rogue Squadron. Unlike Iceheart, Zsinj understood something about the folly of waste—such as murdering subordinates on a whim. But Zsinj's desire to be up-to-date on every operation, to have his fingers in each new plan and enterprise, was extremely tiresome.

Ah, well. As long as Zsinj remained reasonable and kept *Implacable* stocked with fuel, weapons, food, and information, Trigit would remain with him. Far better than setting out on the lonely warlord's road himself.

That is, until he had power and advantages to match Zsinj's.

"Any more?" said Wedge.

Janson consulted his chrono. "It's getting late. But we have only two more candidates to review."

"Today, or total?"

"Total. Your slave-driving habits have gotten us almost through the first phase of the evaluation process." Janson consulted his datapad. "Next is Voort saBinring, a Gamorrean."

"Very funny. You had me going the first time, Wes, but that joke won't work twice."

"He's a Gamorrean."

The green-skinned, pig-faced Gamorreans were found among untrained guard and police forces on many worlds. They were technologically primitive, disinterested in any of the advanced sciences required for technological professions. "It's impossible to train Gamorrean males to something as complicated as fighter piloting. They have glandular balances that make them very violent and impatient."

"He's a Gamorrean."

"Just keep up your little joke, then, and show him in."

Janson spoke into his comlink. A moment later a Gamorrean—1.9 meters of glowering porcine presence, dressed in the standard New Republic pilot's uniform, the bright orange of the jumpsuit clashing nauseatingly with the creature's green skin—walked in and saluted.

Janson smiled ingratiatingly at Wedge. "Yub, yub, Commander."

Whenever the Gamorrean spoke, his natural voice, grunts and squeals not pleasant to the human ear, emerged first. Then, below it, cutting through it, was his other voice, the mechanical one, emerging from the translator device implanted in his throat. "No, Commander. I have not lived among other Gamorreans since I was a child."

Wedge cleared his throat. "I'm sure you understand that this is new to me. But I am curious, how you, well, overcame Gamorrean biology and learned to fly."

"I did not overcome my biology. These were changes forced upon me. By Binring Biomedical Product."

"I know that name. They provide food to the Empire's armed forces. Nasty green nutrient pastes that take forever to go bad. Perfect for stormtroopers."

The Gamorrean nodded. "They also engineer animals to adapt to different planetary environments. They have less wholesome experiments as well. I was one of them. For purposes of espionage, the Emperor wanted Gamorreans with humanlike methods of self-control. They made alterations to our biochemistries. My attention span surpasses human norm. My mathematical acumen registers at the genius level. I do not lose control of my anger."

"This was an Imperial project?" Wedge thought that through. "How many like you are there?"

"None. I am the only success."

"The other transformations were fatal?"

"In a sense. All the other subjects committed suicide."

"Why?"

"If I knew, I would be among them. But I am certain it has something to do with isolation. How would you feel if you were the only thinking human in the galaxy, forced to live among Gamorreans, and all the other humans you met were bloodthirsty primitives?"

"A good point." Wedge sat back and considered that unhappy prospect for a moment. "How did you come to join the Alliance?"

"One of my creators, who had watched his other . . . children . . . kill themselves one by one arranged to have me put through a variety of different simulator training programs to measure my capacity. Or so he said. In actuality, he was doing it to teach me to pilot many different Imperial and Alliance vehicles. Then he arranged for me to escape the Binring compound. Eventually I reached Obroa-skai."

"The library world."

"I learned much there, and eventually chose to come to the Alliance."

"Your, uh, creator—he didn't choose to escape?"

"He was sad because of the projects he had led. He chose to follow his other children."

Wedge winced. "All right. To more immediate concerns. Your record states that you have temperament problems. You're facing a court-martial for striking a superior officer, though that officer is willing to drop charges to get you transferred as far as possible from his command. What do you have to say?"

The Gamorrean took a few moments to respond. "There are two types of pilots in the New Republic. Those who have been Imperial pilots, and may carry with them an irrational dislike of nonhumans. And those who have had bad encounters with Gamorreans."

"I tend to disagree."

"Your experiences do not match mine. And in my experience, a Gamorrean flyer tends to receive an undue amount of abuse from his fellows. Not just pranks. Sometimes sabotage. Lies. Challenges."

"You didn't strike your officer?"

"I have struck several fellow pilots in well-moderated challenge matches. I have never had to strike one more than once. You will notice that charges were filed against me within half an hour of the alleged incident. No one I have ever struck has been able to speak coherently within half an hour of my striking him. Sir, he struck at *me;* I blocked his blow. He has chosen to remember that as an attack. He is willing to drop charges only because he is not strong enough to accept responsibility for the full measure of his persecution of me."

Wedge considered. "Well, that's about all for now. Candidate training begins tomorrow." He rose. The others followed suit, and he shook the Gamorrean's hand. "By the way, what do you like to be called? Voort?"

"I am content with Voort. But many others call me Piggy. I am content with it, too, for I can ignore the definite derogatory component that goes with it."

Wedge and Janson exchanged glances. "The lieutenant and I once knew a very fine human pilot who went by Piggy. There's no 'derogatory component' to it in this squadron. Rather, it's a badge of honor I hope you can live up to."

"I will try to do so."

When the Gamorrean was gone, Wedge said, "I wonder what Porkins would have thought of him."

Janson shrugged. "We'll know better when we've flown with him."

"Well, who's next? A mynock? A womp rat?"

"My, you are getting paranoid. No, next, and last, is a human male, Kell Tainer from Sluis Van. I think he's exactly the leader type you want to replace you when it's time to return to Rogue Squadron. Assuming Myn Donos doesn't return to normal."

"Good. Show him in."

A moment later Flight Officer Tainer entered. *General Crespin is going to love him,* Wedge decided.

Kell Tainer stood nearly two meters tall, with a handsome, sculpted face that holorecorders would adore. Dark hair cut short framed light blue eyes—a couple of shades lighter and they'd make him look like a madman, but at this shade they were piercing, mesmerizing. He was built like an athlete, actually a little too broad in the shoulders to be entirely comfortable in an X-wing's cockpit, but that was a problem for which he would already have learned to compensate.

Kell snapped to a precision salute and held it until Wedge returned it. "Flight Officer Tainer reporting, sir, and a pleasure to meet you."

"Likewise. Let me introduce you to my second-in-command, Lieutenant Janson."

Kell had turned toward Janson and was in midsalute as Wedge spoke. Wedge watched as the pilot's back suddenly locked upright. Tainer's salute pose and salute became iron-rigid. Kell did not meet Janson's eyes, but he did ask, "Lieutenant *Wes* Janson, sir?"

With a bewildered expression, Janson said, "That's me." He finally remembered to return the salute.

Kell turned back to Wedge, kept his gaze focused above Wedge's head. "I apologize, sir. I cannot join this squadron. I withdraw my application. Permission to leave?"

Wedge said, "Why?"

"I'd prefer not to say, sir."

"Understood. Now answer the question."

Kell seemed to vibrate for a moment as his muscles strained against one another. Then, his voice low, he said, "This man killed my father, sir. Permission to leave?"

Janson, his expression shocked, came around to Wedge's side of the desk. His gaze searched Kell's face, and a shadow of recognition crossed his features. "Tainer—your name wasn't always Tainer, was it?"

"No, sir."

"Doran?"

"Yes, sir."

Janson looked away, his eyes tracing something back through the years.

Kell said, "Permission to leave, sir?"

"Wait in the hall," Wedge said.

Kell left. Wedge turned to his second-in-command. "What's this all about?"

4

Janson returned to his chair, finding his way into it by touch; he seemed to look into the past, not seeing anything around him. "My first kill—did I ever tell you that my first kill was an Alliance pilot?"

"No."

"Not something one advertises. Back then, I was a pilot trainee in the Tierfon Yellow Aces. With Jek Porkins."

"Good old Piggy."

"The original. Those were the days when a training squadron might just get picked to do a strike mission that should have gone to an experienced squad—"

"Like today, you mean."

"Well, it's much less common today. You know that. That day, our mission was an ambush of an Imperial freighter and its TIE fighter escort. They were to come in to a landing at a temporary Imperial staging base we'd found out about. We were in Y-wings. One unit of the Yellow Aces was to strafe the base and run, leading off the garrisoned flyers, while the rest was to hit the freighter. To take it, if possible; we really needed the food and fuel."

"So what happened?"

"The first part of the mission went as planned. But as the freighter came in, we saw that the TIE fighter escort was twice as big as advertised. And one of our pilots, a former freighter pilot from Alderaan, Kissek Doran, had a panic attack and took off in his Y-wing. Piggy and I were sent out to bring him back . . . or shoot him down."

"And you did?"

The words exploded out of Janson: "Wedge, I had to! If he communicated on any standard frequency, if he crossed into the base's sensor range, if he bounced high enough that the moon's horizon no longer concealed him; if any of these things happened, we were compromised and the unit might have been slaughtered. Porkins tried to crowd him down to land, but he couldn't, and I—" The words stuck in his throat for a moment. "I shot him down. I had to use lasers. Couldn't risk the ion cannon; its energy pulse might have been detected. The blast cracked his cockpit; vacuum killed him. His scrounged flight suit wasn't up to it."

"It sounds as though you did everything you could to keep him alive."

"Yes, until I killed him. I knew he had a wife and two or three kids back on Alderaan. I figured they'd died when the first Death Star destroyed the planet."

Wedge took up Janson's datapad and scanned Kell's record. "It doesn't say anything here about Alderaan or the Doran family."

"They must have changed their family name, falsified records. The unit commander went to visit them, not long after he'd sent them the official notification of Kissek's death. The story he was going to give her, supporting the one in the notification, was that he died in battle . . . but Kissek's wife had already heard the truth from someone. Accused the Tierfon Yellow Aces not only of killing her husband but of ruining the family name. Maybe she tried to fix things by changing their name and moving away."

Wedge sighed over the datapad. "Look at this. Tainer was a fighter-craft mechanic on Sluis Van. When he came to the Alliance, he trained as a demolitions expert. Served with Lieutenant Page's commandos, then demonstrated a native talent for fighting in re-creational simulators and got permission to train in the real thing. Have you ever met Page?"

"No."

"A good man. Teaches his people well. Wes, we really need Tainer . . . if we can persuade him to stay."

Janson gave him a look that was all mock cheer. "Oh, wonderful. I killed his father. He hates me. He knows how to make *bombs.* Come on, Wedge, how does this story end?"

"If he's an honorable man, you're in no danger."

"So he gets to the boiling point, and then he pops like the cork on bad Tatooine wine."

"All Tatooine wine is bad."

"Don't change the subject. Anyway, keep reading."

Wedge returned his attention to the datapad. "In training, one Headhunter crashed. One X-wing set down hard enough that it took a lot of damage. He claimed unresponsive controls both times?"

Janson nodded. "Typical response from someone who can't accept responsibility for his failures."

Wedge looked up and gave his fellow pilot a piercing stare. "So, back when you were hot to add him to our roster, how were you going to convince me to overlook this little crash-landing problem?"

"Wedge . . ."

"Answer the question."

Janson looked unhappy. "I was going to point out that he could have been correct. The two crashes aren't consistent with his skill index. He's good, and I mean brilliant, in the simulators."

Wedge considered the information on the datapad for long moments. "Well, I'll accept your explanation. I want us to try him out. If he doesn't work out, I'll scrub him. If he does work out and yet the two of you can't work together . . ."

"In the long run, you actually need him in this unit more than you need me." Janson's voice was weary. "In that case, with your permission, I'd transfer back to the Rogues. I can swap with Hobbie."

Wedge nodded, solemn. "Thanks, Wes."

. . .

Janson let Wedge do all the talking. Wedge imagined that it felt better not to have Kell Tainer turn any attention toward him whatsoever.

Wedge explained the situation in a few words, then asked, "Tainer, *are* you an honorable man?"

The pilot, his back once again locked into correct but overtense military posture, said, "I am."

"Do you think Lieutenant Janson is any less honorable?"

Tainer took his time in replying. "No, sir." The words sounded as though they were being ground out of him.

"You took an oath to serve the New Republic, and you have to understand that we need your precise skills more than you need to avoid reminders of what happened to your father. Janson took the same oath, though in his case it was to the Alliance to restore the Republic, back when you were still playing with toys. And he understands that we need his skills more than he needs to be free of the dislike you have for him . . . or of the memory of doing something he didn't want to do. Do you understand?"

"Yes, sir."

"So I'm going to ask you to stay. For now. If you two can't work together, we'll make arrangements. But I have to warn you, with your record, placement in any other unit means you're not likely ever to fly a fighter again. You'll probably end up back in the commandos."

"I liked the commandos."

"Yes, but you'll never be able to repair your father's name there. You'll never show the galaxy that the name 'Doran' doesn't translate as 'pilot and coward.'"

Tainer's head snapped down and he finally met Wedge's gaze. His eyes were as full of rage as any Wedge had ever seen; Wedge resisted the temptation to take a step backward. "How *dare* you—"

Wedge kept his own voice low. "Attention." He waited three long beats, until Tainer again assumed the proper pose and returned his attention to the wall above Wedge's head. Then Wedge continued, "I dare, if that's the word, because it's the truth. I'll bet you've had this dream, a dream of being a pilot and restoring the honor to your family's name, since you were back on Alderaan. Well, you've yet to fly a combat mission and you're already about to wash out of the pilot ranks. Here's your last chance. So, do you stay or do you go?"

Tainer's jaw worked for several moments, but he made no sound. Then: "I stay. Sir." His voice suggested that he was speaking in spite of a deep stab wound.

"Good. Dismissed."

When Tainer was gone, Janson let out a low whistle. "Wedge, I'm not criticizing . . . but that was the coldest maneuver I've seen in a long time."

"You fly through vacuum, you sometimes need cold-space lubricants instead of blood." Wedge slumped wearily back in his chair. Suddenly he felt impossibly tired, and wondered how many pilots would regularly bring him problems like these.

Kell strapped himself into his seat, an effort made a little difficult because the cockpit was so tight around him, and flipped the four switches igniting his X-wing's fusial thrust engines—actually, igniting the ersatz engines on this X-wing simulator. Simulators being as sophisticated and realistic as they were, it was sometimes an effort to distinguish them from reality; they even used gravitational compensators to simulate zero gee during deep-space mission simulations.

Around him, in the viewscreens that simulated the X-wing's transparisteel canopy, he saw a fighter launch bay; he knew the real one was actually half a klick above him, much closer to the lunar surface.

His board indicated that all four engines were live and performing at near-optimal levels. "Gold One has four starts and is ready. Primary and secondary power at full. All diagnostics in the green."

His comm system crackled. "Gold Two, identical report. Ready to fly."

Kell didn't know who Gold Two was; the other pilots in this Gold group mission had been sealed into their simulators already by the time Kell had arrived for the mission. He wondered if they'd been getting in a few minutes extra practice before the exercise. He wondered if he should have been doing the same.

Gold Two's voice, distorted through the comm system, was not deep but seemed to be male; odd pronunciation suggested that Basic was not his native tongue.

"Gold Three, everything is nominal. Ready to go." Those were the mechanical tones of Piggy, the Gamorrean. Kell was interested in seeing how that pilot flew; Piggy was the one candidate trainee who was physically even broader than Kell, even more uncomfortable in the standard X-wing cockpit.

"Gold Four, everything nominal, ready to go." A female voice. Kell had met several female candidates trying out for places in this squadron, but comm distortion kept him from being able to match this voice to anyone he'd met.

Lieutenant Janson's voice crackled in his ear, not distorted at all; Kell stiffened. "Launch in sixty," Janson said. "We have incoming spacecraft, eyeballs and squints, screening a capital ship. Engage and hold them ten klicks from base. Your job is to keep them off us long enough to launch our transports. You fail, we die. Training protocol one-seven-nine is in effect. Control out."

Kell tried to force his shoulder muscles to relax. He switched the comm over to a direct channel to his wingman. "Gold Two, what's training protocol one-seven-nine?"

"We don't know, One."

"We? Who's we?"

"Gold Two, One."

Kell opened his mouth to ask for a clarification, saw that the chrono was down to ten seconds, and decided to wait.

At five seconds he activated his repulsorlift engines and rose a few meters into the air. At one second he nudged the stick forward, made sure he was aligned perfectly with the tunnel exit from the hangar, and kicked in the thrusters. A visual check showed the other members of his group doing the same.

His X-wing punched out through the magnetic containment field at the end of the tunnel, into hard vacuum—

Straight into the incoming fire from a group of four TIE bombers, dupes already so close he could clearly see them with the naked eye.

Kell snapped up on his starboard wing, put all shields forward, bracketed one of the oncoming dupes and pulled the trigger even before the brackets could glow with the green of a laser lock, and pulled up in an arc that carried him to starboard and away from the lunar surface. He saw the rear edges of his control surfaces brighten with the glow of an explosion behind him. Communication from his R2 unit scrolled over his data screen: CONFIRM ONE KILL GOLD ONE.

Panicky, incomprehensible chatter came over his comm system; Kell shouted it down. "Quiet! Strike foils to attack position! Intelligence was wrong, the intruders are already all over the base. Two, stay with me, we're going up after our original objective. Three, Four, do a fly-by over the base and report damage."

He heard a chorus of subdued acknowledgments and saw Gold Two pull up to his port rear quarter. Then he tried the comm again: "Control, come in. Gold One to Control."

No answer.

His sensor unit showed three remaining TIE dupes below, at just above ground level—then two, as Gold Three scored a kill. But ahead and above, now at a distance of four klicks and closing, were thirty-six TIE fighter blips: three full squadrons. They maintained separation, were not converging on Gold One and Two.

Gold Four's voice crackled over the comm system. "One, the launch tunnels are down, all of them. They've been bombed out of existence."

"Even the main tube? The transport exit? That's the only one that concerns us."

"A hundred meters of collapsed rubble, One. Nobody's coming out of that." Four's voice sounded upset even across comm distortion. Kell wanted to tell her, *Calm down, it's only a simulator run. Nobody real is dead.*

But he had other problems. Control had given him a clear set of mission goals . . . and then had changed the mission parameters and invalidated all of them. What should he do now? And what was that damned training protocol Control had cited just before they launched?

"One Group, our mission is scrubbed," he said. "Our status is omega. Three, Four, get to us and we'll punch a hole out of here."

Three and Four acknowledged just as the range-to-target indicator dropped below two klicks. This meant the oncoming enemy was within their weapon range . . . and that Gold One and Gold Two were within range of the enemy's targeting.

They could either bug out and suffer long-range potshots of the enemy on their way back to Gold Three and Four, or try to punch their way through, get back a little of their own, and loop back to their comrades, hoping that their attack might leave the enemy in some disarray. The latter course was potentially suicidal. Kell said, "Gold Two, let's get out of here—"

Gold Two's reply was a weird, warbling yell. His X-wing headed straight toward the oncoming squadron. Little needles of green Imperial laser fire came lancing in, none too close to him.

"Gold Two, return to formation. Gold Two . . ." Kell cursed. Had Two's comm unit malfunctioned? That would be in keeping with the foul-up nature of this mission. "All right, Gold Two, I'm your wing." He continued in pursuit of Two and prepared to cover him.

Two's course carried him straight toward the center of the port squadron. The enemy's laser fire now flashed thick around him, and Kell saw some of it dissipating meters ahead of Two's fighter, stopped by its shields. Two was performing the most dangerous and most effective sort of fighter maneuver, the head-on approach, but against an entire squadron . . . and twelve-to-one odds made it likely he'd end up being vaped.

Time to change those odds. Kell lost a little relative altitude so that Gold Two would be less likely to wander across his field of fire, then switched his lasers over to dual-fire, giving him less punch but a much higher rate of fire. He hit the etheric rudder, slewing his bow to port while maintaining his current course, then traversed his bow back to starboard—and as fast as his targeting brackets panned across the line of TIE fighters and went green to indicate laser lock, he fired, sending streaks of destructive red light toward the enemy. The musical tones of successive laser locks filled his cockpit.

He saw distant light flares indicating he and Two had managed at least to graze some targets. His data screen showed one kill and a graze for Kell, just a graze for Two. He returned more incoming fire and juked as the oncoming TIEs were suddenly on them, then past them—

Time to come around in a tight loop and hit the rear guard if the TIEs had one, fall upon the TIEs from the rear if they didn't. But, dammit, he wasn't lead fighter, the erratic Two was. He found Two visually and on the sensors; the pilot was rolling out and coming around in a tight starboard loop. Kell kept with him.

Sensors showed four TIE fighters coming around to engage them; the other fighters were continuing on toward their objective. Closer to the lunar surface, Gold Three and Four were approaching that remaining line of seven TIEs in the weakened squadron. Good; they were obviously going to plow through the weakest link in the attackers' chain. There were no blips remaining from the four TIE bombers; Three and Four must have finished them.

Two was lining up for another head-on run, but Kell saw the four TIE fighters spreading out in box formation. "Two, break off. They're setting up for you. Follow me in; I'm lead now."

Two ignored him, accelerating even faster and replying with another wavering war cry.

Kell gritted his teeth. *All right. Let's see if I can save him in spite of himself.* He let Gold Two continue to increase the distance between them. He switched over to proton torpedoes.

The oncoming fighters were arrayed like the corners of a two-dimensional box, and Two was headed straight for the lower-left corner. All four TIE fighters began spraying laser fire at him.

Kell pointed his nose up, caught the upper-left eyeball in his brackets. They immediately went red, indicating torpedo lock, and he fired. At this range, the TIE fighter had plenty of time to dodge or range the torpedo . . . but in so doing, he'd have to break off his own attack against Two. Kell rolled up on his starboard strike foil, targeted the upper-right corner the same way, and fired again.

The two TIEs he'd targeted broke off their approach, going to evasive maneuvers in order to elude the torps. The other two continued firing. Kell rolled over to bring the lower-right eyeball into position. That fighter must have had a sensor unit that could detect torpedo locks; it immediately began evasive maneuvers.

He heard comm chatter that reassured him: "You vaped him, Three. I'm your wing." "Got it, Four. There's one coming up on my tail—" "He's mine."

Then Two's X-wing, invisible against the blackness of space, suddenly flared back into Kell's vision. It exploded, an expanding ball of orange and yellow.

A dull weight settled into Kell's stomach. He knew the real Gold Two was unhurt, probably now emerging from his simulator . . . but Control would probably blame Kell for failing to save him. Failing to save him in spite of himself.

He flipped weapons control back to lasers, linking them for quad fire. His target momentarily ceased evasive maneuvers, probably thinking he'd broken Kell's torpedo lock and was out of danger. As soon as his laser brackets went green, Kell fired. His lasers shredded the eyeball, one lancing beam slicing the port wing clean off at the pylon and two others punching through the cockpit. The TIE fighter didn't blow up, but it did explosively vent its cockpit atmosphere and sailed past Kell on a ballistic trajectory that would end on the simulated surface of Folor.

That left Kell with three immediate foes. No, two: One of his torpedoes caught its luckless target, turning him into a rapidly expanding cloud of gas and shrapnel. But his other intended torpedo victim had eluded the explosive device, and that TIE fighter and Two's original target were now wingmates looping around to get behind him.

Kell pulled back on the stick, attempting as tight a turn as the X-wing could manage. TIE fighters were actually more maneuverable than X-wings out of atmosphere, but that meant less if they were being flown by indifferent pilots, as these eyeball drivers seemed to be.

He was at the top of his loop, staring relative-down at his pursuers and the surface of Folor beyond, when red laser fire from moonward sliced through one pursuer and a torpedo from the same point of origin destroyed the other. He checked his sensor board and whistled. "Good firing, Three, Four."

Piggy's mechanical voice: "Thank you, sir. The eyeballs are breaking off. Shall we pursue?"

They were indeed heading off. But why wasn't Kell's canopy fading to black, indicating that the exercise was over?

Kell thought about that long enough to take a couple of deep breaths and steady his nerves. "No, they're heading back to their carrier. Which means we have more incoming. Did anyone ever get a signal from Control?"

"No, sir."

"No."

"Then we have to assume Folor Base is a loss and we're all that's left. Close and follow my heading." Relative to Folor's surface, he stood his X-wing on its tail, then called up his nav program.

Had this been a real attack and Folor Base unable to launch its transports, he would have been expected to get all viable forces to safety and later link up with other New Republic units. So he plotted a quick jump to get them away from Folor and to an unoccupied spot in space—somewhere from which he could set up a more sophisticated course to Allied-controlled space.

The other two X-wings grouped with him. As soon as he had a navigation solution and had left the moon far enough behind to be free of its gravity well, he transmitted the course to the others. "All right. On my mark, three, two, one, execute!"

But instead of elongating into brilliant stripes of light, the first visual sign that a hyperspace jump was being successfully executed, the stars faded to nothingness. Kell's canopy rose and harsh artificial light made him wince.

Janson gathered the four pilots together at a table beside the quad group of simulators and Kell got his first look at his wingman.

Gold Two was not human. He was definitely humanoid, with arms, legs, torso, and head arranged in a comfortably recognizable fashion. But, though nearly as tall as Kell, he was very lean, covered in short brown fur, with an elongated face, huge brown eyes, a broad, flattened nose, and a mouth full of squarish white teeth. His were features better suited to a draft animal than a sapient being—but for the inquisitive, luminously intelligent quality of his eyes. He also had a head of hair that would be the envy of many a human, male or female; as Kell arrived at the table, Gold Two was tugging his hair free of an elastic band and allowing it to shake out into a waterfall of midback-length chestnut brown.

Kell tried to rein in his irritation at the other pilot's blatant disregard of orders and protocol. He extended a hand. "Kell Tainer."

The alien took his hand and shook it in human fashion. "We are Flight Officer Hohass Ekwesh."

"We? Is that a royal we?" That would explain the alien's apparent disdain for procedure.

"No, a collective—"

"Biographies can wait," Janson said. "We're here to review performance, remember?"

Kell stiffened up at the reprimand. "Yes, sir."

"Good. All right. Four, you had two kills and did a good job on your reconnaissance fly-by. Three, three kills, and initiative points for double-checking Tainer's hyperspace calculations."

"Triple-checked, sir. I also ran the numbers in my head."

Kell glared at the Gamorrean. "And did my numbers check out?"

The Gamorrean nodded. "They were inelegant numbers, but perfectly functional, and correct."

"Gold Two, you scored no kills, disobeyed orders twice—though we have to drop one of those because Mr. Tainer yielded lead to you, even if it was a bit retroactive—and managed to get yourself killed through bad tactics." Janson paused over the datapad. He kept his attention on the data before continuing—possibly, Kell thought, in order to keep from having to meet Kell's eyes. "Gold One, very impressive. Five kills, an instant ace if it were real life, including one snap-shot while your strike foils were still in flight position. I'm saving that one for instructional holos. Good choice of new orders when the mission parameters changed. All in all, close to perfect."

Janson glanced around among them. "Now, for scoring. This mission was worth two thousand, with bonuses possible for exceptional performance. Gold Four, thirteen hundred fifty. Gold Three, twelve hundred. Gold Two, twenty-three hundred. Gold One, zero."

"What?" The word exploded from Kell. "Lieutenant, I think you've got that backward."

Janson finally met his gaze, and nodded. "That's right. It is backward. But still correct. Didn't you hear me cite training protocol one-seven-nine?"

"I did, but I don't know what that means."

Janson smiled. "Piggy, it seems to me I heard you telling your wingman over your private channel what that protocol represented. Would you please inform your group commander?"

Piggy cleared his throat; through the mechanical translator, the sound emerged as an ear-popping burst of static. "It is a scoring variation. In order to encourage cooperation, particularly among trainees who have not been together long, each wingman earns the points his wingman scored."

"That's—" Kell heard his voice try to crack. He lowered his tone, tried again, but couldn't keep the anger from his words. "That is manifestly unfair. Is it going on my permanent record that way? A zero for what you called a near-perfect performance?"

"Certainly it's unfair." Janson closed down his datapad. "Take it up with the wingman who ended up with all your

5

It was just over three hundred paces along one broad cut-stone corridor, down a shuddering, clanking escalator, and through a small chamber to the cantina known as Down-Time, and Kell glared at his wingman every step of the way. Finally, in the final chamber before they reached DownTime, the long-faced alien faced him. "I am sorry, Flight Officer Tainer."

"Why did you do it? Fly off on your own, disobey orders?"

"I don't know."

"You *don't know*? If you're going to mutiny, you really ought to remember why."

"It is not so simple." The alien paused to consider his next words, and the delay brought the four pilots into Down-Time.

This was a large chamber cut from living stone back when the Folor Base had been an active mining colony. It was a large gallery, but its size was not what kept visitors from seeing the far wall; the absence of illumination, other than glows from neon decorations and holoprojectors, was to blame.

Kell led them to a four-seat table against one wall, but Piggy pointed to a much longer table nearby. "We'll be joined by other candidates," he said, his mechanical voice cutting efficiently through the cantina's ambient noise, and Kell had to agree.

When they were seated, Kell turned back to the long-faced alien. "You were saying."

Gold Four laughed. Kell turned his attention to her for the first time.

By the standards of DownTime, they had pretty good available light, most of it a glaring cyan from a nearby holo advertising Abrax cognac, so he got a good view of her—and was stunned by it.

If he could have created a holo of what he thought the perfect female pilot would be, Gold Four would have matched it exactly. She was tall and slender, with light hair, probably blond in normal light, worn long in a ponytail. Her features were even and expressive; hers was the sort of face that could go from military blankness to unusual beauty just by assuming a smile, and she was smiling now.

Kell covered up his sudden discomfiture by growling, "What's so funny?" He discovered that his mouth was dry.

She stuck out a hand. "Sorry. Tyria Sarkin. You're just so relentless it struck me as amusing." Her voice was low and she spoke with an accent, a rich roll that was as enchanting as her appearance.

He shook her hand and grinned a little glumly. "It's less funny when you end up with vacuum for a mission score."

"I suppose. I'm sorry."

"I will answer," the alien said. "First, please: I am Runt to my friends and fellows, even when they are angry with me."

Kell frowned. "Why 'Runt'?"

"It is accurate. Compared to my siblings, I am tiny. None of them would fit into a fighter cockpit. So. You asked why I did not remember doing what I did. I am beginning to remember. But I did not recall before because it was not I doing that. It was the pilot."

Tyria asked, "Which pilot?"

"Me."

Kell slumped, momentarily defeated by the circuitousness of Runt's answers, and put his head down on the table. He immediately regretted it: His forehead adhered to some dark, nameless substance there. He pulled himself free and began scraping away the stain left on his skin. "I'm not reading you, Runt."

Tyria said, "I think I am. Runt, are you talking about many organisms, or many minds?"

Runt smiled with the relieved satisfaction of someone who has finally gotten a point across. "Minds."

"You have many minds, and one of them is the pilot?"

"Yes! Yes."

Kell snorted. "Your pilot mind owes me twenty-three hundred points and deserves a good beating."

Runt looked solemnly at him. "We know. We are sorry. He, my pilot, has earned many such beatings. And transfers from many units. I think soon you will see the last of us."

Kell was relieved of the need to respond by the arrival of the waiter, which was heralded by a repetitive squeaking. The waiter was a 3PO unit, a protocol droid, but this one was unlike most of the ones Kell had seen: Most were all gold tone or silver, but the waiter was mostly silver with several gold parts, and squeaked with each step. Kell said, "I'll have—"

"Wait," the droid said pleasantly but firmly, in the melodious voice all 3PO units seemed to share. "In the absence of a hierarchy of rank among you, I will default to ancient protocols and have the lady's order first. My lady?"

Tyria smiled. "Lum. A good one."

Kell said, "I'll have—"

"Wait," said the droid in the same tone as before. "You have now annoyed me twice. This means you will order last of all, but I will still take your order correctly. If you annoy me three times, you would do well not to drink what I bring you." He turned to Piggy. "My lord?"

"A shot of Churban brandy," said the Gamorrean. "And a bucket of cold water."

"That sounds good," said Runt. "The same for us. Me."

The droid turned back to Kell. Kell waited until he was certain the droid was ready for him before speaking. "Corellian brandy. And a wet napkin. Please."

The droid bowed and departed. Kell heaved a sigh. "Not my day. Even the waiters around here are tyrants."

Tyria turned her smile on him. "That's just Squeaky. You'll get used to him. He has a good heart. Or whatever serves droids for a heart."

"Why is an expensive protocol droid slinging drinks in a stony hole in the ground? That doesn't make sense."

"He does what he wants. He was manumitted years ago. The Runaway Droid Ride, you remember?"

Kell frowned. "I don't."

She leaned in close, the better to be heard. "Among droids, and some pilots, he's famous. He was on the *Tantive IV* when Darth Vader captured Princess Leia Organa several years back. The humans aboard ship were killed, but he and the other droids ended up on Kessel. He kept inventories of spice shipments for the penal colony.

"Then, one day, he arranges for a whole bunch of the colony's servitor droids to visit an Imperial freighter that had landed to pick up a load of spice. They arrive over several standard hours, so as not to make the guards suspicious, but they don't leave. And then the freighter takes off and escapes."

"He flew it? I thought droids were forbidden to pilot spacecraft. Deep-down programming inhibitions."

"They are, except for Vee Ones and a few special cases. He didn't actually act as pilot. What he did was reprogram the ship's autopilot to fly them in terrain-following mode a couple of hundred klicks away from the spaceport, out of range of the port's defensive batteries, then punch up out of the atmosphere and jump out of the system. But what he forgot"—her expression turned merry—"was that due west of the spaceport was a series of canyons and mountain ridges, and his terrain-following program was strictly height-above-ground . . ."

Kell caught on before the other two pilots did and burst

out laughing. "So all those escaping droids went on a wild ride."

Tyria gestured with her hand as though she were following the path of a frantic oscilloscope wave. "So imagine you're on this tub of a Corellian bulk freighter, and suddenly you're all over the map, up and down, 'Whee!' 'Aaah!' 'Whee!' 'Aaah!' for more than a hundred klicks . . ."

Runt and Piggy joined in the laughter. Runt's was a hyperkinetic wheezing, nearly an animal bray; Piggy's was a pleasant, deep gruntlike noise, one which his implant was apparently programmed not to translate.

The laughter settled. "Anyway," Tyria said, "they survived, and he came to the Alliance with a bulk freighter and a lot of valuable information about Kessel—such as who was sentenced to serve there and what sort of supplies and defenses the Imperial garrison had. So Squeaky was given his freedom. He doesn't even have a restraining bolt port anymore. And he earns his living like people do."

Kell nodded. "By offering insult to those he serves."

"You know what I mean."

Runt turned to Kell. "So. You would not release us from the subject. We should not release you until it is done. You will forgive us for our mistake?"

"Sure. But tell your pilot mind I'm going to ride him hard if he fouls up again."

"I will do that. He deserves it."

Squeaky returned with their glasses and buckets. Kell went to work on his sticky forehead with the napkin Squeaky gave him. As the droid departed, Tyria glanced at the entryway and straightened up. "The second wave has arrived."

The others turned to look. Approaching them were two men in pilot suits; with them was an R2 unit. Both men had been through rough times in the past: One would have been quite handsome but for the long, wicked scar that puckered his left cheek, crawled across his nose, and marred his left forehead, while the other, taller man had a prosthetic shell over the upper portion of the left half of his face.

The one with the scar said, "More survivors of Lieutenant Janson's bait-and-switch mission scenario?"

Kell managed a mirthless chuckle and gestured for them to sit. "You two just get out?"

The pilot with the prosthetic headgear nodded. The portions of his face still exposed showed lean features, a cold blue eye, and a thin, immaculately trimmed mustache and beard that suggested ex-Imperial warlord more than New Republic fighter. "Ton Phanan. This is Loran and his R2 unit, Vape. The others in our group for the simulator mission were Chedgar and a Bothan who calls himself Grinder. Chedgar was still arguing about the scoring when we left, but I think it's because he knows he's about to be washed out." He leaned back in his chair, laced his fingers behind his head in an attitude of blissful relaxation. "I just made out like a pirate on points; shot down one eyeball and got credit for Loran's three. I could get to like this assignment."

Kell introduced his companions, then took another look at the man with the livid scar. There was something familiar about the pilot, about the man's dramatic shock of black hair and emerald eyes, about his poise and ease among the others . . . "Loran? Not Garik Loran? The Face?"

Phanan sat forward to take another look at his companion; Tyria did likewise. Piggy and Runt merely looked quizzical.

The scarred pilot nodded, looking rueful. "That's me."

"I thought you were dead! Seven, eight years ago. The story broke just before the news about the first Death Star."

"We are sorry," said Runt. "It is obvious we should have heard of this man, but we have not."

"Maybe it's just a human thing," Kell said. "The Face. The most famous child star of Imperial holodramas. Like *The Black Bantha* and *Jungle Flutes*. He made *Win or Die* and Imperial military recruitment went up five percent. You never saw them?"

The two nonhumans shook their heads. Phanan obviously had heard of Loran; he grinned wickedly at this sudden revelation about his companion's past.

Tyria had heard of him as well; her jaw was slightly agape. Finally she said, "I had such a crush on you when I was twelve . . ."

The scarred pilot snorted. "Don't feel bad. I was hand-picked to be the boy most likely to be the subject of crushes."

"What happened to you?" she asked. "Everyone said that Alliance extremists killed you."

He shrugged. "Almost. About the time I was trying to make the transition to teenaged roles, some *ex*-Alliance extremists kidnapped me. They wanted to kill me as a demonstration to those who aided the Empire in civilian roles." His voice was melodious, controlled, exactly what Kell would expect in a onetime actor. "They thought it would be a blow to Imperial morale."

"It was certainly a blow to the morale of young girls," Tyria said.

"But first they decided to show me what the Empire was all about. I got the hard-core briefing on Imperial military and Intelligence activities. Then, when they were set to kill me, an Imperial commando rescue mission struck. That's where I picked up my little facial blemish, a graze from a laser blast. The two sides damn near killed each other, with only a couple of commandos left alive. I was a real mess, emotionally as well as physically, so I hid from the Imps. I decided not to be found until I could sort things out. Since my body was missing and never turned up, they reported me dead and claimed kidnapping me was an approved Rebel mission, which it wasn't."

Tyria looked delighted. "But where have you been all these years?"

"With some members of my extended family. I grew up on Pantolomin, but my people were from Lorrd originally, so when I got back to civilization my parents arranged to send me there. From Lorrd it was an easy step to reach the Alliance. My parents had invested my earnings pretty well, so I never lacked for money when hiding out."

"If you don't mind the question . . ." Tyria looked a little distressed. "Are you allergic to bacta? Is that why you still have your scar?"

"No. I just kept it. A little reminder I earned from people I helped quite a bit when I was young." He shrugged.

Phanan held up a hand. "*I'm* the one allergic to bacta.

That's why I'm twenty percent mechanical, and gaining." He smiled at Tyria. "But every human cell longs to become better acquainted with this lady."

She shot him a look of amused scorn. "Is this going to be one of those units where there's one female pilot, me, constantly being pursued by every jockey with nothing better to do?"

Phanan sat forward and grasped her hand. His voice became low, melodramatic in tone. "Tyria, I've just met you, and already I love you. And don't think I love you for your looks, which are stunning, or your body, which is stellar, or your manner, which is bold and inflames me with desire. No, I love you because I hear you're a Jedi in training, and I need all the powerful friends I can get."

She looked distressed and yanked her hand away. "You heard wrong. And you have the manners of a womp rat."

Kell said, "Are you really a Jedi in training?"

"No. I have just a little, a very little, control over the Force. But I've been working on it for years and haven't improved on it much." She managed a wry smile. "The Force is weak in this one."

Satisfied that his forehead was as close to normal as he could make it, Kell discarded his napkin. "Have you ever met Luke Skywalker?"

She nodded. "He put me through some exercises. A lot of them, really. And he was so nice when he told me he didn't think I'd ever progress very far in my control of the Force. That this dream I'd had for so long was never going to come true."

The scarred pilot said, "You know, if I had even the tiniest control over the Force, what I'd do with it?"

She shook her head.

"On those long missions, I'd scratch that little spot in the center of my back I can never reach . . ."

She stood up fast enough to rattle her tankard of lum. "Go ahead, make fun."

"Oh, come on. You think Skywalker doesn't do that?"

"I don't have time for this. I have things to do." She

headed off toward the exit, her stride suggesting she was furious.

Phanan twisted to watch her go. "Can I walk you to your quarters?" he called after her.

"No!" She didn't look back.

"Can I help you with your things?"

"No!"

"What can I do for you?"

"Shoot yourself!" Then she was out the entryway.

Phanan settled back in his chair, looking morose. "I've done that a couple of times. Shooting myself. Accidents. It's not fun."

Kell glared. "Thanks, Phanan, Face. That helped a lot."

The scarred pilot shrugged, apologetic.

Phanan ignored him. He looked around, raised his hand. "Waiter? Hey, you, the bucket of bolts. We could use some service, right now."

Kell grinned. "Phanan, you just named your own punishment."

The next simulated mission was an ambush on a volcanic world. Kell escaped that one damaged but alive. He heard that Runt had once again been vaporized without scoring a kill, and that Lieutenant Myn Donos, senior ranking pilot candidate, was not required to undergo the scenario; Kell wondered why.

On another simulator mission, Kell was paired with Runt again. In the exercise, Green Squadron and a squad of TIE interceptors converged on an asteroid field; Green Squadron was to defend the space station concealed there, the interceptors to find and destroy it.

Eight klicks from the engagement zone, Runt let out another wild, warbling whoop and kicked his thrusters, moving out ahead of his wingman.

Kell centered his targeting bracket on his partner's X-wing. It went red, the computer giving him the tone of a good lock, a split second later.

A moment later Janson's voice sounded in his ear. "Green Five, what are you doing?"

Kell tensed at the sound of that voice and silently cursed himself for doing so. "Just trust me on this one, Control."

Runt's irritating war cry cut off. Then he said, "Six to Five, are you going to fire on us?"

"Negative, Six."

"Then what are you doing?"

"Getting your attention. Do I have it?"

"Yes, Five."

"Then get back in formation. Right now. I'm lead, you're wing. Do you read me?"

"Yes, Five." Runt decelerated a notch, returning to his proper position behind Kell.

Runt was good until battle was well under way. Then, when he and Kell each had one kill, he belted out his war cry again and rolled out of formation, attempting a pursuit of two interceptors.

Kell hastily said, "You have lead, Six," and followed.

When the lead interceptor tried to peel off and circle back behind Green Six, Kell used his trailing position to cut a tighter circle and vaporized the Imperial craft. It took him a standard minute to pull up abreast of Runt again, and in that time Runt smoked his own opponent with a torpedo.

Kell keyed his comm unit. "Five to Six."

The war cries ceased, but it was a moment before Runt replied. "Six here."

"Just checking. Try to rein your pilot in whenever you don't need him; he's too noisy."

"We read you, Five."

"Good. Keep the lead; I'm on your wing."

Kell ended that episode with only two kills; an interceptor smoked him with a pop-up shot from behind a rapidly twirling asteroid. Still, he didn't feel too bad about it; he was actually getting through to Runt, forcing him to respond.

Kell's canopy seal broke and the simulator canopy opened. Beyond were bright light and Janson.

Kell's gut went cold and he suppressed the urge to stay under cover. Intellectually, he knew he was in no danger from Janson, but he still felt a jolt of fear every time he saw the veteran pilot. In spite of it, he clambered out of the simulator and stood before the squadron's second-in-command.

Janson barely glanced at his datapad. "Average earnings this time around, Tainer. But some unorthodox tactics in"— he hesitated over the words—"personnel management worked pretty well. Some bonus points there. Let's bring up the win-loss ratio a little bit next time; otherwise pretty good. Any questions?"

"Yes, sir. Was it a program that vaped me, or a pilot?"

Janson managed a tight smile. "There's pilot ego for you—unwilling to accept that a standard program took you out. No, you're right. It was a pilot. You've heard of him. Wedge Antilles. Likes to sit in on these missions from time to time. Dismissed."

The training took its toll on the roster of candidate pilots.

Chedgar was gone the next day, the victim, Kell believed, of his own paranoia about officer conspiracies against him. The Quarren named Triogor Sllus was washed out two days later, for backhanding a Mon Calamari candidate named Jesmin Ackbar—the niece, Kell learned, of the legendary Admiral Ackbar. A human named Banna, a decent but not extraordinary code-slicer, was caught "improving" his recorded scores; his bunk was empty the next day. Others vanished with no explanation, and Kell wondered if they'd all failed at their last chance at a piloting career. He wondered if he'd be next.

At one of the pilots' DownTime gatherings, he discussed this with other surviving candidates. "When I arrived to try out for this squadron, I thought I was the only one at the end of my rope as a pilot. But it looks more and more as though all of us are walking in thermal boots on thin ice. Am I wrong?"

Most of the others looked sober. Ton Phanan didn't; he

smiled with diabolic humor. "I have a bit of a problem with luck in combat. Unlike most of you, I've seen some of it—"

Tyria snorted. "Braggart."

"But in five live-fire missions, I've been shot down twice and landed successfully three times. Not a good ratio. Between that and all the new prosthetics, I'm sort of an expensive proposition for any commander."

Runt, his big eyes solemn, said, "We know why we are here. We lose track of ourselves. But Lieutenant Janson says we are doing better, with many thanks to Kell."

Kell smiled. "You're worth it. One day you'll be able to toggle between minds as though they were channels on the holoprojector. Tyria, Face, it's you two I don't get. You two don't act like screwups—"

Phanan glared with his good eye. "Unlike the rest of us, you mean."

"That's right. You especially."

Far from being offended, Phanan grinned at the rejoinder. "Just so that's clear."

Face leaned back, relaxed. "I bought my way into the fighter corps, Kell. That's what my first commander said, and he's right. I used my own money to purchase an A-wing, under kind of odd circumstances, and to get the training I wanted. Flew two missions with Colonel, I mean General, Crespin's Comet Group and had to punch out or eat a bomber torpedo. Bought an X-wing next time just for variety . . . and ended up back at the base run by Crespin, just my luck.

"The general thinks I'm a dilettante who did too much good for the Empire in the old days ever to make up for it. Maybe he's right . . . but when he told me I'd never amount to anything, I snapped back at him like an idiot. I said I was just following in his footsteps. Well, that was it for my career. Until this opportunity came up." He shrugged.

"You're that rich."

"Not rich enough to keep buying fighters, no. I hope to be accepted as a real pilot someday. Enough so that if I lose this snubfighter, the Alliance, rather than my personal accounts, will replace it."

They all turned to Tyria, who looked uncomfortable under their scrutiny. "I don't want to talk about it," she said.

"Fair enough," Face said. "But tell us this: Does whatever it is that brought you here fall within the parameters we've been talking about? Something may have wrecked your chances for advancement?"

She was silent, but nodded.

"Interesting," Face said. "There's something else. I noticed one of the quartermasters delivering Lieutenant Donos a hard-shell case that suggested 'laser rifle' to me—"

Phanan smirked. "There's another vaped career. You know that sim run on the volcano world? I heard—"

Kell's comlink beeped. As he reached for it, each of the other pilots' comlinks also signaled for attention. He turned away from them and activated it. "Flight Officer Tainer."

The voice was female, impersonal, and, he suspected, recorded. "Your presence is required immediately in the X-wing squadron briefing amphitheater. Repeat, your presence is required immediately in the X-wing squadron briefing amphitheater." There was a click as the speaker disconnected. Kell heard the comlinks behind him all repeating the same message.

He looked at the others. "I think we have a unit roster," he said.

6

The briefing amphitheater was a white dome. Several dozen seats were assembled along the wall of one half of the dome; long curved tables, a dais and lectern, and a holoprojector curved along the other half.

Tyria sat at the end of one row of seats. Phanan smoothly moved in to sit beside her, but Kell, uncharacteristically awkward, bumped him out of the way with his hip and sat there instead. "Oh, sorry, Phanan. Were you there? I didn't see."

Phanan smiled, unperturbed. "Perhaps you need an optical enhancement. I could arrange for you to lose an eye; then you could put in for one."

"Thanks, no."

Ten pilots arrayed themselves among sixty seats; then Wedge Antilles and Wes Janson entered the chamber. The door closed behind them. Kell felt his ears pop as a pressure seal activated.

Janson took a chair by one of the long tables; Wedge stood before the lectern and holoprojector. Without preamble, he said, "I'd like to congratulate you on surviving our initial culling process. We had forty-three candidates; you ten survived. We'd actually hoped to have twelve, a full squadron roster of new pilots, but to put it simply, you ten were good enough and the other thirty-three weren't."

Wedge glanced down at his datapad for a moment. "Now to what we're here for. You ten, plus Lieutenant Janson and myself, are forming a new squadron; that much you know. What you probably don't know is that we're doing something a little new.

"Rogue Squadron, the last time it was reorganized, was built with pilots who had a number of intrusion skills. Our new squadron is the reverse: a full-fledged commando unit augmented by X-wing fighters." He looked among the ten pilots, making eye contact. "As much as anything, it is your secondary skills, some of them barely acknowledged in your records, that have earned your places here. We'll be doing as much work on the ground—sabotage, subversion, intrusion—as flying."

Phanan put up a hand. Wedge acknowledged him by pointing. Phanan asked, "Assassination?"

Wedge hesitated over his reply. "If you can find a way for us to infiltrate and surgically destroy an Imperial base without our enemies being able to call it assassination, I want to consult with you after this meeting. Other than that, under my command, members of this unit will never be assigned a task like picking off a speaker at an assembly or walking up to a target and knifing him."

"That's fine. I just wanted to know. I actually don't mind assassination."

Wedge gave him a cool look before continuing. "At the moment, we are designated Gray Squadron. Put in recommendations for a permanent name; if I see one I like well enough to choose it, the submittor gets a three-day leave on Commenor.

"Now, our roster. Most of you know one another. Because of our shortfall of pilots, Lieutenant Janson and I will be flying with Gray Squadron as well as being in command. Janson, incidentally, is a crack shot with hand weapons and fighter weapons systems; anyone who wants some extra weapons training should consult with him.

"Our next ranking officer is Lieutenant Myn Donos."

Kell looked over to where the emotionless Corellian pilot sat, well away from the other nine. "In addition to his flying duties, Donos is our sniper.

"The rest of you are all of equal rank. For this briefing, I'm going to dispense with the tradition of arranging you by the date of your commission or by your specific flight experience; instead, I'll rank you by your scoring during our pilot training. So first among equals of you flight officers is Kell Tainer. He's our backup mechanic when we're away from our support crew and is our demolitions expert. He also served with distinction among the commandos who helped take Borleias last year."

Tyria gave Kell a wide-eyed look. She whispered, "Did you really?"

He shrugged. "I planted charges while my buddies returned fire against unfriendlies. Somebody thought it called for extra recognition."

Wedge cleared his throat to regain everyone's attention. "Next, Garik Loran—" He was interrupted as Face stood and took a bow; several of the pilots offered mock applause. Amused, Wedge gestured for him to sit, then continued. "Face is one of our insertion experts, proficient in makeup, speaks several languages other than Basic—"

Face called out, "Don't forget, master actor."

Wedge nodded amiably. "And sometime cook. You're peeling tubers on kitchen duty tonight. Do you have anything else to add?"

"Uhhh . . . No, sir."

"Falynn Sandskimmer knows a lot about ground vehicles, and is a Y-wing ace." All glanced at the dark-haired woman from Tatooine; she stared back, an expression somewhere between hard-edged and actively hostile. Her look made her features, which under ordinary circumstances would have been attractive, rather forbidding. "In the absence of our support crew, she's also in charge of acquisitions."

Kell raised a hand.

"Mr. Tainer?"

"Speaking of acquisitions, do we have a squadron quartermaster? I'll want to work with him on the matter of spare parts for the X-wings . . ."

"We don't yet, but I'm looking among available personnel for someone who can do that. I'll let you know." Wedge looked down at his datapad to find the name of the next pilot. "Ton Phanan is our medical officer."

Three or four pilots burst out in laughter; the fact that Phanan was at least one-fifth mechanical and not possessed of a healer's manner was well known. Phanan himself grinned.

Face asked, "Corpsman?"

Phanan shook his head. "No. I used to be Dr. Phanan. Fully licensed to cut you open and weld you shut again."

Tyria leaned across Kell and whispered, "Why did you give it up?"

He gave her his most diabolic smile and whispered back, "Because I didn't care for patching up people I don't care about and *do* enjoy killing people I hate."

Tyria drew back with a shudder.

Wedge nodded to the female Mon Calamari sitting on the front row; her chin barbels twitched at the recognition. "Jesmin Ackbar is our communications expert. Voort saBinring, Piggy, is proficient in hand-to-hand combat, and capable of infiltrating Gamorrean units, which will be helpful on certain worlds. Hohass Ekwesh, Runt, has substantial physical strength—nearly three times greater than a human of equal size, and I understand he's small for a member of the Thakwaash species. Eurrsk Thri'ag, whom most of you have met as Grinder, is our code-slicer." The Bothan named Grinder sat upright, his gorgeous silvery fur rippling, and nodded at Wedge. Kell didn't know much about him; he'd kept to himself much of the time, not bonding with any of his flying partners.

Wedge continued, "Tyria Sarkin is one of our intrusion experts; she is a member of the Antarian Rangers from Toprawa, and particularly proficient in silent movement in difficult terrain."

Kell restrained a whistle. He'd never heard of the Antarian Rangers, but he knew the name Toprawa: a human-occupied planet where members of Alliance Intelligence had staged the critical data that led to the destruction of the first Death Star. Not long afterward, Imperial forces had savagely destroyed the world's armed forces, incinerated its cities, and sent the entire native population out of the cities to live in undeveloped wilderness. Kell had heard that the surviving inhabitants had to participate in regular rituals of self-degradation before the Imperial conquerors in order to receive food.

Wedge shut down his datapad. "All right, wingmates and designations. I'm Gray Leader or Gray One. I'm taking both designations to limit confusion. Mistress Ackbar, you'll fly with me as Gray Two."

The Mon Calamari nodded again. "An honor, sir."

"Falynn, you're Three. Grinder, you're Four." Both the woman from Tatooine and the Bothan looked unhappy with the pairing. Kell suspected that neither would be pleased with any wingman assignment.

"Kell, you're Five. Can you guess who's Six?"

"Runt, sir?"

"You're developing into something of a genius, Kell." The others laughed. Wedge continued, "Ton Phanan, Seven. Face, Eight. I want the majority of the squadron's sarcasm concentrated in one wing pair so we can dispose of it more conveniently.

"Lieutenant Donos, Nine, you're with Tyria, Ten. Lieutenant Janson is Eleven, paired with Piggy, Twelve. When we break down into four-fighter flights, I'm in charge of One Flight, Kell's in charge of Two Flight, and Janson's in charge of Three Flight. Any questions on organization?"

There were none.

"Good. You're done for the day. Except you, Mr. Tainer: We've received the first delivery of new X-wings, four of them so far, and I want you and the mechanics to go over them this evening. Join us in the X-wing hangar in fifteen minutes. Tomorrow, live-fire exercises in the real thing." Wedge smiled through the pilots' whoops and cheers, then added, "Dismissed."

. . .

Wedge waited until the last of them was gone. "What do you think?"

Janson stretched; tendons popped. "A pretty good roster . . . if we can keep them out of trouble. Some of them are experienced hard cases."

"How are you getting along with Tainer?"

Janson slumped in his chair and grimaced. "Oh, outwardly, pretty well. But every time he sees me he shoots me this look of pure hate and knots up into a ball of quivering muscle. He spooks me sometimes. I don't like being comforted by the presence of my blaster on base; I'd prefer to be able to relax among allies."

Wedge nodded. "Can you bear up under it for a while longer?"

"I think so."

"All right. I'd appreciate it if you'd dig us up a squadron quartermaster sometime today. I'll be with the new snubfighters and then with our guest if you need me."

Tyria seemed to be in a state of shock as they left the briefing room. Kell asked, "What's wrong?"

"I was the last one he named," she said. "I'm last again. The worst pilot in the squadron."

"No. You're tenth out of forty-three."

She glared at him. "The washouts don't count, Kell."

"Well, let me put it to you this way. You're the lowest-rated pilot in a squadron assembled by Wedge Antilles. You're the worst of this group of elites. Elites, Tyria. And tomorrow, you could be ninth, and the day after, you could be eighth."

Her expression softened. "Well . . . maybe. But let me ask you something, Kell. Have you ever been the worst at something?"

He thought about it. "No."

"I didn't think so."

. . .

The X-wing hangar, so-called because there was only one X-wing squadron on Folor Base and the hangar was given over to its sole use, was cavernously empty. It could have held three full squadrons of fighters, but now was occupied only by nine vehicles.

The largest was the *Narra,* the *Lambda*-class shuttle assigned to Gray Squadron. It had been captured not from the Empire but from a rogue Imperial captain who had turned smuggler. This accounted for the way it had been retrofitted, with a hidden, electronically enhanced smuggler's compartment worthy of Han Solo.

The other eight vehicles were all X-wings. Four had seen combat, the ones belonging to Wedge, Janson, Donos, and Face. Now alongside them were four spotless new fighters. Kell smiled, cheered by the gleaming surfaces, the unscratched paint and canopies, the sentinel-like quality of the sleeping R2 and R5 units tucked in behind the cockpits, the overall appearance of invincibility.

The man beside him said, "How I hate these things."

Kell looked at him. Cubber Daine, the squadron's chief mechanic, was a bit under average height and over average weight, straining a little at the seams of the jumpsuit that might have begun life an orange color but was now so stained with lubricants that it was impossible to be sure. He had intelligent eyes deeply sunk in a face that looked as though it had been sculpted out of chopped meat and hastily decorated with hair.

"You hate X-wings?"

"No, no, no. I hate factory *new* X-wings. They look so sweet. But then you get in under the panels, and what do you have? Factory defects just waiting to blow up in your face. Assembly mistakes no one noticed. And worst of all, they're always making improvements at Incom, slipping in these so-called technological upgrades without documenting them, without fully testing them—"

"And without getting your explicit permission."

Cubber's face broke out in a broad grin. "You *do* understand! All right, kid. Let's pop these things open and see what they've done wrong."

Within a few minutes, Kell decided that Cubber was correct. The rails on which the pilots' chairs were mounted, so that they could be adjusted forward or back to account for the pilot's height, seemed to be a glossy black ceramic instead of the stainless metal he was used to; he had no idea how the things would hold up under hard wear. He resolved to make sure there were some of the old-fashioned rails in the replacement parts inventory. The canopy seal on one of the snubfighters was faulty. The inertial compensators, the anti-gravity projectors that kept the pilot from suffering ill effects from acceleration, deceleration, and maneuvering, were smaller than he was used to and lacked the external kinetic rod array that was supposed to supply their internal computers with data about current inertial conditions. One of the four X-wings had a small, rectangular equipment module mounted on its exterior aft of the cargo compartment, but Kell couldn't find any wiring or other connectors from it into the fighter's interior.

So when Wedge arrived and asked, "How do they look?" Kell pulled himself out of one engine and said, "Terrible." Cubber extracted himself from the next one and said, "The worst batch ever." The rest of Cubber's crew, crawling over the other two new snubfighters, shouted confirmation in explicit and unpleasant terms.

Wedge stared at Cubber and Kell with the ill-concealed incomprehension with which normal people routinely greet the pronouncements of the interplanetary society of mechanics. He heaved a sigh. "Can they be ready for training exercises tomorrow?"

Cubber looked dubious. "Well, two of them, sure."

Kell said, "If we get a perfect run-through, first time, on the inertial compensator checks, maybe three."

Cubber said, "And if a miracle occurs on the extruder valve tests, we could theoretically have all four ready. Maybe."

Kell kept amusement from his face. There was no such thing as an extruder valve on the X-wing design.

Wedge looked unhappy. "Well, do what you can."

Kell saluted. "Will do, sir."

"And when you have a chance, though this isn't necessary for tomorrow, paint out the red stripes on all the X-wings except mine and Janson's. Replace them with gray."

"Will do."

When Wedge had withdrawn to his personal X-wing on the other side of the hangar, Kell asked, "What do you think? One hour, two?"

Cubber nodded. "One. Unless we do the stripes tonight. Which we won't. You play sabacc, son?"

"A little. But I'm not very good at it."

Cubber glared. "Do I look stupid? 'I'm not very good at it,' indeed. My six-year-old daughter is a better liar."

"Well, I lie a little, but I'm not very good at it."

Cubber snorted and pulled himself back into his engine.

Wedge Antilles wandered around the hangar for the next hour, long enough for the mechanics to grow nervous at his continued, needless presence. They got back at him by loudly telling one another stories of amazing mechanical failures they'd heard about, and the great loss of life that had usually resulted therefrom. Their work was done, but Cubber couldn't dismiss them while Wedge Antilles was present; it would fly in the face of the story he'd told of the X-wings' state of readiness.

Finally Kell heard a sound from the far end of the hangar's exit tunnel: Its magnetic containment field hummed into life, and a moment later the heavy doors just beyond it rolled open. Outside, Kell could see dusty lunar surface, blast craters, the silhouettes of other surface buildings of the onetime mine, the distant lunar horizon, and stars.

Then, a light dot in the distance, gradually growing as it approached. When it was several hundred meters from the tunnel entrance, it resolved itself into a shape Kell recognized.

"Corellian YT-1300 Transport," he said.

"Not just any YT-1300." Cubber had moved up beside him. "That's the *Millennium Falcon*."

Kell gave the approaching ship a harder look. "Are you sure?"

"Oh, yes. I was a year on Hoth, passing by that slab of rust and bad wiring every day. I never got to service her—Solo and his Wookiee friend hated for anyone but them to work on her. You can always recognize her by the specific pattern of corrosion."

Kell heard a distant pop as the ship breached the magcon field, which obligingly permitted the ship through but held the tunnel's atmosphere within. The twin-pronged prow of the ship dipped a little as it finished navigating the tunnel and reached the hangar proper. The *Falcon* moved smoothly to the largest bare patch of hangar nearest the tunnel entrance, then rotated in place so the bow was facing back out the tunnel. Only then did it set down, its master displaying considerable skill with the repulsorlift landing engines.

Its boarding ramp descended as Wedge Antilles approached. Down the ramp came General Solo, but not as Kell had seen him on holorecordings. Instead of being an uncomfortable-looking man in a New Republic general's uniform, Solo wore brown pants and vest and a light tunic much better suited to casual travel. He also wore a broad grin that did much for his craggy features.

He and Wedge embraced, then turned toward the hangar exit. Kell caught a few of their words: ". . . flight in . . . diplomatic functions . . . Zsinj." Then they were gone.

Cubber clapped Kell on the back. "There's your brush with greatness, kid. You can tell your children, 'I saw Han Solo get off his ship once. He ignored me completely.' C'mon, let's get out of here."

"Right." But Kell lingered and watched for a moment as a gigantic humanoid mass of hair, doubtless Solo's companion Chewbacca, descended the ramp. The famous Wookiee stood there a long moment, sniffing the air, then uttered a roar—not menacing, but low and resonant, perhaps just announcing his presence or claiming this part of the hangar as his territory. Then the Wookiee ascended the ramp and was gone.

As Kell returned his attention to the X-wing he'd been working on, he heard a scuttling noise. He jumped, then spun around, looking for its source. The sound was what he'd expect if an insect the size of a small floor-scrubbing droid were running around in the hangar. But he caught no sight of such a thing, and the sound ended as soon as he moved.

Cubber was already dismissing the men and waving Kell to follow. "C'mon, kid. Remember sabacc?"

"Right, right." Kell smoothed down the hair that had stood to attention on the back of his neck. He closed up the last of the X-wing's engine panels and followed.

"How was your flight in?" asked Wedge.

"Dull, what do you think?" said Han. "But not as bad as a night of diplomatic functions back on Coruscant. Sorry I missed you when you got back from Thyferra, but I was off on another pointless leg of the search for Zsinj."

They passed through the archway leading into the main access corridor serving most of the hangar chambers.

"You're not still doing that? I was under the impression that you were on the *Mon Remonda* and that the *Millennium Falcon* would be in storage until Zsinj was flushed out."

Han grinned. It was the roguish grin he offered up when he was among friends and enemies, but never at official functions, never in the presence of holorecorders. "I escaped Coruscant and its endless diplomatic functions with the *Mon Remonda* mission, but we haven't had any luck on the Zsinj pursuit in the last few weeks, so it's all dull procedure and maintenance right now. You know how I feel about procedure and maintenance."

"So you escaped your escape?"

Han nodded. "Officially, I'm hand-carrying orders regarding the hunt for Zsinj. Unofficially, I'm here to compare and evaluate on-base gambling all over the Alliance." He sobered. "The orders are variations of the ones Coruscant has sent out recently. They supercede those orders. We're trying to see whether Zsinj and the other warlords have a tap in on those transmissions."

"Meaning that if they set up patrols and ambushes that would be really efficient against the old orders but not as good against the new, you have a problem."

"Right. I have to head out again tomorrow for my next destination—which leaves only tonight for recreation. So, what do you do around here for entertainment?"

"Nothing." Wedge kept his face straight. "There are no women assigned to Folor Base. Because of the general's philosophical beliefs, there's no alcohol, no gambling, and we can't watch broadcasts from Commenor. This has led to a rather high suicide rate, but there's no getting around that. We do have some holorecordings of Coruscant diplomatic functions, if you'd like to see them."

Han wore an expression of growing horror, then it became pure outrage. He pointed a finger at Wedge as though it were a blaster barrel. "You—you—"

Wedge grinned. "I had you going. You believed every painful word. Come on, I'll introduce you to General Crespin, and then to DownTime, which has the moon's greatest supply of Corellian brandy. We'll see if we can put a dent in it."

"I should never listen to you."

"No, you shouldn't."

"Even Leia finally realized that you're a liar."

"Well, she's right."

"She always is. But if you ever tell her I said that—"

"I'll be vaped for sure. I know."

7

Four X-wings raced through the hangar tunnel and punched through the magcon field into the vacuum surrounding Folor.

"Two Group, form up on me," said Kell. "Pack it in close. We're under the eye." The "eye" was another X-wing, Wedge's, already on station half a klick above their position.

Runt, Phanan, and Face formed up smartly around him. This didn't do much to alleviate the tension that had clamped down on Kell as soon as he lit up the engines of the X-wing. Janson wasn't around to cause his concern; no, this was the old trouble, the tightness, the difficulty in breathing that came to haunt him whenever he was in charge of something. It wasn't the same in a simulator; now he was piloting a real snubfighter worth a fortune in a mission where sloppy aim or bad maneuver could cost his life or the life of a wingmate.

He forced his shoulders to loosen, tried to bring himself under control. Maybe Wedge wasn't listening too closely to the comm, couldn't hear his labored breathing. Maybe no one was monitoring the biodata sensors that were sometimes wired into the chairs of novice pilots. Maybe no one would notice his trouble.

He checked out the data currently reading on his navigational computer—very simple data, as it didn't involve a hyperdrive jump or even extralunar travel. He transmitted the data to the others, then brought his snubfighter around toward the south. A visual scan showed the rest of Two Group maintaining their positions; sensors showed Wedge still on station and another blip, doubtless related to their objective, straight ahead klicks to the south.

Wedge's voice broke over their comm systems. "Gentlemen, this is a simple strafing run exercise. The blip on your sensors is *not* your target. That's Lieutenant Janson in the *Narra,* our shuttle. With the shuttle's personnel retrieval tractor beam, Janson will be maneuvering a target, which will be about three hundred meters behind him. Five and Six will perform their run, then Seven and Eight thirty seconds later. Your orders are simple: Arm at two klicks, fire at a klick and a half, immediately disengage and return to base. There is now a governor on your comm systems; Five and Six will not be able to talk to Seven and Eight, and vice versa. If you hear 'Abort,' break off your attack and await orders; it probably means one of you jokers has taken a target lock on the *Narra.* Any questions?"

Kell said, "No, sir," and heard Runt repeat it.

"Good hunting, then."

Kell watched the numbers on the rangefinder spin down at a rapid pace, then saw the faintest shadow of a new blip begin to flicker in and out of existence a short distance behind the *Narra.* Moments later, he saw the *Narra* itself, a distant sliver of lightness against the backdrop of some of Folor's mountains, and saw the target: a sail of reflective cloth about the size of the shuttle when fully deployed. It was not fully deployed now; it twisted and curled in the shuttle's tractor beam.

With its shape and size continually changing, it would be a challenging shot at one and a half klicks. He addressed the R5 unit situated behind his cockpit: "Reset proton torpedo one to a ten-meter proximity fuse. Communicate with Six's R2 and instruct him to do the same."

The R5 beeped confirmation at him. Kell hadn't given a name to the shiny new droid; that was the privilege of the first pilot to be permanently assigned to this X-wing and its astromech.

At two klicks, he called, "S-foils to attack position." He reached up and right to throw the appropriate switch, saw the strike foils to port and starboard part into the formation that gave the X-wings their unique profile.

As soon as they locked into place, his heads-up display faded. Kell had a clear sensor view of the target . . . and no way to lock on to it with his weapons.

"R5, what happened to my targeting?"

The R5's confused whistle tweeted at him over the comlink, and the data board read UNKNOWN.

"Six, I have no targeting!"

"Five, we have no weapons systems. We have a general failure."

"Dammit, dammit . . ." Kell's guts were going cold so fast it was as though an overenthusiastic refrigeration unit had been installed there. He pointed his X-wing in as direct a path as he could toward the target, corrected to a couple of degrees port to account for the speed of the towing shuttle. With seconds remaining, he checked visually and by sensor to make sure that the torpedo wouldn't come anywhere near the *Narra*.

The rangefinder's numbers rolled down to one and a half klicks. Kell fired, saw the torpedo flash toward the target, saw it miss by forty meters or more. As he pulled up and began the long loop around to orient him back toward Folor Base, he watched the torpedo continue on its ballistic path, eventually slamming into the side of one of the distant mountains, illuminating the mountain slope with a brief, brilliant flash.

"Not too good, Five," Wedge said. "Seven, Eight, begin your run."

"Seven, affirmative."

"Eight, affirmative."

Kell frowned. Suddenly he could hear Seven and Eight again. Doubtless, since he and Runt were through with the run, Wedge had reenabled their ability to do so. "R5, can you give me views through their telemetry? Seven's and Eight's?"

The R5 unit hooted in the affirmative. A moment later

two views of the distant target appeared side by side on Kell's main screen—views that were alike but not identical, so they appeared to be an unmerged stereoscopic image.

"Seven, recommend we set the torps to a broader proximity fuse. That target's ugly."

"Good point. Doing so. All right, Eight, strike foils to attack position, now."

"Affirmative."

A moment later one of the visual images went to gray. Kell grinned sourly. Seven and Eight were about to experience the same failure he had.

"Eight, my weapons are gone. Some sort of system failure."

"Seven, my targeting's shot."

"Do you still have weapons?"

"Yes."

"Hold on, I'm transmitting my targeting information to you . . . wait for the lock . . . Got it!"

"Firing, Seven. We have detonation . . . Looks like a kill. But I still don't have targeting sensors."

"Mine show a clean kill. Good shot, Eight."

"You did all the work, I just pulled the trigger. Kind of the way I like it."

Wedge's voice crackled in: "Good work, you two. It's back to base so Three Group can do this. Do not inform anyone who hasn't gone through this exercise of its parameters. That's an order."

"Yes, sir."

"One out."

Kell gritted his teeth. Once again, because of one of Wedge Antilles's oh-so-clever tricks, he had come out looking like an incompetent. He'd worked very hard to overcome that first score of zero in the simulators, worked hard enough to put him at the top of the pilots roster, and now it was starting all over again.

The punching dummy was shaped like a man—that is, if you fed a man until he was so fat that his features half disappeared in folds of flesh, then mounted him on a flexible rod in the Folor Base gymnasium. Kell shook his head; he certainly wouldn't want to be treated that way. Nor would he want to suffer the damage he was inflicting on the dummy.

He started with a one-two combination that rocked the dummy's head, deforming it temporarily; in seconds, the puttylike memory material inside began to restore the head to its proper shape, but until then it bore the marks of Kell's fists. He switched to a knifelike blow with the edge of his hand to the thing's neck, stepped in for a forearm shot to the nose, stayed in close to bring his knee up into the dummy's rib cage twice. Both times, he heard cracking from within the dummy; it was constructed to feel like flesh, to give way like flesh and bone when the assaults were powerful enough, then return to its pristine state.

He danced back, bobbing, weaving, threw a left-hand feint, followed up with a right hook that whipped the dummy's head partway around. Very satisfying . . . though not as gratifying as if it were the real Wedge, the real Janson.

Kell knew he wasn't the best hand-to-hand fighter around. His instructor in the commandos was a woman half his weight, a head shorter than he. She could throw him around the mats at will and could hit harder than he ever could. But he was big, fast, and trained, so he figured he was in the top ten percent of unarmed combatants in the military. It was just something he was good at.

Too bad it didn't help him on Folor Base. He spun, planted a powerful side kick to the dummy's sternum, watched the rig sway far back on its flexible pole and then snap upright.

Just like his tenure here on Folor. If all his skills were as polished as his fighting, all his objectives here seemed as resilient as that dummy. He gave them everything he had and still they popped upright, unmoved, undamaged, unmarked.

"Are you mad at the dummy? Or is this a mad mind?"

Kell spun. Runt was seated on a balance bar, watching curiously, his brown eyes open wider than usual. The fur that covered his body was fluffed and disordered in places, patchy with moisture in others, clear signs of a recent shower and inadequate drying. "Uhhh . . . I guess it's a mad mind," Kell said.

"It seems to be a competent mind. You seem to be able to abandon it when you want. Else you would be attacking us."

Kell smiled. He still couldn't quite work his mind around his wingmate's logic or figure out Runt's circuitous approaches to subjects of conversation. "I suppose so. This 'mind' works better if you can shut it off at will."

"Yes. Our pilot mind is getting better that way. Have you noticed? You can cut through its haze sometimes. This is good."

"I'm glad."

"But you have another mind that worries us."

"Us, as in all of Runt?"

Runt shook his head, sending his ponytail swaying. "Us as in all the squadron. All who admit to worry, that is."

Kell picked up his towel from the floor, threw it over his shoulders, and sat up on the bar beside Runt. "I don't get it."

"You have a bad mind in you. You think we do not see it? It speaks to you when you fail, and lashes you with your failure."

Kell turned away from him, looking back at the dummy. Its features restored to normalcy, it seemed to be grinning at him. Grinning with amused indifference. Or contempt. "There's nothing wrong with that. Identifying failure correctly is just part of analysis."

"Then it keeps at you. For days. Weeks. Eating at you. Like some animal that has crawled into you and now wishes to chew its way out."

"Call it my motivational mind."

"No. It is not. It makes you think things that are not true. It is your enemy. I am your friend. I wish I could turn my guns on it."

There was such bitterness in Runt's voice that Kell turned back to him, surprised. "Don't be ridiculous."

"Falynn and Grinder also failed today's mission. Do you know where they are? In the cafeteria. Eating. Laughing. Looking forward to tomorrow's missions. They and others have settled in around Myn Donos and are trying to make him smile. Where are you? In the training room, punishing yourself and a dummy."

"Is Tyria there?"

Runt blinked at the sudden change of subject. "Yes."

"Have they been there long?"

"No."

"Well, I haven't eaten. I think I'll take a quick shower and join them. You coming?"

"I do not think you have heard what I have said."

"Of course I have. I'll see you there in a few minutes."

As he walked toward the showers, Kell heard Runt breathe a long sigh.

It was as Runt had said. Most of Gray Squadron was at the longest table in the officers' cafeteria. Falynn and Jesmin had Donos pinned between them. They were laughing as Kell approached; Runt waved him toward a seat beside him, but Kell took the one beside Piggy, opposite Tyria and Phanan.

Face was speaking. "So here I am stark naked, locked out of my quarters, running around the corridors looking for a towel, a rag, anything, and I turn a corner and bump right into the executive officer. He has about the same sense of humor as a Wookiee with a rash. So I throw my best salute and say, 'Major, I regret to report only partial success with the Personal Cloaking Device.'"

The others burst out in laughter. Even Donos, slowly stirring some sweetener into his cup of caf, managed a faint smile. Falynn asked, "So, what did he do?"

"He turned out to be all right. He made me hold salute for a while, looked me over, returned my salute, and said, 'It's obvious this project was a failure. I suggest you go and cover up its shortcomings.' So I did."

Falynn snickered, then asked, "What about the lieutenant?"

Face shrugged. "She had a sense of humor like mine. Probably why we got together, and certainly why we got apart just as fast. The next day, they found my clothes just in front of the intake door of the food reprocessing plant. There was a note on them saying, 'I cannot live with what I have done. Think of me whenever you have a bite to eat.' She signed my name, of course. I got away clean, so to speak, with the naked-in-the-halls thing, only to be written up for my 'practical joke.' I had to clean everyone's dress uniform boots for graduation."

Phanan said, "So, Lieutenant."

Donos looked up. "We're off-duty. You can call me Myn."

"So, Myn, do they do that sort of stuff in the Corellian armed forces?"

Donos nodded. "A long and honorable tradition. I'll tell you sometime about the dead gurrcat that wouldn't stay buried."

Grinder sniffed. "Practical jokes. A ridiculous waste of time."

The others looked at him. Face said, "You've never sliced into someone's secure files and changed them, left messages or something, just for your own amusement? Or to make them look stupid?"

"Certainly not."

"You're not like any code-slicer I've ever met."

The Bothan smiled. "I'm better."

Falynn turned away from him and back to Donos. "So, were you really a sniper?"

The lieutenant nodded.

"Did you ever have to . . . you know . . . I mean, don't answer if that's too personal."

"Did I ever shoot someone in cold blood? Without giving him a chance?"

She nodded, somber.

"Yes. Three times I did that. I didn't much care for it; if I did, I'd probably still be doing it. But better to have dead enemies than dead innocents." He glanced at his chrono. "Speaking of which, I need to suit up and get in some practice out on the range." Folor Base had an interior shooting gallery for blaster pistol practice, but the distances for which a laser sniper rifle was best suited were much greater. Donos and Janson had put together a target site on a hilltop outside, in hard vacuum; Donos would be sniping on it from several surrounding hills. "Ten, are you still going with me?"

Tyria nodded. "I'm certainly not going to let you wander around out there alone."

Jesmin said, "Please, let me. I need the vacuum suit practice." She rose.

Donos followed suit and, with a short nod for his squadmates, left with the Mon Calamari flyer.

"He certainly opened up," Phanan said. "It makes me feel all warm inside, seeing the barriers come down. I think we should get him a toy bantha to cuddle at night."

"Oh, shut up," said Falynn. "He *is* better. He talked, a little. He even smiled."

"Imagining Face naked would make anyone laugh."

Falynn glared at him. "Ton, would you die for Myn Donos?"

The cyborg chuckled. "Maybe some other day."

"Would he die for you?"

"I don't know."

"He would. I'm sure he'd die for any of us. He wanted to die for his last squadron, but his responsibility wouldn't let him. As far as I'm concerned, that makes him better than you. Ton, what's it like to be constantly making fun of people better than you?" She rose, not waiting for an answer, and stormed out of the cafeteria.

Phanan raised his eyebrow. "I say she's sweet on him." He turned to Face. "Want to bet? I'll give you three to one."

"No, I'm betting your side."

Grinder leaned in. "I'll have some of that. I am an expert in human psychology. She is too independent and pragmatic to have romantic yearnings for him. She is merely responding to the pain of a hurt animal. This is a human female instinct. She wants to nurse him back to health."

Phanan grinned. "Twenty creds?"

"Fifty."

"Done."

Kell fixed Tyria with a stare. "What do you bet?"

She shrugged. "They may both be right. Some women see

a man who is a mess, feel the urge to repair his problems, and then fall in love with him while they're working on him."

"Emotional distress as an attractant. Say, Tyria, I have a sharp pain in my childhood memories."

Phanan winced. "What a terrible line. I wish I'd thought of it."

Tyria stood and turned an indulgent eye on Kell and Phanan. "You two go play your boy games. The rest of us have some studying to do. You know we're going to have a hyperspace nav mission soon. How are your nav scores?"

Kell shrugged. "So-so. But Piggy's the navigational genius."

"That's right." She turned to walk away, but called back over her shoulder. "That's why we can be sure Wedge will forbid him to help."

"You know," Face said, "she's right."

Phanan looked glum. "I hate it when that happens."

The file appeared on Admiral Trigit's datapad, its title "Recent Morrt Project Data-Gathering Results and Conclusions." Its listed author was Gara Petothel, the code-slicer who had been so useful to him in providing information leading to the demise of Talon Squadron.

He brought up the file and read its contents, then skimmed them again. Finally he crooked a finger to summon his XO.

"Prep the TIE squadrons," he said pleasantly, "do full diagnostics on our weapon and shield systems . . . and tell *Night Caller* to prepare a load of the new Empion mines. We'll plant them in the unoccupied systems closest to Commenor, and then head on to Commenor system itself. It looks as though the Rebels are staging from the moon Folor . . . and I think it's time for us to put an end to it."

8

Over breakfast, Kell told her, "I think I'm in love with you."

They sat again in the officers' cafeteria, but this time it was Kell and Tyria alone at one of the smaller tables, early enough that only Face of the other members of Gray Squadron was eating at another table; there were a few of the A-wing pilot trainees about. Kell had arisen early, adjusting himself to Tyria's hours in order to catch her alone here.

Something like exasperation showed in Tyria's eyes. "No, you aren't."

Kell nodded. "I know you think I'm probably kidding. Like Ton Phanan always does. But I'm not."

"Oh, I'm sure you're not kidding. You're just wrong."

He laughed. "How could you possibly think that? How could I be *wrong*? Love is love. You're not making any sense."

She stirred listlessly at a nameless green puddinglike mass on her plate, then shoved the plate away. "All right, let's hear your reasons."

"Reasons?" He stared at her, genuinely surprised. "Reasons why I love you?"

"Reasons why you think you do, yes."

He sat back, the cold of panic beginning to spread through his gut. She was not responding the way he thought she would. He'd prepared himself for acceptance, for refusal, for confusion, and let's-talk-about-it-later, but not this cold-blooded call for analysis.

He took a couple of deep breaths to steady his nerves and organize his thoughts. "Well, it boils down to this: You're everything I want in a woman. Smart, talented, brave, beautiful. I've been attracted to you since that first simulator run."

"Yet you've barely talked to me."

"Well . . ."

"You're aware I have no family?"

"Well . . . yes." Face had mentioned that to him in passing, that her family had died when her world of Toprawa had fallen, that she had survived by her ranger skills for years until a New Republic Intelligence reconnaissance mission had brought her and a few other rescuees offworld.

"Now, what I want to know is this. Is my lack of a family a draw because I'll bring you no in-laws to complicate your life, or because you get to bestow me with the boon of your own family and make me happy again?"

He drew back. "That's uncalled for."

"Not the sort of thing you'd expect me to say, is it?"

"No."

"Proving my point that you don't know me. You've just decided that I match the concept in your mind of what your perfect mate should be, so now you're in love. We'd be the perfect couple. I'm tall, so you wouldn't have to bend over too far to kiss me, and we'll look good on the holograms together. I'm a pilot, so we can be partners. I assume, back when you were in the commandos, that your perfect mate would have been a commando. Right?"

The coldness in his gut solidified into a solid block of ice. "You're wrong. You're wrong about me."

"Then tell me," she said, "how much time you spent thinking about me yesterday."

"What?"

"That's a simple question. How much time? Six standard

hours? One? Ten minutes? Kell, give me a truthful answer. Set Honesty to On."

He thought it over, and as the answer came to him he felt his heart sink. "About fifteen minutes."

She smiled without humor. "You don't spend very much time dreamy-eyed for a man who's hopelessly in love, do you?"

He looked down at the tabletop and didn't answer. She continued, her voice ruthlessly gentle, "The good thing about fantasy lovers is they don't need much of your time. They're very low maintenance. Unlike real people. I'm very flattered that you feel you've fallen in love with a fantasy Tyria. But she isn't me, Kell." She rose and was gone.

Miserable, he stared into his cup of caf—not seeking answers, just avoiding the eyes of those around him.

She was right. Tyria was his idea of perfection. But the real Tyria? How close did she match his idea? He didn't know.

Face wandered by on his way out. "She shot you down?" he asked.

"Vaped me. One shot."

"Cheer up. Maybe this was just a simulator run."

Nor did the day's trials end there.

Kell stopped in at his locker to retrieve his datapad. He keyed in his personal code and pulled the locker door open.

Something shifted inside as he did so, then a mass of wriggling tentacles leaped out at him, landing on his chest, wrapping itself around him.

Kell let out a yell, tore the slick creature from him, and hurled it to the ferrocrete floor. He gave it a fast kick to send it skidding up along the aisle of lockers. He drew his blaster from where it hung inside the locker and aimed at his attacker.

It lay there on the floor, a collection of greasy tubes and metal springs. Its parts waved in the air, slowly settling down to stillness.

Chuckles and laughter broke out from all directions. Kell

looked around. Other pilots, X-wing and A-wing, peering in down the aisles, ducked away as his gaze fell across them.

Face was one of the other pilots, but he didn't pull back. "A prank."

"Very funny. Ha, ha." Kell wiped the sudden sweat from his brow and returned his blaster pistol to the locker. "That's the last thing I need. To be reprimanded for shooting up the locker room."

"Well, maybe the prankster will turn his attention to me. Won't that be fun? I'll destroy him psychologically. Put him in fear for his sanity. Cost him the will to live."

"Sounds good to me. Of course, I don't know that you *weren't* the prankster."

"True." Face shrugged.

Most of the rest of the squadron gathered for breakfast a little later in the morning.

"So, I'm curious," Phanan said. "Commander, Lieutenant, who do the old-timers think of as the greatest fighter pilot in the galaxy?"

Wedge and Janson exchanged a look. "Well," said Wedge, "we can hardly speak for the old-timers. As a matter of fact, you're older than I am."

"I'm sorry. I actually meant your generation of pilots."

Wedge sighed.

"It depends," Janson said. "What are the criteria for 'greatest pilot'? I mean, I've seen plenty of pilots with brilliant skill. Luke Skywalker is one of them. On the other hand, he didn't fly regular combat missions for as long as most, so his kills aren't up there with other pilots who have been around longer. Other pilots were extraordinary, too, but ended up drifting into the path of some Imp gunner and were vaped."

He glanced at his commander. "If you want to go by numbers and survivability, of course, there's only one pilot who has survived two Death Star runs. From that perspective, Wedge Antilles is the best pilot ever."

Falynn snorted with amusement. The rest looked at her. Janson asked, "Something funny, Sandskimmer?"

"Oh, no offense, *sir.*" The sarcastic edge to her voice suggested that avoiding offense was nowhere in her mission parameters. "But piloting is for the young. I'm sure Commander Antilles was very good in his prime. He may have *been* the best pilot at one time, long ago. And I know he's a good trainer even today. But, Commander, you're what? Forty?"

Wedge managed to look amused and regretful at the same time. "Twenty-eight."

"Exactly! Your reflexes are shot. There's only so far experience can go to overcome that handicap."

Janson said, "Sandskimmer—"

Wedge said, "You're only nine years from that same grim fate."

"If I should live so long, I'm sure I'll find some way to make myself useful. Just like you have."

Wedge stood. "Come along."

"I'm not through eating, sir."

"You're young. You can afford to miss a meal." Wedge reached over and drew Falynn's tray away from her. "Come on."

Reluctant and annoyed, she stood. "Where?"

"We're going flying. A little competition. If you're up to it."

"Now, wait. That's not fair. Until I'm through training, you still have some points on me in X-wings."

"How about repulsorlift ore haulers? Do you give up any points to me in those?"

"No, sir!"

"Come along."

The rest rose to follow, but Janson waved them down. "Finish your breakfasts and assemble in the briefing room. I'll follow and transmit. This should be interesting."

It was the oldest, dingiest hangar on Folor Base, and not truly in use by the New Republic military. It held vehicles from the mining colony that had originally inhabited Folor, vehicles that were still functional but not in use by the base garrison.

Among the vehicles on hand were three repulsorlift vehicles large enough to carry four X-wings nose to tail, with beds deeper than a man is tall. The vehicles still bore scratched traces of their original gray coats of paint and their beds were littered with dust and pebbles from the last ore loads they carried, years ago. None of the three had an enclosed cockpit.

Datacards still in place in their simple computers indicated they'd been serviced within the last year, and all three started up when activated. Wedge and Falynn listened to all three, agreed on which two engines sounded best, and flipped a decicred coin to see who'd get the best one. Falynn won.

Minutes later, wearing vacuum suits, they guided the open-air vehicles through the hangar's magnetic containment field and headed at a leisurely pace toward the near end of the Pig Trough.

The Pig Trough was an anomalous geographical feature of Folor. It was a meandering lunar fissure, created at some distant time when the moon's surface was not quite cool and tectonic plates were still in motion. Its near terminus was only a klick from Folor Base, and the lengthy geographical feature wandered for thousands of kilometers to the northeast, then cut sharply northwest for an even greater distance. The nearer portions of the trough were too broad, with curves too gradual to be of any use to the trainers, but more distant portions were used by pilot trainees for trench maneuvering and bombing practice.

On the lip just above the first descent into the Trough, Wedge and Falynn brought their ore haulers to a halt. "Comm check," Wedge said. "You receiving?"

"Yes."

"Wes?"

"I'm here. I've dropped a flare four klicks up the trench. That's your goal."

"Sandskimmer, you ready?"

"I've been ready since I confirmed seal on my suit."

"Go." He issued the command in a mild tone, but there was nothing restrained about the way Wedge kicked his ore hauler forward, roaring down the Trough's shallow slope as though he were in command of a fast-moving combat assault vehicle.

"Cheater!" Falynn was only a split second behind him. Well before they reached the bottom of the slope, she'd drawn almost even with him to the left. She sideslipped into him.

Wedge felt rather than heard the impact, but it didn't maneuver him out of line. He grinned. Only the greenest pilot would have failed to anticipate the maneuver and compensate for it. He gunned his engines and leaned into his leftward slide. The nose of his hauler was still a few meters ahead of hers and thus able to push hers out of line. He shoved her until her left side began to scrape along the rift wall; the sudden friction slowed her and he shot out ahead.

"Keep trying, Sandskimmer. I'm old. I might be tiring already."

Her curses lit up the comm unit.

The other pilot trainees gathered in the briefing room and watched the visual sensor feed from Janson's X-wing. Janson was pacing the ore haulers at an altitude of about fifty meters. Kell guessed that Janson was running on repulsorlifts, occasionally hitting the thrusters, else he wouldn't be able to move slowly enough to keep them in his sensor view.

Donos said, "She's actually moving that bucket around pretty well. She was probably a pretty hot stick back on Tatooine." He sounded more analytical than admiring, but it was the longest single statement Kell had heard from him.

Kell shook his head. "I've serviced rigs like that. They're not like recreational skimmers. Their repulsor fields extend out ahead several meters. They have to be anticipatory to keep those haulers from gutting themselves on rough terrain. If she doesn't know that, she'll bounce—there she goes." Indeed, the front end of Falynn's hauler rose an additional two meters as the craft approached a boulder outcropping. The hauler went skyward, gaining enough altitude to lose repulsorlift contact with the ground, and Wedge's vehicle gained another handful of meters on her.

Donos said, "She'll take him."

Kell pulled a handful of coins from his pocket. "Ten credits."

"You're on." Donos's coin joined his on the tabletop.

The other pilot candidates rummaged through pockets and began pulling out coins, money-transfer cards, jewelry, pieces of candy.

They ran now with Falynn's bow to Wedge's stern. Whenever she sideslipped to try to pass, he broke in that direction, blocking her move. The richness and color of her nonstop cursing were testimony to his success.

It couldn't last forever. She slid rightward, he followed suit—and noticed too late that the maneuver led him right onto a nest of boulders. Their proximity kicked his bow up into the air and she slid around to his left, passing him before he reestablished contact with the rift surface.

He laughed. "Not bad, Falynn. You've proved you can learn at least one thing a day."

"You're going to look funny spitting out lunar dust while you're teaching me, *sir*."

Ahead, the rift turned leftward. Near the right wall was a tumbled pile of stone; between it and the wall itself the floor curved gently upward. Left of the pile was broad, open ground.

Falynn headed for the broadest open area. Wedge slid rightward, angling between the stone pile and the wall. As he squeezed between them, his repulsors kicked loose stones from the pile of boulders, raining them down on Falynn's hauler. Her reflex slid her leftward and he gained on her going around the turn; he was a few meters ahead as they came out of the curve.

"Obviously you can't win by flying fair, *sir*. What happens when we get to the end? Do you shoot me?"

"I'm thinking about it."

The end of the run was within sight, a distant red glow where Janson had dumped his flare. The rift bottom was flat and smooth to the right of the straightaway, but grew stony and broken along the center.

Falynn drifted right. Wedge drifted left, toward the more difficult terrain. He saw Falynn turn to look at him; he couldn't read her expression through the vacuum suit's polarized shield, but knew she had to wonder what his plan was in giving up the speediest approach to the finish line.

She gained on him as they approached the rockiest portion of rift floor. But as they reached the point where the tumbled boulders were worst, he sideslipped right and his nose crossed over the highest of them. The move kicked him up several meters.

And he came down right on top of her hauler.

His vehicle's weight forced hers down, compressing her repulsor emissions, slowing her vehicle. His own repulsors kicked him forward off her hauler. He held his control wheel on course by brute strength. His hauler straightened out as it came fully down off hers and onto the rift floor—and a second later he passed the glowing flare, Falynn's hauler tucked in right behind him.

"You—you—"

"That's right, Sandskimmer. I won."

"You *cheated*."

He laughed as he slowed his hauler and swung its nose around. "Falynn, consider this. When an Imperial laser cuts through your canopy and hits you, the energy will superheat the water in your tissues. They will literally explode. If there's enough of your X-wing to retrieve, they'll have to hose down the inside. When that happens, will you complain that the TIE fighter pilot cheated?"

Her voice was grudging. "No, sir." She followed him through his maneuver.

"What will you say?"

"I won't say anything. I'll be dead."

"So to keep one of these bad boys from cheating until you're dead, what are you going to do?"

"I guess I'll have to learn to cheat, sir."

"Congratulations. You've proved you can learn *two* things in a single day."

• • •

At mission briefing that afternoon, Wedge announced, "We have two pieces of good news. Our other four snubfighters are in, and Cubber's crew has cleared them for use." He paused as the squadron applauded, then continued. "Also, we now have a unit designation. Courtesy of Tyria Sarkin, we are Wraith Squadron."

Several of the pilots made appreciative noises. Face merely looked disgusted.

Runt asked, "What is a wraith?"

"Something I heard about in my childhood," Tyria said. "Dark things that come in the night for you. That's what I think we are. For the Empire, for the warlords, we're the phantoms under the bed, the monsters in the storage cubicles."

Runt smiled, showing big teeth, and narrowed his eyes. The expression made his long face look sinister. "We like that."

Wedge said, "So Tyria wins the three-day pass . . . but not today; we still have a run to do. A full squadron run, for the first time. Other news: we now have a squadron supply officer. Please come on in."

The pilots turned toward the entrance. The supply officer's arrival was heralded by a set of rhythmic squeaks.

"We are in trouble," Kell said.

Squeaky, DownTime's 3PO server, walked in and up to the speakers podium. He turned to the pilots. "Let me begin by saying that I am delighted to bring my years of experience to this novice squadron. I expect that my skill will keep some of you alive."

Phanan whispered, "Inevitably, some of us will prefer to die."

Squeaky continued, "I am also pleased once again to be serving a fine officer named Antilles. A pity what happened to the last one. I am sure we will all pitch together to keep fate from repeating itself."

Wedge looked pained. Most of the pilots knew that a Captain Antilles, no relation to the commander, had been master of the *Tantive IV* and had died at the hands of Darth Vader.

"In dealing with you," Squeaky said, "I will match courtesy with courtesy, insult with insult, incompetence with incompetence. I have transmitted requisition forms to your astromechs and to your datapads; please use them, and always check your spelling. Thank you." He bowed to Wedge and moved to sit by Lieutenant Janson.

Wedge's mouth twitched as he too obviously restrained a smile. "Thank you, Squeaky. Wes?"

Janson stood and tapped his datapad. The room's holoprojector glowed into life, and on it appeared a dark field with a few dozen glowing points arranged within it: a small-area starmap.

He pointed into the mass of stars at a bright golden one. "Here's Commenor. You are here. Here's Corellia and more Core systems. Farther out, we reach border and then Rim territories. This star is nicknamed Doldrums for its lovely, featureless, uninhabited planets. That's our destination.

"Each of you is to spend an hour with your astromechs putting together a three-stage course to get us to Doldrums and a two-stage course to bring us back. These navigational paths should follow normal security guidelines for limiting observers' abilities to follow our course or trace our routes.

"When you're done, transmit your course to Control. We'll choose the one we like best, the one that burns the least fuel and appears the most elegant . . . and then we'll fly it as a test of your hyperspace skill and accuracy. Questions?"

There were none.

"Good. We'll see you in the hangar in an hour."

The pilots rose to head toward their X-wings and astromech droids. Face looked rueful. "I can't believe you, Tyria. I thought I had that pass locked up."

"What squad names did you suggest?" she asked.

"Well, there was Silly Squadron."

She shook her head. "We'd have to repaint the X-wings."

"Then there was Rogue Squadron."

"Taken."

"I know, but it was a good idea. Then there was Dinner Squadron."

"I take it you were faint from hunger when you were coming up with these."

"How did you know?"

Less than two hours later, Wraith Squadron was skirting Commenor, preparing to slingshot past it to get clear of its gravity well and into the proper orientation for the first leg of Piggy's proposed course. Folor was moments from disappearing behind Commenor's horizon when Jesmin transmitted, "Wraith Leader, this is Two. I have transmissions on an Imperial channel."

Kell knew Jesmin had installed an upgraded communications and sensor package in her X-wing, appropriate to the squad's communications expert.

Wedge's voice was next. "Squad, break off the exit maneuver. Circle here at a diameter of fifty klicks. Two, are they transmitting in the clear?"

"No, sir, it's encoded. I'm working on that. But there's something else. It's a tight-beam transmission, and the origin of the transmission is pretty close to our flight path from Commenor. Two possibilities are that they're waiting there for us, or they're using Commenor as a backstop for the signal so it won't reach Folor."

"Right. I'll inform Folor. Wraiths, maintain station. Make yourselves useful."

Kell gritted his teeth. Another test. The crucial duties, of warning the base and breaking the transmission code, were assigned; Wedge obviously wanted to find out what additional use the other Wraiths could make of themselves without suggestion from him.

Almost immediately, Face's voice came back: "Twelve, here's an idea. Query Two's R2 unit for the signal she's receiving. Analyze it for waveshift and see if you can determine how fast the signaler is coming."

Piggy's voice, distorted by the comm unit, was completely mechanical and inflectionless: "Will do, Eight."

Kell's shoulders tightened. Once again, Face was jumping right into a useful task, showing leadership qualities. If Kell wasn't careful, Face would grab control of Two Flight. Kell had to respond, to do something just as useful. He had to think fast.

Commenor was a planet fringing on Core worlds territory. Its government dealt and traded with the New Republic, with the shrinking Empire, even with warlords. So if the incoming vessel or vessels, which were either Imperial or warlords because they were using Imperial frequencies, were transmitting to Commenor, they were either announcing their arrival or making requests of the government. "Four, this is Five."

"I hear you, Five."

"In all the time you've been here, have you sliced into Commenor's official computer system?"

Grinder was slow in responding. Finally, "Yes, Five. Just to keep in practice."

"Good. Can you slice in now, with the gear you have on your snubfighter?"

"In no time, Five. I have my list of key codes with me. Always."

"Right. Punch in now. We're going to look for a few things."

"Making contact, Five. Starting the approval dance. What are we looking for?"

Kell thought back to the sorts of record changes the commandos had taught him to look for. "First, any new mobilizations of government forces. Second, new reservations for ship berths. Sort by ship class, prioritize for military ships and hyperdrive-equipped shuttles. Take reservations made for tomorrow as well as today. Sudden large-block hotel and resort reservations, especially the cheaper ones, just in case there will be some rest and recreation for a capital ship. Also, I want astronomical data, if possible, from any observatories pointed out toward the origin of Jesmin's signal."

"Would you like breakfast in bed with all that, Five?"

"That's right, Four. But that's after everything else."

They waited in silence for a few minutes.

"Five, this is Four. I read one government shuttle assigned in the last few minutes to convey documents and an observer to the incoming flight. Granting it the right to perform military exercises above Folor."

"Thanks, Four. Leader, that marks the base as their probable target."

"Leader here. I read you, Five."

"Five, there's more. Orbital Spaceyard 301 has been ordered to clear a servicing berth for private yacht *Implacable*."

Kell frowned. "*Implacable* is the kind of name they give to Imperial capital ships."

"Five, the berth they've cleared is the largest they have. This is no pleasure yacht."

"Five, Four, this is Leader. You're correct. *Implacable* is an Imperial Star Destroyer commanded by Admiral Trigit. He went rogue when Ysanne Isard died. Good work, you two. We're going back to Folor, and we're going to set up a greeting for Admiral Trigit that he's going to remember for a while. Form up on me."

Admiral Trigit beamed as he viewed the moon Folor through the bridge's transparisteel windows. An ugly, mountainous, frost-coated thing, it was well positioned to be of considerable use to the Rebels. He'd put an end to that.

An aide appeared beside him. "Sir, we have low-level beacon transmissions and encrypted transmissions on Rebel frequencies from the far side of the moon."

Trigit nodded. "Pinpoint the transmissions, then set a course for that location. Launch the TIE squadrons at a thousand kilometers to target. They'll escort us until we order otherwise."

"Yes, sir."

General Crespin's voice echoed in the ears of all the Wraiths. "They're coming in on the most obvious heading. They're a few minutes from arrival. Transports are loading. Four A-wings each from Gold Squadron will escort them. Blue

Squadron, Gray Squadron, remain on station for delaying action."

Wedge's voice came back immediately, "*Wraith* Leader acknowledging." Other voices, pilots of the transports and squadron leaders, responded likewise.

Wraith Squadron sat on an icy field between two hill ridges about ten kilometers from Folor Base. They'd landed as per squad organization, with each group of four snubfighters one hundred meters from the other, arranged in a triangle.

Kell decided against another, unnecessary check of his power levels and weapons readiness. His right leg was getting twitchy, refusing to sit still, a sign of his growing nervousness. He switched the comm system to Wraith Squadron's frequency and dialed it down to a transmission strength not likely to extend beyond this valley. "Commander, this is Five. Shouldn't we be up there, engaging them, slowing them down so the transports can launch?"

"That's a negative, Five."

"But they're going to arrive and pound their target flat!"

"That could well be, Five."

"Sir, I don't understand."

"That's affirmative, Five."

Kell shut up. He could imagine the other Wraiths, especially Janson, snickering over that rejoinder. Rather than humiliate himself further, he restored the comm system to its default settings and waited, seething.

"No sign of defensive measures, Admiral."

The *Implacable* was one hundred klicks from the target. "We'll just have to lure them out," Trigit said amiably. "Dispatch the bomber squadron and a screen of fighters."

"Yes, sir."

A moment later two squadrons of TIEs blasted past the *Implacable,* approaching from the rear, popping over the aft command tower and diving so that they seemed to swarm before the bridge viewports as they sped toward their target. As each TIE fighter or bomber dropped into view, it waggled its wings, a show of respect.

Trigit smiled. He appreciated the showmanship. Those squadron commanders deserved a little reward. He'd have to think about that. "Keep me updated on their defensive posture."

"All squadrons, all ships, this is Folor Base. We read multiple bombing runs and strikes on target." It was General Crespin's voice again.

Kell looked to port, to the west. If the report was true, he should see bright flashes of light limning the tops of the hills between their position and the base. But there was nothing.

Crespin continued, "All ready transports, Gold Squadron, launch. Good luck, and the Force be with you."

Kell sank back in his seat as the truth dawned on him.

"Coming within bombardment range now, Admiral."

Trigit looked at his sensor screen, which showed the Folor Base site. It was a broad plain of ice situated between two mountain ranges. Now it was littered with craters; the one or two sets of buildings he could make out seemed to be burning. Doubtless they were fuel or chemical depots; otherwise they could not burn in the vacuum around Folor. He frowned. Idiotic of the Rebels to have surface-based fuel depots. "Any communications from them?"

"No, sir. Their beacons are still transmitting, and their coded signals became more agitated, but they haven't responded to our hails."

"Commence bombardment." Why did the matter of the surface fuel stations bother him? Ah, yes. Commenor's files on the abandoned mining facilities on the moon mentioned numerous surface buildings. The plain Trigit viewed was almost entirely clear of such construction. Obviously, the Rebels had destroyed or concealed the ruins in order to make it harder to find the base. A sensible measure, yet more work than the shorthanded Rebels were typically capable of performing. Nor was it sensible for them to remove most surface traces and yet allow surface refueling depots to remain. It was the contrast that worried him.

His sensors officer looked up at him from the crew pit. "Sir, I'm reading launch of a capital ship. A Gallofree medium transport, from its sensor echo and maneuvering characteristics."

Trigit stared unbelieving at the little sensor screen on the arm of his command chair. "Where?"

"On the other side of Folor, sir. It just cleared the horizon."

A cold wash of realization went through the admiral. "Lieutenant Petothel." He kept his voice cool, calm.

His new favorite data analyst looked up from her station's screen. She was a lean woman with medium-length hair and a beauty mark on her right cheek. Her features were elegant, mesmerizing; he often had to make an effort not to stare. "Sir," she said.

"Call up the maps Commenor provided us of Folor."

"Done, sir."

"Establish the location of the mining facilities suitable for Rebel occupation."

"Yes, sir."

"Where are they?"

"They're . . ." She winced. "They're halfway around the moon, sir. The base is at this same latitude one hundred and eighty degrees around."

Trigit slammed his fists down on the arms of his command chair. A simple trick: plant beacons and false buildings far from the true base location, light them up when trouble is spotted. All he had to do was make sure the base they were targeting was in the same position as the mining facilities . . . but he'd let the Rebels make a fool of him. "Navigator, set course for the coordinates Lieutenant Petothel will give you. Get us there as fast as possible. Communications, transmit that location to the squadrons; they're to stay before us as a screen." There was little to be gained by dispatching the fighters and leaving *Implacable* vulnerable to an ambush.

"Yes, sir."

Trigit watched the squadrons in the viewport as they

heeled over and vectored north, the across-the-pole route being the shortest one to the target. The horizon tilted as the *Implacable* slowly followed suit. He couldn't feel the maneuver take place, couldn't feel the tilt of the ship; inertial and gravitational compensators eradicated the sensation.

He could feel annoyance. And a certain admiration. Well, if he couldn't destroy Folor Base with its entire staff complement inside, at least he could annihilate the stragglers, destroy the base itself, and deny it to the Rebels forevermore. A partial victory.

Crespin's was now the mechanical, condensed voice of a fighter pilot in a cockpit. Wedge wasn't surprised; if he knew the aging general, Crespin would personally lead Blue Squadron into combat. The training squadron would benefit from his long experience and might, just might, get out of the conflict alive. "Confirm *Implacable* and escorts oncoming by the most direct course," said the general. "*Borleias, Bright Nebula,* are you ready to lift?"

Wedge couldn't hear the transmissions of the two transport captains, but a moment later General Crespin came back. "*Bright Nebula* reports ready to launch; they'll be away before the TIE squadrons get here. *Borleias* is still suffering a malfunction on the ion engine initializer. Blue Squadron, Gray Squadron—I mean, *Wraith* Squadron—we're going to have to buy them some time and hope they can make use of it. Commander Antilles, any suggestions?"

"Yes, sir. If I remember Folor's geography right, a straight polar shot from the false base to the real one has to bring the invaders across some portion of the Pig Trough."

"That's correct, Wraith Leader."

"I suggest we calculate the interception point the TIEs and the *Implacable* will most probably pass. Send a unit of spotters to some point even farther north of that point to confirm their arrival, have them power down so they won't show up on routine scans. When the TIEs reach the trench, Wraith and Blue Squadrons pop up out of it and chew them up. Our spotters can either fall on them from behind or hit the *Implacable,* if it's close enough, to cause them some consternation."

"Wraith Leader, you plan is approved. You send two spotters, I'll send two."

"Wraith Five, Wraith Six, get out there. Run along the Pig Trough to bypass any sensor packages they might have ahead of their squadrons."

"Wraith Five, acknowledging." Kell powered up his repulsorlifts and turned in place to orient himself toward Folor Base.

"Wraith Six also acknowledge."

Crespin's voice came back, "Blue Nine, Blue Ten, join them. Same approach. We'll transmit your destination and the most likely intercept point when we have them."

Kell heard acknowledgments from Crespin's A-wing pilots. Then he brought thrusters up to full and shot toward the closest hill pass between this position and the start of the Pig Trough.

9

Kell and Runt reached the opening into the Pig Trough seconds ahead of the A-wings from Blue Squadron; Kell saw them visually moments before the X-wings banked and entered the mouth of the trench.

No one had said, "X-wing or A-wing, the first fighter to reach the assigned location is the winner," but everyone involved knew that was the challenge. It was always the challenge. And A-wings were just plain faster than X-wings.

Blue Nine and Blue Ten caught up with them on the first straightaway, blasting past without difficulty; Kell saw the pilot of one of the fighters wave jauntily at him. *Keep celebrating, Blue Boys,* he thought. *Just tell yourself you've already won.*

By the time they reached the end of the Trough's first long straightaway, many kilometers of it, the A-wings were out of sight ahead. At the first of what would be numberless bends and zigzags, Kell said, "Follow my lead, Runt," stood his X-wing on its starboard wing, and roared through the turn, slewing so close to the fissure wall under his hull that he could make out small cracks in the stones.

Runt's response was his pilot mind's war cry, but for

once Runt didn't try to pass Kell by. He stayed close on Kell's tail, a demonstration of precision flying to make his squadmates proud.

After a few minutes of wall-hugging corners and precision turns, Kell caught sight of the A-wings' thrust emissions ahead. Moments later they could see the speedier fighters, and with each turn in the course of the fissure they found themselves closer.

One more turn, and Kell nearly smashed into an A-wing, his keel to the A-wing's top, as they navigated a sharp angle in the fissure's course. The A-wing pilot veered out of reflex to get clear, and since he was already standing on his port wing the maneuver popped him up above the fissure rim for a moment. Kell rolled until he could see the pilot's helmeted head, waved cheerfully, continued the roll until he was inverted from his previous angle, and whipped around the next turn.

Then there was no sight of the A-wings for several torturous minutes of precision flying. Kell knew that shortly after the Pig Trough turned northwest again they'd reach the broader portion of the fissure where the Y-wing bombers liked to make their runs, a straightaway that would allow the A-wings to regain much ground. If only he and Runt could build up enough of a lead in the winding, snakelike portions of the fissure, they'd be able to keep their lead . . .

A short straightaway gave Kell time for a moment of reflection. Here, now, though a single slip could put him against the side of the fissure and kill him instantly, he knew no fear, no tension. It was just him and his fighter against the challenge of speed and obstacle. If he fouled up, if he died, Runt would take that as a warning, slow down fractionally, reach the observation sight alive. Or the A-wings would get there. No one was really depending on him, and that was the way he liked it.

Thirteen, his R2 unit, recently assigned to him on a permanent basis when the final X-wing assignments were established, beeped at him. He glanced at his main display. It now showed the path of the Pig Trough, his location, the A-wings' locations, the oncoming TIE fighters and Star Destroyer, and two projected sites: the spot where the TIE fighters would theoretically cross the Trough, and the spot from which Kell and companions were supposed to surveil the enemy. That was a spot just on the lip of the Trough several kilometers northwest of the projected intercept point.

If Kell had it calculated correctly, he'd be able to give Wraith Squadron and Blue Squadron a bare few minutes of warning from point of first sighting to the time the TIEs reached the Trough. That meant the two New Republic squadrons had to be under way already, following Kell's path at somewhat less reckless a speed.

Owing to a programming error, Kell's R2 unit initially responded to any request for a random number with the value thirteen. Kell had arranged for Grinder to fix the programming glitch, but had given the astromech unit Thirteen as a name. He suspected the R2 actually liked it, for it implied that the droid was the thirteenth member of the squadron.

They reached the first bend that would angle them northwest, through the main bomb run and to their destination. "Six, take lead. I'm your wing."

Runt bellowed out an incomprehensible reply and moved up past him. Kell concentrated on duplicating his wingmate's maneuvers, anticipating them as much as he could, flying wing just as precisely as Runt had flown it for him.

Then they were in the bombing run. They leveled out and put all energy to thrusters. Kell glanced behind him. Still no sign of the A-wings. Moments later they were halfway along the straightaway and the other fighters had not shown themselves.

Kell felt a sudden grip of guilt. Had he and Runt flown too well? Had the A-wings, wishing not to be shown up by the more experienced pilots, overflown themselves and been destroyed against the fissure walls? But no, just as they arrayed themselves to enter the narrow continuation of the Trough, Kell saw the A-wings' lights behind, just entering the bomb run.

A bare minute later, with their lead over the A-wings still solid, Runt reduced power to the main engines and cut in the repulsorlifts. Kell followed suit. The two of them angled northward and rose smoothly along a jagged cliff face, clearing its top by a mere two meters, and set down twenty meters from the dropoff.

"Six, cut all power," Kell said, "except life support, communications, visual sensors. No cockpit lights. Tell your R5 to shut down its exterior lights."

"Will do," Runt acknowledged.

A shadow fell across Kell's cockpit as the two A-wings settled in beside them. Kell switched his comm system from the squad frequency to the general New Republic frequency, but kept power scaled so far down that it would be unlikely for anything more than a klick away to pick them up. "Glad you two could join us. We've been here awhile; would you relieve us while we take a nap?"

"Ha, ha," came the reply. A woman's voice, Kell thought. "Who are we talking to?"

"Kell Tainer, Wraith Five. To my starboard is Hohass Ekwesh, also known as Runt, Wraith Six." Kell saw the two A-wings powering down and was relieved he didn't have to remind them.

"Dorset Konnair, Blue Nine. The pretty boy to my port is Tetengo Noor, Blue Ten. You two got some fair speed out of those outdated piles of junk."

"Why, thank you."

"Of course, we would have beaten you if Tetengo here hadn't remembered he'd left something in the oven back at base. We went back for his supper."

The other pilot's voice cut in. "I didn't want to go into combat on an empty stomach."

Kell snorted. The affection A-wing pilots had for their fighters' speed was legendary, as was their contempt for any vehicle slower than theirs. "Let's just keep that little story to ourselves," he said. "We don't want Blue Wing pilots to pick up a reputation for turning tail."

Blue Nine made an outraged noise; it sounded like a giant insectile buzz over the comm transmission. "Ooh, you'll get it for that."

"You have your visual sensors oriented toward their projected arrival zone?"

Blue Nine said, "Naturally."

Blue Ten said, "Oops."

"Snap it up, Ten."

For a few minutes they didn't speak. Then Blue Ten's voice cut in: "I have them."

Kell panned his visual sensor around but couldn't pick up the enemy. "Blue Ten, feed me those coordinates."

A moment later his screen brightened with a jittery view of numerous tiny glows—TIE fighter ion engines, far to the north.

Kell fed that sensor data to Thirteen and received back the precise map coordinates of the point on the Pig Trough the incoming fighters could cross—that, and the exact time of their arrival there, assuming they did not change speed. Kell said, "This is Wraith Five. Did anyone else run the numbers?"

"Blue Nine here."

"I'll show you mine if you'll show me yours."

Their numbers agreed to two significant digits. Kell transmitted them, encrypted, a short burst aimed directly at Folor Base; with luck, the attackers wouldn't pick up the signal, wouldn't be able to track it, or would dismiss it as irrelevant.

Kell waited with his hand on the power-up switches. Four minutes until the TIEs reached the Pig Trough. They'd be a long four minutes.

"Wraith Five, I have the Star Destroyer."

Kell checked his sensors, saw the blip moving in along the wake of the TIE fighters, several minutes back. "The signal wouldn't be this strong if they didn't already have their shields up. The captain in charge of that Star Destroyer is pretty cautious. Blues, do you think there's anything we can do about that capital ship?"

"Wraith Five, Blue Nine. I don't think so. I suppose we could crash into her bow like bugs hitting a speeder bike. That might upset their frail temperaments."

"A charming image. Thanks, Blue Nine." Kell tried to let go of the idea of hindering or diverting the massive vessel, but he couldn't. If the vessel joined the impending fight between the TIEs and the New Republic fighters, more of his friends and allies would be killed; if it reached Folor Base before the last transport lifted, that ship would never see freedom. He felt the muscles in his upper back begin to knot.

What would turn the Star Destroyer away from its mission, even temporarily? A greater perceived threat? How would they simulate one?

Perhaps a greater prize for the captain to gain . . . Kell sat upright. "Blues, Wraith Five. Our astromechs are factory-new. No sense of history to them. Does either of you have in your computer records any of the older encryption codes? The expired codes?"

"Blue Ten. I've got a whole string of them."

"Good. Here's what we do."

On this final stretch of the Pig Trough, Wedge didn't bother to check on the formation of the other nine members of Wraith Squadron accompanying him. They'd formed up tight on the straightaways, loosened up for the stretches requiring tight maneuvering, but always formed a screen forbidding General Crespin's A-wings to pass them.

Up ahead was the fissure bend that marked their exit point—the place where six TIE squadrons would be passing overhead any moment, if Kell Tainer's math was right. He glanced up above the rim of the cliffs and saw the first of their targets, an oncoming wave of enemy fighters mere seconds from passing overhead.

"Strike foils to attack position," he said, and followed words with action. "Wraiths, hit the interceptors first if there are any, then bombers if possible. Follow me in—"

"Damned Blue Squadron!" That was Grinder's voice. Wedge glanced back just in time to see the A-wings, no longer needing to maintain secrecy, rise above the fissure walls and kick in their full acceleration, firing up out of the fissure faster than the X-wings could follow.

"Four, this is One. Refrain from personal comments. Wraiths, they seem to be going after the lead eyeballs and the dupes they're escorting. That leaves us free to hit the squints.

Let's go." He pulled back on the stick, punched up both the thrusters and the repulsorlift engines.

Wedge's X-wing cleared the lip of the fissure wall by only a few meters, but its proximity to the lip kicked in the repulsorlifts, which bounced the X-wing up faster and harder, giving him an extra edge in altitude. He was pleased to see Jesmin Ackbar still with him; she had to have been proficient with the same little trick to do so.

Above and ahead, less than two klicks away, were six full squadrons of TIEs. Wedge set his jaw; they faced three-to-one odds. This was going to be bad.

He homed in on the squadron of squints, interceptors, and swept his targeting brackets across them. The brackets immediately went red and he fired, sending a proton torpedo toward them. He saw other reddish streaks of acceleration as four more Wraiths fired their torps, then pure red needles of light as the remainder cut in with quad-fired lasers. Wedge saw no less than four of the interceptors flare out of existence from that first barrage.

Almost directly above, TIE fighters and bombers flared into incandescence and faded into nothingness as General Crespin's Blue Squadron hit them. Then all six flights of TIEs were dissolving into flurries, pairs of fighters rolling out and diving toward them, already firing green laser lances.

"Two, stay on me." He corkscrewed upward, gaining altitude west of the main body of descending TIE fighters.

"One, we have three oncoming."

"Target the one to starboard, Two." Wedge transferred more energy to the bow shields.

Three TIE fighters dove toward them, firing continuously. Wedge almost smiled at their lack of marksmanship. Wedge closed with them, half rolling his fighter back and forth to present a more confusing profile, and switched to lasers, linking them for quad fire. He waited until he had a solid lock on the port eyeball and fired.

The shot melted and tore away the entire starboard side of the fighter, sending its severed wing in a plummet toward the lunar surface. The TIE fighter banked as though the pilot were still futilely trying to regain control, then exploded.

Wedge saw a quad pattern of laser fire hit the starboard fighter, coring it through the center of the cockpit. The eyeball, still virtually intact, heeled over and began its final descent to Folor.

Yes, they were beginners. The third pilot panicked, rolled out to begin his escape, and presented both Wraiths with a beautiful side shot. Both linked sets of lasers hit it, melting it to slag in the brief instant before its twin ion engines lost integrity and detonated.

Wedge and Jesmin wheeled around, seeking the area where the interceptors were most likely to be. Over the babble of instructions and outcries occupying the airwaves, Wedge heard Piggy's voice: "Seven, this is Twelve. Recommend you dive . . . *now*. Eight, recommend you fire . . . *now*."

Wedge frowned. Piggy needed to be fighting, not acting as ground control. But Janson was the Gamorrean's wingmate and could control him. Wedge picked up the blips of a cluster of fighters, probably eyeballs, at the extreme range of his lasers. He evened out his shields, said, "Two, fire at will," and began taking target-of-opportunity shots as his brackets flashed green.

Then across his comm came the last thing he expected to hear: "Han, can't you coax any more speed out of that pile of junk?"

Admiral Trigit switched his chair monitor to the plotting graphic showing the fighter engagement. He frowned. They no longer had three-to-one odds; the Rebel fighters were putting up a ferocious fight after an ambush of considerable efficiency. Of seventy-two fighters, Trigit had lost twenty-one, with only two kills among the enemy.

That would change. Numerical superiority would eventually make the difference. But these losses were costly.

"Admiral, new target, designated Folor-Three. About forty klicks to the west and heading west, slowly."

"Identify it, please."

"It looks like two groups of X-wings and a ship of unknown type. We're picking up transmissions."

"Put them through routine encryption, let me know if you get anything. If they're headed away, they're not a threat to us."

"They're already decrypted, sir. They're using an older code, one we cracked a couple of weeks ago."

"Well, put them on. From the start."

The voices were crackling and full of mechanical buzz. "Han, can't you coax any more speed out of that pile of junk?"

A female voice answered: "Han can't come to the cockpit right now. He's up to his armpits in what's left of the main engines. We've got only repulsorlifts running."

"Princess, repulsorlifts aren't going to get you off Folor. If you can't get those engines up in a couple of minutes, go to ground and hide out. We'll try to come back for you."

"That's very encouraging, Rogue Two."

Trigit snapped upright. "Sensors, does this 'ship of unknown type' match the parameters of the *Millennium Falcon*?"

"Sir, they don't match anything. Some sort of odd-shaped thing with an oscillating shield system we can't get a good fix on. Those shields can't be offering too much protection, though. Uh, records indicate that the *Millennium Falcon* has had three distinctive sets of parameters just since the death of the Emperor—"

"Yes, yes. Continual retooling, and all that." Trigit drew his sleeve across his brow to wipe away the sweat that had suddenly appeared there. Han Solo and Leia Organa here? Escorted by units of Rogue Squadron? Why? He was under the impression that their respective missions for the Rebels currently had them separated, with the *Millennium Falcon* not even in service.

But he knew it had to be them. The base was surely abandoned by now, so why would the base's A-wing and X-wing trainees be waging such a furious defense? It only made sense if they were covering the flight of the princess, one of the most influential figures in the New Republic.

"Pilot, close with target designated Folor-Three. We're going to capture some famous Rebels." He smiled at the cheers of his bridge crew and returned to his command seat.

"That's very encouraging, Rogue Two."

Wedge realized his mouth was hanging open, and shut it. Rogue Squadron and Leia here? When the *Millennium Falcon* had arrived and departed without the Rogues days ago? It made no sense.

Then he caught sight of the data screen and the information his astromech unit, Gate, was scrolling across it. These transmissions had been encrypted in the Derra-114 protocol, a code they'd been instructed to abandon weeks ago when they learned the Warlord Zsinj's forces had cracked it. It was the same as broadcasting in the clear.

New Republic fighter voice transmissions were often crude, part voice and part static buzz. This wasn't because the New Republic couldn't afford better transmission gear; it was a tradition dating back to the earliest days of the Alliance. New Republic comm units, by reducing voice data to the smallest set that would convey data and be recognizable, were able to broadcast transmissions across a wider set of subfrequencies, making it more difficult for enemies to jam them. The data reduction had another effect that was vital back when the New Republic was a rebellion: The voice distortion made it next to impossible for Imperial investigators to conclusively match transmissions with those who had sent them, so it was difficult to prove that a given person was the pilot at a given fight. Still, Wedge thought he caught some of Kell Tainer's vocal mannerisms in the voice of "Rogue Two," meaning the supposed *Millennium Falcon* group had to be Kell and his three companions. It was some sort of ploy.

"Leader, Two. *Implacable* is breaking off."

The sensor screen showed Jesmin to be correct; the Imperial Star Destroyer was turning slowly to the west, away from the fighter engagement. Wedge smiled broadly. "Wraiths, this is Leader. We've been given some extra time. Make the most of it."

Ahead was the thickest swarm of the dogfight, at least twenty TIEs mixing it up with half that many New Republic fighters. Wedge set his lasers to dual-fire and angled in toward the swarm. "Strafing run, Two. Fire at will."

Engines wailing, they dove into the thickest of the dogfight, firing as fast as their targeting computers showed green. Green return fire and red crossfire from their own allies flashed before them, above, below, beside, but Gate gave him no indication that he'd been hit.

The comm was live with the fog of communication: "Blue Three is gone, I repeat, *gone*." "Somebody get this mynock off my tail!" "Wraith Four, this is Twelve. Spin out, *now*. Three, your target should be coming into range . . . *now*." "Blue Four, this is Three. I'm still here, where are you?" "Then who's that cloud of debris—"

Wedge emerged from the far side of that cluster of fighters certain that he'd hit a TIE fighter, equally certain that he'd vaped an interceptor and winged one or two other enemies. He glanced beside him and was reassured to see Jesmin still on his wing. "Two, this is Leader. Status?"

"Leader, I'm hit. I show significant damage to etheric rudder."

"Can your R2 patch it up?"

"I think so. He's shrieking at me not to maneuver, though. He says it will tear apart the few connections I have left."

Wedge bit his lip. If that report was accurate and Jesmin returned to the fight, she'd probably lose maneuverability fast—and that would make her an easy target for opportunistic TIE pilots. "Two, break off. Return to Folor Base, maneuvering by engines only. Take up station there and keep me updated."

"Yes, sir." Even with comm distortion, there was no mistaking the resignation in her voice. Wedge felt for her; he knew she'd be berating herself for failing the squadron. He'd felt that way himself eight years ago, when ordered to break off his attack on the first Death Star. But he had no time to play morale officer now. He waited until she locked her strike foils back into cruise formation and began her long, gentle curve back toward base, then he looped around in a tight arc and headed back toward the fight.

Sensors showed the TIEs dropping at a good rate, though battle damage was taking its toll on the X-wings and A-wings. If the *Borleias* didn't launch soon, Wraith and Blue Squadrons were going to be in deep trouble.

Blue Nine and Blue Ten flew wingtip to wingtip with a precision that made Kell jealous. He'd always thought of A-wing pilots as being a little sloppier than X-wing pilots, because their crafts were not quite as maneuverable, but Blue Squadron was putting the lie to his suppositions. He revised his opinion of General Crespin from "pain in the rear" to "pain in the rear but a fine trainer."

Wraith Five and Wraith Six paced the two A-wings, and their rate was appallingly slow—about the same as a fast human sprint, the maximum rate of some repulsorlift engines. Though their course was a straight line northwest, they kept the Pig Trough within a kilometer of their position.

Kell checked his monitor, still showing sensor data. The fighter battle was a confusing blur of specks far in the distance. Closer, the *Implacable* gained on them with frightening speed. They were already within range of the Star Destroyer's bombardment cannons . . . though those weapons were not accurate against fighters at this distance.

"Runt, anything from Folor?"

"Negative, Five."

He switched back to the Derra-114 encryption and boosted his transmission power. "Princess, they're gaining on us. I give you two minutes before we have to cut and run."

Blue Nine's voice was a plea: "Just hang on a little while, Rogue Two. We're almost there."

Kell grinned. He and Blue Nine were pretty bad actors, but the crew of the *Implacable* apparently hadn't noticed. Maybe, if he survived, he'd get Face to teach him some of the tricks of the trade.

"Five, this is Six. *Borleias* reports launch."

"*Falcon,* sorry, you're on your own. Go to ground, get to cover. We'll meet up with you at, uh, New DownTime."

"I read you, Rogue Two. Be strong in the Force. *Falcon* out."

That was their bug-out signal. Kell instructed Thirteen to cut the power boost to the X-wing's transponder and shields; Runt would be doing the same, and this would drop the signal strength to that appropriate to a pair of X-wings instead of two groups of them. The A-wing pilots would now be shutting down the program that oscillated the energy going to their own shields, which had yielded the odd signal Blue Nine had hoped would attract the *Implacable.* If this all worked, a presumed *Millennium Falcon* and six or eight X-wings would magically transform, on the *Implacable*'s sensors, to a mere four fighters.

The four rolled to port and blasted their way to the Pig Trough, now only half a klick away, then dropped back into the fissure and headed southeast again.

The sensors officer looked confused. "The signal changed. I think they're trying to jam us. They've certainly gone into that prominent canyon formation."

"Pilot, new course, due south. When you get to these coordinates"—Trigit tapped the point where their southern course would intercept the fissure—"hover. Weapons, prepare the tractor. We'll pluck them out of that ravine like a Gamorrean plucks morrts."

"Admiral, this is Tactical. The Rebel fighters at the main engagement are breaking off. We also show another transport well out ahead of them, clearing Folor's gravity well."

"Tell the interceptors to keep on their tail, pick off stragglers, plot their jump course if they jump."

"Sir, the interceptors are all gone."

Trigit looked up. "Wait. There was another transport?"

"Yes, sir."

The admiral felt his stomach begin to sink. "Pilot, bring us to flank speed. I want us over that canyon *now.*"

"Coming to flank speed, sir."

• • •

Janson's voice crackled over the comm unit, "*Borleias* reports she's away and within a couple of minutes of entering hyperspace."

Then Crespin's voice; Wedge was pleased to hear that the aging pilot was still among the living. "Blue Squadron, Wraith Squadron, break off and regroup. We'll reunite at Rendezvous One."

"Blue Leader, Wraith Leader. Acknowledged. Best of luck." Wedge, just having completed another head-to-head run-through of the most energetic swarm of fighters, began a long circle. "Wraiths, you heard him. Break off. Form up on me."

The surviving TIEs, reduced in number by half and never reinforced by the presence of the *Implacable,* let them go—all but a pair of overeager eyeballs who pursued and were vaped almost immediately by Janson and Piggy.

Wedge brought Wraith Squadron around to a southward course, toward base. "Wraith Five, Wraith Six, do you read?"

"We read, Leader. We're coming. Too busy to calculate ETA."

The *Implacable* slowed to a full stop with its main tractor array poised over the fissure.

The sensors officer immediately spoke up. "Four ships incoming along that geographical formation. But they're not target Folor-Three."

Trigit frowned. "What do you mean? Who are they?"

"Two X-wings, two A-wings. No Corellian YT-1300s."

No *Millennium Falcon.* Trigit closed his eyes. Twice. He'd been fooled twice in one day. Not even his own children, bright and malicious as they were, had ever done that to him. He rubbed his forehead, at the headache that had suddenly appeared there. "Forget the tractor," he said gently. "Maximum laser bombardment. I want them dead."

• • •

Kell finished his transmission with the *Implacable* almost directly overhead. Then the Star Destroyer's laser cannons began raining columns of pure destruction down on them.

The first blast hit the fissure wall less than a hundred meters ahead, filling the fissure and sky above with blinding light and melting stone debris. Kell headed to starboard of the blast's center, flying by memory while his sight and sensors were useless, and cleared the blast field, only to run right into another one. He heard stone shards hammer against his cockpit, against the side of his fighter. "Six, we're in trouble."

"Five, I'm taking lead." It was Runt's voice, but different, neither the polite Runt of ordinary conversation nor the inarticulate screamer who did his best flying.

Kell saw Runt overtake him, could barely pick him out visually and by sensor. Runt continued, "Blues, follow me in. This is an easy one."

Obligingly, Kell brought his fighter up on Runt's wing. Each debris cloud they cleared brought them into another one, more hammering sounds of stone shrapnel, more buffeting from the suddenly expanding clouds of gas that used to be ice and solid rock. But Kell maneuvered when Runt did and, miraculously, avoided tearing himself to shreds on the fissure walls.

Then, a sharp right turn and they were beyond the bombardment. Laser blasts the diameter of fighters hammered the fissure rim above them but did not reach the depths. Runt led them down to the fissure bottom and reduced their speed from insane to merely near-insane velocities.

"Great work, Six. Who was that?"

"The student. The one who remembers, who studies for tests."

"Tell him he just scored very high." Kell brought diagnostics up on his main monitor. They showed minor damage to both port strike foils and a slow leak, a very slow one, of cabin pressure. "Blue Nine, Blue Ten, status?"

"We're chewed up, Wraith Five. But we can make it back to the group."

"Good. This far from the *Implacable,* I think we'll save fuel and jump out of the Pig Trough, head in straight."

10

Ten X-wings and the squadron's *Lambda*-class shuttle, the *Narra,* were already lining up for departure as Kell and Runt arrived. The late arrivals slid into formation with Phanan and Face, then Wedge brought the squadron up to speed and oriented them away from Folor.

Wedge's voice came over the comm unit. "Wraiths, I have the pleasure of reporting no losses among our forces. Ton Phanan has reported some minor injury; fortunately, he has our doctor with him. Everyone else has sustained some vehicle damage, none critical. For a unit's first engagement against a numerically superior force, that's brilliant flying."

"Leader, Eight. How did Blue Squadron make out?"

"Not so well, Eight. Five lost, serious damage to most of the rest. We have two kills today for Face, which brings his total to six—you're an ace, Loran."

"Do I get a trophy with that?"

"No, but someone may buy you a drink. I also need to commend Wraith Five and Wraith Six for exemplary tactics in drawing the *Implacable* away from us—"

"Thank you, sir!"

"Pipe down, Five. Also to mention that I'm thinking of putting you two on report for that stunt with the clear-air broadcast to the *Implacable*. What were you thinking?"

"Uhhh . . . I guess we weren't, sir. I was just shot through with adrenaline because I'd survived."

"Well, I expect it all balances out, and by way of reward and punishment I'll just hammer medals straight into your skulls."

"Thank you, sir. Uh—who's piloting *Narra?*"

Another familiar voice cut in. "It's Cubber, Five. I have Squeaky with me."

Wedge said, "That reminds me. Wraiths, be advised that instead of taking the first transport off this rock, Squeaky raided your quarters and lockers, bagging anything he thought would be of importance to you, especially personal items; they're all aboard the *Narra.*"

There was a chorus of thanks, whistles, and short cheers over the comm. Then Squeaky's voice: "It was enlightened self-interest, I assure you. Had I not done this, I would have been barraged with requests for replacements for your lost goods. I'm far too busy to attend to such irrelevant requests."

"Leader, Five. What's our destination?" Folor had shrunk to a small coin-sized disk of silver-gray behind them; their current course was taking them around Commenor in a wide arc.

"As before, Doldrums. We're going to take the same navigational exercise as before. We'll be joining the rest of the Folor Base evacuees at Doldrums."

"They're going there, too? That's an odd coincidence."

"No coincidence, Five. When I reported the *Implacable* coming in, I also told General Crespin of our training mission and mentioned that Doldrums would be a good site to stage a regrouping. The rest of the evacuees are going there in one jump; we're going to do our exercise just because we can use the practice. Which reminds me—I need fuel reports from each of you."

·   ·   ·

Malicious cheer clearly visible on his face even through the wavering hyperspace connection, Warlord Zsinj's hologram smiled at Trigit. "Well?"

Trigit didn't bother to conceal his glum mood. "I have both good news and bad to report. The good news: the base on Folor is gone, and I think I gave it enough of a pounding to make it impractical for the Rebellion to reestablish it."

"Good! And?"

"Due to some unanticipated reconnaissance and some superior tactics on their part, the Rebel garrison got away without significant loss. We, on the other hand, had substantial losses. Twenty-six TIEs of various types destroyed, another eleven damaged so badly that they withdrew from the engagement. I've already transmitted a requisitions request to your bridge."

"Apwar, Apwar! They outmaneuvered you with such ease, and you expect me to replace your losses?"

"Yes, of course. I don't ask for unnecessary excesses of supplies when I perform brilliantly for you, and I do ask for ordinary replacements on those few occasions I come up short. So far, I believe you have little to complain about." Trigit finally let a smile spread across his face. "Besides, I had already set some activities in motion to capture possible evacuees. With luck, I'll have some better news to report to you in the near future."

Zsinj sighed, rippling the holographic image. "Very well. I'll signal you when I have replacements available for you. In the meantime, keep—"

"—you informed. As ever, sir."

Zsinj gave him a frosty smile and wavered out of existence.

Before they made the jump to hyperspace, Wedge switched his comm over to give him a private channel with Janson. "Wes."

"I'm here."

"What was Piggy doing?"

"I'm not sure how to describe it. I think he was running

like a tactical planning computer. In addition to doing all his own flying—he vaped one interceptor—he seemed to be keeping track of all the Wraiths and their current opponents. He offered a few suggestions at critical times and gave us a handful of kills we wouldn't have had otherwise."

"I've never heard of anyone able to do that."

"Well, he's not human. He's not even exactly Gamorrean."

"What's your assessment of the overall squadron?"

"They're not as good as Rogue Squadron was when you reorganized the squadron. But they're still pretty good. Why?"

"They're just . . . different. Hand them an ordinary set of instructions and they'll carry them out in an ordinary fashion. Hand them an objective without instructions and they accomplish it some strange way. Like that whole fake *Millennium Falcon* ploy, and what Piggy was doing, and the data they got off Commenor's planetary computer net. I'm having a hard time anticipating them."

"Hey, you picked them."

"I—*I* picked them? What were you doing during those pilot interviews?"

"Daydreaming."

"Traitor." Wedge hit the comm key to send a click, signaling the end of the conversation, and switched back to squadron frequency. "Wraiths, thirty seconds to jump."

During the first of three long jumps leading them to Doldrums, Kell forced himself to calm down, to settle his nerves.

He couldn't quite extinguish his jubilation, though. In his first combat mission as a pilot, he hadn't so much as fired a shot at an enemy, but he'd executed tactics that might have saved the *Borleias* from destruction or saved some of his fellow Wraiths from death under the guns of the *Implacable*.

Even Wedge Antilles had been impressed—at least, more impressed than annoyed.

The jump was long enough, though, that he couldn't just reflect on his recent victory. There was Tyria to consider.

How would he persuade her that she was wrong about his feelings for her? First, obviously, he'd have to think about her more during the day, to answer her objection on that score . . . What else did he need to do?

He considered that, approaching the problem from a dozen logical angles, but an answer he had not expected and did not like began to lurk at the periphery of his thinking. Finally it moved in, squeezing aside his other trains of thought, and demanded that he pay attention to it.

Tyria hadn't been wrong. She was right. You don't actually love her.

Kell frowned at the traitorous voice. *What are you, one of Runt's leftover minds?*

You don't love her. You feel about her the way you did about Tuatara Lone when you were fifteen.

Tuatara Lone was a holo actress on Sluis Van. Short, shapely, so cute she was toxic, she was particularly adept at portraying madcap girls with odd lifestyles or nosy investigators capable of bluffing their way out of any problem. For three years, Kell had been mesmerized by her, seeing every one of her comedies and dramas, agonizing at night over her beauty, projecting himself into fantasy situations where he'd rescue her from harm or solve a crisis threatening her happiness.

Then he'd learned that the actress was in fact extremely happily married, with two children and another on the way. Kell, finding himself out of the running in a race he had actually never entered, was crushed. He moped around his home and was nearly fired from his job as a mechanic. Only when he entered the New Republic armed forces and was too busy to do anything but work and sleep had he forgotten his pain.

Now she was back, Tuatara Lone in all her beauty, hovering before him alongside Tyria. And that drove it home, his two obsessions side by side, as no previous argument had: He really was in love with holograms, images that only dimly reflected the real women they represented.

Tyria was right. You don't love her.

I know. Shut up. Just go away. He sighed, dejected.

Thirteen beeped at him. Startled out of his painful reverie, he saw the timer on his main monitor counting down one standard minute—time until arrival in the Xobome system, the uninhabited first stop on their route to Doldrums. He did a visual check around his X-wing, seeing only the usual effect of a hyperspace jump, the corridor of light formations in endless, beautiful motion. Everything normal, and he had enough fuel, just barely, for the two farther stages on to Doldrums.

At twenty-seven seconds until the end of the jump, the stars appeared as elongated columns like millions of laser beams extending into infinity, and then snapped into a motionless starfield. Immediately a bright glow swallowed the stars, erased them.

Kell's instrument panels and forward viewports went dark. A bright flash of light rocked his snubfighter. A shower of sparks erupted from his main monitor, landing on his flight suit, threatening to set his legs on fire. There was more smoke in the cockpit than those sparks could have produced.

He cursed and batted at his legs to put out the sparks. His vision and the viewports cleared, the starfield outside returning to normal. In the distance, he could see one star that was noticeably brighter than all others; if this was indeed the system they were aiming for, that was Xobome, but they'd arrived well outside the region they'd targeted. He could see another X-wing half a klick or so to his starboard, drifting slowly away; he couldn't make out the pilot, but if it was the closest snubfighter to him, it should be Runt.

His instruments remained dead, and there was no hiss of air to indicate his life-support systems were functioning. Glancing back, he could see lights flickering on Thirteen; the droid seemed to be in the middle of startup procedures.

Kell pulled off his flight suit gloves, then reached under the instrument panel, unhooked latches there, and swung the whole panel up. Here was the source of some of the smoke, several wires burned and semiconductors fried—all delicate diagnostics circuitry, it appeared.

The wiring and circuitry associated with his restart system seemed intact, so he swung the instrument panel back into place and dogged it down. Then he reached past his left shoulder, pried open a small, innocuous panel there, and depressed the red button beneath it. He held down the button there until he heard the comforting, familiar whine of a snubfighter trying to bring itself back on-line.

Immediately words appeared on his data screen: R2-D609 IS ACTIVE. HOW MAY I SERVE YOU?

Kell frowned. "R2-D609, what's your name?"

The R2 unit beeped irritably at this simple test. I AM R2-D609.

"Can you give me a random number?"

13.

"Dammit." Thirteen's temporary memory was gone; it had returned to its default memory and settings, the ones burned permanently into its circuits.

They'd been hit by some sort of ionization bomb, he was sure of it; in his experience, only an ion cannon could scramble all a snubfighter's electronics this way. But what had hit them was more powerful, and ion cannons couldn't cause a ship in hyperspace to pop back into real space prematurely.

His communications board lit up and immediately he had voices: "—is just drifting. I have one engine coming up; I'll try to maneuver over to him." "Do that, Three. Is anyone else active?"

"Five here," said Kell. "I'm in the middle of a cold start."

"Four."

"Eleven."

There was a noise over the comm, something like an animal grunt.

"Twelve, this is Eleven. Was that you?"

Another grunt.

"Piggy, is your translator burned out? Once for yes, twice for no."

One grunt, a short, irritable one.

"Are you injured? Has it done any damage to your throat?"

Two short grunts.

"Good. Stand by."

"Sir?"

"This is Leader. Who's speaking?"

"Sir, Shiner isn't responding." Shiner was Donos's R2.

"Nine, is that you?"

"Sir, Shiner isn't responding."

"I read you, Nine. Are you injured?"

"No, sir. But Shiner—"

"Isn't responding. I understand. Let him be for the time being."

"Yes, sir."

Kell frowned. Donos didn't sound like himself. He did sound like someone suffering a concussion or other injury.

Within the next couple of minutes, the remaining Wraiths had reported in, all but Runt, Phanan, and Grinder. Most also reported electronics system damage, some of it trivial, though several engine units and a couple of astromechs were not coming on-line.

Everyone reported total electronic memory loss—from the X-wings' configuration choices to the astromechs' full memory banks to the contents of the pilots' datapads and chronos. That meant their nav course to Doldrums was erased. Even a return to Commenor system was impossible.

Wedge doggedly worked his way through their options. They didn't have enough fuel to go looking for a safe landing zone in another system; the X-wings were running close to dry.

The *Narra* had nearly a full load of fuel. The Wraiths could improvise a fuel transfer between the shuttle and the X-wings, but under these conditions this would take hours. If, as Wedge suspected, this attack would result in pursuit by their enemies, such a tactic would doom them.

Or the shuttle could dump all its cargo, the pilots could assemble on board, and they could jump around until they reached a system where they could reacquire navigational data. That would bring them to safety . . . but would cost them twelve X-wings, eight of them new. That would probably be the death knell of Wraith Squadron.

On the other hand, if he had the *Narra* use its personnel retrieval tractor to drag the inoperable snubfighters to available cover, where they could be repaired, the energy-expensive effort would burn off enough of the shuttle's fuel to make the squadron's escape impossible. But they would be operable and perhaps able to take out the pursuit vessels.

Finally Wedge said, "All right, Wraiths. Two reports a planet and satellites not too far away. I'm pretty sure that it's Xobome 6, the outermost planet of the system, and it has an atmosphere warm enough for us to effect some repairs, and an asteroid ring—just the thing if we're being pursued, and I'll bet my Endor patch that we are. We'll transit there, with the *Narra* towing the three nonfunctional fighters with its pilot retrieval tractor."

"That'll be slow going and a significant power drain, Lead."

"I know, Eleven. But we don't have another choice that will keep the unit in one piece. Once we're in position, we'll try to effect repairs, first on the fighters that are out of commission. That means—Five, how's your suit integrity? Can you stand a few seconds of hard vacuum to make a cold transit to the shuttle's emergency airlock?"

"My suit diagnostics are down, too, sir, but I think the suit's otherwise intact."

"Good. You and Cubber will put on vacuum maintenance suits Cubber stowed on the shuttle and effect repairs as best you can. I'm assuming that we're going to have pursuers on our tails soon, so work fast and be as messy as you have to. Everyone but Four, Six, and Seven head on over to Xobome 6. Land and effect what repairs you can, all but Five—you remain in orbit. I'll stay on station with the inert fighters while *Narra* tows them in one by one. Execute."

Kell, who had four engines showing ready, brought his fighter up to speed and in line beside and aft of Wraith Twelve—even at proper trailing distances he could recognize Piggy by his profile in the cockpit.

"Demolitions."

Kell jerked upright. In commando operations plotting, he knew he might be referred to as Demolitions instead of Wraith Five. A check of his comm board told him this was a private communication from Wraith Leader.

"Yes, Control."

"What do you think hit us?"

"Nothing I've ever heard of. But I think I could build something to do this—though I could bank the money and live off it for the rest of my life instead."

"Describe it."

"You'd need four basic components. No, five. First, a pretty standard ion projector, probably rigged for a single detonation instead of multiple shots. Second, an electromagnetic pulse generator, with the same area of emission. Third, a sensor rig that can detect hyperspace anomalies—that is to say, ships jumping into the system. Fourth, a gravitational pulse generator like the ones off the Imperial Interdictors. And fifth, a communications device—probably a one-shot hypercomm unit, something to throw off a single alarm at the time of detonation."

"So you're talking about a bomb that detects hyperspace arrivals, puts out a gravitational pulse to bring them out of hyperspace prematurely, and then hits them with both ion pulse and electromagnetic pulse."

"That's about the size of it."

"I don't buy it. Energy dropoff is such that it couldn't be made practical. What if you arrive in a system and this bomb is on the far side? It would detonate and do no harm to the arrivals."

"I thought about that, sir. And if I think as a bomber, not a demolitions professional, it occurs to me that you plant bombs where people are most likely to be."

"Explain that."

Up ahead, a tiny white dot, Xobome 6, appeared among the stars and began to grow. "Sir, most nav courses are plotted from the point of departure to the center of the system where you plan to arrive—that is, the sun. It's simple and it's safe; you taught us that. You can set distance so you drop back into real space short of the system, with no chance of hitting any natural gravity well, or you can fire straight into the system, and if you hit a gravity well before you reach your destination, it pops you back into real space before you're close enough to the center of gravity to endanger you. Correct?"

"Correct."

"So everyone knows that most courses are aimed at the sun of the arrival system. And if you already know that there's going to be a jump from Commenor to Xobome's sun—"

"Oh." The word emerged as a bark. "You set up your bomb on that straight-line path, just short of any normal arrival point at the system, and you're almost sure to bag your target. Meaning that someone knew, or suspected, there would be traffic from Commenor to Xobome."

"And since there's no trade between the two systems, it had to have been planted by the forces that attacked us. They knew we'd flee, and knew or suspected that some of us would flee by way of Xobome."

"Right. That makes sense. Thanks, Demolitions. Control out."

Kell had had a little training in zero-gee, hard-vacuum work. He'd done some exterior repairs on a cruiser over Sluis Van and had gone through the standard demolitions training in planting charges on a vessel in orbit.

That didn't make him proficient. That didn't mean he liked it.

In the cumbersome vacuum maintenance suit, which had built-in maneuvering jets, he could move around and stay warm. But he and Cubber didn't have tools rated to the cold of space, just toolboxes cobbled together from the X-wing hangar back on Folor, and this left them cursing over frozen and vapor-locked hydrospanners while Grinder, safe inside his cockpit, watched them impatiently.

Still . . . Kell could look up for an unimpeded view of an infinity of stars, the sort of vista he could never see on any world with atmosphere and never had time to appreciate while in the cockpit of a snubfighter. He could look down past his feet to see the world of Xobome 6, rotating with a slow majesty. Somewhere down there, on a high plain blasted by freezing winds, most of the Wraiths were trying to make repairs to their own less-damaged X-wings. They were probably looking up now and envying Kell his comparatively warm environment suit.

Kell floated beside the open hatch to Grinder's port dorsal engine. Its internal diagnostics said it was on-line and ready to supply power, but it was receiving no data from ship's controls. Kell brought himself back to his task. "Could all four data relays have been shorted?"

On the other side of the X-wing floated Cubber; even through their respective polarized faceplates Kell could see the mechanic shake his head. "All of them identically? No, it's got to be an interruption farther up the line."

"Think you could get into his cargo hatch and splice into the data feeds under the cockpit? I'll monitor here."

Cubber shrugged, an exaggerated motion. "I'll give it a try." Tiny jets vented at intervals across his back, turning him toward the X-wing's bow, moving him forward.

"Kell?" The voice was faint, eerie . . . and emerging from within Kell's own suit.

Kell's mouth went dry. He used his tongue to hit the microphone-off switch, then said, "Who's there?"

"Kell, it's Myn."

"How did—" Kell sighed and relaxed. Donos had apparently patched in to Kell's own private comlink, the one he carried in his breast pocket. Kell tugged his helmet forward so he could angle his chin down past the bottom of his helmet, making it easier for him to make himself heard. "Myn, call me on the main squadron channel."

"No, no. I need privacy for this. I need your help."

"Go ahead."

"Shiner's still down, Kell. I need for him to be up."

"We have more important problems right now. Shiner can wait."

"*Please*, Kell."

Kell frowned, troubled. The pain and worry in Donos's voice were clear enough to carry even over standard comlink distortion. "What's he doing?"

"Nothing! He won't respond to verbal commands for a

warm start, and the reset switches for a cold start don't do anything. I think he's . . . dead."

"Probably just in need of repairs. Stop worrying." The droid's power converter could be down, or it could be powered up but with its programming locked, unable to begin a restart sequence until power was actually shut off throughout the unit and the system was restarted. "Hey, try this. Do you have a restraining bolt? You or any of the others?"

A long pause. Then, "Yes, you have one."

"All right. Insert it. In him, I mean."

Donos didn't laugh at the joke. "It's in. But nothing's happening."

"Right. Now switch it over to power-down."

"Done. No change."

"Now switch it back to power-up."

"No— Hey! It's working!"

Kell smiled. Among the many features of the standard restraining bolt, an attachment designed to maintain control over a fractious or independent-minded droid, was an external means to shut off a droid's main power converter. Kell's guess had been right, and this external shutdown had flushed the droid's locked-up programming and allowed it to begin a cold start.

"Call me again if you absolutely have to—but don't call me just because his memory's gone. All their memories are gone."

"Right, right. Thanks, Kell. Myn out."

Cubber summed it up. "Commander, we got Grinder and Runt mobile in record time, but Phanan's X-wing is a loss until we can get it into a full shop setup." Within his cockpit, Phanan looked pale. He said he'd gotten bandages over his injuries, but there was no doubt that he couldn't give himself full medical attention within the cramped confines of the cockpit, without the medical kit now occupying his cargo bay. He also wasn't moving too well; it was evident some of his cybernetics were still malfunctioning.

Wedge's voice sounded resigned. "All right. Pop the

hatch and get him into the shuttle. Don't forget his medical gear.

"In the meantime, we can assume that the bomb that stuck us here also sent out a signal to whoever planted it. Meaning they'll be coming soon. If it was a hyperspace communication and they were signaling the *Implacable,* the Star Destroyer could be here in another couple of hours. We could make a blind jump to deep space or the nearest star to get away from them, but that'll probably end up killing us; we don't have enough fuel to do any significant exploration. Anybody have any ideas?"

Cubber, floating beside Ton Phanan's cockpit, pressed his faceplate against the transparisteel and began speaking. The words didn't come over the squadron frequency. From the slow pace and deliberate way he was shaping his words, Kell assumed he was shouting; the sound would conduct through faceplate and canopy, and Phanan would be able to hear him. He saw Phanan nod listlessly.

"Leader, this is Eight. I say we leave Seven's X-wing up in orbit for them to find, and when they pull it in, we board and seize them."

"Thanks much, Eight. Anyone else?"

"Sir, I'm serious. I've been thinking about this."

". . . Very well. Give it to me step by step."

"Well, we leave the fighter in orbit broadcasting a distress signal. Put up some debris with it to suggest that maybe another X-wing has been destroyed. Among the debris we have someone in one of the extravehicle suits, carrying Donos's laser rifle for maximum firepower."

"And they draw the suit in and the pilot inside starts shooting?"

"Yes, sir."

"They do this even when their sensors say there's a live body in the suit?"

"Uh . . . I'd forgotten about that."

Atmosphere began venting from around the seals of Phanan's cockpit. Kell saw Phanan check and recheck the integrity of the bandages he'd slapped onto his pilot suit where shrapnel had cut through it.

"Next plan?"

Kell keyed his microphone. "Sir, wait a second. We could put our intruder in the *Narra*'s smuggling compartment. Its systems will conceal the presence of a living person. Pull it out of the shuttle, attach a battery pack to maintain its electronic countermeasures, and float it among the debris."

Squeaky's voice was distinctly irate: "Cubber, we have an additional compartment in here and you didn't tell me? I could have packed more gear, more supplies—"

Wedge cut him off. "Continue, Mr. Tainer."

"Well, that's all I was going to say."

"And what do we do if they don't tractor in our intruder?"

"Make sure he can play some solo games on his datapad?"

"Not funny, Mr. Tainer."

Face cut back in. "Could we mount a propulsion unit to the compartment? The thrusters from an ejection seat?"

Kell said, "Yes."

Wedge said, "But it would be pointless. Can you imagine trying to aim a rig like that before firing off the thrusters? Odds are a hundred million to one that he'd miss and shoot off into space. And those are odds even a Corellian will pay attention to."

Kell said, "Put the thrusters at one end and an astromech at the other end. The astromech can feed visual data to the intruder's datapad. The intruder steers with the datapad, and the astromech translates that into precise thruster control. That makes the odds pretty good that he'd make it where he was aiming."

"That's crazy, Mr. Tainer."

"With all due respect, no it's not, sir. It's merely desperate. Speaking of which, the sniper rifle may not be rated to hard vacuum and the cold of space. It might freeze up. And we can give our intruder a much better weapon anyway."

"Such as what?"

"Well, if we're using a battery to keep the smuggling compartment powered, we might as well use the 04–7 power generator off Ton's X-wing. And if we have that much power available, we could pull the guts out of one of the laser cannons, cable it to the power generator, and rig it with a trigger. That'd give our intruder a few shots with something powerful enough to cut through bulkheads, much less through stormtroopers."

"A laser cannon is nine meters long, Five."

"Not the essential components and housing, sir. Strip out all the computerized aiming and synchronization equipment, the diagnostics, the flashback suppressor, I think we could chop it down to a meter and a half, two meters."

The canopy on the X-wing came up and Phanan clambered out, surrounded by the distinctive glow of a personal magcon field. He immediately began to drift away from the craft. Kell saw from Phanan's expression that cold was already eating its way through the atmosphere around his compromised suit. Kell and Cubber closed on him, each grabbing one of his arms, and began to maneuver him toward the *Narra*'s emergency airlock.

Wedge took a long time to answer. "Face, Kell, that's the craziest idea I've heard in a long time."

Face said, "Maybe, sir, but we've answered all your objections. We can do this."

"Let's say you're right. We have one pilot with a powerful, crude, prone-to-failure weapons rig, and he's in a hangar on an Imperial Star Destroyer. What then?"

"Leader, Eleven. A couple of ideas. If he could get to a computer interlock, he might be able to load in a program that would broadcast a distress to the New Republic. The rest of the pilots might be able to hide out until rescue. Or it may not be *Implacable*. It could be one of their support vessels, and we might be able to take it."

"You, too, Wes?"

"Yes, sir. I think this plan is marginally better than dying of asphyxiation or starvation out in empty space, and it has the virtue of novelty. *Implacable* couldn't anticipate we'd do it. Only crazy people could anticipate we'd do it."

"True." Wedge's voice sounded resigned. "Cubber, your professional opinion: Can you do this? Patch this aberration together in an hour or two at most and make it work?"

Cubber shut the airlock hatch on Ton Phanan as he answered. "With the kid's help . . . yes, sir."

"The chrono's running, gentlemen. Do it. And may the Force be with you. You need it."

Face said, "I have some Force here in my pocket. Kell, Cubber, you can have it if you need it. Oops, no, it's gone. Maybe it's in my cargo."

"Eight?"

"Yes, Leader?"

"Be quiet."

Weary, Wedge sat back in his pilot's chair. He switched the comlink over to his private connection with Janson. "Wes?"

"Here."

"They're doing it to me again."

"That's right."

"I haven't reached my thirtieth birthday, Wes. And once again I feel like the conservative old man in charge of a new generation of insane young pilots."

"That about sums it up."

"Thanks for the moral support, Wes."

II

They had to tell Squeaky and Phanan to squeeze into the shuttle's tiny airlock—fortunately, both were thin—then depressurize the *Narra*'s interior and open its main boarding ramp. Cubber and Kell could then enter and disassemble the mounting concealing the smuggling compartment. As soon as they had the compartment unplugged and towed back out into space, they saw where their plan couldn't succeed.

"It's not big enough," Cubber said. "These suits, with all the thrusters and life support, are too damned bulky to fit into the compartment. And I don't recommend we cut 'em down to fit."

"Good point." Kell sighed. "Well, our intruder will just have to wear a standard pilot's suit. This compartment is supposed to be airtight, that'll help."

"Airtight enough to fool mechanical sniffers, true, but it's only rated for pressurized environments. The seals aren't strong enough to hold in atmosphere against hard vacuum. Also, we're going to be drilling holes in it to mount the thrusters, to cable the battery to the countermeasures, to get the data feed from the R2 . . ."

"So we don't put the intruder into our fake debris field until the last possible moment."

Cubber shook his head. "And if they just take a few extra minutes to creep up on the site, our intruder freezes to death. It's not going to work, kid."

A new voice cut in, a strong and harshly mechanical one. "It can work."

Kell smiled. "Piggy! They got your voice working again."

"Grinder and his datapad got it started. I feel much better. And I should be the intruder."

"Why is that?"

"Physical structure, Kell. My body is swathed in heavy layers of fat. Humans find it unappealing, and it is a detriment in hot environments, but my fat will sustain me against starvation and will insulate me from cold temperatures. In an ordinary pilot's suit, I'm rated at half an hour's survival after ejection into space, rather than a few minutes. Too, my suit is intact."

Kell whistled. "Well, unless we get a better idea, Piggy, I think you're our man."

"Your Gamorrean."

While Cubber and Kell assembled the jury-rigged vehicle, which they nicknamed the *Lunatic,* Grinder and Piggy worked out the programming of the R2 unit and control datapad. Occasionally Kell listened in on the conversation—Grinder and Piggy had to work from within their cockpits and communicate via comm.

"What sort of targeting model do we use?" That was Piggy.

"Visual pattern recognition, I think. With the starfield as the primary element—it will be static. Perhaps we can limit it to stars of a certain brightness; that will reduce the amount of data to be processed. If the ship is a recognizable type, the R2 can add a detailed map of its configuration to the pattern; otherwise you'll just have to aim at what you think is a cargo hatch and pray."

"What if imbalances or faulty thrusters throw me off course?"

"Well, we have to have some sort of correction built in to the R2's programming. The crudest way is to have it evaluate its visual input and correct—overcorrect, really, with the time involved—if the visual image traverses too far."

"Very crude. Prone to error. And to overcorrecting, as you say."

"Yes. Hey, Kell?"

"I read you, Grinder."

"Is there any way to put some sort of mass sensor in our insertion vehicle? Something to calculate load balance, center of gravity, that sort of thing, to improve flight accuracy?"

Kell thought about it. The X-wings had such a system, of course, which used pulses from the inertial compensator to calculate the snubfighters' mass characteristics several times per second. "No. Not a chance. I'd have to have exact data on all the components going into this cobbled-together rig, I'd have to have a precise graphical model of it, Piggy would have to remain as still as if he were in a pilot's seat, and you'd have to have even more time to do all the physics-heavy programming."

"Forget it, then. Thanks."

Within an hour the *Lunatic* took shape. The storage compartment, roughly the size of a large coffin, was the main element. At one end, Phanan's R2 unit, Gadget, was mounted by way of crude brackets—metal strips cut from some of the cargo crates on the *Narra,* attached to the compartment's hull through simple bolts. At the other end were mounted the fuel pods and some of the thrust nozzles from Phanan's ejection seat; other nozzles were attached near the R2, pointed in four directions horizontal to the plane on which Gadget was standing, to give the rig as much maneuverability as was possible. Metal tubing carried fuel from the pod to the nozzles. A data cable ran from one of Gadget's ports through a hole drilled in the compartment; inside the compartment, it was attached to the datapad that now held Grinder's and Piggy's maneuvering program. A power cable ran from the electronic countermeasures socket on the outside of the compartment, through another hole, into the compartment; it currently floated free.

When Piggy was placed in the compartment, he'd be carrying on his belt the bulky main components of the Novaldex 04–7 power generator from Phanan's snubfighter. The cable powering the electronic countermeasures would be inserted temporarily in the power regulator fitted to one of its power-out sockets, while another socket was fitted with a cable running to the crude, six-foot-long cylinder that was what remained of one of Phanan's laser cannons.

"This is, without doubt," said Cubber, "the most inelegant rig I have ever had the pleasure of working on. Not counting the first still that I ever built, which was even more dangerous."

"Tests all show in the green. I think we're done."

"Call it in to the commander, kid."

In his cockpit, watching the universe spin around the asteroid on which he'd landed, Wedge relaxed with the calm of the seasoned New Republic pilot. He knew the others, excepting Janson and maybe Donos, would be fretting, ready to go; if they lived long enough, they'd learn to conserve their energy, to catch catnaps whenever they could.

The Wraiths' X-wings, as repaired as they could be during their stay on the ground, now rested on some of the planet's larger asteroid satellites in power-down mode. The *Narra* waited with power up, ready to go, with Piggy standing by in the airlock. Phanan's X-wing, some stony debris retrieved from the asteroid ring, and *Lunatic* spun lazily in an orbit closer to the planet's surface than the asteroids. The X-wing's comm system continuously broadcast a distress signal, a plea for help recorded by Face; Wedge could not but admire the skill of Face's performance, the realistic pain and fear he injected in his voice as he begged for rescue.

The comm unit popped. With power output turned so far down, no ship entering the system would be able to pick up their transmissions; in fact, some of the X-wings were having trouble reading them. "*Narra*, this is Five."

"Go ahead, Five."

"Cubber, wasn't Seven's fighter the one designated 3–0A when it came in?"

"That's right."

"Do you remember some sort of attachment mounted toward the aft end of the cargo bay? A rectangular thing, no ports or screens?"

"No. None of the X-wings have anything like that."

"Well, one of them did. It was about twenty-five centimeters long, maybe six broad and four thick. It was painted in standard Alliance gray."

"I'm telling you, kid, there's nothing like that on any of the X-wings. Wait, hold on."

A long silence, then Cubber's voice was replaced by Squeaky's. "Flight Officer Tainer, there is an attachment like that at the bottom of the main drive unit of the *Narra*. I noticed it because it wasn't identical to the drive units on other *Lambda*-class shuttles. I saw it several times during the many, many trips I made loading the *Narra* up with the pilots' personal gear."

"Cubber, I've serviced the *Narra*. There's nothing like that back there."

"I know, kid. Something's very wrong."

Wedge started to request that one of the X-wings ease out of the asteroids and make a visual check of *Narra*'s aft end. But before he could speak, his wingmate's voice came in: "Wraiths, this is Two. I have faint chatter on Imperial frequencies. Encrypted."

Wedge finally did speak. "*Narra*, this is Wraith Leader. Place your package, then scram back to one of the big rocks and power down. Wraiths, observe communications silence. Piggy, good luck."

He watched as the *Narra* drifted to within a few meters of the insertion vehicle. The shuttle's airlock opened and Piggy pulled himself out, hampered by the bulky belt he wore and man-height pole he carried. He shoved off from the airlock with confidence and drifted over to the insertion vehicle, which he grabbed.

The impact of Piggy's mass sent both pilot and *Lunatic*

drifting away from the wrecked X-wing and debris. But, as Piggy pulled open the compartment's door and began to squeeze in, the drift suddenly stopped. *Lunatic* moved slowly back to its original position relative to the X-wing.

It hung there, rigidly unmoving in the grip of the shuttle's tractor beam, as Piggy hooked up his belt power generator to the compartment's electronic countermeasures, then pulled the compartment door shut.

Wedge breathed out a sigh. Now it was all in Piggy's hands.

The compartment interior was lit only by the glow from the datapad's screen. Piggy patted at the gut of his flight suit, assuring himself that his blaster and the one Grinder had given him were still tucked away there, that the datacard containing the program that might force *Implacable*'s computers to send out a rescue message was still in his pocket, that the suit's seal was still intact. Then he seized *Lunatic*'s control datapad. "Status?" he said. His suit comlink was at minimal output power and set to the standard datapad channel.

Gadget's reply appeared as text on the datapad screen: OPERATIONAL. I CALCULATE A CHANCE THAT I WILL NOT REMAIN OPERATIONAL.

"I'll get you out alive, Gadget."

The words MOVEMENT DETECTED appeared. The screen switched from pure text to graphics on top, text at the bottom, and Piggy got a crude, monochrome view of the stars. From the way the starfield was moving, Piggy supposed that the *Lunatic* was now rotating slowly, and that Gadget was turning his hemispherical head to keep the camera within it aimed at his target.

A tiny white dot moved across the starfield and slowly began to grow.

More text appeared: THEY WILL DETECT THAT I AM OPERATIONAL.

"That's all right. They won't consider an astromech droid to be a threat. R2s are built for hard-vacuum repairs, so many of you have survived the ejection of their pilots into space."

The dot grew until Piggy could make out its shape. It was not the *Implacable,* nowhere near so formidable a vehicle: it was a Corellian corvette, a long, narrow vessel with a blocky engine housing at one end; at the other end, the bow looked like an ancient war-hammer head turned sideways.

Even at this distance and through the crude imager of the datapad, Piggy could see a bright vertical slit of light appear at the bow as the hold doors there were opened. Two large silhouettes emerged from the light and rapidly grew as they came closer.

They resolved themselves into TIE fighters.

The two starfighters roared past Phanan's X-wing and its debris cloud, close enough that Piggy imagined he could feel their wake. They looped and came back, then decelerated for a close view of the X-wing.

THEY ARE QUERYING ME.

"Respond truthfully, but only with data you have in your defaults. You don't know what happened to your pilot, you don't know how you came to be here." Piggy magnified the image of the corvette on his datapad screen, focusing in on the open bow hold. "What's our range to target?"

THREE HUNDRED METERS.

"Can we make that?"

THE VEHICLE IS COMING STRAIGHT AT US ON AN UNVARYING COURSE. IF WE MAKE NO MISTAKES, WE CAN.

Piggy took a deep breath and brought up the crude targeting brackets Grinder had added to his cobbled-together flight program. He set the brackets in the center of the open bow hold and hit the execute button.

He felt faint pressure against his back as one or two of the *Lunatic*'s top thrusters fired, orienting its "bow," Gadget, toward the corvette. Then it was as though he were in a turbolift, sudden weight as the thrusters beneath his feet fired off, and the image of the corvette's open hold began to grow.

He was suddenly banged up, down, and sideways by thruster corrections and could no longer keep his attention on the datapad. Then gravity had him and he was standing on his head.

He heard a wild, musical shriek, Gadget emitting a sound of pure droid terror, and there was an impact. Something gave way under the blow. Piggy was slammed forward, banging his head, then slammed onto his back.

He had heard Gadget screech; they had to be within atmosphere. He popped the seal on his pilot suit and dragged out one of the blasters with his left hand, then kicked open the hatch of the smuggling compartment. Bright light flowed in to blind him.

He couldn't wait for his eyes to adjust. He squeezed out of the compartment.

He was on his back on a metal floor. It was a miniature hangar space, mostly filled with four gigantic metal racks situated side by side; the two end racks held TIE fighters upright. He was almost directly beneath the starboard-side TIE fighter. Forward was the open hold door framing starfield and the planet Xobome 6. He could not see the magnetic containment field holding in the hold's atmosphere, but if it were not there, he'd already be strangling on vacuum.

The sound of a laser blaster's discharge and the impact of the bolt on the metal bracket nearest him made him jerk. He rolled over onto his belly, dragging the chopped-down laser cannon out of the compartment after him, and aimed the blaster pistol.

Nothing directly ahead but metal stairs going up. But above them was a gray catwalk, and on it men in mechanics' overalls running toward an exit. And two men in standard stormtrooper armor, aiming rifles his way . . .

He snap-fired at one, hitting the wall behind the man, and tried to crawl backward from the smuggler's compartment and under the cover offered by the nearest TIE fighter. But as he crawled the *Lunatic* came after him. It wasn't as heavy as it should have been; he saw that Gadget was no longer attached, and the brackets that had held him there were bent and broken.

He swore to himself, a Gamorrean grunt, as he realized the power cable from his belt generator was still plugged in to the compartment's electronics. He got two fingers of his blaster hand on the cable and yanked it free; a blast from the second stormtrooper hit the compartment dead-on, chewing a head-sized hole in its metal side.

Piggy got back under the cockpit of the TIE fighter. A marginal improvement; they couldn't see him, but he couldn't see them.

He felt the air pressure change, then a wash of heated gas rolled over him from behind. Shrapnel clattered across the TIE fighters and little pieces stung the back of his legs. Something had happened just outside the bow hold door, but he couldn't turn back to look.

Tactics. The stormtroopers would be separating on the catwalk, moving in either direction to bracket him with fire. He half stood and put his shoulder against the TIE fighter's wing.

The sturdy starfighter resisted his efforts, but some of the brackets holding it in place broke. The TIE fighter rotated, the remaining brackets acting as a pivot, and suddenly he could see the right-most stormtrooper. The trooper fired at him but the TIE fighter's solar wing, held before Piggy like a shield, absorbed the bolt. Piggy returned fire with the blaster pistol, saw black charring appear on the stormtrooper's chest, saw the trooper collapse to the catwalk, twitching.

He continued pushing against the wing, rotating the eyeball farther still, firing almost blindly as he went, until the second stormtrooper came under his gun. He hit the trooper twice. The trooper smashed back into the wall behind the catwalk, then stumbled forward and went over the rail.

A moment's breather. The hold crewmen had all escaped through the door. Then there was also the open hold door leading to space. These were the only ways out.

"Gadget?"

An irritable, nearly musical chittering from the far side of the hold reassured him that the R2 was functional.

Tactics. If he were the ship's captain, he'd shut the internal door and turn off the magcon field, venting the bay's atmosphere into space and suffocating Piggy or launching him into the void. Well, he'd have to do something about that possibility.

Wedge saw both of the TIE fighters rotate, trying to track the *Lunatic,* but only one managed to maneuver fast enough to get off a shot. The shot missed the wildly rocking assembly of parts. Then, at full speed, the *Lunatic* shot into the open bay door.

Wedge realized his mouth was open. "I'll be damned. They did it." He hit his comm key. "Wraiths, power up and target those eyeballs, lasers only, do not abandon your positions." He switched channels. "Attention, TIE fighter pilots. This is Commander Wedge Antilles of the New Republic. We have you under our guns. Surrender or be vaped."

The two TIE fighters ceased drifting. One came up to speed, heading toward the corvette, and the other spun back toward Phanan's X-wing. That eyeball fired, its green lasers shredding the derelict snubfighter.

Wedge grimaced. "Amateurs. Wraiths, open fire."

Not all the Wraiths had angles on the eyeballs, but enough did. The fighter approaching the corvette was hit by two quad-linked bursts, the one that had destroyed Phanan's craft by three. Both exploded.

His blaster pistol once again tucked away and the chopped-down laser cannon hanging from its power cable, Piggy climbed the TIE fighters' landing brackets. He kept a strong grip on those brackets; if the atmosphere vented, he didn't want to be pulled out with it. He saw the door through which the hold crew had run begin to close.

At the top of the brackets, he was only three feet from the hold ceiling. If he remembered the layout of Corellian corvettes from the training he'd received, there would be a floor of officer and guest quarters above the hold, and the ship's bridge would be immediately above that. If his cannon would chew holes in both ceilings and he could find a means to keep climbing, he could be in the bridge before anyone knew he was coming.

He dragged up the cannon, pointed it at the ceiling, averted his eyes, and fired.

The light produced by the shot was overwhelming, dazzling him even when reflected from the canopy of the TIE fighter below. The noise was incredible, a shriek of metal and displaced air. Melting metal scraps fell all around him—and on him, burning through his pilot's suit.

He ignored the pain. As his eyes cleared, he clambered up atop the bracket beams and leaped up through the hole he'd made—

Into the bridge. Around him, lying on the floor where they'd leaped for cover, running toward the exit, reaching toward holsters for blasters they'd never grasp, were the members of the bridge crew.

Where was the officers' quarters floor? It didn't matter. Piggy shouted, "Stop where you are! One move and I fire!"

And he aimed the still-smoking laser cannon toward the bow of the bridge, where metal walls and transparisteel windows were all that held in the chamber's atmosphere.

The bridge officers glanced at one another, then at an officer wearing the insignia of an Imperial naval lieutenant. The lieutenant nodded glumly and raised his hands.

Only when ash began to drift down from the ceiling did Piggy glance up, there to see what was left of another ship's officer.

"Captain Voort saBinring of the New Republic corvette *Night Caller* hailing Wraith Squadron. Wraith Squadron, come in."

Wedge couldn't restrain his grin. "*Captain?* That's a sudden promotion."

"A temporary promotion, sir. I am in command of this vessel. I thought a captaincy would be most appropriate."

"Oh, it is. Permission to come aboard?"

"Granted. And please hurry."

12

Inconvenient as the planet's weather was, they brought *Night Caller* down to the surface of Xobome 6 to perform their examination. Jesmin Ackbar remained on station in orbit to alert them to any other enemy arrivals.

Wedge stayed on the bridge, accumulating information, while the Wraiths performed their duties as fast as possible. Wedge could see them, dim shapes moving among the rocking X-wings while the wind drove ice particles past the bridge windows and obscured his vision. He was careful to stay well away from the hole melted in the floor. The object fried to the ceiling above that hole, remains that had once been a man named Captain Zurel Darillian, had fallen free during the ship's landing and dropped into the TIE fighter hold; Falynn Sandskimmer, unperturbed by their grisly nature, was dealing with them.

Squeaky, just back from his initial tour of the ship, seemed fascinated by what he'd seen. "It's all so very clean, sir. The captain must have been quite a stickler for cleanliness."

Wedge gave him a rueful look. "Usually a sign of a diseased mind . . . What about the structural modifications?"

"It has been very heavily modified from the standard corvette, Commander. Where the *Tantive IV* had a luxury quarters deck beneath the bridge, *Night Caller* has eliminated the deck, I suspect to make extra room in the bow hold for the four TIE fighters. The bow has also been widened, the hull armor on the sides of the bow narrowed, electronic apparatus that should be between bulkheads there moved somewhere else. The topside hold has been converted into a skimmer hangar. There are no laboratories; that's where the luxury quarters are located."

Wedge nodded. "It appears that this was no retrofit job. It came out of the shipyards this way."

"I agree, Commander."

From the main weapons console, Janson said, "They've given up one of their bow turbolaser twin cannons and installed a tractor beam instead."

"Most ships this size have a tractor."

Janson grinned. "I mean a *real* tractor beam. Something suited to a frigate or larger war vessel, not just a beam suitable to drag a fighter around."

Grinder, bent over one of the bridge's data consoles, called, "Oh, Commander." He made the rank sound like part of a song. When he straightened and turned, Wedge could see the Bothan's teeth bared in a meat-eating smile.

"Yes?"

"Piggy got to the bridge so fast—oh, this is sweet. They didn't have time to shut down, to purge the memory, to activate the most basic security. They have a state-of-the-art Imperial HoloNet system, a real luxury on a vessel this size, and it was hot, ready to go—and they didn't even get a message off."

Wedge blinked at him. "Whatever fleet it came from is unaware it's in trouble?"

"Completely. I pulled up its mission profile, its standing orders, its schedule, everything."

"Tell me."

"It belongs to Zsinj—"

"No surprise."

"No surprise. But it's temporarily assigned to Admiral

Apwar Trigit. Its mission is to lay mines, Empion mines, a type I'm not familiar with—"

"Ask Kell about them. I think I had him redesign them in his head earlier today."

"Right. Anyway, it's supposed to plant them, to monitor their hypercomm frequency for alerts that they've been triggered, to inform Admiral Trigit of the results when they go off."

"Go on."

"I also got their schedule, mostly visiting unaligned planetary systems and demonstrating that Zsinj has muscle, also some routine meetings with refueling ships. A schedule they're supposed to return to once this minelaying is done."

"Show me."

Grinder brought up a list on-screen. Wedge read off the list of planets. "Viamarr 4, Xartun, Belthu, M2398, Todirium, Obinipor, Fenion. Can you plot that for me?"

"I'm way ahead of you."

"That seems to be a short description of my recent command history." Wedge looked over the star chart Grinder brought up. It tracked a course through Rimward planets just outside the New Republic's current zones of control. "And Trigit doesn't know we've captured this vessel."

Grinder shook his head, sending ripples through his silver fur. "Sir, he can't."

Wedge whistled as the first elements of a plan began to percolate in his mind.

Cursing the cold, Cubber and Kell staggered against the gale-force winds of Xobome 6 and reached the stern of the *Narra*.

There, as Squeaky had described, tucked neatly away in one of the recesses beside the main thruster of the main drive unit, was a rectangle of the dimensions Kell remembered. This one was black to match the surrounding components of the drive unit.

The two mechanics looked at each other. "Doesn't belong here," Cubber said. "Let's pull it off."

"Let's *scan* it first, Cubber. Remember my other occupation?"

"Oh, yes. I'll wait over there. Behind the outcropping."

Kell pulled out the sensor pack Squeaky had saved for him, the one optimized for demolitions work, and hoped that it would hold up in this cold environment. He moved it slowly across the surface of the mystery box and carefully watched the sensor's display.

The heat-based visual display showed intricate electronic components inside, some of which were consistent with advanced comm gear, none of which seemed to include the sort of nondifferentiated material that usually made up the explosive portion of a bomb. There seemed to be some sort of armature attachments on the other side holding it to the shuttle's surface.

He waved Cubber over, then carefully gripped the box and pried at it. It resisted him; then, as he applied more pressure, it came away from the shuttle. Four mechanical limbs, each articulated, half a meter long, and ending in gripping hands, hung limply.

"I think it's dead," Cubber said.

"What do you want to bet that the bomb that scrambled our droids' memories did the same thing to this?"

"No bet. Let's get inside where it's warm and find out for sure."

Jesmin remained at her station in orbit; Falynn and Runt guarded fifty-plus ship's officers and crewmen now crowded into the stern lounge. The rest assembled in the small meeting room that was part of the captain's quarters.

"First," Wedge said, "I want to commend the principal parties involved in the capture of *Night Caller*. Piggy, Face, Kell—excellent work."

There was general applause, and Piggy said, "Can I keep the ship?"

"If you mean as a personal possession, no. If you'd like to remain in command, the answer is probably yes."

Piggy looked startled. "I was joking."

"Well, the question would have been a joke in the Imperial navy or the Corellian fleet or a lot of other places, but it's actually a reasonable one in the fleet of the New Republic. It's all because many of our traditions are rooted in the more piratical times of the Alliance's first days. Still interested?"

Piggy nodded, silent. His expression was made up of surprise and confusion.

"The first thing you'd do is transmit an informal request for command of *Night Caller* to Fleet Command. Then you'd submit a formal application for transfer out of Starfighter Command and into Fleet Command. I'd have little choice except to approve it, and the Navy is nearly one hundred percent likely to accept you. They have a keen appreciation of officers who capture ships to add to the fleet, after all.

"Then you'd receive a crash course in naval traditions and capital ship command, along with a promotion to naval lieutenant . . . and an immediate *temporary* promotion to captain. Because of your lack of experience, you'd be given very simple missions for your first several months—guarding convoys of ships carrying nonessential goods, for example. Eventually, within the year, I'm certain, they'd become aware of your competence, begin giving you more critical missions, and make that last promotion a permanent one.

"Let me just say, though, I personally think it would be a shame to take a promising fighter pilot like yourself and turn him into a barge driver. But I have to admit that those are the words of an irredeemable X-wing jockey."

Janson barked out a laugh, which Wedge ignored. Wedge continued, "What about it, Piggy? Naval captaincy within a year? Still interested?"

Piggy was still for a moment, then slowly shook his head. "Perhaps I am selfish. But everyone remembers Lando Calrissian and Wedge Antilles and what they did at Endor. Who remembers the name of the captain or the gunner on the *Home One* at the same battle?"

Wedge smiled. "I do. But I know what you mean. And I appreciate the fact you're staying." He turned back to the others. "All right, back to *Night Caller* and our current situation. Cubber, fuel?"

"We're good. *Night Caller*'s tanks were almost full, and they have proper refueling equipment. I've siphoned off enough to top off the *Narra* and all the X-wings except Jesmin Ackbar's."

"As soon as we're done here, I'll bring her down and send Myn up so you can refuel her as well."

Jesmin's voice came out of the intercom on the table. "Thank you, sir."

"Oops. Forgot you were listening. Grinder, did you transfer the nav data?"

The Bothan nodded. "We can jump out of system at any time."

"Phanan? Your status?"

Ton Phanan looked less pallid than he had up in orbit, but he looked no less unhappy. "They blew up my snubfighter."

"Your physical status, I mean."

"Oh. The damage to flesh was all trivial. I didn't lose any limbs or organs this time, which is quite a treat, I assure you. The damage to the prosthetics is not all fixed yet, though. My left leg isn't receiving proper neural input and drags a bit. And my right hand works just fine for most things, but when I start to work with a datapad, there's some sort of leakage of signals and it just goes crazy." Phanan waved the hand in question. It ordinarily looked like a normal hand, but now it twitched continually, the ring finger jerking rhythmically and the flesh on the back of the hand crawling in an inhuman fashion. Phanan did not seem disturbed by the phenomenon. "But with a little more work with the ship's computers, I should be able to set everything right."

"Cubber, Kell, the attachment on the shuttle?"

Kell shrugged. "It's hard to tell with its memory blown out, but I think it was some sort of parasitic communications device. It was mobile and had a camouflage coating; it can alter its color to match whatever vehicle it's attached to. It also has a very small, very limited hypercomm ability . . . but again, with its memory gone, I can't find out where it was transmitting to. My guess is that it went from ship to ship and occasionally broadcast its current location to its maker."

Grinder said, "Which is nothing if there's only one of them . . . but important if they could build hundreds or thousands. They could build up a map of anomalous hits and find all sorts of things. Smugglers' bases. Deep-space assembly points."

Wedge said, "And hidden Alliance bases. Jesmin, add that to the report we're sending to Command. 'All ships, be advised . . .'"

"Understood."

Wedge checked the next item on his list. "All right. We've faked up a report in Captain Darillian's name, with all the appropriate security checks on it, explaining that he jumped into this system, found the abandoned X-wing, assumed that the pilot had ejected, sent over a party to retrieve it—and it blew up, some nasty treachery on the part of its original pilot. We've sent that report off. We hope it will forestall any further inquiry on the matter of the Xobome system. Now, we're going to take some time, rotating you among the guard duties, but giving everyone a chance for a few hours' rest. When we're all feeling a bit more recovered, we launch."

Kell said, "Doldrums, here we come."

"No, Mr. Tainer. Not Doldrums. First we're going to three different uninhabited systems to pick up three unexploded Empion mines. Then we're going to the Viamarr system."

Kell frowned, confused. "If I may ask, sir—"

"Why this schedule? Because that's the order of business for *Night Caller*. Ladies, gentlemen, I'm acting on my own initiative and sending off a request that High Command approve my new plan. Which is this: We've just become crewmen in Warlord Zsinj's fleet . . . and we're going to do his bidding until we can find a way to strike at him."

Kell emerged from his temporary quarters wearing a black TIE fighter pilot's jumpsuit—one that was, miraculously, large enough for him—and toweling his hair dry.

Night Caller seemed eerily quiet. They were still on the ground, so the ship did not tremble from the efforts of her engines, and she was massive enough to be immune to Xobome 6's winds. With most of the old crew collected in the stern lounge under guard, and with Wraith Squadron spread thinly through the rest of the ship, there were few noises to be heard.

He headed forward, toward the bridge, along the main corridor running the length of the ship. When he was almost to the bow, he heard voices drifting down a stairwell to port.

He followed them up. Off the main corridor of Deck One, he found himself peering into the ship's main communications bay, a smallish chamber whose walls were solid, modular blocks of communications gear.

Jesmin and Face were seated there, and another man was with them—a hologram, actually. The man, thin, clean-shaven, with hawklike features, was dressed in a sharp-looking black uniform with Imperial captain's bars. He was seated in an imposing command chair and was much given to irritating theatrical gestures as he spoke. "We have been charged," he said, "with weaving the net that will capture any Rebels who are so fortunate as to survive the destruction of the base on Folor and flee. Our assignment: lay Empion bombs along the four most likely escape routes and then wait at the astrographical center of that array to snatch up whatever poor insects fall into our trap." He leaned forward, eyes glittering. "Personally, I hope some of them can effect repairs in the time it takes us to get to them. I could do with a bit of a fight."

The Wraiths burst out in laughter. Jesmin hit a button on the main console and the captain's image froze there, his expression still suggesting he had just let the viewers into his confidence with that little revelation.

"What is this?" asked Kell.

Face leaned back and stretched. "That's our former ceiling decoration, Captain Zurel Darillian. He apparently kept the ship's log in full holo."

"What an ego." Kell shook his head. "That must take up massive storage."

Face said, "The ego or the graphics?"

Jesmin turned one eye admonishingly toward Face, then

nodded toward Kell. "Oh, it does. But I thought that since Face was an actor, he should see this man's performance. I have seldom seen anything so florid, so self-satisfied, so . . . repellant."

"Oh, I have," Face said. "I once sat in Ysanne Isard's lap."

Kell and Jesmin stared at him. Kell said, "You're kidding."

"Oh, no, I'm not. *Win or Die* had just been released Empire-wide. I played a little boy, a son of two patricians of the Old Republic, only I know that the Empire is the way to go and I try to run away to safety with the new Emperor. But my dad doesn't see it that way and shoots me in the back, and I die in the Emperor's arms, begging him to finish conquering the galaxy so that the evil of people like my parents can be eradicated . . ."

Jesmin burst out in gales of laughter, then clamped both hands over her mouth while she shook. When she had herself under control, she said, "Face, that's horrible."

Face grinned. "That was the old propaganda machine. So I got a trip to Imperial Center, I mean Coruscant, to meet the real Emperor. But he'd been called away to deal with some problem—I heard later that he had just received one of the early reports informing him of the degree of organization the Alliance actually had, and he wasn't in a very good mood. So I saw Ysanne Isard instead, and she sat me in her lap and told me what a good boy I was."

Kell finished with his hair and slung the towel over his shoulder. "What was that like?"

"Something like being stroked by a poisonous reptile wearing a human suit, only not quite so comforting." Face shuddered. "The most crushing blow I ever felt after joining the New Republic was learning that Rogue Squadron had killed Isard—meaning that I wouldn't be able to. Anyway, Captain Darillian is nothing in comparison. He was just a petty guy who reached his ultimate level of usefulness driving a minelaying barge for a warlord and then had to be scraped off the floor."

Jesmin said, "You'd better finish getting ready, Kell. We take off in half an hour."

"How are we doing that? I mean, with most of us returning to the X-wings, who's going to pilot *Night Caller* and who's going to deal with the prisoners?"

"We landed four X-wings in the topside hold, strapped them down tight almost on top of one another so they'd fit," Jesmin said. "And the *Narra* is hooked up to the corvette's port docking station. Commander Antilles will be piloting the corvette—he says he used to pilot Corellian freighters—and Phanan, Face, Grinder, Squeaky, Cubber, and I will be aboard." Her voice turned sarcastically sweet. "I think we will be able to manage."

"Well . . . all right. You have my permission." Kell reflected. "Say, since we're sending messages to Warlord Zsinj, why can't we just track them along the HoloNet and find out where he is?"

Jesmin said, "Face asked the same thing. And it might be that simple if we had regular communications with him in the usual fashion. But *Night Caller* is not actually using the HoloNet for reports. We're to send hypercomm transmissions along specific courses."

"Meaning Zsinj's ship, or just relay satellites, can be anywhere along those courses . . . across hundreds or thousand of light-years."

Jesmin nodded.

"That's why I'm Demolitions and not Communications. Much simple just to blow things up." Kell gave them a mock salute and left.

In the corridor leading back to the temporary quarters, Kell saw Wes Janson headed his way. The two men passed without comment, each moving as close to the opposite side of the corridor as decorum would allow.

At his quarters, he nearly bumped into Donos emerging from the cabin next door. "Myn. How is Shiner?"

Donos looked rested and uncharacteristically cheerful. "Shiner? He's fine. Why?"

"Well, you seemed so concerned about him the other

day, I was wondering if he'd suffered some sort of physical damage I'd need to repair."

Donos shook his head. "No. I, uh, we just . . ." He stopped for a moment and appeared to be organizing his thoughts. "Kell, we leave them hanging out in hard vacuum. I just think we need to protect them."

"Right." Kell tried to relate that answer to Donos's behavior of a few hours ago and couldn't. "Well, I'm glad to hear he's in good shape." He pushed into his quarters and escaped the peculiarly uninformative lieutenant.

It took them the better part of two days to retrieve the three undetonated Empion mines and return them to *Night Caller*'s belly hold. The X-wing pilots were rotated through duties on the corvette so that everyone got an almost-adequate amount of sleep.

Kell suggested some changes to Wedge and ended up pulling a succession of corvette shifts while he and Cubber implemented them.

They welded metal sheets approximately the size of TIE fighter solar array wings between the escape pods hanging from the corvette's flanks. They stowed two of the ball-shaped escape pods in the belly hold and painted the others the same dark Imperial shade as TIE fighters. Then Wedge personally flew the two remaining TIE fighters to dock them at the empty escape pod hatches. The end result was that from any scrutiny except close examination, the TIE fighters looked like escape pods—and would actually be faster and safer to launch than out of the bow hold.

With the TIE fighters out of the bow hold, Kell and Cubber disassembled the braces designed to hold them. They used that metal and more from the belly hold to fabricate a new set of braces and rails, three rows of them, one above the other, built at the very rear of the hold.

It would require delicate piloting, but an X-wing could now use repulsorlifts to back into the bow hold and accept instructions from a ground-guiding crew member to slide into rails spaced to accommodate their strike foils. Once they reached the rear of the rails they could be locked there by metal brackets lowered into place.

This gave them an array of three X-wings by three, the strike foils on each row overlapping one another slightly. With the bow doors open, the X-wings in the center column could launch quickly and in relative safety; the six along the sides would have to launch a little more slowly, but the guidance rails would probably keep accidents from happening.

With nine X-wings in the bow hold and two more up in the top hold, *Night Caller* could now carry eleven X-wings and two TIE fighters.

Cubber cackled and rubbed his hands together. "More than a squadron's worth, by virtue of superior engineering."

Wedge said, "Not bad. Not bad at all." He reached out to grasp the nearest vertical brace and heaved against it. The bracketing rig didn't budge. He smiled.

Night Caller was ready for action.

13

The records said Viamarr 4 was an agricultural world, somewhat higher in gravity than Coruscant standard; its chief export was a subterranean fungus whose offshoots and tubers sometimes grew to the diameter of a kilometer or more. The fungus, inaccurately called Viamarr Blackroot for its color, was well liked for its meaty texture and nutrient balance.

"Who has TIE fighter experience?" Wedge asked. "Even in simulators?" He held up his own hand.

So did Piggy, Falynn, Face, and Janson.

"Piggy, how were the simulator cockpits for you?"

"Terrible, sir."

"All right. I want Wes to remain on *Night Caller*. Falynn, suit up. You and I are going to buzz the capital of Viamarr 4."

The somber woman from Tatooine gave one of her rare smiles.

Wedge continued, "Squeaky informs me that there's a TIE fighter simulator in the stern lounge. Not too surprising, since this corvette is trying very hard to be a pocket carrier. I recommend that the rest of you get some experience in it. We may be flying a number of TIE fighter missions."

.   .   .

Wedge looked over the half-familiar array of controls and monitors, let out an irritated sigh, and flipped two switches. The TIE fighter immediately hummed, indicating it was powering up. "We have two lit and in the green," he said. Automatically, he glanced to port and starboard, a visual check of his surroundings, and bit back another annoyed remark. There were no windows to the sides; had there been any, their view would only have been of the fighter's wing pylons and large, hexagonal solar array wings. The TIE's only viewports were forward and above. They showed endless starfield, reminding Wedge that he was hanging from what until a few days ago was an escape pod dock.

No shields. No ejection seat. TIE fighters were disposable attack vehicles for disposable pilots, and Wedge never cared to feel disposable. "Laser cannon readings nominal. How am I transmitting?"

Jesmin came back, "Sir, until you launch, your communications are coming in over direct connections."

Wedge grinned. "Sorry. I'll ask again after launch. Gray Two, what's your status?"

Falynn's voice sounded a bit nervous. "Twin ion engines are live and running at optimal. Ship's systems all in the green. Two laser cannons at full power. Shields—damn. I mean, uh, sorry, sir."

"That's all right, I feel the same way."

"And I don't look forward to landing this thing. Sir, even in the simulators, I've never landed straight onto a docking station."

"You'll do fine. Just remember to crank the hand yoke over to minimal responsiveness. That'll make you feel like you're crawling along centimeter by centimeter, but you won't crash into anything on landing. Watch what I do." Now, he had to match action to words. He cranked the knob on his control yoke down as far as it would go, then cut the connection with *Night Caller* and kicked in the ion engines.

He drifted free of the corvette. When the rangefinder said he was fifty meters from the ship, he rotated in place, looking back across *Night Caller*'s belly. On the far side, Falynn's TIE fighter was also in a slow, smooth descent relative to the corvette's keel. "Good," he said. "Ready to fly?"

"Ready, sir."

"Gray Flight away." He pulled back on the yoke and twisted its adjustment knob, feeding more power into the engines. The TIE fighter glided smoothly forward; he heeled it over toward the distant planet of Viamarr 4. He was pleased to see Falynn follow him with adequate skill; apparently her simulator time had been put to good use.

A while later they dove into the atmosphere of Viamarr 4 and headed toward Velery, the planetary capital, a community of a hundred thousand on the largest continent of the southern hemisphere. The land surrounding the capital was largely forested, with numerous tiny communities of wooden buildings.

Finally someone was alerted to their presence: "Incoming craft, this is Velery Station. Please identify yourself. Do you read?"

Wedge switched his comm to broadcast in the clear. "Velery Station, this is Gray Flight, escorting private yacht *Night Caller*."

"Ah, yes." The voice became noticeably more agitated. "Gray Flight, please come to heading two-five-five and make landing here at Velery Station."

"Can't do it, sorry. Not in our mission parameters." The mission assigned to *Night Caller*'s TIE fighters was a simple one: Buzz the town of Velery a couple of times, spook any air traffic, ignore attempts by the local government to impose its authority, and return to the corvette. Simple. The agrarian settlers of the planet didn't have any significant defenses— nothing even to make TIE fighters worry.

"Uh . . . may I inquire as to what those parameters are?"

"Stay where you are and you'll see them in just a minute." He could see the interruption in the forest ahead that had to herald the presence of Velery.

The sensor board beeped a strident signal Wedge recognized. He switched to *Night Caller*'s frequency: "Follow me,

Two, someone's trying to paint us for laser fire." He pulled back on the yoke and went skyward.

As he climbed and then looped backward, he could see their pursuers through the viewport atop the TIE fighter's cockpit. Two stubby fighter craft, their noses similar to X-wings except for the bubble canopy—"Headhunters," he said. Evidently Viamarr had picked up some fighter defenses when Zsinj wasn't looking.

"Mark Ones," Falynn said. "See the swing wings? They're pretty old."

"Maybe, but they're as good as TIE fighters in atmosphere, and their lasers can cause you to have a bad, bad day." Wedge saw the Headhunters climb in an effort to stay on the TIE fighters' tails.

Then they were on the comm: "Gray Flight, this is Blackwing One. You need to comply with Velery Station's instructions. Right now." The voice was male, young, rustic.

Wedge shook his head. Farmboys in Headhunters trying to point laser cannons at him. "Oh, we can't have that."

He snap-rolled and dove, pushing the TIE fighter's atmospheric capabilities to their limits in an effort to come down in firing position behind the Headhunters. Atmospheric drag on the solar arrays caused him to slew to port, but he kept the fighter in line through experience and brute strength.

He had a moment's worry wondering if Falynn could keep up with him, tried to spot her visually and couldn't, then caught sight of her blip on the sensor monitor. She had lost ground to him, but was in control.

Mere meters above the treetops, he rolled upright and began another climb, this time with the port-side Headhunter in clear sight. He brought up the TIE fighter's targeting equipment and immediately had the Headhunter's jittery silhouette bracketed. "Blackwing One, if I were in an irritable mood, one of you would be dead now."

"So you say. These things can take a lot more punishment than those pasteboard boxes you're flying." The Headhunter in his brackets juked left, then rolled up on its starboard wing and began a tight roll to starboard.

"And they'll do just that if you don't stop annoying me."

Wedge easily stayed on the Headhunter's tail, anticipating the fighter's banks and turns, gaining on the older vehicle until he held at a mere fifty meters back.

He glanced at his sensor board. Falynn wasn't talking, but she was still behind the other Headhunter, mimicking its maneuvers. Finally her voice came across on *Night Caller*'s channel: "Sir, it won't be hard, but I really don't want to vape these plow-pushers."

"Keep your guns on them and outfly them, Two. Maybe they'll grow a brain stem."

Wedge's target rolled left and suddenly lost altitude, diving straight toward the trees. Wedge followed him in, blinked in amazement as the Headhunter crashed down through the top layer of branches.

Follow or break off? That pilot was young and arrogant, but didn't seem suicidal. Wedge followed.

He felt his solar arrays tear through branches, then suddenly he was below the level of the treetops. His target was angling to starboard, following the course of a low river. Wedge tucked in right behind him. "Blackwings, are you ready to break off and go home?"

"Gray One, you're about a second from me turning around and giving you six laser cannons' worth of dental work—"

The voice of Velery Station cut in again. "Blackwing Flight, break off and return to station. That's an order."

"*Sir* . . ." Blackwing One's voice was sulky, frustrated.

"That's straight from the governor. Or do you want your pilots' licenses transferred to tractor operations?"

"No, sir." With no further taunts for the TIE fighters, Blackwing One reduced speed, then punched up through the light canopy of tree branches. On the sensor screen, Blackwing Two was also headed toward the Velery Station coordinates.

"Good flying, Gray Two. Now, let's buzz their administrative buildings."

"Sounds like fun, One."

.   .   .

Jesmin leaned back from the comm station. "Lieutenant, we're receiving a communication from Velery House. That's their capitol building. They're asking for a specific encryption that's in our computer. Obviously they've talked before."

Janson, lounging in the captain's seat, looked confused. "There's no provision in the mission profile for this. They weren't supposed to call. They were supposed to batten down hatches and ride out the TIE fighters' overflight."

Jesmin gave him a very human shrug. "I know."

"Well, take the call. Tell them the captain is taking a bath or something."

"Sir, *Night Caller* followed Imperial protocols under Captain Darillian."

"Meaning?"

"Meaning it wouldn't have a Mon Calamari communications officer."

Janson uttered an irritable hiss. "Well, I can't take the call. My face is fairly well known."

They both looked at Face, seated at the navigational console. He straightened up. "Uh, even with my scar, they might recognize me. Some of the Wraiths did."

Janson didn't bother to conceal his frustration. "Face, you're an actor. Do something."

Face stood, looked frantically around the bridge. There wasn't much on hand: items dropped by the bridge crew behind consoles, plus Cubber's toolkit over where the mechanic had been cutting the sharp edges away from the hole in the floor, preparatory to putting down a metal sheet.

He ran to the toolbox, pulled out Cubber's welding goggles. Then a cylinder of orange paint used to mark spots on a ship's exterior where repairs were necessary. He sprayed the interior of the goggles until they were opaque.

Containers of grease, hydrospanners, cables, sensors, tubing . . . He took a tube half the length of his forearm, inserted one end in his nose, the other in his right ear. Then he put the goggles on, resting them on his forehead, and hunted up one of the bridge crewmen's hats. "Give me the chair."

Janson vacated it. Face settled in, pulled the goggles over

his eyes, pulled the hat down low on his brow. "How's that look?"

He couldn't see their faces, but Jesmin responded with gales of laughter. He could barely hear Janson's reply: "It's disgusting."

"But they won't recognize my features. All right, put him up on the screen." He turned toward the bridge's main viewscreen.

He could dimly see the light intensity in the room change, then he heard a voice: "Captain D— Oh, my."

Face took a deep breath and ran his voice down into the bass range where it could vibrate rocks and desktops. "Captain Darillian is having his bath. I am Lieutenant Narol. Who are you? What do you want?" He injected both boredom and contempt into his voice.

"Um, I am Governor Watesk. I would very much like to speak with Captain Darillian." The man's voice was a plea.

Face angled his head down so he could peer between the top of the goggles and the bottom of his officer's hat. The face on the viewscreen was of a graying, bearded man, dressed in rustic brown tunic but with expensive wood paneling behind him. "Was Basic your first language? Do you not understand? The captain is in his bath."

"You could give me voice-only access."

"He's dictating his memoirs and doesn't want to be disturbed."

"In the bath?"

"Of course, in the bath!" Face's tone was an explosion of anger. "Where else? The captain is a very busy man! He's not some deskbound colony governor with enough time to pick his nose with one hand and skim the cream off taxes with the other! If you have anything to say, you can say it to me. Or perhaps we'll just jump on to our next destination and I'll give the captain a report of your bad manners. And the manners of your pilots, who for some unknown reason decided to play tag with ours."

"No! Lieutenant, please forgive me." The governor looked appropriately contrite. "Our air force is very new, the pilots not yet very experienced. They acted on their own initiative. They will be punished. But that's not what I'm calling about."

Face contrived, with posture and the set of his mouth, to look bored. "Go on."

"I'm calling about the agreement. I'm ready for Viamarr to become a signatory. A *proud* signatory."

Face glanced at Jesmin. Her fingers flew over her communications console. Then she began a wild pantomime that said clearly to Face that there was nothing about this in the ship's records.

"It has been a while," Face said smoothly. "What makes you think that the original offer is still available?"

The question caught Governor Watesk off guard. The man had to take a couple of gulping breaths before he answered. Before he could reply, the wall panels behind him vibrated and Face could clearly hear the sound of a TIE fighter screaming by near the governor's position. The governor tracked the TIE fighter's movement with his eyes, then returned his attention to Face. "Sir, the warlord *said* I'd have until your next visit to decide."

Face gave him a cold smile. "And what did the warlord say *after* the last time he talked to you?"

The governor looked stricken. "I don't know, sir. I couldn't possibly know."

"Correct. Well, you tell me what you think the warlord offered and I'll tell you what part of it is still on the table."

Janson smiled broadly and gave Face a thumbs-up of approval.

"Uh, yes." The governor glanced down, apparently looking at a datapad or documents the screen didn't show. "We are to provide his army with supplies equivalent to one-tenth our exports."

"And?"

"And you are to . . . and you would give us a location where we could transmit requests for aid in case of attack or invasion. You'd protect us."

"And?"

"And we would of course provide you with information

about any dealings with the New Republic, the Empire, other warlords."

"Of course. And?"

The governor's lip trembled. "That was all."

Face looked steadily at him. There was something in the governor's manner, something that said obsequiousness was his nature but that he was actually simulating it now. That suggested he was holding something back.

Face turned to the side. "Ensign Ack—" He coughed. "Ackran, inform Gray Flight that they should blow a few things up before returning to us. We'll be jumping out of system as soon as they return."

"No, wait!" The shrill desperation in the governor's voice seemed real. "Sir, you have to realize, the warlord told me not to talk about the last part with anyone but him."

"Well, after you've convinced me, I will support your claim to the warlord that you told me nothing. Now, go ahead."

"The land is ready."

"Ah, good." Face waited.

The governor looked more confused. "That was all."

"No. Does the land conform to the warlord's specifications? Location, size, documentation?"

"Of course it does!"

Face slammed his arm down on the armrest. "Of course it doesn't! It doesn't until I know it does! I don't see the file appearing on my datapad, Governor. Where are those specifications?"

"But—"

"But nothing. Unless you transmit me that information, I have no way of knowing whether you've given him exactly the location he wanted. And you've probably sliced back the dimensions of the property to save yourself a few credits—"

"No, sir!" The governor's voice was at full bellow, the yell of a new soldier inductee just learning to fear the non-commissioned officers. "I'm transmitting that information now, sir!"

Face glanced over at Jesmin, waited until she nodded to

indicate that she'd received the file. "Lieutenant, does this data match what we're supposed to be getting?"

She shrugged, at a loss for how to answer. Out of the corner of his eye, Face saw Janson nodding. Jesmin said, "It does, sir."

"Good." Face turned back to the governor. He made his voice pleasant, soothing. "Watesk, I commend you. You are unusually cooperative and forthcoming for a planetary governor."

"I am?" The man sagged in relief and used his sleeve to blot at the perspiration sheening his forehead.

"You are. And the warlord will be pleased. We'll forward to him the information of your acceptance, and he will arrange for a formal document to be delivered that everyone can sign. Will that be satisfactory?"

"Oh, yes, Lieutenant."

"Good. I look forward to sampling some of your fungus. Narol out."

Jesmin cut the signal.

Face slumped and pulled off the hat and goggles. "I hate improvisation."

They gathered in the ship's conference room.

"What in the name of the Sith is Zsinj up to?" Wedge asked. "A trade of supplies for protection I understand. But land deals?"

"There's more," Jesmin said. "The records they sent us have the land transfer registered to a person named Cortle Steeze. I must assume that's an alias for Zsinj, but we should look for the name anyway. Whoever Steeze is, he has his choice of how the land is to be subdivided and zoned."

"How much of it is there?"

"A good-sized island. Fifty klicks long by about thirty wide."

"Interesting." Wedge glanced at Face. "Good work. By the way, you still have some of that paint on your face." Around the lines and spots of paint, the unscarred portion of Face's skin was red from scrubbing.

"I know." Face's voice held a hint of complaint. "It won't come off."

Cubber snorted. "It's not supposed to. It's supposed to mark work sites. Very reflective, and shows up very well under ultraviolet. You need the solvent to get it off."

"Solvent? Do you have some?"

There was malice in Cubber's smile. "Sorry. Used the last of it cleaning out my goggles."

14

When they jumped into the Doldrums system, two ships were on station waiting for them: the transport *Borleias* and the Mon Cal MC80 Star Cruiser *Home One.*

Wedge, piloting *Night Caller,* whistled as he saw the smooth, almost organic lines of the cruiser. "Admiral Ackbar's command ship. Maybe our recent communications struck a nerve."

Ton Phanan, at the sensors station, snorted. "Let's hope we can off-load a whole lot of whining, mewling, boring prisoners and take on some decent food to replace the slop they stock their galleys with."

"Communication from *Home One,*" Jesmin Ackbar said. "A request from the admiral to come aboard. He's sending a shuttle over."

"Acknowledge, with permission and greetings, of course. Starboard docking station, please."

Wedge's tour of *Night Caller* began and ended at the bridge. Admiral Ackbar looked off through the viewports at his own vessel in the distance and said, "Am I mistaken, or are your methods becoming even more unorthodox?"

Wedge smiled. "I think you're mistaken. It may just look that way because the new unorthodox methods are stacking on top of the old ones."

Ackbar's barbels twitched with amusement. "So. Well, I come with news in addition to congratulations." From a pocket he pulled a datapad; Wedge brought his own out in case Ackbar decided to transmit files.

"First," Ackbar said, "based on this training squadron's exemplary performance at Folor, Xobome, and Viamarr, I have the pleasure of declaring you fully commissioned and operational."

Wedge rocked back on his heels. "I'm . . . delighted to hear that. Thank you."

"You are also worried that it is premature?"

"No, sir. The Wraiths are a little rough around the edges, but they perform like a unit that has completed training. I'd just forgotten that we *weren't* officially operational."

"Ah. How anticipatory of you, General Antilles."

"How anticipatory of *you*. It's still Commander Antilles, sir."

"Of course. Second, we are in the process of alerting the armed forces about the small parasitic droids you described. We'd already had reports of rectangular apparatuses with melted parts aboard some ships; it appears the devices do have a self-destruct mechanism that fuses their interiors when they are forcibly detached from their host vehicles. But with your examination of the one you captured—and the device itself, if it is still intact—"

"I'll have Grinder deliver it to you, sir. And one or more of the Empion bombs."

"With a sample to examine, we should be able to capture more of the parasites 'alive' and begin releasing others with false data. Use them as a tool against Zsinj instead of simply suffering their effects. And with the Empion bombs, we may be able to equip our ships with shielding against the precise frequencies they emit, in order to reduce damage.

"Third, we have brought you some replacement equipment and supplies. Including gear, suited to commandos, from Special Forces and Intelligence."

"I'm glad to hear it. Do we have a replacement X-wing, sir?"

"No, not yet. None to spare, but you're at the top of the replacement list. The *Borleias* will deliver to you one of the X-wing simulators and backups of all your astromechs' memories. We also have food, fuel, X-wing replacement parts, and a piloting and maintenance crew for this corvette so you can free up your own pilots. Have your supply officer transmit requisitions for further items."

Wedge nodded. "I know we've needed some vacuum-rated tools. I'll have Squeaky get on that."

"Not Squeaky the 3PO unit? Of the Runaway Droid Ride?"

Wedge nodded.

Ackbar shuddered, then returned to his list and continued. "Fourth, your plan for retaining *Night Caller* and continuing on with its orders—that has neither been approved nor disapproved. I must know, what end do you hope to serve?"

"After some additional thinking, sir, my plan is to let *Night Caller* go through her assigned duties, but in those systems that are obviously in collusion with Zsinj, Wraith Squadron jumps in shortly afterward and makes strikes against the collaborators. Eventually Zsinj or Trigit should get the idea that somebody is following *Night Caller* around. My hope is that we can lure Zsinj out that way—have him arrange a trap for us and trap him in it instead."

"How appropriately vague." Ackbar considered. "For the time being, consider your plan approved. But how long do you think you can keep up this deception?"

"Quite a while, sir. The fact that Warlord Zsinj obviously had some special, unrecorded instructions for Captain Darillian is a problem; it may trip us up. But we're going to try to compensate with a trick or two of our own. For instance . . . Flight Officer Ackbar, is the demonstration ready?"

"Standing by, sir."

"Orient it toward us instead of the captain's chair and initiate."

Jesmin went through a series of control manipulations. Then the air hummed as a hologram appeared before Admiral Ackbar and Wedge.

The hologram showed a man in a control chair, his uniform black and nattily spotless, his manner energetic and haughty. He looked up as if startled and said, "Who in the hells of the Sith are you?"

Ackbar glanced at Wedge, who gave him no cue to go by. "I am Admiral Ackbar of the New Republic. Identify yourself."

"I am Captain Darillian, master of the private yacht *Night Caller*. I demand to know why you have interrupted me." The captain glared at the Mon Calamari officer; his anger was so palpable that if holograms had been able to project energy Ackbar would have been struck dead by lasers.

Ackbar turned back to the commander. "I thought you said he was dead."

Before Wedge could speak, Captain Darillian roared an interruption: "Dead! I'll show you dead! Ensign Antilles, kill this intruder."

Wedge barked a laugh. "*Ensign* Antilles, now? I'm all over the rank chart today. That'll be enough, Face."

Captain Darillian smiled. He reached to his right farther than the sensor on him could track and his hand disappeared. He must have manipulated something, for his image wavered . . . and became that of Face Loran. "Yub, yub, Commander." Then he disappeared.

Ackbar turned both eyes toward Wedge. "A holographic overlay of some sort."

Wedge nodded. "That's right. Captain Darillian was such a massive egotist that he kept his ship's journal and personal journal in full holo. That gave Grinder Thri'ag a huge sample that he could encode. He compiled a computer model of Darillian's body from the waist up, and his voice into an overlay, both of which we can project over Face. We have near-instantaneous translation of sight and sound. As long as we don't have to let anyone meet Darillian in person, and as long as Face can bluff his way through situations where the enemy knows more than we do, we can keep fooling them."

"I see. Very encouraging." Ackbar consulted his datapad again. "Fifth . . . Could you relieve Flight Officer Ackbar of duty for a few minutes, so that my niece and I might visit?"

"Consider it done, sir."

There weren't many places to go on the cramped *Night Caller*. Jesmin led her uncle first to the bow lounge and was lucky enough to find it unoccupied.

"You will understand my surprise," the admiral said, "when first I hear that Commander Antilles is assembling a squad of pilots who are chronic misfits . . . and shortly thereafter I see your name on the list of pilots assigned to that squad. I am not displeased to see you serving with him . . . but I do not understand. Your record is spotless, exemplary."

Jesmin gave him the barbel-twitch of knowing amusement. "My record shows I am a complete failure, Uncle."

"No."

"Try to understand. I was first in my class on graduation. Then, whatever unit I was assigned to, whatever type of fighter or field of engagement, I ended up flying routine scouting missions . . . or desk assignments."

"With your marks?"

"With my *name*, Uncle. My commanders were afraid of putting me in the line of fire, for fear that I'd be killed . . . and that you'd blame them."

The admiral rolled his eyes in different directions. "That is preposterous. General Cracken's son Pash has been in the path of danger since he joined the military. He even flew with Rogue Squadron, hardly the safest place in our armed forces."

"Perhaps there's still some Imperial-style overprotectiveness of females—or contempt for us—also at work, Uncle. But preposterous or not, I was a waste of training. I wasn't doing anything. I can't tell you how happy I was when Commander Antilles accepted me to the new squadron . . . and how much happier I was the first time I was put out in the line of fire. Finally, I am a pilot instead of a waste of volume." She gave him a steady look. "If I do come to my death in this unit, I hope you will not hold it against Commander Antilles."

"Are you happy here?"

"I am."

"Then I will hold him blameless. But if you do everything he says and learn whatever he tries to teach you, you might not ever give me cause for such grief."

"I'll try, Uncle."

After the last of the prisoners had been transferred over to *Home One,* the next shuttle trip brought them their new crew for *Night Caller.* Wedge was introduced to a small, neat man with a weathered face, Captain Choday Hrakness of Agamar, the new ship's captain, and to a tall, elegant-looking brown-haired woman of Coruscant, Lieutenant Atril Tabanne, his second-in-command, as well as to a number of technicians and mechanics.

Together they all watched *Borleias* and *Home One* jump out of system, then they set about reorganizing *Night Caller.*

The expanded mechanics crew, under Cubber's direction, reinforced the brackets holding the X-wings in the bow hold, making them steadier and more durable.

Officers and crew were assigned permanent quarters. Since many of the former crew of *Night Caller* had been stormtroopers and had not been replaced by New Republic ground troops, their departure left the ship comparatively empty. Every pilot received his own small stateroom, and Wedge, as commanding officer of a provisional group that now included the corvette, Wraith Squadron, and Rogue Squadron, was obliged to accept the huge and garishly over-decorated captain's cabin. He immediately sent the velvet drapes and antique furnishings collected from around the galaxy off to the hold and converted the captain's private audience chamber into a second conference room.

Meanwhile, the pilots settled into a new routine.

For Kell, it was less than a pleasant one. *Night Caller*

was a much smaller environment than Folor Base, and consequently he could not avoid running into Wes Janson several times a day. Most were simply incidents of passing one another in the hall, but even those brief and innocuous encounters brought cold fear to his belly and the lockup of all the muscles in his back.

After one such ordinary encounter, Runt told him, "You think he means you harm."

"I think he's waiting for me to make a mistake. I just don't know whether he intends to send my career into a trash receptacle or literally vape me in combat."

"I think you are wrong," Runt said. "I think your bad mind is imagining things."

"I think all *your* minds ought to go out and play in a mine field sometime so that only one or two come back."

Runt responded with a braying laugh. Kell shook his head; he could never tell what his wingman would find amusing.

Runt, too, was putting new skills to the test. Because of the multiplicity of his minds he was charged with reading the mail the ship's former crewmen had received and writing responses for those who had been active correspondents—a small number, fortunately. He submitted his efforts to Face for both a human's and a performer's input, then broadcast them. He told Kell that the duty was strange and sometimes tedious, but was very helpful at teaching him to switch from one mind to another with greater speed and less effort.

Meanwhile, the ship's two simulators were almost continuously occupied. The X-wing simulator became the near personal property of Tyria, who flew its missions obsessively, trying to bring her scores out of Wraith Squadron's basement. Meanwhile, Falynn Sandskimmer monopolized the TIE fighter simulator, a tactic, she admitted, she hoped would make her the default choice for a wingman whenever Wedge flew TIE fighter missions. Tyria prevailed upon Grinder to program simulations of launches and landings in the difficult bow hold of *Night Caller*.

.   .   .

In the ship's mess, Kell and Phanan settled in on either side of Tyria. Intently studying her datapad, she was slow in noticing their arrival. "Oh. Hello."

"We're the committee to force you to relax once in a while," Kell said.

Phanan nodded. "According to our mission chrono, it has been thirty-six standard hours since you enjoyed any aspect of your life, and twenty-three since you even cracked a smile."

She managed one now, a very faint one.

Grinder, seated opposite her, said, "You'd think she was facing her final pilot's examination. Relax, Tyria. You made it."

"You don't know anything about it," she said. "Besides, I'm still the bottom-rated pilot in this unit."

"Not in kills," Kell said. "Because of the way Folor Base came off, Runt and I still have zero. You got one there."

She waved away his objection. "You sacrificed one combat's worth of kills and came up with a tactic that probably saved the *Borleias*. That's a bright spot on your record, Kell, not a black one."

"Well," Grinder said, "there are ways to bring up your scores. Techniques a lot more effective than flying simulators hours every day until you're bone tired and stupid from lack of food."

She looked at him dubiously. "Such as what?"

"Well . . ." He looked around conspiratorially. "I shouldn't do this, because if you improve your rating, that leaves me at the bottom of the squadron. But I don't particularly mind. I could slice into your simulator records and bump them up a few points. Put you out of the danger zone. By way of compensation, I wouldn't ask much—"

She came over the table at him, knocking him off his bench to the floor, and landed on him hard. She struck him in the face three times, over his shouts of pain and surprise, before Kell and Phanan could shake off their shock. They scrambled around the ends of the table, converging on her, and seized her arms before she could continue turning Grinder's face into a bloody mess.

The other diners, a tableful of Cubber's mechanics and technicians, watched in surprise; some were laying down bets just as Kell and Phanan yanked Tyria upright.

Her face was flushed, her expression not just furious but hate-filled as she glared down at the Bothan. "You *bastard*," she said. "How dare you—"

"You want me?" Grinder scrambled to his feet, his nostrils streaming blood. "A fair fight, not an ambush? Bring her to the lounge, boys—"

"Attention!"

All of them snapped upright, mechanics included. Wedge and Janson stood in the doorway. Both pilots looked grim as they strode in. "Explain this," Wedge said.

Tyria didn't immediately respond; she seemed to be concentrating on catching her breath. Phanan said, "Well, sir, we were discussing some fine points of a specific hand-to-hand combat takedown maneuver, and—"

Wedge looked as pained as if Phanan had stabbed him. "Flight Officer Phanan. How many times do you suppose I've heard that 'We were discussing a boxing maneuver' excuse?"

Phanan looked confused. "I, uh, don't know, sir."

"That was a rhetorical question, Phanan. Do not reenter this conversation."

Pale where his skin could be seen under his skull prosthetic, Phanan shut up and stared off through the near wall.

Wedge dropped his voice. "Grinder, Tyria, come with me."

In his ridiculously well-appointed office, with Janson beside him, Wedge glared at the two junior officers and asked, "Grinder, did you do anything to provoke this?"

If possible, the Bothan's posture became even stiffer. "I didn't think so initially, sir. But in jest I did offer to do something unethical for her. I suppose she may not have gotten the joke."

"Tyria, did you 'get the joke'?"

"I suppose I didn't, sir."

"Grinder, a good comedian adjusts his jokes for his audience. Watch Face and Phanan sometimes. They're annoying, but proficient. Dismissed."

Grinder saluted and made good his escape.

Wedge turned his full attention on Tyria. "It appears to me that your response was completely out of proportion to the offense."

"Yes, sir."

"Explain yourself."

"I have no excuse, sir."

"I'd like to help you here, Flight Officer Sarkin. Your record already has one notation for gross insubordination. It would be good not to make it worse."

Tyria bit her lip. Wedge could tell that she recognized that his use of her full rank and name meant this discussion had reached a more official level. "Thank you, sir. But I have no excuse, sir."

"Very well. Consider yourself on report. For the time being, your X-wing will be reassigned to Ton Phanan. Dismissed."

For a moment she could not keep the dismay from her face. Then she recovered herself, saluted, and followed Grinder's escape vector.

Wedge sighed. "Any ideas?"

Janson shook his head. "This really came out of the asteroid belt. I thought she was one of the most steady of them."

"Me, too. Do me a favor and write up this incident report, would you? But keep the language flexible. I'd like to be able to monitor the situation and make adjustments to the report up until the time I have to file it."

"Will do. You going to make her apologize?"

"No, I'm going to find out if she apologizes. A forced apology is worth nothing."

"True."

"How are things going with Tainer?"

Janson grimaced. "Worse than ever. And now I understand he's received some demolitions components from *Home One*."

"I told you, you don't have to worry about that."

"You also told me Tyria was one of the most steady of them."

Wedge glared in mock anger. "You don't want to get into a 'let's recall who has screwed up the worst' contest with me, Wes."

"I think I'll be off to write up that report. Sir."

"Good."

Tyria entered her quarters and switched on the lights.

At her table sat Kell and Phanan.

"Oh, great," she said. "One reprimand, you get one pilot in your quarters. Two reprimands, two pilots."

"You may doubt this," Phanan said, "but we're not part of your punishment. We're worried about you."

She fell over, full length, onto her bed and buried her face in the pillow. Her voice came out muffled. "Well, don't be."

Kell dragged his chair beside her. "Tyria, what happened in the mess was crazy. We'd like to help, but we can't if we don't understand it."

Phanan said, "Your wingman ought to be in here. But Donos is about as warm, tender, and helpful as a methane ice comet. So we're here. Tyria, we're your friends."

"No, you're not. You just want to jump into bed with me."

Phanan looked crestfallen. "I'm sorry if I gave you that impression. Yes, I *do* want to jump into bed with you. It's nothing personal. You're talented and beautiful, and for some reason I find that appealing. But I'll break off my most ardent pursuit, forever, if you wish, if you'd only talk to us."

She pulled some of her flowing hair from over her eye and stared at him. Then she looked up at Kell. "You, too?"

He winced. "Whatever you like. I really wasn't assigned to this unit to make you feel worse."

She managed a low chuckle. Then she rolled up on her side, her back to the cabin wall, and looked them over frankly. "Look, you two. I'll tell you this, but if it gets out, it's the end of my career. Literally and without recourse."

"I understand," Kell said. Phanan nodded.

"All right. I got into the New Republic Academy pretty much for one reason: because I demonstrated I had a little control over the Force."

Phanan said, "They were hoping you'd train up to be a new Luke Skywalker."

"That's right. But in my early simulator work I flew more like a drunken dinko. I was on the verge of washing out when I was transferred to a squadron for, well, remedial pilots in training.

"The unit commander, Colonel Repness, seemed to be a pretty good instructor. My scores came up into the acceptable range. Then, just before final examinations, he came to me and said, 'Would you like to make sure your final examination and average scores don't just earn your wings, but also bump you out of the bottom quarter of this class?' "

Kell grimaced. "I can see where this is going."

"Well, maybe not. He wanted me to take a training run in an X-wing and simulate equipment failure. A very sophisticated simulation, backed by transmissions from my astromech. I'd ditch in the ocean and the rescue crews would pick me up . . . but the X-wing would have sunk thousands of meters to the bottom, where no one could recover it."

Phanan nodded. "Except Repness would actually have been waiting for you at the ditch site and would make off with the X-wing. Which he could put on the black market."

"That's right."

Kell whistled. "What did you do?"

"I said no. And I said that I was going to turn him in. He seemed shocked. He started begging. He said, please wait, give him a day to tell his wife and set his affairs in order." She took a deep breath and released it slowly. "Like an idiot, I told him I would. I was actually naive enough to think that I was the first one who'd ever refused him, that I was in charge of the situation."

Phanan grimaced. "So naturally he took the extra time to cover his tracks and set you up."

"Basically, yes. I reported for duty the next morning and found out that he had put me on report for gross insubordination. He claimed that I had made *advances* toward him—

talk about unchecked ego—and had also made horrible disparaging remarks about his wife. With a blot like that on my record, I'd have to score very high on my final examinations and keep my record clean for a long time afterward to stay in the service.

"So I went to him and told him to take that off my record. And he said, 'You can either turn me in and see your career go straight into the incinerator, or leave the record as it is and go on to a career as the mediocre pilot you're destined to be.' I didn't understand what he meant until he showed me. He'd been falsifying my records all along, since the day I transferred to his unit, recording my scores as higher than they were—I'd actually have washed out weeks before. If the truth about his offer to trade my services in stealing an X-wing for grades went on the record, so would my true scores." She looked very, very tired.

"So you kept quiet," Kell said.

"Yes, I did. I shut my mouth and accepted the reprimand and graduated at the very bottom of my class. And immediately the offer to try out for this squadron came in—and I later learned that it was just because of my Ranger experience. I've tried so hard to improve . . . and now Grinder comes up to me with this same suggestion—"

Phanan's voice was gentle. "I truly doubt that he was offering to raise your scores for profit, Tyria. He was just being a code-slicer."

"Maybe. I didn't think about that. I wasn't capable of thinking. I just wanted to smash his face in. To smash Colonel Repness's face in."

Kell said, "Another thing you have to understand. Wedge Antilles would never let an inferior pilot into a squadron he commanded."

"He's probably anticipating that I can learn more control of the Force. He's investing in that. He hasn't yet figured out it's never going to happen. In the meantime, Ton here gets my X-wing."

Phanan said, "I'm sorry."

"Which means," Kell said, "that whenever Falynn is asleep or something, you should be training in the TIE fighter simulator. You might get some time in one of the TIEs. And also do some shuttle training. I'll drop a word in Cubber's ear and see if I can get him to give you some instruction there."

"All right," she said.

"So," Phanan said, "are you going to hold me to my deal?"

She looked confused. "What deal?"

"You did talk to us. Must I now abandon my pursuit of you? That would sadden me beyond measure—"

Tyria's pillow bounced off his face.

"Ah. Well, I'll just put it on hold, then."

"Tell me about these Rangers," Kell said.

She gave him a curious look. "Why?"

"Because I'd like to know."

"All right." She turned on her back and stared up at the featureless ceiling. "It's an old order, the Antarian Rangers. Founded centuries ago to aid Jedi Knights. A few of them, anyway; most of the Jedi tended to be pretty solitary. But some of them appreciated having loyal, reliable warriors to help them. Freedom's Sons were one such order, and the Rangers were another.

"To be a Ranger meant knowing how to move in any environment. To blend in with the forest or grassland, to sail, to swim, to dive, to pilot. To be masters of our surroundings. We were good spies, good warriors, very adept at intrusion and escape.

"In the old days, there were communities of the Rangers on several worlds, including Toprawa. There was some inter-marrying between the Jedi and the Rangers, which may be where I inherited my own nearly useless talent with the Force. Gradually, there were fewer and fewer Rangers around. The Clone Wars killed off whole clans, and then most of the rest were purged with the Jedi. The rest went underground. My family stayed hidden for decades, and then before we could emerge, Toprawa was bombed into barbarism by the Empire. That's when the last of the Antarian Rangers on Toprawa died."

"Except you," Phanan said.

"I'm not sure it's a matter of 'except me.' I expect that I

will die in this service, without continuing my line. The Sarkins are gone. I'm just a living reminder, hoping to make something of myself before I join them. That's why I make few plans for the future." She turned toward Kell as he opened his mouth. "Don't say it. Don't tell me that I may doom myself by being fatalistic. I've heard it before."

"Then why haven't you listened?" he asked.

Instead of being offended, she smiled. "Kell, I've failed at everything I wanted to do in life so far. I failed to keep my family alive. I failed to learn the ways of the Force and uphold my family tradition. I failed to enter the fighter corps on my own merits. But I got in anyway, by way of a cheat I shouldn't have accepted. Now all I want to do is find some sort of grace, something that will make up for my failures. Just once before I die. Can't you understand that?"

Kell thought back to his family's last days on Alderaan, the meticulous scrubbing of their true family name from every aspect of their lives, the way his mother cursed and mourned her husband at the same time. "Believe me, I can."

"Then you don't need to preach to me that what I'm doing is the wrong path." She motioned as though to shoo them away. "Go on, you two. Let me get some rest." As they rose, she added, "And, Ton?"

"Yes?"

"Take care of my snubfighter. I want it back."

15

"Captain Darillian and the warlord will be *very* pleased," Face said.

This time, he was not wearing a disguise cobbled together in a matter of seconds.

His entire face was covered in a sheath of flesh tone polymer that allowed his skin to breathe yet concealed his true features and scars. The polymer took makeup well and was decorated with a luxuriant mustache and the usual assembly of small scars, moles, and other defects a normal person acquires over a lifetime. He could not feel the nighttime wind in his face, but otherwise the mask was fairly comfortable. Face also wore an Imperial lieutenant's uniform, modified to bear the extravagant rank insignia unique to *Night Caller*.

The man before him, Governor Nojin Koolb of the Outer Rim world of Xartun, smiled in appreciation of Face's words. "I am delighted to hear it."

Face brought his voice down, made it a trifle ominous. "One thing disturbs the warlord, however. The fact that Xartun is a recent signatory to the New Republic. Do you not feel a certain conflict between the word you've given the Provisional Council and the one you've just given the warlord?"

Governor Koolb did not lose his smile or aplomb. "Of course not, Lieutenant. It was my illustrious and so widely mourned predecessor who signed the accord with the New Republic. I did not. My loyalty is with Zsinj . . . even if practical circumstances prevent me from declaring it publicly at this time."

Face smiled in return. "We'll see to it that you can make your true feelings known as soon as possible." He extended his hand.

The governor shook it. "I look forward to it. By your leave." He and his subordinates withdrew from Face and the shuttle, standing far enough away on the ferrocrete landing pad that an ill-considered pivot of the shuttle on takeoff would not carry the thruster wash across them.

Face trotted up the shuttle's boarding ramp, felt it rising to close even before he reached the top. He dropped into the copilot's seat beside Cubber, who wore the uniform of an Imperial ensign. "Are they on station?"

"They should be, by now. Let's find out." Cubber double-tapped a button on the shuttle's comm.

Face looked out across the ferrocrete. Ahead of him, the first of Xartun's two suns was just beginning to rise over the innocuous bunker where he had just spent a couple of informative hours; the governor had given him the very detailed grand tour reserved for Captain Darillian. Face had seen the underground levels, the manufacturing equipment that turned out transparisteel products such as blastproof windows and fighter canopies. All of it, the governor explained, now owned by Lord Houghten Ween . . . another alias of Warlord Zsinj.

Beyond the bunker was the parking area and arrival zone where the plant's day laborers left their personal vehicles, and beyond that was the land road leading to the nearest community. All around the complex was thick forest . . . forest where the commando team was now supposed to be waiting. But Face saw no signal, heard nothing over the comm. "No sign of them," he said.

"Look at your chest."

Face glanced down. Dancing around on his chest was a

bright red spot, the wrong end of the laser targeting sight from Donos's sniper rifle.

Face half crawled out of the chair before he could bring himself under control. "All right. They're ready." He took a couple of deep breaths to bring himself under control. The red light disappeared. "I'm going to get him for that."

"Sure you are."

Face took off his lieutenant's cap, pulled the concealed device from within, and plugged it into the shuttle's communications console. "Tour data compressing . . . compressing . . . Ready to go." He turned on the comm. "Shuttle *Adder's Bite* ready to depart. Requesting communications signal integrity check."

"*Adder's Bite,* this is Tower Six, copy. Go ahead."

"Prepare for thirty seconds of nasty Verpine music, then report signal strength." He hit the transmit button.

The file began broadcasting. Coming in over an audio link, it would sound like discordant, jarring shrieks only a very few alien species could love. Acquired as data and then translated by a program written by Grinder, though, it would expand out into a holographic record of Face's tour through the manufacturing bunker.

The file cut off. "Signal strength nine," Tower Six reported. "And that's nasty."

"Don't let your children listen to it. They might get a taste for it . . . like mine did. *Adder's Bite* out, and away."

"Good luck, and good flying. Tower Six out."

Cubber cut in the repulsorlifts and the *Narra* smoothly rose off the ferrocrete pad. As she rose, her wings came down from their upfolded position and locked into cruising configuration. Cubber elevated the bow and cut in the thrusters, punching the *Narra* up toward space at an abrupt angle.

Face, bounced around by the crude maneuvers in spite of the inertial compensators, hurriedly strapped himself into place. "Hey, where did you earn your pilot's license?"

"*License?*" Cubber broke into laughter. "Listen to the boy. I don't have anything as fancy as a license. Just a few hours instruction from a couple of pilots I did some favors for. You want a smoother ride? Give me some lessons."

"Oh, yeah? Will you trade a favor for them?"

"Sure. Something mechanical?"

"A modification to Vape, my R2."

"Sure. Just let me station this flying can at our waiting zone and you can tell me all about it."

A hundred meters from the landing pad, in a glade a few meters from the forest edge, Grinder looked over his datapad. "It uncompressed fine. I told you."

Kell squatted down beside him. "Don't be defensive. I just like to have things run through over and over again."

"You're obsessed with preparation."

"Yes, I am. Meaning I want you to study that recording until your eyes bleed. I'm going to do the same."

Grinder sighed.

They wore dark jumpsuits in dark green broken by irregular swaths of black—camouflage wear suited to deep forest or nighttime in most overgrown areas. All the Wraiths but Face were present . . . and despite the rank disparity between them, Wedge had assigned command of the mission to Kell, due to his specific commando experience.

"All right," Kell said. "Everyone, settle in for some sleep. I'll take first watch; Janson, you take second. We go at nightfall."

As the day progressed, large personnel skimmers and private vehicles delivered workers and managers to the factory. From their vantage point, the commando party couldn't see much of what went on at the front, or business, end of the complex. But shortly before noon, four X-23 StarWorker space barges landed and took on cargo through the bunker's rear cargo doors. Kell and Wedge took notes on their registry numbers while Jesmin recorded all transmissions. The barges took off an hour later and Kell went off-duty, settling into sleep.

He woke as dusk was settling. He was a little stiff and suffered from new aches, his sleeping roll not being adequate defense agains the hard ground and tree roots beneath him or the local stinging insects. The other Wraiths looked as though they felt the same.

Runt, his fur spotted with twigs and crumbled pieces of leaves, handed him a hot and extra-stout cup of caf. Kell took a sip and winced. "More of Cubber's solvent?"

Runt looked at him in slight confusion, then something in his eyes and manners changed and he uttered a soft chortle. "I understand."

"Has everyone eaten?"

"Everyone but you." Runt picked up a small gray case a third of a meter long and pressed a recessed button at one end. The whole package began to crackle as its contents, Kell's supper, began to cook within.

"Good." Kell raised his voice slightly to get everyone's attention. "People, do your final equipment checks. We'll move out as soon as it's fully dark."

He ignored his own directive; he'd done his equipment check before falling asleep. Shaped charges. Grenades. Explosives. Adhesives. Detonators. Detonation comlinks. Miniature datapads optimized to detect complex sets of circumstances and then trigger detonators. Sensors. Tools. Hand lights. Headband lights. Lights with temporary adhesives to stick to all sorts of walls and other surfaces. A full-sized datapad with permanent memory stuffed full of data about explosives in use by the Empire, by the New Republic, by warlords and individual worlds. All of it arranged by straps or in pockets so he could find any item by touch. All of it was fine. He opened his meal case and began absently pulling nameless meatlike balls from it and eating them.

Grinder waved a hand to get his attention. Kell moved over to him, still unsteady from sleepiness, and drank more of the poisonous caf.

"I have something for you," Grinder said. He was staring intently at the oversized screen on his datapad.

Kell moved to loom over him. "Show me."

On the screen was a panoramic camera view of the front of the bunker. Kell knew it had been taken through the fisheye camera rig in Face's hat. With the touch of a button, Grinder set the view into motion; the heavily armored door

into the bunker slid open, the planet's governor and some of
his cronies moved ahead of the camera view into the small
vehicle hangar beyond, and Face's point-of-view followed.

One of the governor's men pointed, drawing Face's attention toward a long, open vehicle, which Kell recognized as
an Ubrikkian cargo skiff. This one was different from the
standard model; at the rear was a small passenger bay enclosed in a globular transparisteel canopy. Inside was a reclin-
ing couch large enough for two. The governor's man wore an
expression Kell interpreted as amused, and the camera vibrated a little, possibly from Face laughing.

"Here," Grinder said, and paused the image. He tapped
the lower-left corner of the display. It showed a man holding
a comlink, but not orienting it toward his mouth. Grinder
started the image in motion again. The man pressed a button
on the comlink. Behind him, in the corner of the display, the
bunker door began to close. "What does that suggest to
you?"

"The door closed on a signal instead of a wall switch or a
timer," Kell said. "And possibly the governor's man drew
Face's attention away to keep him from seeing it; that whole
scene in the corner would have been behind him as he looked
at the skiff. That suggests a security measure. Maybe an
alarm on timer; if they don't switch it off with the comlink
within the appointed time, the alarm goes off."

"That's my guess, Demolition Boy."

"I'm leader here; call me Demolition Boy Sir. Uh, roll
that sequence back to the point at which he hit the button on
the comlink."

Grinder did.

Kell consulted the numbers on the text screen of the
datapad. "Jesmin, how long have you been recording?"

The Mon Calamari stood at attention. "Since we came
on station, Demolition Boy Sir."

Kell gave her a look suggesting she had just betrayed
him to the Imperials. "That's an awful lot of time to record,
isn't it?"

"Not really. My gear records everything off the airwaves,
but analyzes it as it goes, and only commits discrete strong

signals or repeating patterns to its memory. So after hours of recording I have perhaps an hour recorded."

"Did you record a transmission at two hundred oh eight oh three?"

She picked up her heavy communications gear pack and opened the flap giving her access to the main control screen. After a few moments, she said, "Something within eight seconds of that time, sir. Acceptable within normal variations on individual chronos. The transmission was fairly complex but lasted less than half a second."

"Make sure that eight seconds is the interval between your gear and Grinder's datapad." Kell frowned at the Bothan. "Didn't I tell you to synchronize the chronos between everyone's datapads?"

Grinder looked abashed. "I have no excuse, sir."

"Oh, so when you're in trouble, I stop being Demolition Boy?"

Grinder grinned.

"That's the interval," Jesmin said.

"All right. Note that transmission and be prepared to broadcast it, in the frequency it came in on, at my command."

There was a faint rustle in the trees between them and the landing pad. Wedge, Kell, and Tyria had blasters in their hands within a split second and had them trained on the intruder before he, Donos, emerged from the trees.

Donos blinked at them. "The suns are down and the last of the worker transports is gone."

"Good," Kell said. "People, remember: Once we reach the bunker, always use your numbers. Never your names.

"Here are the final orders . . . until circumstances and screwups dictate that we alter them. Ten, break trail, with One as your backup." Tyria and Wedge nodded. "Four and I follow fairly closely." Grinder, obviously still abashed from his failure to calibrate chronos, merely hoisted his pack onto his shoulders and saluted.

"Nine remains on station here as our long-distance spotter and sniper." Donos nodded. "The rest follow in a group until we get to the bunker's rear door. Eleven, you'll set up at that door as our secondary spotter." Janson gave a brief nod.

"Inside, Three will choose one vehicle for our escape; I recommend the cargo skiff, but you're the expert on the condition of these crafts, so make your choice at your own discretion. Disable the rest. Twelve, you'll stay with her as her guard and ears." Falynn gave him a thumbs-up; Piggy nodded.

"The rest of us will enter, acquire all the data we can, plant the charges, and get out. Questions? No one? All right. Move out."

Wedge, trailing Tyria at a distance of eight or ten meters, marveled at the way she moved.

Hers was not a steady progress. She stopped to listen to animal noises, stray crackings of twigs or other unexplained sounds, and when there was no noise at all. But when the wind stirred the trees, she glided forward at a steady pace, the wind completely blanketing whatever noise she might have made.

Wedge tried to follow her example. After so many ground missions in the last few years, his own intrusion skills were not inconsiderable. On the other hand, he hadn't needed them to survive day after day for years as she had; it was hardly embarrassing to discover she was better at them.

They skirted the forest edge alongside the ferrocrete landing pad until they reached the closest approach to the bunker. Keeping low, they moved across open ground until they reached the bunker's shadow, then hugged the bunker wall all the way to the door. Tyria nodded and Wedge clicked his comlink twice to indicate success. The two of them crouched, motionless, blasters in hand, and covered the approach of the next team.

Within a minute Kell and Grinder joined them. "So far, so good," Kell whispered. "Minimal security."

"On the outside, anyway," Tyria amended.

Kell clicked his comlink twice, then nodded to Grinder. The Bothan held a small light in his mouth and looked at the access panel beside the door to the hangar. "Standard model," he mumbled around the light.

Kell snorted. "With Zsinj involved? Don't believe it."

"I don't." Grinder brought out a small sensor and ran it around the join where the access panel was sealed shut. "Ooh," he said. "Standard keypad. Underneath, simplified circuits. Behind that, a denser circuit panel. Not standard."

"What's that mean?" asked Wedge.

"False layer to trip up . . ." Drool ran out of Grinder's mouth around the penlight and he shut up, scowling.

"If you open up the panel," Kell said, "you'll probably get something that looks like the standard wiring you find in these panels. Odds are good you can even patch into it to run a bypass and get these doors open. But it's a fake, and the circuitry beneath it will be busy alerting every guard on this hemisphere of the planet. The trick is to open both top layers at once and not trip the security, which is really tough—"

Grinder popped open the access hatch. A panel of dense circuitry in a pattern unfamiliar to Wedge glinted at them. Grinder turned to smirk at Kell.

"All right," Kell said, "maybe not so tough."

Wedge had to work to keep a smile off his face. The Wraiths were still surprising one another with what they could accomplish. A good sign. He just wished Kell were not so tense, so rigid; he'd been that way ever since Wedge had announced Kell was leading this mission. *Not* a good sign.

The others moved up fairly quietly behind them. "All accounted for," whispered Janson.

Grinder plugged wires and bypass circuitry into the access hatch's naked circuitry, then flipped a tiny toggle on an equally tiny capacitance charge. The hangar door groaned and slid open before them. It was pitch-black beyond, and the moons, still arising on the far side of the bunker, offered no light.

Tyria pulled her night-sight gear over her eyes and switched it on; it made a faint hum. "Everyone move in, no more than six paces; we're clear to that point," she said.

They did as she said, all but Janson.

"Two."

"Yes, Five."

"Can you transmit that signal by touch?"

"Yes, Five."

"Do so."

The door moaned behind them until it was shut again.

"Hand lights on," Kell said.

The commandos' handheld lights sprang to life, tiny beams illuminating small portions of the spacious hangar.

"You all know your assignments," Kell said. "Let's go." He headed toward the doors that gave access to the hallway with the bunker's main freight turbolift; all but Falynn and Piggy followed.

In the hall, Grinder took only a minute to bypass the turbolift controls. Then he tried to lift the turbolift's massive top-closing door. It stubbornly refused his efforts.

"Allow us." Runt stepped in, affecting a swagger Wedge hadn't seen before, and put his fingers under the door's bottom lip. He straightened easily, lifting the door to waist height. He showed big teeth in a near-human grin. His long, furred hands were steady as they held up the door's enormous weight.

Kell ducked to peer inside. The turbolift shaft went down six or more stories, more than the three Face had been shown; the lift car was far below in the dimness. There were access rungs on one side.

On their way down, Grinder spoke to Kell; Wedge barely heard the whispered words. "I haven't seen any cameras. Microphones. No wiring for them in the wall behind the turbolift access panel."

"Have you seen enough to be sure there aren't any?" Kell said.

"No. I'm giving you an impression."

"Keep looking." Face's tape hadn't shown any armed guards, either. The bunker complex might rely on other types of defense . . . and not knowing what they were had Kell worried.

The turbolift was a freight model, with no roof to impede them. They dropped the last six feet to its floor. Grinder immediately got to work bypassing the door's electronics, then

Runt, with little apparent effort, heaved the car's door and then the armored exterior door up.

The door opened onto a loading area. It was full of loading carts and even some repulsorlift vehicles, with transparisteel products loaded onto some of them.

There were crystal-clear cubes three meters on a side, with small circular holes and an opening, one meter by one meter, cut into the side; there were large, thick sheets shaped as irregular polygons; there were curved disks over two meters in diameter, looking like enormous lenses.

Wedge looked at these last items. "TIE fighter front viewports," he said. "And the big sheets, unless I'm mistaken, are bridge or lounge windows for a capital ship."

"Sounds like support for Zsinj's Super Star Destroyer," Kell said. He dropped his voice to a whisper, tones probably too low for planted microphones to pick up. "But then why wouldn't Eight have been shown this level?"

Wedge frowned as he considered the question. He responded in a whisper. "The governor on the other world was reluctant to discuss things with Eight when he'd obviously talked about them with Captain Darillian. My guess is that Zsinj is compartmentalizing information about himself. Structuring things in cells, like a resistance movement, so that information is contained."

Kell nodded. "When one cell falls, the rest remain safe."

Grinder hissed at them from the doorway to an adjacent chamber. They joined him.

It was an operations control center, banks of computer consoles and black viewscreens that probably showed crucial areas of the manufacturing chambers when live. "The home of data," Grinder said.

"Drain it dry," Kell said. "Replicate everything you downlink into Two's comm gear memory."

Grinder's face twisted. "That'll take extra time."

"Not much. Do it."

Wedge guarded Kell while the mission leader explored other chambers of the sixth subterranean level.

This was just another manufacturing floor; it received superheated transparisteel ingots from the larger foundry floors above and shaped them into parts best suited to Imperial warships and fighters, plus those large, inexplicable cubes they'd seen. Kell seemed to pay little attention to the function of the rooms he was in; he simply chose support beams, retaining walls, and power generators on which to plant his demolition charges. Both men preferred to keep conversation to a minimum while Kell was setting up his explosives.

Wedge felt a slight change in air pressure. He turned away from the support pillar Kell was rigging; he moved his hand light beam around the room.

Nothing. Just conveyor belts, receiving receptacles, polishing machinery, phototropic shielding equipment.

Then his beam flitted across something moving. He caught the barest glimpse of the thing, something taller than a man, moving fast and silently. He flicked the beam in the direction he thought it had been heading, but there was nothing there.

"Trouble," he whispered.

He heard a faint whine as Kell activated the timer on the latest charge, then a scrape of metal on leather as Kell drew his blaster.

It came at them from the side, claws and pinchers extended—

16

"Ten."

Tyria looked up, in the direction of Runt's call. Runt was still on station near the door to the turbolift. His eyes were wider than normal. "Yes, Six?" she said.

"Did you hear something? We heard something."

Tyria glanced toward the door to the operations center. Ton Phanan was still on guard duty there, his blaster pistol up and at the ready. He was peering into the op center and did not look alarmed.

She turned back to Runt. "No, nothing."

The silhouette materialized out of the gloom behind Runt. Before Tyria could say anything it ran him down, smashing him to the floor like a runaway speeder bike.

An ungainly silhouette, round and heavy on top, trailing arms or tentacles like some invertebrate sea life, it came on straight at Tyria.

The attack caught Kell and Wedge off guard. The mass of the attacker hit Kell head-on, slamming him to the metal flooring. Wedge twisted with the attack, took a grazing impact to the arm, and went down rolling; he ended up under a control console, aiming and firing before he'd come to a stop.

His blaster shot was on-target, hitting the attacker dead center. The laser blast charred what it hit but did not penetrate; it merely illuminated the attacker.

It was a floating mass of machinery. The main portion was a roughly spherical body, the top and bottom hemispheres divided by a narrowed equator that Wedge knew allowed the two portions to swivel independently. A half-dozen articulated limbs trailed below it. The designation A3 was painted on the upper hemisphere. The spherical portion was studded with sensor ports and blaster nozzles. The top hemisphere rotated, bringing one of those blaster nozzles in line almost instantly.

Wedge ducked behind the console support as the thing fired. The blaster shot hit the console, burning through it, showering Wedge with sparks.

Imperial probe droid. Wedge came up in a half crouch, running behind this console and the one adjacent. Beyond it he could see Kell's foot. The big man was not moving.

Wedge grabbed Kell's leg and hauled him behind the console. The probe droid fired again, the shot melting into slag the metal deck where Kell had just been lying.

Tyria ducked behind one of the carts loaded with TIE fighter viewports. She fired at the oncoming droid, hitting it once, twice beside the characters A2 painted on the upper hemisphere. Surface armor charred a little but the thing was not slowed.

It fired a return shot. It hit the TIE fighter viewport Tyria hid behind. The viewport instantly opaqued and the laser blast did not penetrate; the transparisteel slowly began to fade to glasslike clarity.

She breathed a sign of relief. These viewports had already gone through their phototropic shielding treatment. They'd stop anything short of the blast from a tripod-mounted laser cannon.

The probe droid sideslipped to get around the impediment of the viewport. A blast fired by Phanan hit one of its sensor eyes, shattering it, but the droid returned fire almost instantly; Tyria saw Phanan duck back behind the doorway to the op center.

"We're under assault," Wedge said. "A probe droid, military model. Our hand blasters aren't going to do it much harm."

Kell's eyes opened. "I know that."

"I'm talking to Jesmin," Wedge said. "They're under attack by another one."

"Shouldn't we be keeping comm silence?"

"If the probots are active, the locals know we're here, Tainer."

"I can kill ours." Kell lifted his head and groaned. "But I'd like a nap first."

"No time for a nap. You're going to use explosives?"

"Of course."

"How do you plan to plant them?"

Kell grinned. "I was sort of hoping you'd lead the droid around so I could get a good approach on it."

"Great."

When the droid glided around the side of Tyria's cart, she broke the other way, running straight toward one of the repulsorlift carts. Phanan fired a steady stream of blasts to cover her movement; the droid returned fire, superheating the op center's metal doorjamb to a dripping, golden, glowing mass.

Tyria jumped into the driver's seat and fired up the engine. Immediately the cart rose a meter into the air. It held a load of large windows, her only protection. She threw the cart into reverse and backed straight at the droid.

It fired at her, the blasts stopping against her transparisteel cargo. Then the cart hit the probot, the great mass of vehicle and cargo pushing it backward. Tyria kept the thrust at full until the cart slammed into the wall; then she held the thrust, pinning the droid in place. It struggled to wriggle free and fired blast after blast into the transparisteel windows. The windows darkened and began to melt under the barrage.

Wedge made a complete circuit of the manufacturing chamber, running along the maintenance alley behind the banks of control consoles. He varied his pace so the probot couldn't time his passage and take an accurate shot at him as he crossed the gaps between banks. It followed him throughout his circuit, staying on the other side of the consoles. Its accuracy was high and two near misses had charred his clothes— and slightly burned the skin beneath—at shoulder and thigh.

He passed Kell where the demolitions expert crouched. Just before the next gap between consoles, Wedge skidded to a stop. The droid fired, a pattern of three blaster shots flashing between the consoles and melting holes in the wall.

From the corner of his eye, Wedge saw Kell's attack. Kell rose in a smooth motion, his height and long legs enabling him to step up on the high console counter, and threw himself atop the probe droid.

He bounced off immediately and hit the floor rolling. The probe droid grabbed at him with a claw, missed, and brought a blaster into line, but Kell was already behind the room's bulky master control console.

Wedge suppressed a groan. "Don't tell me I have to do the whole thing again!"

"Get behind cover!"

Wedge ducked down fully behind the console just as the droid's top hemisphere erupted like a volcano. The blast shattered console gauges all across the room and smashed the probe droid into the floor, crushing its trailing armatures.

Wedge rose. "Pretty slick. I didn't see you plant the charge."

Kell returned to pick up his bag. He cupped a hand behind his ear and mouthed something.

Wedge realized there was a ringing in his ears. "What?"

He dimly heard Kell's reply: "What?"

· · ·

Tyria struggled with the cart's controls, desperately aware that she was losing the battle to keep the probot pinned.

Phanan continued firing at the probe droid. Bit by bit, his shots were chewing away at the droid's armor. At this rate, he'd have the thing dead in a couple of days.

There was an explosion from the main fab chamber. Tyria froze, momentarily frightened that Kell's demolitions were going off prematurely . . . but there was only the one blast. She hoped Kell was well clear of it.

A mass of transparisteel goods slid into place against the wall beside the probe droid. Tyria looked up to see Runt, weaving like a sailor just back from a night of tavern crawling, his flat nose streaming blood, finish positioning the cart and then lock down the parking brake. Runt waved drunkenly at her and ran, with a weaving gait she didn't imagine he'd be able to duplicate when unhurt, to grab the maneuvering handle of another cart.

He'd just slammed that one home on the other side of the droid and locked it down, blocking Phanan from firing further, when Wedge and Kell emerged from the fab chamber.

Kell shouted, "We're omega!" He waved the commandos toward the turbolift shaft. Grinder and Jesmin followed Phanan out of the op center and all scrambled into the turbolift shaft.

"What happens when that probe droid gets free?" Tyria asked.

"What?" said Kell.

"What?" said Wedge. He cupped a hand behind his ear. She shouted, "Probe droid! Will get free!"

Kell shook his head and pulled a timer charge from his bag. "No. Get clear."

"What if there are more?"

Grinder said, "They're mine. Trust me."

Kell shouted, "Six, open up the doors to the fourth and second levels as you go!"

Runt, pressing his sleeve against his nose to stop the flow of blood, nodded.

"Why have him open those doors?" Tyria asked. Realizing that Kell and Wedge were having trouble hearing, she repeated the question, shouting this time.

"Still have to plant charges on the support beams," Kell answered, unnecessarily shouting. "Hold the top floor. If I'm not out in seven minutes, finish the evacuation."

"If *we're* not back," Wedge corrected, also shouting. "You still need someone to guard your back."

"Obviously so." Kell grinned. He skidded the charge under the blockade of hauling carts. Its timer was already counting down from ten.

They ran.

Kell wasted no time. On the fourth basement level and then the second, he ran from support pillar to support pillar, slapping his explosives in place, keying in the countdown, and activating the charges, all at a record pace.

Wedge kept alert for more probe droids, but none appeared. He thought he might have glimpsed something rising through the turbolift shaft, but it was gone before he could sight in on it.

Probe Droid A1 rose into place, hovering in the shaft at ground level, then floated forward through the door.

Grinder, his back to the wall just beside the turbolift, hit the button on the wall.

The turbolift door, its safety governors disabled, slammed down atop the probe droid, crushing its spherical body nearly flat. Lights dimmed in its sensor eyes. Sparks shot out of new tears and rents in its surface.

Grinder raised the turbolift door and smashed it down twice more, then raised and locked it. He stared in satisfaction at the damage he had done. "Do I get to paint a probe droid silhouette?"

Phanan snorted. "Sure, on your datapad."

"Quiet," Jesmin said. "Nine and Eleven report we have new arrivals. A flatbed skimmer full of troops and two TIE fighters just landed on the pad outside."

. . .

Outside, just beside the hangar door, Janson lay perfectly still and whispered into his comlink. "I count thirty or thirty-five troops. Some of them are deploying around toward the front; I assume they'll be hitting us from two sides. The TIE fighters are oriented so they can fire in through the hangar door, but the troops back here aren't approaching yet. I think they're waiting for the others to get in position. When I give you the go, I want you to open the hangar door just wide enough for me to get in."

"Acknowledged," said Jesmin.

Donos did not call in with unnecessary queries about what he should be doing. Janson was sure he would not announce his presence unless ordered to or circumstances meant he had to fire to save a fellow Wraith. In the meantime, he'd provide additional intelligence information when needed.

A minute later, one of the infantry commanders waved forward. He and a half-dozen men, armed with rifles and wearing helmets and breastplates that looked like cast-off stormtrooper scout armor, advanced in a half crouch.

Janson shot the commander in the faceplate. The man dropped, dead before he knew he was hit. The half-dozen men looked at him for a moment. Janson shot a second man in the chest. Then, as the survivors began to drop to the ground, he hit another faceplate and said, "Open up."

The hangar door began to grind open as the storm-troopers opened fire. Laser blasts hit the door and bunker wall above and around him. Janson grimaced. With that caliber of marksmanship, there was little chance any of the attackers could hit him deliberately, but there was always the possibility that someone firing blind or a ricochet could hit him.

Janson scrambled sideways toward the opening in the door. He fired three more times, scored two hits that he was sure of.

Then someone grabbed his ankles and hauled. He was suddenly inside the hangar, looking at metal floor.

He turned to look up. "Thanks, Twelve."

"You're welcome."

He wriggled back up so that he could see through the partially open doorway. The troopers had not yet begun to advance again. He continued firing steadily, scoring hits against several targets; the others began to withdraw toward the comparative safety of the vehicles on the landing pad.

Grinder, looking over his datapad, plugged by standard interface into a communications interlock on the wall, said, "They're in the building. Through the east doors."

Janson asked, "Is the corridor with the freight turbolift the only approach to us?"

"Yes."

"Who's there?"

"Six and Ten."

Janson frowned. Neither Runt nor Tyria was a true marksman. Then again, the approach to the freight corridor, from what he'd seen of Face's tape, was open and the corridor was short. It would become a killing ground if the enemy charged.

Kell and Wedge emerged from the turbolift shaft a full minute under Kell's margin.

To their left was one set of doors out of the corridor. A cargo hauler was parked before them; on either side of it were Runt and Tyria, firing through fresh laser blast holes in the doors.

To their right, the doors into the hangar were locked open; on the far wall, the big door leading outside showed a gap and a little night sky. Janson and Piggy were there, firing at intervals. The door shuddered and moaned as return fire from outside hit it.

Grinder and Jesmin were both plugged into communications interlocks on the wall. "Are you all right?" Jesmin shouted.

"We can hear again," Kell said, "no need to shout. Is everyone accounted for?"

"Yes. But there are troops and TIE fighters on the ground outside."

Wedge and Kell moved into the hangar. Falynn was at the aft end of the cargo skiff; the bubble top was up and she was lounging on the control couch, fiddling with the controls. Kell said, "Three, can you reenable any of these other vehicles? In seconds, I mean, not minutes?"

She said, "Yes. Which ones do you want?"

"Any landspeeder that can be flown off autopilot or remote. Or even off a datacard plug-in."

She pulled her datapad from a pocket and pointed it at a flat-bodied XP-38 Landspeeder, so new its paint still gleamed. She hit a button and the skimmer's console lit up; it rose a meter in the air and hovered, waiting. "Consider it reenabled."

"Brilliant. Twelve, move that over near the door. Program it to move straight out ten meters, turn ninety degrees to starboard, and run as fast as it can."

Piggy nodded. He jumped into the skimmer's passenger seat.

"What's the plan?" asked Wedge.

"Send out the skimmer as a lure. I expect the troopers and TIE fighters to fire on it. That'll draw their aim off the doors for a few seconds. We shoot out in the skiff and we can overrun one of the TIE fighters. That reduces the effective odds against us by nearly half. Then we only have to worry about the other TIE fighter."

Wedge smiled. "If we're fast enough that's not a worry. We're in a cargo skiff, remember?"

"Uh-huh?"

"With a cargo skiff's load lifters?"

Kell laughed.

"Six, Ten, fall back!" Kell waved them toward him.

Everyone but Runt, Tyria, and Piggy were already in the floating skiff. Runt and Tyria abandoned the riddled door they were guarding. When they reached the skiff, the others hauled them over the rails.

"Hit it, Twelve."

The Gamorrean pilot slapped the control against the

wall. The hangar door began to grind farther open, screeching where its now-deformed surface dragged across the adjacent wall. He ran to the floating skimmer, tapped a control on its console, then leaped up on the skiff and was aided over the rail.

The troopers outside began firing on the skimmer before it began moving, before the door was completely open. Two blasts hit it, slagging the windscreen. Then Piggy's timer ran down. The skimmer moved forward onto the ferrocrete landing pad, executed an abrupt right turn, and accelerated.

Almost immediately the Wraiths heard the distinctive sound of TIE fighter lasers joining the barrage of hand-laser fire. Kell called, "There, go!"

Falynn put the skiff into motion, slewing at the last moment to bring the craft into the proper orientation to leave the hangar. The Wraiths knelt, each gripping the rail hard with one hand, keeping a blaster pistol ready with the other.

Outside, fifty meters away, two TIE fighters were on the ground flanking a parked personnel skimmer. Men all over the ground and both starfighters were firing away at the ruins of the landskimmer. Some of the infantry noticed the skiff's appearance, shouted, began firing on the Wraiths.

Falynn sent the skiff in a straight course toward the portside TIE fighter. The Wraiths opened fire at the ground troops, keeping the troops pinned down.

The first TIE pilot apparently did not notice the skiff bearing down on him; the starfighter did not budge.

The skiff's bow hit it just above the forward viewport. The impact rolled the starfighter backward on its solar wing arrays, and Falynn brought the skiff's nose down as much as she could so the hull stayed in contact with the TIE's bulb-shaped cockpit as the skiff passed over. The skiff shuddered from the contact, and a moment later the Wraiths looked back past the stern to see the still-rolling TIE bouncing along behind them.

Falynn banked to starboard, a move that slewed the skiff's keel and nearly threw the port-side Wraiths over the rail. She brought the skiff in line with the second TIE.

This TIE fighter was already in motion, repulsorlifts

kicking it up into the air, wheeling so it could bring its guns to bear on the skiff. Falynn gained altitude and kept the skiff's turn tight, not approaching the TIE fighter head-on, angling to pass it port side to port side.

The TIE fighter fired, a snap-shot that passed the port rail and ignited some treetops forty meters away. Then the two vehicles were abreast, passing less than a meter apart.

Wedge, on the port side, activated the skiff's port cargo loader and swung its armature out. The huge electromagnet hit the TIE fighter's port solar array and snagged it, yanking the starfighter along beside the skiff. The skiff shuddered but did not slow.

Falynn dropped a few meters' altitude and the TIE's solar arrays hit the ferrocrete below, jarring the starfighter so that it looked to the Wraiths as though it were vibrating. Wedge could only imagine what was happening to the pilot within.

Falynn banked again, headed back toward the other TIE fighter. It lay on its back, one of the solar arrays bent so that it half covered the forward viewport. She glanced at Wedge. "It still has repulsorlifts!" he shouted. "Take it!"

She nodded and came up alongside it, keeping to port of the half-wrecked fighter. Kell, on the starboard cargo loader, swung out his armature and grabbed the second TIE as they passed.

Falynn kept her altitude down—dragging the twin fighters so they jerked and vibrated from continued contact with the landing pad—and headed straight for the verge of trees due south. When the skiff's prow was within twenty meters, she shouted, "Go go go," then gained altitude and banked to starboard.

Wedge and Kell cut power to the two cargo lifters. The TIE fighters continued bouncing forward until they hit the screen of trees. Wedge saw the starboard wing pylon shear off his starfighter as it hit a tree; the other rolled to a stop and the twin ion engines in back lit off like one of Kell's demolition charges.

A hundred meters along the verge of forest, Falynn brought the skiff to a stop. None of the troopers near the bunker was still firing; Wedge saw them streaming into the bunker. He shook his head.

Donos came out of the forest at a run and swung up over the rail. "You people are terrible cargo haulers," he said.

Wedge smiled. "Probably why we were demoted to be fighter pilots. Let's meet the *Narra*, people." He waved at Falynn to continue forward.

Behind them, the roof of the bunker swelled like a balloon, chunks of ferrocrete firing up in the air, then collapsed. The rumbling roar of explosions followed them as they raced toward their pickup zone.

17

"I've consulted precedents on this matter," Kell said, "and it appears that the TIE fighters will end up being chalked up as gunnery kills for Commander Antilles and myself, rather than as pilot kills for Falynn. Sorry, Falynn."

The woman from Tatooine smiled. "I still may be the only woman to have dragged two Imperial starfighters around like boat anchors. I want that logged."

"Consider it done."

It was the day after the commando strike and the Wraiths, now parsecs from the Xartun system, were debriefing in *Night Caller*'s conference room. Most of the work was done; they were now cleaning up incidental details.

Kell, as mission commander, had been chairing the meeting, but Wedge leaned forward to assume control. "We've had the facts on what we found. Now I want some speculation based on your respective areas of expertise. What is Zsinj up to?"

"This is just a guess," Grinder said, "but it looks to me like they're setting up a financial empire to support Zsinj's ambitions. We know he controls a large area of space; what we didn't know was that he had such a network of business interests outside his space."

Kell nodded. "I also think he's doing it to support *Iron Fist,* his Super Star Destroyer. Here he makes replacement transparisteel parts. At another place, he refines fuel. Somewhere else, twin ion engines—or maybe complete TIE fighters."

Tyria said, "I think we're agreed that he's almost organizing it as though he were a resistance organization. Cells kept isolated from one another, with ships like *Night Caller* being the only connection."

"It makes me feel a little odd," Wedge said. "In a sense, we're becoming the Empire and warlords like Zsinj are becoming the Alliance. We've become a legitimate government with fixed locations we have to reinforce and protect. They're operating from secret bases, mobile bases; they're using the hit-and-run tactics we perfected. The galaxy has turned upside down since the Emperor died."

Falynn looked surprised. "It sounds as though you miss the old days."

Wedge looked at her and shook his head. "No. These days, we can wear our uniforms with pride to most worlds we're likely to visit. We get cheers, or at least words of appreciation, instead of getting turned in to the Imps. Still, I like to think that I can adapt quickly to new tactics . . . but I know there are plenty of military officers and government representatives in the New Republic who *can't.* That's what worries me."

Face spoke up, his voice quiet, reflective. "Zsinj is doing something else, too. Something motivational. Those probe droids weren't made here and weren't sold to the government on the open market. They're something Zsinj had to have brought. Maybe the TIE fighters, too. I think that in addition to providing protection to the worlds he's dealing with, he's offering goodies to his government contacts. Technology they couldn't get anywhere—or at least couldn't get without leaving records everywhere. He's offering his partners toys their legitimate rivals won't have. That can be a powerful inducement."

"Unresolved detail," Phanan said. "What were those big transparisteel cubes, anyway?"

Obligingly, Grinder keyed his datapad. The room's holoprojector brought up the appropriate sequence, from Jesmin's camera, of the large transparent objects.

"They're cells," said Piggy. These were his first words since seeing the recording the first time.

The others looked at him. Janson asked, "Prison cells?"

"Something like that." Piggy jabbed a finger at the image. "See the long side with the holes cut in it? That's the back side of the cell. This hole is for sewage pipes. This one for clean-water plumbing. This one for air ducts. This one for data cables. The big hole is fitted with an access hatch, though the hatch is almost never used. The other side is unmarred. That's the side that faces the control room where the observers work. The subject never has privacy."

Wedge listened to his explanation with interest. "Where have you seen such an arrangement?"

"I grew up in one."

They all looked at him. Wedge asked, "At Binring Biomedical Product?"

"Yes."

Janson whistled. "Piggy, do you mean these are *like* the one you grew up in, or are they identical?"

"These are the same. Exactly the same."

"So either," Janson said, "this is a standardized piece of equipment, or Zsinj has some connection with Binring Biomed."

"I haven't seen this model before," said Ton Phanan. "Either when I was a practicing doctor or later. They aren't, for example, the same as the cages in which General Derricote kept his test subject for the Krytos Plague. I'd say they weren't a standard design."

Wedge nodded. "We may just have to add Binring's home base to our list of targets. Piggy, where is that?"

"Saffalore."

"That's in the Corporate Sector, isn't it? Currently independent?"

"Yes, sir."

"Very well. Unless we have any further questions, it's time to issue some new orders." There were no inquiries, so Wedge continued. "We had a good, successful run this time. No losses. Information gained. But we can't just hope that each official who has dealt with Darillian gets in touch with us and lets us force or trick him into revealing where Zsinj's new property is, then blow up that site. Zsinj will figure out what we were doing in no time. We want to leave Zsinj with the impression that *Night Caller* is being followed—not that the ship itself is responsible for the attacks.

"So, first, General Cracken has said that he's dispatching Intelligence teams to each world on the list I sent him. Our hope is that they can provide us with information as we get there.

"Second, Grinder, I want you to research the ship's logs. Call up information on every planet *Night Caller* has visited since the Emperor's death and note the dates. Since Captain Darillian didn't make notes of his audiences with these collaborators, if General Cracken's team hasn't been able to do so, you'll try to code-slice into planetary records when we visit those worlds and figure out which properties were switched to new owners during or just after *Night Caller*'s visits. Then we investigate them . . . and if they're Zsinj operations, we take them out. Always a few days after *Night Caller*'s visit, always when the ship is already in another system."

Grinder nodded. "Understood."

"Face, if the planetary governor or anyone reveals to you that he's Zsinj's collaborator, that's just sheer informational profit. Relay the information as fast as possible to Grinder so he can dig out appropriate information. But don't pry for additional information yourself unless Grinder comes up dry; in that case, you can contact Zsinj's stooge later and try to get the data."

Face smiled. "If the miracle Bothan fails, Captain Darillian the Magnificent will save the day."

Wedge gave him a steady stare. "You don't have to get into character now. In fact, we might have to shoot you if you do."

"Alliance audiences are always the toughest audiences."

"Piggy, I'm sorry to ask this, but I want from you a full, detailed report on your stay with Binring Biomed. Personnel, the site where you grew up, impressions, odd things you noticed that didn't mean anything at the time, whatever you can remember."

Piggy took and released a deep breath. "I will do it."

"Everyone else, standing orders apply. Back to work."

Face was standing by as Tyria emerged from the X-wing simulator. "Better this time?"

She smiled. "Better. Always better, bit by bit. But if I were you, I'd give it a few minutes to air out before climbing in. I had quite a workout in there."

"Thanks for the warning. You are a lady and a gentleman."

She activated the hoist to pull her R5 unit, Chunky, from the slot at the rear of the simulator. X-wing simulators could also simulate astromech interactions, but missions were more realistic if the pilots had their own astromechs plugged in.

Once Chunky was settled on the deck, Tyria glanced at Face's R2 unit, Vape. "Hey, he's had a new paint job." Indeed, the red trim had been replaced with a proper Wraith set of gray stripes.

Face snorted. "That's actually just a cover for some modifications I've had made to him."

She gave him a suspicious look. "Modifications. A pop-up screen and a complete set of your holodramas?"

"That's not such a bad idea. Maybe that will be the next mod. No, this is one anyone can appreciate." He looked around to make sure no one else was in the lounge. "Vape: cold one."

A trapezoidal panel on the top of Vape's dome pulled aside, leaving a hole open. Vape made a noise like an airgun firing. A bottle leaped up a meter from the hole. Face snagged it on its way down and twisted the cap off.

He handed it to Tyria. "Elba beer. Chilled. For you. I'll have one myself after my sim run."

She looked at him. "Do you know, you're getting stranger and stranger."

He smiled. "Good."

Things went as Wedge predicted. At least, they did at first.

By the time they reached Belthu, the next world on *Night Caller*'s circuit, Grinder had already found two likely candidates for Zsinj's contact: the chairman of the coalition of mining company presidents who effectively controlled the wealthy colony world, and one of the board members, president of the second-largest corporation.

The New Republic Intelligence team on-planet was too newly arrived to offer much information of value. However, Face's routine communiqués with planetary officials bore fruit.

The chairman of mining company presidents spoke with "Captain Darillian" and helpfully provided a price list for the world's latest stockpile of ores. The other suspect, the company president, privately let the disguised Face know that a shipment of refined durasteel awaited the arrival of Zsinj's next bulk cargo hauler. Wedge transmitted that data to the Intelligence team.

After *Night Caller* jumped out of system, General Cracken's people spent a day tracking down the site where the unrecorded durasteel shipment waited. Rather than sabotaging or stealing it, they simply noted its location. They also delivered Grinder into the corporation headquarters and helped him ferret out details of the transfer, to another false Zsinj identity, of a small, somewhat outdated durasteel foundry. Two days after Grinder rejoined the Wraiths, the Intelligence team blew up the foundry.

The next stop in sequence was not a settled world; in fact, the planetary system had only a number designation, M2398, in the New Republic and Imperial records. Without any ordinary way to smuggle agents into the system, General Cracken had chosen not to send in a team.

Despite the fact the system was supposed to be uninhabited, *Night Caller*'s records clearly showed a stop here, though there was no mention of contact with local authorities.

Night Caller jumped to a position well outside the orbit of the outermost planet and took sensor readings on the M2398 system. Within minutes they had trace communications emissions from a moon of the third world, a gas giant featuring a beautiful dust and asteroid ring. The transmissions were coded, but Jesmin, in the comm center, cracked the encryption in a matter of minutes. She called it in to Wedge, who was pacing the bridge, to the amusement of Captain Hrakness. "Simple mathematical substitution," Jesmin said. "It's probably only good for one battle or so, just long enough to keep their enemies from knowing what they're saying."

"Put it on," Wedge said.

First there was a hiss of static over the comm unit, then a man's voice. "How is it, Guller? Cold?"

A pause, then another man's voice. "Shut up."

Pause. "I mean, I know it's cold. But is it just cold, or is it *really* cold, or is it your-parts-are-numb cold, or is it your-parts-are-falling-off cold?"

Pause. "Shut up."

Pause. "You see anything?"

Pause. "No."

Pause. "But are you not seeing anything because there's nothing to see, or are you not seeing anything because your eyes are frozen?"

Pause. "Shut up."

Wedge asked, "Two, that interval—I assume it's transmission lag?"

"Yes, sir. I calculate that they're about a hundred and fifty thousand klicks apart. I'm pretty sure that 'Is it cold' is broadcasting from the largest moon, and 'Shut up' is in the asteroid belt."

"An outpost of some kind." Wedge considered. "Sound like a pirate nest to you, Captain Hrakness?"

The smaller man leaned back comfortably in the command chair. "Out-of-the-way system, unprofessional and

credit-wasting exchanges between members of the group
. . . Probably so."

"Very well. Jesmin, set up the Captain Darillian simulator and call Face to the comm center. Falynn is to get into
Imperial pilot gear and take TIE Two; I'll be in One. All the
other Wraiths to the X-wings. Tell Tyria to take her own
snubfighter—she's temporarily restored to duty—and Phanan
to take Falynn's. Captain Hrakness, call battle stations. I
want everyone standing by hot as we go in, but looking cool;
we don't want them to know we're ready."

As he began his start-up checklist, Wedge heard the comm
pop. Swearing in a female voice immediately came over the
communications speaker. He took a look at his comm board.
The TIE fighter was still docked, with external communications off-line; this had to be the direct connection to the other
TIE fighter port. "Gray Two, is that you?"

The swearing broke off momentarily. "Yes, sir!" Then it
continued.

"Refrain from personal comments over this channel."

"Yes, sir!" Her voice sounded resentful.

"What's the matter?"

"Nothing with the TIE fighter, sir. I just had a dead body
drop on me out of my closet."

"What?"

"A pressure suit. Sealed and inflated. With a knife taped
to its glove. When I slid open my closet door to get my Imp
flight suit out, it fell on me."

"A prank?"

"What else?"

"Are you all right?"

"I'm fine. But it's not funny. And if I were as clumsy as
some of the old men in this squadron it would have stuck
me."

"I'll do something about this when we get back."

"I don't need any help, *sir*."

"Maybe you don't, but your prankster does. Are you
live?"

"Two engines green, weapons live."

"Drop to a trickle charge and prepare for what may be a long wait."

From his seat in the comm center, Face watched the monitor, saw the hyperspace's lines of light shorten into stars. Directly ahead was the red and orange brilliance of the third world. Face nodded in appreciation; *Night Caller* had dropped out of this second hyperspace jump not far from the world, as close as its gravity well would permit.

Almost immediately the comm board lit up as the unseen parties out there began communicating. "Glit One, Glit One, we have unknowns." Pause. "Got you, Nest. I read one Corellian corvette. Looks like Captain Dandy is back." Pause. "Confirm one dandy, Glit One. Glit Five, are you on-line?" The next pause was much longer, then Glit One's voice came back, resentful: "Shut up."

Face scanned the comm equipment. He knew the basics of handling a comm unit, but didn't have the training to try to seek and amplify what had to have been a third transmission point out there.

Then a new voice, a strong broadcast from the occupied moon: "*Night Crawler,* this is Blood Nest. Respond at once."

Face toggled his comm and the switch governing the instant translation to Darillian's voice. "Bloody Nose, this is *Night Caller*. What do you want?"

"We want to tear your face off and vent what's left into hard vacuum."

Face snorted. Was this piratical posturing, or did these people intend to attack Captain Darillian? "You're welcome to if you can, Bloody Nose. But first, tell me about your wife. I want to know something about the woman I'll be consoling tonight."

There was a long pause. Then the voice returned, more somber than before. "Darillian, I told you not to come back."

"I recall you *requesting* me not to come back. Do you remember us talking about the possibility of mutual profit?" Nervous, Face tugged at his collar. He was guessing now, presuming that Darillian had followed what seemed to be his predictable pattern in dealing with these people. "Have you really decided to close off all my avenues to more wealth, more power?"

"No . . . of course not. Very well, *Nutcracker*. I'm clearing you to land on Berth Two. We'll dine, we'll talk. Follow the signal in."

"Excellent. *Night Caller* out." Face disconnected both the microphone and the Darillian voice simulator.

Immediately the comm unit indicated a single strong signal coming from the moon that must house Blood Nest. "Captain Hrakness, this should be your homing beacon."

"It is, Face. We've got it, thanks."

Night Caller's TIE fighters were mounted outside the corvette's artificial gravity field. Wedge, waiting in his cockpit, didn't care to spend time in zero gravity, but he decided it was marginally better than being shot at.

His right hand twitched. He tightened it into a fist and tried to ignore it. In one of his few protracted zero-gravity experiences, he'd had to keep two components of the external triggering mechanism of a self-destruct device from coming together. He'd done so the simplest way possible: exiting his X-wing into hard vacuum, relying only on his flight suit's magcon field and a life-support tether to keep him alive, and jamming his hand in between the closing components.

In the long minutes he'd waited, he'd been battered by conflicting thoughts. He'd resigned himself to dying, yet hoped rescue would come. His flight suit inadequate to the task of retaining his body heat, he'd begun to freeze, yet he'd waited there, marveling at the beauty of the starfields above the sanctuary moon of Endor.

When rescue, in the form of Luke Skywalker, had come for him, he'd torn himself free of the mechanism and almost lost fingers doing it . . . and now those fingers became a bit twitchy whenever he found himself in zero gee for any length of time. The emotions returned, too. He could even taste the bacta they'd dunked him in to heal him after the ordeal. He tried to will the taste away and concentrate on his surroundings.

Just as at Endor, there was beauty here. The gas giant was an extraordinary pattern of warm colors, a mesmerizing painter's palette.

Eventually the moon of Blood Nest came into view, a large but dismal brown thing. *Night Caller* descended into its thin, unwholesome-looking atmosphere. Wedge felt himself settling into the cockpit restraints as gravity began to pull at the corvette. There were no seas below, only pockmarked brown and red desert; the corvette passed above it, heading toward high mountains in the distance.

As they approached the first set of foothills, Wedge saw a curved portion of ground below and to the side of *Night Caller*'s course curl up and retract.

For a moment it made no sense. Then the picture fit itself together into elements he could recognize.

A crater, concealed from above by some sort of colored or dust-covered fabric. Beneath it, a laser artillery cannon, its barrel elevating straight toward the unshielded keel of *Night Caller*—

Wedge powered up and hit the crude escape-pod ejection switch Cubber had wired to his control board. His TIE fighter dropped. He oriented immediately toward the laser rig. "Bridge, bring up all shields! Gray Two, launch! Follow my lead. Fire at will." He suited action to words, firing as soon as his laser cannons oriented on the artillery unit below.

His first shot creased and blackened the unit's barrel housing. "Wraiths, launch. We're under attack." He fired again, not yet bothering to arrest his plummet, and saw the TIE fighter's green lasers penetrate the cannon housing halfway between the barrel end and the control pod at its base.

The cannon operator fired his compromised weapon. Wedge saw the upper half of its barrel glow red, then yellow, then white from heat as it melted from within.

Gray Two sideslipped into position and fired. Her shot penetrated the phototropically darkened bubble over the control pod. Wedge saw the pod light up from within. Inside was a fuzzy-edged human silhouette that almost instantly lost resolution and was absorbed by light. The pod vented gases.

Captain Hrakness's voice was cool over the comm: "Wraiths, Grays, we have incoming from dead ahead."

The bow hold doors were sliding open as Hrakness transmitted his message. As soon as they were separated enough to allow an X-wing to exit, Kell saw the distant thruster trails of the incoming fighters.

He was lucky enough to be the centermost of the nine X-wings in the hold. That meant he launched first, and he wasted no time with repulsorlifts, punching forward with a burst from his main thrusters. He'd helped build the blast shield behind the X-wing's housing racks; he knew it could take punishment from his engines.

He emerged from the hold into dirty air and checked his sensor panel. "Wraiths, I read two full squads of snubbies unknown types, mixed types, distance two point five klicks and closing."

"*Night Caller* is vectoring." That was Lieutenant Tabanne. She sounded as calm as her captain. "Wraiths, compensate for the maneuver or refrain from launching for a moment."

Kell nodded. *Night Caller* couldn't approach oncoming fighters with her bow hold open. Even with shields up, if a laser blast or proton torpedo penetrated them, there would be no ship's hull to take the shot; X-wings still in the hold could be vaped. So could any of the mechanics on duty there; or the blast could angle up against the ceiling and penetrate the bridge. Hrakness's maneuver was simple self-preservation, and Kell prepared himself to fly alone for a few long moments.

18

Tyria's voice came over the comm: "So, you're making it a challenge?" Kell glanced back to see the corvette in midmaneuver, Wraith Ten firing out of the bow hold. Tyria stood her X-wing up on its port strike foil and angled straight toward Kell.

"Wraith Two away!" Jesmin's snubfighter was next.

That cleared the center column. The other six X-wings in the bow hold, closer to the sides of the hold, would have a slightly more difficult launch; even ignoring the corvette's maneuver, they'd be several more seconds. But now Piggy was following Janson out of the topside hold, arcing around to join the group, and the TIE fighters of Wedge and Falynn were rising toward them.

Kell's R2 unit shrieked at him as the cockpit alarm indicated an enemy laser lock. Without waiting for authorization to break, Kell rolled up on his starboard strike foils and continued the roll, spinning and diving; he could see the other Wraiths break and roll.

Wedge heard Janson's voice: "They're Uglies." Uglies were hodgepodge rigs assembled from components of normal fighters; they were unpredictable to both their pilots and their targets, sometimes characterized by terrible flight performance, sometimes by unusual and effective weapons combinations.

Wedge added, "Wraiths, this is Leader. Fire at will. Forget the standard wing assignments. Form wings as you launch. Three, stay with me." He shook his head. This was bad. The Wraiths were uncoordinated, still half off balance despite the destruction of the ambushing laser cannon.

His sensors showed a trio of bandits headed his way. He desperately wanted to snap off a proton torpedo to shake up their formation, to put extra energy into his forward shields, but the TIE fighter didn't give him either option.

Instead, he gave his yoke a little sideways tug, felt the moon's thin atmosphere yank at his solar wing arrays, and was hurled to starboard. His engines screamed with the change in course. The maneuver was just in time; green lasers cut through the air he had just occupied. Sensors showed Falynn performing a similar sideslip to port.

His Imperial-style targeting screen showed a lock on the closest oncoming enemy. It was visible in the viewport, an unlikely assembly of parts: a classic Headhunter body augmented by TIE fighter solar wing arrays mounted horizontal to its plane of flight on each side. TIE fighter wings were designed to recharge ship's lasers and to provide some armor, and were never particularly aerodynamic; in this rig, they were wobbly, far too awkward to provide lift in flight, and probably provided tremendous drag. The vehicle had to be entirely dependent on repulsorlifts. Wedge fired at the patchwork vehicle, a snap-shot, and watched it shudder its way into a starboard rising turn. This made its profile longer, larger, and his second shot sheared through its midsection, just behind the cockpit. Wedge saw components and perhaps crew falling out of either portion of the bisected, doomed craft.

He reversed his lateral slide, turning portward again, gaining altitude, and spinning into a corkscrew.

Falynn shot out ahead of him, then abruptly climbed into a loop. In a moment she'd be inverted, then diving, firing. It was a canny move, considering her inexperience in the TIE fighter: If she maintained a course without the slightest port or starboard deviation, regardless of how she gained or lost altitude, she wouldn't suffer the buffeting TIE fighters took in atmosphere and could keep her engines at full thrust, full speed.

One of the oncoming Uglies, a ball-shaped TIE fuselage attached to a top-mounted fixed wing and a rear-mounted rudder, took the bait and climbed to follow. Wedge oriented toward him, fighting with his stick, and almost immediately got the jittery glow of a laser lock. He fired into the Ugly's underside, scoring a direct hit on the ionic engines. The Ugly detonated into a brilliant shower of sparks and flaming debris.

At less than a klick, the third Ugly, which looked like a wingless, rudderless Imperial shuttle, fired on Wedge—thin streams of red lasers, a seemingly endless number of them. He juked left, continued that way as the broadening pattern of energy pursued.

He saw the Ugly's side gout—a side-mounted tube firing a concussion missile. There had been no warning from the TIE's sensor-lock alarm and the missile came in straight at him at less than a klick's distance, a blur accelerating so fast there was no chance he could maneuver out of its way.

"Ten, you're my wing. Let's go high road." Kell stood his X-wing on its tail and bled power from his bow shields into his thrusters. He'd have to trust his sensors to warn him of weapons locks for a few long moments.

"Five, acknowledged." Tyria followed his maneuver almost point for point.

"Nine is away. Two, I'm your wing."

"Nine, understood."

Sensors reported twin concussion missile launches from the oncoming squads of Uglies. Kell put on a bit more speed, but Thirteen gave him no indication they were coming after him. Two fighters at the rear of the Ugly formation were showing increasing altitude, however—climbing after him and Tyria.

"Six are away! Bring on your Uglies, your wretched rigs of cast-off parts, your—"

"Six, Twelve. No recitations."

"Yes, Twelve."

Kell frowned. Runt wasn't in his pilot mind; that personality never spoke intelligibly. More changes going on in his usual wingman's mental processes . . .

"Four away. Six, I'm your wing."

Wedge relaxed the pressure on the pilot's yoke. In the split second his twin ion engines lost thrust, he dropped back into the wash of laser fire he'd been avoiding.

Lasers splashed across him. The concussion missile flashed past his viewport, missing him by maybe ten meters. Then he emerged from the other side of the laser pattern . . . unscratched.

He smiled grimly. He'd realized almost too late that there were two ways a fighter that size could fire lasers so continuously. One was to have a highly advanced, experimental power generator worth a squad of A-wings. The other was to fire targeting lasers, beams bright enough to see but not to do damage . . . bright enough to spook a fighter into fleeing before them in a predictable path, right into the line of a fixed missile tube.

Falynn's TIE fighter roared down from above, linked lasers firing. Her shot hit the shuttle fuselage, crisping a black circle at the aft end. Wedge expected the shot to destroy the shuttle's engines, sending it into a helpless dive, but the Ugly merely lost altitude, trailing smoke. Its movement suggested that it had been flying all along on high-altitude repulsors.

Falynn dove past, firing once more, hulling the craft at nearly the same point. She leveled off below it, inverted, and climbed toward its belly.

"TIE fighter, break off. We surrender!"

She must have heard; she broke off her firing run, climbing in a dizzying spin until she was on station above and aft of the craft. Wedge grinned, imagining the volatile Tatooine woman cursing at having to give up a kill. Her voice, over the comm, was a furious sputter: "You Kowakian-ugly flying wreck, get to ground right now or I'll vape you, surrender or not."

"TIE fighter, we acknowledge. Don't shoot." The bizarre shuttle heeled over and began a faster descent.

At the top of his arc, Kell inverted and dove.

The two Uglies that had been climbing to engage abruptly broke off and fled at ninety degrees to his flight path. He rolled down onto his port wing and pursued.

"Five, Ten. I don't think they're running. This is strategic."

Kell eased back on his stick. "What makes you think so?"

"I don't know."

Strategic. What would this strategic retreat bring the enemy?

He eyeballed their flight angle, calculated that it would take them beyond the engagement zone, over a series of craters, over one large crater in particular—

"Pig Trough," he said.

"Five, what?"

"Ten, tighten up. Stay on me." He dove to the lunar surface and headed through the broadening engagement zone, angling to reach the far side of the battle and beyond.

Jesmin kept up her streaming fire against the nearly stock Headhunter in her brackets. Finally the atmospheric fighter's durasteel armor gave way under her lasers. The deadly red beams penetrated into the fighter's aft end. A moment later the Headhunter bent, arching its back like a wounded animal, as the engines detonated, venting through the craft's belly, tearing the fuselage in half.

"Good shooting, Two."

"Thanks, Nine. That's five!"

"Five here."

"No, Kell. I mean, that's five kills. I'm an ace!"

"Two, wait for the debriefing. In this unit, your wingman may get credit for your kills. But congratulations."

"Very funny, Five." Jesmin vectored toward a pair of oncoming Uglies at the far side of the formation. Abruptly they veered away at right angles to her flight path.

She rolled up perpendicular to the ground and followed. Nine stayed on her wing.

Janson smoked a double-hulled monstrosity that had been firing eight-way-linked laser cannons—firing them inaccurately, fortunately for Janson—and took a look around.

At the very center of the engagement, two X-wings were in trouble, juking and weaving their way through the heaviest fire, diving out of the path of one set of Uglies only to find themselves immediately in the path of another. Janson's sensors identified the Wraiths. "Seven, Eight, how are you doing?"

Face's voice: "Not good, Eleven."

"Seven, what are you doing here?"

"My job in the comm center was done. Do you mind? I can go back if you like—"

"Never mind. Hold tight. I'm coming in to help."

But help was even faster than that. The entire sky seemed to light up and one of the Uglies—a huge ball that seemed to be made up entirely of TIE fighter solar wings—evaporated, leaving behind only a glowing afterimage and tons of falling liquefied metal.

Janson leaned away from the painful brightness. "What the—" Then he caught sight of the vehicle that had scored the kill. "Good shooting, *Night Caller*."

Lieutenant Tabanne's voice came back, "Can't let you toy drivers score all the kills, Twelve. Hold tight." The oncoming *Night Caller* fired again, her laser cannons converging on a wingless TIE ball that had been firing concussion missiles indiscriminately. The spherical craft emerged from the beam intact, or so Janson thought at first; then it rotated and he saw that one half had been burned entirely away.

Half a pilot drifted out of the cockpit and joined it in its plummet to the lunar surface.

Kell heard two more Ugly pilots surrender. His snubfighter roared over the moon's surface, mere scores of meters above the irregular ground, occasionally dropping closer as he and Tyria headed over deep impact craters.

They skipped over the ridge that was a common border between two such craters and saw them—treaded vehicles peering just over the far rim. Even as large as this crater was, they were already in weapons range, only a couple of seconds away.

"Switching to torps," he said. "Firing."

"Firing," Tyria repeated.

Their proton torpedoes flashed almost instantly across the distance separating firer from target.

Almost instantly. The treaded vehicles also fired, lasers and concussion missiles, aiming at distant targets. Then the torpedoes caught up to them. Kell's hit the big one on the left, the too-tall construction body atop a military crawler's treads, while Tyria's hit the smaller laser-cannon-armed crawler in the middle. All three vehicles were caught up in the dual blast. They dropped out of the bottom of the resulting ball of smoke and fire, tumbling down the crater's slope, throwing off treads, doors, shreds of weapon components, chunks of armor, all charred and warped almost beyond recognition.

The comm crackled with Jesmin's pained voice. "I'm hit."

Kell and Tyria cleared the crater a moment later and vectored in behind Jesmin and Donos.

The Mon Calamari pilot and her temporary wingman were still together, but both were hit, trailing smoke, and drifting apart.

Jesmin seemed to be the one damaged worst. Kell guessed that the blast had been one of a pulse barrage; nothing else was likely to have been able to knock down her shields and penetrate before the shields came back up. A laser blast had hit her on the port side of her cockpit; from the angle and the deepening black score along the cockpit's flank, Kell gauged that the blast had done the majority of its damage just behind and below the pilot's chair. Jesmin also could have caught some of the wash of damage.

Her X-wing was also standing on its starboard strike foils and was in an arc heading toward one of the nearest hills. "Jesmin, straighten up. Two, can you hear me?"

"Hear . . . you . . . Five . . ." If anything, her voice sounded worse than before.

"Level off, Two. Right now."

"Can't . . . reach . . . stick . . ."

She was too badly hurt to reach the pilot's yoke? That was bad, but—then he realized the truth. Her words, and the way she was struggling to say them, added up to one thing: her inertial compensator was shot. The device that made pilots immune to the centrifugal effect of fighter maneuvers was no longer working, and she was being crushed back into her seat by the high-speed arc she was performing.

She was seconds from hitting the hillside. He said, "Thirteen, instruct her R2 to cut her fighter's thrust by half."

Thirteen's answer came up immediately: HE CAN'T. HIS LINKS TO COCKPIT CONTROLS ARE GONE. HE SAYS GOOD-BYE.

"No! Jesmin, punch out!"

There was no answer.

There was other comm traffic going on. Kell ignored it. He was aware only of Jesmin's dying X-wing meters in front of his own. Of the rapidly growing hillside beyond that.

He closed his strike foils into cruise position and goosed his thrusters until he was just to the side of and beneath Jesmin's X-wing.

Janson's voice: "What are you doing, Five?"

Wedge's: "Let him go, Eleven. I see what he's up to."

With his port wing a meter beneath Jesmin's starboard wing, Kell rolled gently to starboard. His wing contacted hers with a scrape, putting a shudder through his snubfighter, checking and reversing her roll. He drifted to starboard and continued his roll until he nearly completed a three-sixty.

Now he stared at the bottom of Jesmin's fighter, at the damage to her side and at cables trailing out of it. Because the impact of wing against wing had rolled her, her fighter had gone through nearly ninety degrees of a rotation to port. For the moment, her X-wing was angling away from the hillside, but the roll was continuing. As delicately as he could, Kell rose toward the underside of her fighter.

The hillside flashed below him and was gone. Jesmin's roll brought her port wing down on top of Kell's. The stick under his hands shuddered. Behind him, Thirteen shrieked and Kell felt the bump of the R2 unit's impact with the underside of Jesmin's fighter.

As Jesmin's rotation forced his port strike foils downward, Kell's flight stick jerked and his fighter tried to roll to port. He fought it, trying to keep his fighter in line through sheer strength. If he could just bring Jesmin's nose up, he might angle her out of the atmosphere, enable the *Narra* to catch up to her—

He heard a crackle, felt his body tingle. Thirteen made another noise of dismay.

His text display lit up with diagnostics reports:

ETHERIC RUDDER NONFUNCTIONAL.

PORT FUSIAL THRUST ENGINES NONFUNCTIONAL.

STRIKE FOIL CONFIGURATION HYDRAULICS NONFUNCTIONAL.

REPAIRS COMMENCING.

Kell's port-side engines whined and shut down. Jesmin's X-wing, now headed in a long arc toward the ground, leaped out ahead of him.

"No! Five to Two, come in."

Nothing.

"Thirteen, can you query her pilot chair's electronics?"

THEY REPORT LEVELS CONSISTENT WITH UNCONSCIOUSNESS IN MON CALAMARI.

"*Night Caller,* can you snag her with your tractor?"

"She's out of our line of sight, Five. I'm sorry."

Jesmin had only ten or fifteen seconds to live unless he managed something. "Ten, where are you?"

"Five, this is Leader. Ten is with Nine. She can't help you."

"But I've got—I've got—"

"I'm sorry, Five."

Jesmin's fighter hit the lunar surface. It didn't detonate; it shredded instantly into tons of shrapnel, rolling across the rocks and pockmarks of the moon below, coming to a rest in a swath of litter half a kilometer in length.

Kell wiped tears away from his cheeks. Then the real pain of his failure hit him.

"Nine, answer me." Tyria tried to keep her voice calm and level. Flying above and behind Donos, she could see that damage to his X-wing was minimal—unless she counted the charred crater that was what was left of his R2's docking station. If there were any fragments of Donos's astromech, Shiner, remaining, they would have to be dug out of a deep layer of slag and carbon scoring.

The dialogue between Kell, Jesmin, and Wedge was becoming more desperate. She tried to ignore it, to keep it in the background of her mind. "Myn! Answer me!"

There was a little burst of static that may have been a word.

Tyria pressed her helmet closer to the side of her head, hoping it would help her hear. "What did you say? 'Gone'?"

It came again, Donos's voice, still faint but understandable: "Gone."

She glanced at her sensors. Jesmin wasn't gone yet, but it didn't look as though there was much hope for her. Tyria started to correct Donos—then the import of what he was saying hit her.

She dialed her comm system down to minimum transmission power and hoped that her signal wouldn't carry back to the other Wraiths. "Myn, do you mean Shiner?"

"He's gone."

"Myn, damn you, he's only a droid! Jesmin Ackbar may die and all you're worried about is a hunk of metal!"

There was no answer.

She accelerated and dropped down in front of Donos. "Wraith Nine, this is Wraith Ten. You're my wing. Do exactly as I do."

Again, no answer. She sideslipped a little to starboard but Donos didn't follow. Exasperated, she moved back in front of him.

Then she saw it, just as, minutes ago, she'd imagined the two flying Uglies leading Kell off to his death. "Talon Leader, this is Talon Two. Do you read?"

There was a delay, then Donos's voice came back strong and calm. "Two, this is Leader."

"Leader, you're damaged. Injured. I'm going to lead you back to base. You're my wing. Do you copy?"

"I copy, Two, and thanks."

She slowly rolled up onto her starboard wing and came around in a gradual arc back toward *Night Caller*. Behind her, Donos skillfully duplicated her maneuver.

She wanted to feel relieved, but trying to imagine what must be going on in Donos's mind made her shudder.

Then the dot designating Wraith Two winked out on the sensor board.

Wedge and Janson finished the tour of the bandit base in silence.

The base was an elderly, damaged Kuat Super Transport VI container ship. With its engines in the shape they were, Wedge doubted the vessel would ever lift, even from the half-standard gravity of this moon. The engines were just barely functional enough to provide power for artificial gravity, life support, and communications. A smaller hauler, an aging Corellian bulk freighter, apparently served to haul half squads of Uglies through hyperspace to whichever areas they chose to patrol. They had enough firepower to intimidate de-cent-sized cargo vessels, and their supplies of stores suggested the pirates had been doing quite well.

In the base's filthy mess hall, the surviving pilots, eleven of them, plus about twenty support crewmen waited under guard. Falynn and Grinder, grim-faced, kept them under the cover of blaster rifles; the two Wraiths stood behind upended tables that would give them some quick cover if one of the pirates produced a holdout weapon the searchers had missed.

Wedge stood before the pirate captain, a beefy, black-bearded man who had admitted to the name of Arratan. "Stand," Wedge said.

Uneasy, the man stood. "We have a right to be here. We have a right to attack intruders."

"What right?"

"We're colonists. This is an unclaimed system. There's no law here."

Wedge sighed, suddenly made even more weary by the lie. "Very well. You're free to go."

The pirate chief blinked. "What?"

"You're free to go."

The bearded man looked among his men and nodded. They slowly stood.

"Of course," Wedge said, "there's no law here. So my pilots are free to shoot you if they want to."

The pirates sat again, all but Arratan.

"Furthermore, since there's no law here, my crew and I are going to help ourselves to whatever supplies we need. Then we're going to take off and blow a hole in your beloved Blood Nest, venting the atmosphere. Then we'll inform the New Republic military that there's a nice hard-vacuum warehouse here full of other stolen goods and a lot of depressurized bodies."

Arratan's face twitched. "You can't do that."

"Of course we can. There's no law here. This is unclaimed territory. Would you or any of your men like passage to some other system before we blow this base to pieces?"

"Maybe."

"Then *maybe* you should spend some time thinking about what you have to offer us for passage. Not goods; we'll take what we want anyway. Information." Wedge leaned close to the pirate. "Be advised. You filth killed one of my pilots to protect your right to have no laws. So I'm going to be very hard to please."

Rattled, the pirate chief leaned back from Wedge. The backs of his legs encountered the table bench behind him and he sat clumsily.

Wedge spun on his heel and left the mess, Janson following.

19

On the way back to the wobbly, unreliable-looking extruder tube where *Night Caller* was docked, Wedge said, "New orders."

Janson pulled out his datapad.

"Test all the fuel they have in reserve. Whatever's up to the standards of our snubfighters, transfer to the corvette. But I want Kell to look at everything first in case it's wired to blow."

"Kell's in sick bay."

"Was he hurt?" Wedge was aware that trailing power cables from Jesmin's X-wing had shorted out some of the systems of Kell's snubfighter. Perhaps he'd taken too much electricity himself.

"Violent nausea."

Wedge gave him a surprised look. "What does our doctor say about that?"

"He says Kell is a real mess and shouldn't be given a job frying tubers for the Alliance, much less flying X-wings."

"That sounds like Phanan. Was that on the record?"

"No. He's hoping Kell will surprise him. By coming out of it."

"Me, too. I'll talk to Kell. Any other injuries?"

"Myn Donos. A concussion from the explosion that did all the damage to Jesmin's snubfighter. Or so Phanan says. I wasn't able to talk to Myn; Phanan had already sent him to his quarters for rest."

"Fine. Oh, and transfer Phanan's R2 unit—Gadget?"

"Gadget."

"—to Myn."

They entered the airlock providing access to the extruder tube. Wedge closed the inner airlock door and opened the outer, then stared dubiously at the shifting length of stained man-height tubing. Somewhere beyond its curve was one of *Night Caller*'s airlocks. "I'd almost rather suit up against the atmosphere."

"Oh, come on, Wedge. If it's good enough for those upstanding citizens, it's good enough for us."

Wedge managed a faint smile. "Then you go first."

"Ton, a few minutes privacy?"

Wedge stood just inside the door to sick bay. Phanan gave him a stiff nod and left without a word.

On one of the bay's beds lay Kell Tainer, somber, pale. He gulped, obviously aware he was in for a dressing-down.

"I don't know how you do it," Wedge said. "You do such good work. Then you screw everything up."

Kell nodded. "It's my fault Jesmin is dead. I know that."

"Not that, you *idiot*. It's that tank driver's fault she's dead. It's the fault of a failed inertial compensator. It's her body's fault for failing her, letting her fall unconscious, when she could have used those extra seconds you gave her to reach her ejection control. The maneuver you pulled, trying to rescue her, was crazy and brilliant. Most pilots in Starfighter Command would've cracked up performing it."

Kell drew back from the anger in Wedge's voice. He looked confused. "Then what—the screwup—"

"It's this." Wedge waved at him, at the sick bay. "You think you've failed. You go to pieces. Every one of us lost a friend today, and who's in sick bay? You. Myn Donos has a concussion and he's just sleeping it off. You need a doctor's care."

Kell started to say something, then clamped down on it.

"Now, get up, get back into uniform. I want you to search the pirate base for explosives. I don't want any of us losing hands—or our lives—when we're exploring. We need you."

Kell started to rise, then pain crossed his face. To Wedge, it looked like a massive cramp.

"That's part of it, too, isn't it?" Wedge kept most of the scorn out of his voice—leaving in just enough for Kell to detect. "Someone needs you and you go to pieces. Well, we do need you. We're relying on you. Our lives depend on you. Right now. What's it going to be?"

Kell stood up. His face was a curious mixture of fury and pain. That pain doubled him over, but he straightened up almost instantly. "Permission to speak freely, sir?"

"Go ahead."

"Every time you make one of these motivational speeches I want to beat you to death."

"And how do you suppose I feel about *you* whenever some responsibility sends you into vaporlock?" Wedge turned and left.

In the corridor, he realized what his next task had to be. He resisted the urge to turn back. He'd rather argue with Kell for hours than perform his next duty. He'd almost rather let Kell beat him to death than perform it.

He could put it off for a while. He had to dictate the report of the assault on this pirate base. He had to put in a recommendation that the New Republic seize this site, just in case it became useful in the war against the warlords and the Empire. He even had to put in a recommendation for a citation for Kell Tainer—even if the man folded up in a pinch, his efforts today were above and beyond the call of duty.

But then, ultimately, he had to write Admiral Ackbar to tell him that his niece was dead.

Wedge sat under a single light in the captain's quarters that had once been lavish but were now echoingly empty.

He began writing on his datapad's touch pad. A terminal keyboard would have been faster, but he knew it was not the interface that would slow him tonight. Slower still would be finding the right words.

He wrote, *Sir, I'm afraid this letter comes to you as a bearer of bad news.*

He looked at his words. *A bearer of bad news.* A trite phrase, and it wasn't correct. The letter wasn't the bearer. Whoever brought Ackbar the letter would be the bearer. Perhaps it would just be a wall terminal.

He hit the clear button and the words winked out.

Sir, I wish I could find some way to soften the news—

No. With a preface like that, Ackbar, if his emotional patterns were like those of humans, would merely feel a mounting fear of dread . . . just before realizing his dread was justified.

He hit the clear button.

Sir, I regret to inform you that your niece, Jesmin Ackbar, is dead.

Ackbar knew that Jesmin was his niece.

He hit the clear button.

Sir, I regret . . .

Even that was formal, impersonal. He and Ackbar were not friends; they were fellow officers. But he had great respect for the Mon Calamari naval officer and felt that Ackbar had similar respect for him.

He felt for Ackbar and his loss. He'd known that loss himself, the day a pirate's escape had destroyed the refueling station where his family worked and lived. He'd lost his home, his family, his past. All that was left to him was his future, one that had then seemed threatening instead of inviting.

But that was just the opposite of what Ackbar would experience, wasn't it? Jesmin was not his past. If anything, she was a piece of his future. Was that not even worse? Suffering the pain of the loss of a loved one . . . and of the future she represented?

He took a sip from his drink and tried to settle his thoughts. He'd had to perform this task so many times. He should be good at it by now. But he felt just a little touch of pride that he wasn't, that it never came easy to him. That he could never be glib about it.

He hit the clear button.

He wrote, *Sir, it is my sad duty to report to you the death of Jesmin Ackbar.*

Kell had peeled halfway out of his coveralls when the door to his quarters slid open. Tyria stepped in and hit the door-close button.

He looked at her. She didn't speak; her expression was tight, worried.

Finally he said, "Isn't one of us supposed to make a joke?"

"Some other day, maybe. What have you been up to?"

"Making sure Blood Nest wasn't rigged to blow. Which it was. And trying not to throw up. Fortunately, I succeeded at defusing and failed to keep my stomach under control, rather than the other way around." He turned his back to her, shoved his coveralls down to his ankles, and stepped out of them on the way to his little closet. He felt light-headed; working for hours on a stomach that was empty and violently protested any attempt to fill it made him that way. "How's Myn?"

"I don't know. Ton Phanan doesn't know. Myn just lies there, staring off into nowhere. He'll eat if you put food in his hand, drink if you put the cup to his lips. But he's gone somewhere."

Kell selected a clean jumpsuit in TIE fighter pilot black and began to put it on. "How long do you think you can keep it under cover?"

"I don't know, Kell. Long enough to shake him out of it, I hope. Ton says that if this, this collapse goes on his record, that's probably it for his career as a pilot."

"Maybe it should be. Maybe he's too close to dissolving to fly again."

"That's not for you to say."

He finished pulling the jumpsuit up and zipped it up. "I know. That's why I'm going along with this, this scheme. In spite of the fact that it might kill *all* our careers." He shrugged. "It's the least I can do. I failed to save Jesmin. Maybe I can help with Myn."

"Don't say that. I heard what you tried with Jesmin. That was . . . tremendous."

"It would have been tremendous if it had worked. Since it failed, it was just futile. Can I ask you something?"

"Sure."

"You knew those two Ugly pilots were lures. You probably saved my life by making me take the time to think about it. Was that something you'd run into before?"

She shook her head. Her ponytail swayed slowly. "I just . . . felt it. I almost saw you being vaped."

"Could that have been the Force at work?"

"I don't think so. I wasn't concentrating on using the Force."

"What's it like when you do concentrate?"

She gave him a bitter little smile. "It's like putting my toe into a nice warm river back on Toprawa, and starting to slide in, and then looking over my shoulder and seeing that my ancestors for twenty generations back have all lined up behind me with stern expressions to make sure I'm doing it right, and I suddenly realize that I can't swim well enough to make them proud of me. If I go into the water I'll drown. That's what the Force is like to me."

"No wonder you want so badly to learn to use it."

She looked at him as if trying to figure out whether to be offended.

"All right. It was a limp joke. But it was a joke. It fulfills my obligation."

"Good night, Kell."

"Good night."

Wedge reviewed the words on the datapad.

Sir:
     It is my sad duty to report to you the death of Jesmin Ackbar.

On the largest moon of the third world of System M2398, Wraith Squadron encountered and defeated a numerically superior foe, a pirate nest that had been in communication with Warlord Zsinj. Jesmin shot down three opponents in that engagement and earned her status as an ace of the New Republic, an event that pleased her. Shortly afterward, a laser cannon attack from ground units damaged her X-wing and sent her into an uncontrollable descent into the lunar surface. As far as we have been able to determine, she was, at the time of impact, unconscious from uncompensated acceleration and did not suffer.

In the time Jesmin served with Wraith Squadron, I found her to be an excellent flyer and a superior officer. Her skills with communications equipment saved Folor Base from a disastrous assault; every person stationed at that base at the time of its evacuation owes her his life. Even in the elite units of the New Republic's armed forces, there are too few pilots who share the courage and dependability she exhibited as a matter of routine.

I cannot begin to appreciate your loss, but in reflecting on her death, I have come to a conclusion that is important to me. I no longer believe that the momentum of a life headed in a worthwhile direction ends when that life does.

Jesmin Ackbar shot down five enemies, all of whom served evil men. Had she not done so, their actions would have led to further evil, but her actions take their place instead, broadening like a firebreak into the future theirs would have occupied.

Jesmin Ackbar saved hundred of lives at Folor. Had she not done so, a bow wave of suffering would have rippled out from Folor, scarring survivors, leaving behind nothing but loss.

In the future, staring at each new class of graduating pilots, relaxing in the company of friends on some world that has been on the verge of commitment to the Empire but has become an ally of the New Republic, I will never know how much good surrounding me is a legacy of

Jesmin's life. Her future will be invisible to me. But invisible is not the same as nonexistent. I will know that her deeds and accomplishments still move among us, phantoms that represent everything good the New Republic stands for, and I am grateful·for it.

    With respect,

    Cmdr. Wedge Antilles

That, at last, was what he meant to say.

The corner of the datapad showed the time. It was an hour before he was due to rise. He'd lost the whole night trying to express his regrets to Admiral Ackbar. But he never would have been able to sleep until he was done; the short hour he had would, at least, be a peaceful one.

He switched off the light and stretched out on the captain's bed, finally able to surrender himself to temporary oblivion.

Two days later, a New Republic cruiser came to deal with the fate of the Blood Nest pirates.

They'd been talkative during those days, offering all they knew of Captain Darillian, Warlord Zsinj, and their own piratical raids. But ultimately, they were nothing but a bunch of freebooters, conscienceless men who were too stubbornly independent to join Zsinj's operation and too stupid to find a tactic other than attacking Zsinj's emissary.

Still, the fact that Zsinj was interested in dealing with men of this caliber was interesting. It suggested that his standards were lower than the New Republic had realized. What role would they have played in his organization: disposable shock troops? Wedge didn't know.

"We jump out of system this morning," he told Janson.

"We're resuming *Night Caller*'s original schedule?"

Wedge nodded. "What's our squadron status?"

"About like it was yesterday. We're down two X-wings, two pilots—though in Myn's case it's a temporary thing. With the TIE fighters, we have a full squadron's worth of fighters."

"Find out if any of *Night Caller*'s crew has any aptitude for TIE fighters. Lure them to the simulator with brandy or sweets if you have to."

Janson grinned. "Fuel and food supplies at full. We're doing pretty well."

"Very well. I'll issue the orders within the hour."

They stood on *Night Caller*'s bridge, all the surviving Wraiths but Donos and Wedge. In his X-wing, Wedge hovered fifty meters off the bow, oriented, as *Night Caller* was, toward the sun of this forsaken system.

Face concluded, "Lacking even her mortal remains to say farewell to, in the manner of her people or ours, let us make this show of respect. Let us send out a physical beacon to mark her passing in the hope that there will be a spiritual one to guide her to her destination."

Kell decided that Face made a pretty good speaker for the dead. He wished he knew how much of this speech, of the emotion Face projected, was genuine, from Face's heart . . . how much was merely the artifice of an actor. But he didn't need to know right now.

Wedge, acting not as Wraith Leader but as Jesmin's wing-man one last time, fired. His proton torpedo shot toward the distant sun and detonated a few moments later, ten kilometers away, creating for a brief moment a brilliant beacon in the sky. But like the mortal life it symbolized, the proton burst quickly faded from sight.

Wedge's X-wing slowly maneuvered downward, toward the open bow hatch and out of sight. The mourners, all but the bridge crew, began to leave.

"Tainer."

Kell stiffened. "Yes, Lieutenant Janson."

"*Night Caller* did take a couple of shots during the battle. No significant damage, but it appears to have knocked some couplings and fittings loose around the ship. I'd appreciate it if you would join the mechanics in fixing them."

Kell saluted the man who'd killed his father and watched him leave.

It was punishment detail. He was sure of it. He'd fouled up the rescue of Jesmin Ackbar and would be receiving point-less tasks like this for the duration of his stay with Wraith Squadron.

In the hallway leading to the officers' quarters, he caught up with Tyria. "Any change?"

She shook her head. "He's still the same. Another day or two and we're going to have to convince them that he's re-turned to duty. We might be able to take some of his work shifts and just sign his name to them . . ."

"It gets more and more dangerous."

She shrugged, obviously aware of the truth of his state-ment. "Should we only risk ourselves for the safety of civil-ians?"

"No." He sighed. "I can't help you with him today. I have tug-and-plug duty. Maybe it won't take too long."

"Good luck." She rose on tiptoes and absently gave his cheek a quick kiss, then headed off toward Donos's quarters.

Kell rubbed his cheek. Now, what did that mean? Just when he was at his most wretched, she showed some faint sign of affection . . .

Ah. He understood. That conversation with the others about wounded males and females who tried to nurse them back to health. He'd finally reached such a low point that she cared about him.

Well, to hell with that. He might have thought differently a few months ago, but now, given the option of feeling as he did and winning her affection, or finding some worth in him-self and no longer being miserable enough to attract her, he'd have to go for the second choice.

He headed off to find his tool kit.

"Shall we trade?" asked Warlord Zsinj.

Admiral Trigit expansively gestured. "You go first. You *are* the warlord."

"True. You remember *Night Caller.*"

Trigit snorted. "One of your TIE fighter corvettes. Thank you for forwarding their reports to me. I'm grateful to *Night*

Caller, my lord. It's good to know there is a ship undergoing an even less eventful mission than my own."

Zsinj twisted his face into something like an indulgent smile. "What if I told you that *Night Caller*'s last several stops have all been visited—or, to be more accurate, smashed—by Rebel forces? Sometimes commandos, sometimes X-wing squadrons?"

Trigit took a half step back. "The ship is being shadowed."

"Correct. I would appreciate it if you would take care of the matter."

"At once. Well . . . perhaps not. The matter I called you about may be of more importance."

"Go on."

"You've heard of Talasea, in the Morobe system?"

Zsinj frowned. "Some sort of agricultural colony world, wasn't it? An economic failure?"

"That's correct. It was abandoned. Not long ago, it was temporarily used as a secret base by Rogue Squadron."

"Ah, that's it. One of Ysanne Isard's other pets assaulted them there. And failed to exterminate them, obviously."

Trigit kept his smile frozen to his face, but the comment about Iceheart's pets rankled him. Zsinj obviously considered him one of those pets. "Yes, yes. Well, the Morrt Project is recording an unusual number of hits from Morobe. The visual data we're receiving suggests a wide variety of ships. X-wings, A-wings. Rebel transports. One of them was the *Borleias,* the last transport to lift from Folor Base."

Zsinj took a deep breath. "Anxious to avenge yourself on the Folor survivors, Apwar?"

"I'm not too proud to admit it."

"Then, by all means, deal with it. I'll send you, oh, *Provocateur* as support. *Night Caller* and *Constrictor* likewise. That should be a sufficiently lethal fleet for a new base, even if elements of the Rebel fleet are lingering there."

"Thank you."

"Then you can run off and deal with these forces shadowing *Night Caller.* I think I can trust you to eliminate an X-wing squadron and a commando unit by yourself."

"Your faith in me makes my heart drip with goodwill."

Zsinj gave him an irritatingly superior smile and waved farewell. His holoimage faded.

Trigit gritted his teeth. Owing to Trigit's failure at Folor, Zsinj had been able to fling out far more barbs in their recent conversations than Trigit could defend himself against. That had to end soon. Perhaps at Morobe Trigit would do well enough to quiet the warlord.

He could only hope.

In a service conduit above the corridor accessing the officers' quarters, Kell Tainer hung upside down.

It wasn't a pose he preferred. But the relay box he was servicing was in the vertical conduit halfway between the corridor and the horizontal service shaft above. At this late hour, he could go wake up Cubber or one of the other mechanics and find out where they'd stowed the ladders, or he could hook his legs over the lip where the two shafts met, hang upside down for a couple of minutes, and fix a conductor relay that had been shaken loose by battle damage.

So he played a game with himself, seeing if he could get the relay reseated before the blood rushing to his head made him dizzy.

He had the cover off the relay box and was wrestling with the relay itself when he heard them, footsteps and voices beneath him. He heard the name "Donos" and went very still.

The first voice was Wedge's. "The first time we have to scramble for action, the secret's out."

The second was Janson's. "Is there anything we can do? We could arrange things so that only a half squadron of Wraiths was standing by at the next target zone. We could arrange it so that Donos was part of the off-duty pilot group—"

"And risk the lives of the others if it's another ambush like the last one? No, Wes. But keep thinking about it. If you can find anything I can reasonably do—reasonably—I want to hear about it."

"Yessir."

Footsteps moved away. Kell looked down. By arching his back, he could see just the back of Janson's head. The lieutenant didn't move; he had his head down. He had to be thinking the situation over.

Thinking about Donos. Kell suppressed a whistle. Wedge and Janson both knew about Donos—knew, at least, that he had been incapacitated. They knew the Wraiths were covering it up. But none of the Wraiths had realized that those two were doing the same, giving them time. Time to give Donos a chance to pull out of it.

The thought hit Kell like an electrical jolt. *But that meant—*

He grabbed the far edge of the perpendicular shaft, levered his legs free, and dropped to the corridor below.

Janson spun at the sound of something hitting the metal floor behind him.

It was a big man in a crouch—Janson threw himself backward, slamming into the bulkhead wall, and grabbed at his blaster. But his hand came up empty; the weapon wasn't on his belt.

Then the big man straightened and Janson recognized him. "Sithspit! Tainer, you almost gave me a heart attack! Where did you come from?"

"I'm a Wraith, aren't I? We strike from nowhere." Kell's face wore a weird expression, a combination of intensity and bafflement that made the flesh crawl on Janson's neck.

"What do you want?"

"Why didn't you turn him in?"

"Who?"

"Myn Donos."

"For what?"

"Don't. Just don't. I know you know."

Janson let his face settle into determined lines. "Then you know why."

"You're giving him a chance."

"That's right."

"I'll be damned. I didn't think you'd do that. For any-one."

"What do you mean?" Janson didn't bother to hide his confusion.

"I thought, I always thought, with you it was one real mistake, and boom."

"Boom." Realization hit Janson like the bow wave of a proton explosion. "No, Tainer. Not with Myn. Not with your father. Not with anyone."

"I never would have believed that before just a moment ago."

"But you do believe it now?"

Kell looked away from Janson for several long moments, finally meeting the lieutenant's eyes again. "Janson, you're always going to be the man who killed my father. I don't think I'll ever be able to look at you without that coming to mind. But maybe, the other stuff—everything I thought went with it, Janson the Killer, Janson the Lurker—maybe that was just a kid's fears."

Kell crouched. Janson stepped to the side, bracing him-self for the leap of attack, but Kell jumped straight up, scrambling into an overhead shaft.

Janson watched the pilot's booted feet disappear. Kell's face did not reappear overhead. Janson turned away and headed back toward his own quarters, rattled.

20

Twelve X-wing snubfighters roared down into the atmosphere.

This was a dark world with a polluted sky, its atmosphere formed from gases and smoke hurled from hundreds of active volcanoes. Four kilometers ahead, the TIE Interceptor, fastest fighter of the Imperial forces, was distantly visible; it stayed well ahead of the X-wings, though the sparks and gouts of smoke issuing from its engines, unseen but reported by sensors, suggested it could soon lose speed.

Myn Donos, the X-wing squadron commander, looked around in confusion. This wasn't right. He'd been through this already. This mission could lead only to . . .

Death.

No. He was imagining things. He had a job to do. But what was next?

Tentatively he said, "Leader to—"

Damn. What was his comm specialist's name? What, in fact, was his call number?

Oh, that's right. "Eight. Leader to Eight. Has there been any change?"

"No, sir. We're the only ones broadcasting. There's nothing on the sensors but us and the Interceptor."

"Thanks, Eight." Eight's voice had changed. It was more resonant and lacked its usual rustic accent. Things were otherwise as he remembered them. Well, that was all right. Eight would be dead soon, anyway.

Donos's head swam as he recognized the simple cruelty of that stray thought.

The Interceptor abruptly lost speed and heeled over to starboard. Donos smiled. Its engine trouble had to have worsened. It headed straight toward the gap between two giant volcanoes, straight toward the trap.

The ambush. They were all about to die.

"Talon Leader to squad, break off! Omega signal!" He rolled up on his port wing and curved in a tight arc away from the volcanoes. Away from death.

The other Talons did not follow. They sped down their destined path toward annihilation.

"Leader to group! Break off! Follow me!"

A woman's voice: "Can't do it, sir."

"Twelve, is that you?"

"Yes, sir."

"Follow me. That's an order! The others die down there. You follow me. Maybe you can make it out this time."

"No, sir. What does it matter whether I die down there or on the way out?"

Donos continued his arc until he completed a full circle. He now sped on in the wake of his pilots. But no matter how much power he diverted to his engines, they seemed to gain on him, heedlessly rushing toward their own dooms.

"It matters, Twelve. Break off." He felt an unfamiliar weight crushing his chest. It wasn't acceleration; it was the inevitability of those pilots' needless deaths. "*Please,* Twelve."

Her voice turned scornful. "Don't '*Please*' me, Lieutenant. If someone said, 'Please live' to you, you'd just ignore him or spit in his eye."

"That's *crazy*." The pilots ahead of him were moments from entering the pass between the volcanoes. The pressure increased, squeezing his chest so hard he didn't think his heart could beat.

"No, it's not. You don't care enough about yourself to live. So you don't give a damn about us."

"You're wrong. Turn back."

"Swear it."

"I swear it! Turn back!"

The canopy of his X-wing went black and the roar of his engines died. A white slit appeared where his canopy should rise, but when it did come up, it opened on a port-side hinge rather than on a hinge behind him.

Sweating, trembling, he stared into the faces of Face, Tyria, Falynn, and Kell. They wore headsets and somber expressions.

The pressure in Donos's chest snapped. It became a ball of pure rage. He lunged at the faces before him but was restrained by his pilot's harness. "You *bastards*—"

All but Kell pulled away. Kell merely pulled his headset off and handed it back to Face.

Donos got his harness off, stood in his pilot's seat, and leaped at Kell. The force of his leap, the force of his anger, should have taken the big man off his feet, but Kell pivoted, caught Donos's right arm, and spun Donos down to the flooring almost gently. The walls of *Night Caller*'s lounge, their colors chosen by scientists to be soothing, twirled around him as Kell manhandled him.

But Kell didn't pin him. From his kneeling position, Donos took a swing at the big man's groin. Kell got a hand in the way, angled the blow to the side, and took it on his thigh.

"I'll *kill* you." The force of his scream scoured Donos's throat raw. "How could you do that to me, put me through that again—"

Kell didn't speak. He was concentrating on Donos's movements, which made Donos even more furious. It was Tyria who answered: "What choice did you leave us? You were just lying there. Trying to die."

"That's my right!" Donos stood and threw his best punch at Kell's face. Kell managed to get his hand behind Donos's elbow, shoving Donos off balance. Then Kell turned away as if to leave, completed the spin, and Donos felt his legs being kicked out from under him. He slammed down onto the hard floor of the lounge.

"You don't have the right," Kell said. "Do you remember swearing an oath?"

"Shut up!" Donos kicked out at Kell, but the other man anticipated the move and drew back a pace. Donos's boot fell short and rang on the lounge floor.

Kell continued, merciless: "Do you have the right to mourn a droid so deeply that you don't give a damn about Jesmin Ackbar dying?"

"Shiner . . ." Suddenly all the fight left Donos. Grief so strong it was like a physical thing, like a hole in his body, bent him double.

He became aware that Tyria was bending over him, shaking him. "Myn, don't go away. We need you here. We need you flying. We need you watching our backs. We're your squad now."

"Shiner . . ."

"What is it about that droid?" Her voice was at once worried and angry. He looked up at her, saw her incomprehension.

"The last . . ."

"The last what?" She stared down into his eyes, then she looked startled. "The last Talon. He was the last Talon, wasn't he?"

Unable to speak, Donos nodded.

"And as long as he was still . . . alive, you hadn't let them all down, had you, Myn? You hadn't failed the whole squadron? You still had him to protect."

Donos spoke around his grief. It made his words thick. He himself would barely have understood if he weren't speaking. "He's gone now."

"Myn . . ." Tyria looked lost, desperate. "We need you to protect us now. We're your friends."

"Don't want friends. Friends die."

"Dammit!" She pulled him to her so his head was in her lap. He stared up at her, hoping she'd stop speaking soon so he could go back to sleep. "Myn, I agree with you. When I joined the Alliance, that was my motto. Friends die, so don't make any. Just go out, kill the enemy, and when death comes, I'll know I've done my best."

"Then you know."

"I changed my mind, Myn. When Jesmin died. How could I look her in the eye if I just threw my life away? She fought to live. She'd be angry at me for wasting what she didn't have a chance to enjoy."

Donos didn't answer. He didn't have a reply for her.

"What about the Talons? Do they want you to die?"

"They must."

"Stop that. You knew them. Would they want you to die?"

"Their families would."

"No."

"They'd want me to die because I led their fathers and brothers and sisters and cousins off to some nothing world to die for no reason." He looked beyond Tyria's shoulder to where Kell and Face stood. "He knows. Muscles there."

Kell said, "I know what?"

"You want Janson to die."

"No."

"Don't lie! He killed your father."

"How did you know that?"

"Someone told me." Donos shrank away from the question. No need to implicate Grinder, regardless of whether Donos chose to live or not.

Kell knelt beside Tyria and looked gravely down at Donos. "I used to want him to die. I killed him hundreds of ways in my imagination. But I changed my mind."

"Just so you could argue with me!"

"No." Kell seemed to sag. He looked tired and years older. "I doubt that I'll ever play sabacc with him, Myn. But I want him to live. Because with him in an X-wing, it means that every year there are fewer Imps and warlord flyers out there endangering my sisters. My mother. My friends. And the families of the dead Talon Squad pilots will think even better of you than I do of Janson. Unless you kill yourself. If you kill yourself, they'll tell themselves, 'My father didn't even have a chance; he was led by a coward.' If they know you were a courageous pilot, they'll say, 'He died fighting for us.' "

Donos blinked, and for a moment he was far away from *Night Caller,* flashing at hyperspace speeds through the homes of the families whose members he had led to death. As he'd done so many times in the days and weeks after Talon Squad was obliterated. But this time, the faces he saw were not masks of anger and vengeance. Just sadness, sometimes; sometimes they were just curious and reflective faces turned up toward the stars.

"I'm sorry about Jesmin," Donos said.

Tyria nodded and brushed a lock of sweat-drenched hair out of Donos's eyes. "We all are."

Donos looked up at Falynn. "I'm sorry about you."

Falynn came forward. She wore an expression compounded of pain and even, Donos thought, jealousy at Tyria's ministrations to him. "What do you mean?"

"I thought you wanted to get close. I kept you away. I was cold to you."

"I understand why."

"I think I need to go to bed now."

Kell rose and helped Donos up.

Tyria also rose. "Will you be all right?"

"I don't know." Donos shrugged. "Maybe."

"Breakfast is at eight hundred. We'd like to see you there."

Donos nodded. "I guess I'll be there."

On the way back to his quarters, he felt so strange . . . All the pain he'd known since Talon Squad died was still there, but the exhaustion that had accompanied it seemed to be gone. It was as though toxins he'd been building up for ages had been bled out.

He fell onto his bed and was unconscious in moments.

The others watched him depart the lounge. Falynn followed him at a discreet distance, making sure he made it back to his quarters. Then Face slumped against the lounge bar. Kell sat heavily on one of the long couches. Tyria reached in to the simulator unit to power it down, then sat beside Kell.

"Well, that was fun," Face said.

"It worked," Kell said. His voice sounded as heavy as he felt. "And neither Commander Antilles nor Lieutenant Janson walked in on us. We got lucky."

Tyria leaned back and closed her eyes. "Now, all Myn has to do is actually get up in four hours and we can say we did it."

Kell said, "Now maybe Runt will get some sleep."

"Oh?" Tyria asked. "He's been sleeping badly?"

"On the shifts he pulled to sit with Myn, he talked to him endlessly. Tried every way he knew to get Myn to 'switch to a less damaged mind.' Something his people do with fair ease, even the ones who are mentally ill. He's been lashing himself for his failure to help Myn do the same thing."

Face said, "Four hours? What am I doing awake? I'll see you two tomorrow." He strode from the room.

The two of them sat in silence for a few moments. Then Kell said, "That was a pretty good idea. About Shiner being the last Talon in the weird way Myn was thinking."

"Thanks."

"Another insight? Like the other day and the ambush those pirates set up for me?"

"Something like that."

"I bet it's the Force. I bet you can only use it when you're not thinking about it."

"Oh, that's great. That's just what I need. How would you like to be the best pilot in the galaxy, but only when you're outside a cockpit?"

He snorted.

"Was it true what he said?" Her voice was unusually gentle. "About Janson and your father?"

"Yes." Kell reached out for the deep wellspring of hatred he'd carried for Janson all these years, but it was still gone. *Mostly* gone. "Every day, I wish it hadn't happened. But Janson had reason." He shook his head, trying to dispel the mood of gloom those memories always invoked. "Was it true what *you* said? About giving up that whole attitude of 'I might die tomorrow, probably shouldn't make any plans'?"

She took a while to answer. "Yes, I meant it."

"Um."

"Um? That doesn't mean anything."

"You remember a while back, when I told you I loved you, and you told me it was just a puddle on the floor, and then you put my face into that puddle?"

She looked at him as if to gauge his mood. Seeing that he wasn't mad, she managed a sympathetic smile. "Of course I remember."

"Well, I have something to tell you. After I realized you were right, I decided that it was enough to be your friend."

"Good."

"Then I fell in love with you again."

Her expression became one of dismay and exasperation, "Oh, Kell—"

"No, bear with me, just for a minute."

"It's just the same words again."

"Same words . . . different Kell. This time I know what I'm talking about."

"Of *course* you do. So. Set Honesty to On?"

"Honesty to On."

"How much time did you spend thinking about me today?"

"Every chance I got. Every chance I had when Commander Antilles and Janson weren't working me."

"Ah, but in how many of those little fantasies of yours was I wearing any clothes?"

He snorted in amusement. "Lots of them. Most of them." The words, the truth, came easily to him. "I saw us together in quiet times. When the war with the last bits of the Empire was over and we could argue and be confused about what to do next. Deciding things together. I saw myself presenting you to my family . . . and saw them making a place in their lives and hearts for you." He saw distress in her expression but pressed on anyway. "I saw a hundred ways for our lives together to be, and the only thing that made me sad was that we couldn't explore all of them."

He sighed. "But now, like the galaxy's worst general, I've told you my objective—I'm going to win your heart. I just don't know how I'm going to do it, you being forewarned and all—"

She lunged at him. Her tackle took him off the end of the sofa. Suddenly she was atop him on the floor, her arms around his neck, embracing him but glaring furiously.

He rubbed the back of his head where it had hit the deck. "Ow."

"Shut up." She kissed him.

That went on a while and felt better than a three-day bender on Churban brandy—even better, for the rising heat and excitement he felt were something no brandy could ever simulate. In spite of his confusion, he remembered to wrap her up in his arms so she couldn't escape when she regained her senses.

Finally she broke the kiss and returned to glaring at him.

"Well, that wasn't bad," he said. "But I thought you didn't feel the way I did."

"Of course you did. But then, you're a giant adolescent with no sense. A big shaved Wookiee with no grasp of human emotions."

"Granted. But how long have you wanted *me?*"

Her expression went from angry to plaintive in an instant. "Since I met you."

"What? Then why didn't you—"

"Because you were in love with that other Tyria, the one who doesn't exist. We established that weeks ago." She managed a little smile. "But I think you're finally over her."

"I am."

"You have to prove it."

"How?"

"Oh, we'll find a way."

Wedge stepped into the officers' mess, took a quick look around, and froze.

Donos was among the other Wraiths. Chatting. Laughing, despite the new gauntness to his features.

Face, on the other hand, didn't look at all well. There were circles under his eyes. He had obviously lost sleep. But he seemed cheerful enough.

Kell and Tyria looked just as bad, sleep-deprived and weary. Yet they seemed even more than cheerful.

Wedge's sudden appearance caught the Wraiths' attention. Their conversation cut off and they turned to look at him.

Wedge straightened and nodded sardonically at Face. In a mild tone, he said, "Captain Darillian to the bridge."

Face scrambled up and out the door. He wouldn't be going to the bridge, of course; Darillian's seat of command was the comm center.

Wedge jerked his head for Janson to join him. His second-in-command was at his side in an instant. They headed toward *Night Caller*'s true bridge.

"What's with Myn?" Wedge asked.

"I don't know. They're not telling me. But he seems to be functional."

"Good. One crisis averted. What's with all the tired faces?"

"I, well, don't know. Maybe a late-night sabacc game they don't invite senior officers to?"

"Fine. Anything else you don't know?"

"Yes. Something happened with Kell yesterday."

"What?"

"I don't know."

Wedge stopped short and gave Janson a reproving look.

"No, really, I don't know. We talked. About his father. I got the impression that he'd been thinking of me as some sort of avenging monster who vaped people for screwups. I also got the impression that he really hadn't been plotting my death every time he came within a few meters of me . . . in fact, that he might have been scared stiff."

"That can actually look the same."

"Anyway, this morning, things had changed. For the first time, he didn't become a tower of knotted muscles when I sat down to breakfast."

"Good." They swept into the bridge. "Lieutenant

Tabanne, put the compiled transmission up on the main monitor."

"Yes, sir."

Face sat at the comm officer's chair, activated the voice and visual translators, and put them through the fastest possible diagnostic check. Both came up in the green. The computers controlling the comm center's cameras thought they were tracking his body motions correctly.

He sat back, thought for a moment about an aging prima donna of a leading man he'd worked with once, and was instantly in character for Captain Darillian. He turned toward the comm center's main holoprojector, hit the button to activate transmission, and prepared to speak to Admiral Trigit.

The three-dimensional image of Warlord Zsinj materialized before him.

Face took an extra-deep breath and broadened his smile to cover his surprise. "My lord. I am honored."

Zsinj's smile was one of condescension and amusement. "But not honored enough to do your job correctly."

Face let his eyebrows rise. How had Darillian responded to scorn in his memoirs? With outrage. But the man would never direct an angry response to Warlord Zsinj. No, hurt was the order of the day. "My lord . . . I have failed you in some way? You have called to tell me I no longer deserve your patronage. It's the life of a pirate for Darillian . . ."

"Oh, stop being such a baby. It leeches all the fun out of scolding you." Zsinj heaved an annoyed sigh. "I received the relay of your report on the visit to Blood Nest."

Pretending not to be fully recovered from the wound to his pride, Face shrugged. "A pity they chose to reject your offer. But since my avoidance of their ambush was so brilliantly successful, I feel I have left them with something to think about. Perhaps they will be more cordial when I return."

Zsinj shook his head. "I don't believe so. Blood Nest is gone."

Face leaned forward and assumed an incredulous expression. "They fled?"

"No, and that's the problem. Sometime after you departed, Blood Nest was destroyed. In fact, every site you've visited in the last several weeks has subsequently been visited . . . by Alliance pilots or agents."

"No." Face knew he looked shaken and hoped Grinder's program was up to having Darillian show the same expression. "At the next stop in my mission, I'll pretend to jump out, then lie in wait for them. I'll destroy them."

"Yes. But not yet. I have a more important mission for you." Zsinj smiled. "You're going to help that fool Trigit finish off the survivors of Folor Base."

Once everyone was reseated at breakfast, Piggy asked, "Can the Alliance muster enough firepower to Morobe in time to take out *Implacable*?"

Wedge nodded. "That firepower is in place. We know which system Trigit's going to strike, even though Zsinj, with his customary caution, hasn't told us yet. If Zsinj were going in himself, we'd have to draw so many frigates, cruisers, and Star Destroyers away from other duty that Zsinj would be alerted . . . but, fortunately or unfortunately, *Iron Fist* isn't joining in this mission.

"We do have a real problem, though. He told our Captain Darillian to make rendezvous with the supply ship *Hawkbat* to replenish expended fuel and supplies. And to pick up a load of surveillance satellites we can deploy at our next scheduled stop so they can acquire data on our 'pursuers.' He also says he wants the *Hawkbat*'s master to come over for an inspection tour of the ship and a talk with Darillian."

"Oh, wonderful," Kell said.

"Also, if *Night Caller* is participating in the battle at Talasea, Zsinj is probably going to expect us to field our full complement of TIE fighters. Which is supposed to be four, not two."

"The TIE fighters are no problem," Falynn said.

"They're all over the galaxy. Set the Wraiths down on any planet and we can steal two and fly them back."

"Speaking of which," Janson said, "we have two more TIE pilots if we need them. Both Captain Hrakness and Lieutenant Tabanne are Imp Academy graduates. He's done simulators and soloed, and she actually flew a few missions."

Wedge tried to keep any emotion from his face. "Kills?"

"No. Only since defecting and joining the New Republic Navy."

"Good." One of the problems with the New Republic was that many of its pilots had literally and violently been at odds in the past. It sometimes caused trouble when a pilot now under New Republic command had shot down other New Republic pilots. But some people Wedge absolutely trusted had been Imperials: Tycho Celchu, current leader of Rogue Squadron; Hobbie Klivan, who had defected with Biggs Darklighter and the rest of the crew of the *Rand Ecliptic;* even Han Solo had been an Academy graduate and briefly an officer.

"The rendezvous is no problem," Phanan said. At Wedge's curious look, he said, "We simply need to get to the rendezvous site and say, 'Oh, no, we're all down with the Tastiged Flu. Sure, come over. Hope you don't mind when we have sneezing fits all over you and infect you.'"

Wedge shook his head. "We're dealing with an enemy who is proficient at intelligence work. I think that a sudden inconvenient contagion would tend to alert him."

Face smiled. It was a crooked smile better suited to a member of Black Sun, the criminal underworld of Coruscant. "What if it's not us who gets contaminated?"

"Go on."

"Zsinj transmitted us the *Hawkbat*'s current schedule so we could arrange a rendezvous at our mutual convenience. That means we know where they're going to make planetfall over the next several days. We choose the planet where they're most likely to be offering shore leave; we send the Wraiths over there; and we expose them to some sort of disease. Then it's the *Hawkbat*'s captain who has to report we couldn't meet physically because of an 'inconvenient contagion.' Zsinj can investigate all he wants . . . because he won't be investigating us."

Wedge rubbed his chin and resisted the urge to say, "That's crazy." Instead, he asked, "Where do we get the contaminants?"

Phanan said, "Every modern planet has a hospital, Commander. Some even have centers for disease containment. One of those would be a street market of disease for us."

Wedge stood. "Wes, Phanan, let's go back to my conference room and see if we can actually hammer this into a plan. The rest of you—I think a day's rest is in order. Get some sleep."

They broke into laughter at his words and he didn't dare ask why.

21

As the world of Storinal grew in *Narra*'s viewscreen, the Wraiths still hadn't finalized their plans.

There were too many unknown factors, Wedge reflected. Storinal was still under Imperial control, but at the very edge of Imperial space, and said to be leaning toward possible alliance with the New Republic or Warlord Zsinj. The Wraiths could count on running into Imps, and might run across factions of the other two groups. Possible complications there.

Exactly which disease agent they'd be using on the crew of the *Hawkbat* was an unknown. Phanan wanted to make that decision at the last minute, based on what was available on the planet's surface and what they could find out about the crew of the *Hawkbat*. It wouldn't do to use a biological agent that meant mild illness for most of the crew but death to others. Fortunately, many of Zsinj's ships appeared to follow Imperial recruiting doctrine—employ no nonhumans if at all possible—which helped limit that danger.

There was the matter of stealing a pair of TIE fighters. The planet was probably swarming with them . . . but how good was Imperial security? The mission called for the

Wraiths to locate and select their target fighters and perform all steps of their acquisition except the actual theft . . . and then wait until other elements of the mission were completed before launching for space with their new acquisitions. In the middle would be a wait that could be very dangerous.

The whole mission offered little but questions at this stage. *Fortunately, it will offer nice scenery while we're chewing the details,* Wedge decided. *Night Caller*'s library record of Storinal displayed image afer image of lushly green countryside, rivers cascading down stepped hillsides, forest-sized tropical flower gardens, and cities of graceful lines and dimensions occasionally interrupting the world's natural vistas. The people of Storinal were said to be steeped in a philosophy of beautification that extended to their world, making it one of the most gorgeous in what was left of the Empire, and a favorite center of tourism among those who enjoy natural delights. Falynn, of course, had looked through the data and decided, "Looks humid."

Then there was the problem of clearing customs. Were they coming down to the planet aboard a cruise vessel or as part of the crew of a large military ship, they could blend in with fair ease and be accelerated through the routine inspection offered to large, precleared groups. But they'd be arriving in a private shuttle. They'd receive close, individual inspection. Face's plan was to make them stereotypes, types very familiar to customs officials so their inspectors would dismiss them and give them the minimum likely inspection . . . but that could go wrong, too.

There were even unknown factors among his own team. In the space of two days, things had shifted, changed as though a rock slide had come through. Donos was functional again. Falynn Sandskimmer was cozying up to him once more, but this time he seemed to be reciprocating the sentiment. Kell and Tyria, though they did not advertise it, made no attempt to hide the fact that they were together. Kell himself seemed looser, more at ease, his very presence no longer causing fits to Janson. All these changes seemed to be improvements, especially in light of how down the Wraiths had been after Jesmin's death . . . but Wedge was slow to embrace so many changes all at once.

At least they did have one piece of simple good fortune involving Storinal. The planet, despite its Imperial ties, had a small but visible population of Gamorreans. Most were guards whose chief role was to be visible and exotic for the entertainment of tourists. So Piggy would be able to move with the other Wraiths.

"Routine planetary inquiry," Kell announced. "Means we've wandered into their outermost sensor zone. Grinder, you'd better get under cover."

The Bothan heaved a much-put-upon sigh. He moved back into *Narra*'s cargo compartment and tapped an intricate rhythm against one of the bulkheads. A plate popped open along a weld line, swinging out as a lateral door . . . giving him access into the same scanner-shielded smuggling compartment Piggy had once used as a vehicle. With one last injured expression directed back toward the cockpit, he swung up into the compartment and pulled the access closed behind him.

"Falynn," Kell continued, "weld it shut. Make it airtight."

Falynn smiled but didn't move from her seat.

Wedge suppressed a smile. It was better for the government of Storinal not to know there was a Bothan on board; ever since the participation of an Alliance-friendly cell of Bothan code-slicers in the acquisition of the plans for the second Death Star, the Imps held all inhabitants or descendants of Bothawui under even more suspicion than other nonhumans. Grinder would serve best by staying an unknown, a wild card for them to draw when needed. Runt, too, was acting as a wild card, charged with the very uncomfortable duty of parking his X-wing on one of Storinal's distant moons and waiting for an emergency signal. He could be there for three days, eating preserved food, breathing recycled air, and having only a plastic tube-and-bladder rig for a 'fresher, but he was determined to remain of use to the other Wraiths.

"Transmitting passenger manifest," Kell said. "By the way, not one of you has paid for his ticket."

"Take it up with a judge," Phanan said. "You're in an awfully good mood for a man putting his head in a noose."

"Maybe it's because you're in the next noose over. All right, we're cleared for approach. Anybody forget his papers?"

Everyone checked pockets or bags for the requisite identification cards, all forged by Grinder with data provided by New Republic Intelligence. Wedge saw Janson, ridiculous in his red carnival costume and long white beard, grow increasingly panicky as he checked pocket after pocket. "Something wrong, Wes?"

"It's here somewhere," the lieutenant said.

"Check your boot," Falynn said.

"Check under your seat cushion," Phanan said.

"Check your other boot, too," Wedge said. "Falynn really meant both boots, but she doesn't realize you wouldn't necessarily understand that."

Janson straightened up from his searching long enough to shoot his commander a betrayed look. "Why isn't Hobbie here to take this abuse?" A moment later he straightened again, wearing an abashed expression. "It was in my other boot."

"Yub, yub, Lieutenant."

"Thirty seconds to atmospheric entry," Kell said. "Strap in, people."

Five minutes later they were gliding over those beautiful green vistas on a government-dictated course toward the spaceport of the entertainment-complex city of Revos. Grinder's innocuous consultation of the city computer's records indicated that ship's crews enjoying rest and recreation there included the crew of *Hawkbat*.

Narra's scanners indicated that a fighter was pacing them, trailing them by a kilometer and a half and one klick higher in altitude. This would have been unfriendly attention on some worlds, but Donos said that many worlds with law enforcement agencies designed to maintain the tourism industry would employ such tactics as a matter of course; it didn't mean anything.

"Pretty," Face said. He stared at the gleaming view of Revos appearing before them. The city seemed to be made all of tall, curving towers built of creamy pastel marble in a variety of colors.

The spaceport, built outside the city walls, came into view a minute later. It did not share the idyllic architecture of the city; it was a duracrete circle two or more kilometers in diameter, with landing circles and wartlike ferrocrete bunkers, gaily painted but somehow no less ugly for it, scattered across its surface. The Wraiths counted several small cargo ships, shuttles of various types, light atmospheric craft, and even a few TIE fighters among the vessels clustered around the various bunkers.

Kell landed where he was instructed, at one of the outermost ring of bunkers. A viewscreen on the bunker wall displayed primitive line graphics instructing Kell how to maneuver the shuttle to its exact landing pad and orientation. Two guards in stormtrooper armor were in position on either side of *Narra*'s nose before the shuttle had quite settled down.

"Doran Spaceways welcomes you to Storinal," Kell said in his most official voice. "Be ready to show your documentation to all officials of the planetary government, and enjoy your stay." He lowered the shuttle's main ramp. "First-class passengers first, please."

Wes Janson tugged at his lengthy white beard, a gesture that looked habitual but really served to assure him that it was still attached properly. He squared his shoulders, assumed a properly haughty attitude, and descended the ramp, his bodyguards flanking him—Falynn left, Lieutenant Atril Tabanne right, and Piggy, in the full regalia of a Gamorrean warrior, complete with vibro-ax, behind.

The end of an inspection tube connected to the bunker swung out before the shuttle, and a planetary official stepped out from it to join the guards. Doubtless the man thought himself natty in his emerald-green longcoat and shining gold buttons, but Janson knew himself to be a far more brilliant, and possibly ridiculous, spectacle.

Janson wore a glittering red coat cut in the style of a naval officer's, complete with epaulettes and a double row of buttons, plus matching peaked cap and well-tailored black pants. White belt and gloves, shining black boots and blaster holster completed the ensemble. The clothing ensemble, that is; Janson also wore thick white hair, beard, and mustache, and makeup that roughened the skin on his face and hands. Wes Janson's face was too well known in Imperial-controlled space to risk a less elaborate disguise.

His bodyguards, in contrast, were beacons of sobriety. Falynn and Atril wore body stockings in light-leeching black. Their leather accoutrements—boots, belt, bags, and blaster holsters—were matte black. Their hair was drawn back in severe braids, and Face had insisted both women dye it black, too, explaining that it was appropriate for the sort of all-controlling personality Janson was supposed to be to have matching bodyguards.

Janson stopped before the government agent, who held out his hand. Janson cleared his throat in what he hoped was an appropriately blustery manner, and Atril handed the official four sets of identicards.

The official slid the first one into his handheld scanner. "Senator-in-Exile Iskit Tyestin from Bakura," he said. He frowned. "Bakura."

"Don't bother to tell me that Bakura is hardly a friend to the Empire these days." Janson struggled to keep that elusive element of harumph in his voice. "If she were, I would still be there, in my home, instead of here, loyally serving the Empire."

"Of course. What is your business on Storinal?"

"Business. I'm raising funds for the Bakuran Loyalist Movement. We continue to put pressure on the government to sever ties with the Rebels and return to her true allegiance."

The official's hand-reader pinged and he looked at it. "You are in our records. A loyal friend of the Empire."

Janson harumphed, straightened with pride. The Senator Tyestin identity matched a real person, one of the last of the Empire's supporters to be elected to the senate of Bakura before that world decided to join the Alliance. The real Tyestin never made it offworld; his escape craft was destroyed when he attempted to flee, a fact that was not yet lodged in the Empire's datanet.

The official dropped each of the other cards into his reader. "My lady Anen of Bakura. Profession, bodyguard. Licensed to carry exposed and concealed weaponry. Please don't use it, Mistress Anen; even the most legal and reasonable of shootings leads to tedious investigations. My lady Honiten, likewise, likewise, and likewise. And Guardsman Voort." He peered at the Gamorrean. "Does it understand Basic?"

"A few words," Janson said, his tone a grumble. "Too few."

"Please observe the signs outside each establishment about who and what may enter." He returned the cards to Atril with a polished smile. "Welcome to the fair world of Storinal. Enjoy your visit."

Ton Phanan, wearing false prosthetics to conceal even more of his flesh, and playing the part of a test pilot obviously down on his luck—and running ever lower on human components—passed inspection easily, as did Tyria, portraying his long-suffering wife. Then it was time for Wedge, Face, and Donos . . . potentially the most dangerous part of the deception, as Wedge's face was on holographic wanted memoranda all over Imperial space.

Wedge tugged at the furious mustachios he wore. They were nowhere near as elaborate a disguise as the set of false prosthetics he'd worn to penetrate customs on the world of Coruscant, but he shouldn't need such difficult and expensive measures here. And the continuations of his disguise on either side of him should draw attention away from his features.

He and his two companions wore nearly identical clothes. Their rough-country ponchos were woven from a heavy brown cloth that looked gritty and sand-filled even when scrupulously cleaned. Their trousers and shirts were a lighter weave of the same stuff, hard-worn—aged in just two days by having the Wraiths take turns marching across them for hours. Their broad-brimmed hats had received similar, though less extensive, treatment. Their hair and false mustaches were cut to identical lengths. Face again wore false skin to conceal his scars and had managed to mold it to make his features a bit more like Wedge's. All in all, Wedge knew they looked like three yokels who'd blown their savings on a single trip to a more civilized world.

They descended the ramp and handed their identification cards to the official with an identical flourish. The man looked at them, an expression somewhere between amusement and horror on his face.

He recovered enough to slide the first card into his reader. "Dod Nobrin of Agamar."

Agamar, an Outer Rim colony world, was a rough place whose inhabitants had to be equally rough to survive. Not surprisingly, the rustic ways, stubbornness, and durability of the men and women of Agamar earned them an undeserved reputation for stupidity across the Old Republic and the Empire. Even today, half of the jokes told in Basic about stupid people cast them as men and women of Agamar. Face had developed the trio's clothing style and mannerisms after careful consultation with Captain Hrakness, a native of Agamar, to match the most common stereotypical depiction of the people of that world.

Face nodded, a head-bobbing motion more suited to a carrion bird than to a man. Wedge duplicated the motion. A moment later Donos caught on and did the same. The official looked between them as if mesmerized.

"I'm Dod," Face said. He jerked his thumb at Wedge. "This is my brother Fod. Also from Agamar." He gestured at Donos the same way. "This is my brother Lod."

"Also from Agamar."

"Oyah. That's right. You're pretty sharp for a city man." The official shook his head with the motion of someone resigning himself for a long, long day at work. "Your business on Storinal?"

Face beamed. "Women."

"Entertainment, then."

Face looked indignant. "No."

"Business?"

"No! That's not the sort of business we're in."

Wedge said, "Brides."

Donos, keeping his voice low, repeated, "Brides." He stretched the word out as though it had some cosmic significance.

Wedge said, "There are only six beautiful women on all Agamar. And they're all married."

Face said, "There are only five."

Wedge shook his head adamantly. "Six."

"Five. Ettal Howrider got shot."

"Gentlemen . . ."

"Who shot her?"

"Her cousin, Popal Howrider."

"I thought he was still laid up from getting bit and the wound festering and all. That awful smell . . ."

"Gentlemen!" The official's color had risen. "I'm going to put 'Entertainment' on your temporary visa. If you're not here to do financial transactions with someone, you're here for 'Entertainment.' You understand?"

Face nodded agreeably, and again Wedge and Donos matched his bobbing motion. "Oyah. We understand." Then Face caught sight of something off to the side. "Look at that!"

Everyone, the guards included, looked in the same direction, but the only thing to see was the motion of people walking inside the near bunker, just on the other side of a gallery-length window.

The official asked, "What?"

Face grabbed his tunic, pulled him close, pointed. "Her, her! She's nearly naked!"

One of the passersby was in a golden, reflective garment that showed a considerable quantity of leg and shoulder.

The official tried to pull himself free. "That's merely summer wear, sir—"

"What's her name?"

"I don't know." The man tried to pry Face's hand off but made no headway. He cast a beseeching look over his shoulder toward one of the guards, and Wedge tensed, but the armor-plated trooper didn't move. He was, Wedge saw, shaking with laughter.

"You don't know her name? You live in the same village with her!"

The official finally got Face's hand free. "It's a city, not a village, and it's too large for me to know everybody." As quickly as he could, he cycled Wedge's and Donos's cards through the reader.

"That's not very neighborly." Face accepted the cards and passed them out among his brothers. "Say, if you could direct us to where the beautiful women looking for husbands are, it'd be worth a credit to you."

The man looked at him, too drained to be stunned. "A whole credit."

"Oyah. Always pay for the best, that's what I say."

"Try the Howler. It's a bar. It's where you'll find locals with an itch to get offworld but not enough money to do so."

"Sir, you're gentleman." Face dropped a credit coin into the man's palm and walked into the inspection tube opening.

"A gentleman," Wedge repeated, and followed. He heard Donos grunt, "Gent," and come stomping after him.

Kell ambled down the ramp. He saw the inspector's tired expression and gave the man a knowing smile. "Imagine being trapped aboard a shuttle with them for three days." He bobbed his head up and down in a fair simulation of Face's distinctive nod, then handed his identicard to the man.

"Do you think they'll be any trouble . . . Captain Doran?"

"Call me Kell. No, none of them is any trouble except the old senator. Just stroke his ego . . . and don't shoot against him. I accepted a competition challenge from him,

and lost. That's why I had to carry his damned Gamorrean."
Kell took a step to the side and looked up at the *Narra*'s
flank. The words "Doran Spaceways" and the name *Doran
Star* on the shuttle's side still looked appropriately weathered,
belying the fact that they'd been painted on three days ago
and then partly scraped off again.

"Thanks. I'll make sure the appropriate parties know."
The official handed back Kell's card. "Are you carrying them
back again?"

Kell answered by shuddering.

"Ah. Well, your loss is our gain, provided it's soon.
Please wait in the inspection area. Pending a scan of your
shuttle, you're clear."

"Thanks."

As soon as they cleared inspection, the party of Senator-in-
Exile Tyestin, known informally on this mission as the Joyride Group, checked into the lodging nearest the spaceport.
After they swept their suite against the possibility of listening
devices and found none, Janson said, "No reason to go farther away to find TIE fighters. There are some here . . . and
traffic of lots more strangers than on an Imp military base."

"Atril and I can switch in and out of disguise a lot more
easily than you," Falynn said. It was true; for the two
women, all it took was a change of clothing and addition of a
wig to cover their severe black hair. "You and Piggy should
stay here, in character, for the time being. Let us do the
groundwork."

"Because my disguise is inconvenient," he said.

"Yes."

"Not because I'm old and feeble like Commander Antilles."

She smiled and looked away. "I suppose I've had to re-
vise my opinion about old, feeble pilots."

"Well, you children go and have a good time. I'm going
to order expensive meals and expensive entertainments. This
is on one of the New Republic's covert expense accounts, and
for once I feel like running up a nice big bill."

. . .

Phanan's group, including Tyria and Kell, was charged with acquiring disease agents. They took the repulsorlift rail passage from Revos to the capital city of Scohar, home of the planet's largest spaceport and of a medical center designed to deal with diseases both domestic and alien.

The Revos-Scohar railway was a marvel of engineering and public relations. The conveyance itself was a series of lengthy repulsorlift cars coupled together, traveling for the most part along a featureless tunnel. But every so often the train would rise into the open air, long enough for the passengers to enjoy one of the planet's most beautiful vistas—here a spectacular view of snowcapped mountain peaks, there a long look at valleys purpling under the setting sun—and then descend again. Kell decided that it was a good compromise between giving the tourists the show they wanted and marring the carefully maintained landscape.

Scohar was much like Revos, only far larger, and dotted with recreational complexes that included thrill rides that simulated danger without ever harming a visitor. The Plague Group, as they called themselves, stayed away from the most tourist-heavy portions of the city and checked into lodgings near the Scohar Xenohealth Institute—the innocuous name the government of Storinal had given to their center for disease control.

Wedge, Face, and Donos, informally the Yokel Group, found lodgings at the Revos Liberty, a hostel catering to large ships' crews on shore leave. Because of its orientation, rooms were small but inexpensive; services and amenities would be rare. However, half the rooms, including the Wraiths', opened directly out onto an artificial riverside beach.

Face excused himself for a few minutes and returned with a pile of brightly colored cloth. He handed out individual portions to the others.

Wedge shook his out. A short-sleeved tunic in orange and yellow tropical fruit patterns and short pants in lavender. "I'm going to throw up."

Face smiled. "That would be the final bit of trim on the ensemble, wouldn't it? I recommend you keep the hat. That really completes the image of an Agamaran stereotype with no taste and no sense."

"I wish I didn't agree with you."

"Yub, yub, Commander."

Donos looked mournfully at his outfit: a shirt with thin red and green horizontal stripes and shorts with black and white vertical stripes. "Sir, permission to kill Face?"

"Granted. But keep your hat, like Face says."

Face unfolded his own fashion disaster. A black silken shirt with a variety of insects picked out on it in glittery silver, shorts in a brighter, more painful orange than that of New Republic pilot's suits, and a red kerchief for his neck. "As you can see, I saved the best for myself. Time to find some brides, brothers."

22

"Really," Wedge said. "I thought all you Imperial Navy boys were TIE fighter pilots. Every one."

They sat in the Sunfruit Promenade, actually an extensive roofed patio flanked by flower gardens. The lounge was thick with recliner chairs and interrupted occasionally by musicians' pits, most of which, at this late-afternoon hour, were occupied by musicians, male, female, and droid, playing a variety of stringed and percussion instruments.

The three yokel brothers were there, in the midst of a veritable sea of *Hawkbat* crewmen. Most of the crewmen were doing some light drinking in preparation for going out after dark and doing their heavy drinking. Some were accompanied by local women and men; the recliners were built to accommodate a cozy two. But Wedge, Face, and Donos, garish and loud, were by themselves.

The man opposite Wedge, a long-time Imperial Navy NCO, if Wedge was any judge, built like Kell but even bigger and deeper in the chest, smiled at Wedge's stupidity. "Now, think about that, Dod—"

"I'm Fod. This is Dod. That's Lod."

"Fod. Even an *Imperial*-class Star Destroyer only carries

six squadrons of TIE fighters. That's seventy-two. Even with relief pilots, you're talking about ninety or a hundred pilots on one of the big ships. Do you think a Star Destroyer can manage with just a bridge crew and a hundred pilots?"

"Well, I didn't think about it, really."

The *Hawkbat* crewmen immediately around them laughed.

The big NCO, whose name was Rondle, looked sadly into his almost-empty glass.

Face, his motions those of a profoundly drunken man, jerked upright. "We can't have that. Hey, server! Another one all around." He collapsed back into his simulated drunken stupor.

The *Hawkbat* personnel were more than happy to have the Nobrin brothers around. The boys from Agamar obligingly bought drinks for everyone in their vicinity and seemed oblivious to the barbs the spacemen aimed at them. Wedge had noticed some of the spacemen bringing dates to see the supposed men of fabled, idiotic Agamar. He felt like an animal in a cage viewing a procession of zoo-goers.

Wedge continued, "So when it's time to go home you don't all just hop in your TIE fighters and blast off for space."

Rondle smirked. "No. I'm an unarmed combat instructor. Partus over there, she's the one with the red face, is a navigator. That's someone who tells the ship how to get where it's going. Dewback Kord over there, he's a ship's mechanic. No, when it's time to leave, we all hop in a shuttle and go up."

"A shuttle? A *Lambda* shuttle? I was in one of those once."

Rondle nodded distractedly and accepted a drink refill from the droid server.

"Is yours the *Doran Star*? That's the one we were in."

Rondle fixed him with an aggravated stare. "Now, you just arrived from Agamar in whatever bucket brought you here. If that was our shuttle, too, how would we have gotten groundside before you got here?"

"Well, I don't know."

"No, ours are the *Hawkbat's Perch* and the *Hawkbat's Vigil.*"

"Oh. Hey, that's some kind of coincidence. Ending up with two shuttles with names kind of like your big ship's name."

Rondle covered his eyes with his hand.

"I wish Grinder were here," Phanan said. He tapped irritably away at the suite's terminal keyboard, cruising through layer after layer of helpful organizational screens.

Kell and Tyria were behind him, squeezed into an over-sized stuffed chair that would have easily accommodated two ordinary-sized people. Tyria said, "What's wrong? You don't seem to be encountering any security."

"No, but I can't just issue a command for the system to give me information on all biological agents being stored over at the Institute, not without raising some alerts, and I bet Grinder could. Plus, I have to deal with roommates making obnoxious snuggling noises while I'm hard at work." His tone was only half joking. He'd been annoyed ever since Tyria suddenly made her preference known.

Kell said, "We can go take a walk."

"You've already done your initial look at the Institute's exterior—hold it. News retrieval. Disease outbreaks. Sort by mechanisms. This won't be as comprehensive, but it'll tell us what has actually gotten out into the Storinal population. And whatever's been out there is sure to be in the Institute's vaults."

Tyria and Kell came up to lean over his shoulders.

"Bothan Redrash," Phanan said. "Too hit-or-miss. Plus, Grinder might catch it, and we'd never hear the end of it. Bandonian Plague, too severe. Blastonecrosis likewise, also disgusting. Big tourist planet like this has seen some odd ailments. Hey." He abruptly focused on one of the entries on the screen and brought it up to read more.

Kell leaned in closer. "What is it?"

"Bunkurd Sewer Disorder."

"Yecch," Tyria said. "Sounds disgusting."

"Not as bad as it sounds. A couple of centuries back, on Coruscant, the Bunkurd Corporation engineered a bacterium that does a better job of breaking down sewage for recycling. Something like a twenty percent improvement over previous bio-agents used for the same purpose. And believe me, Coruscant needs all the help it can get, that way. But if this bacteria gets in the human digestive system, it basically attacks what you eat as soon as you eat it, making it less nutritional . . . and giving you the equivalent of food poisoning. It takes a predictable amount of time to incubate and responds very well to standard medicines, so there's no danger of loss of life except in isolated areas."

"Sounds like our stuff," Kell said. "Now all we have to do is get some."

"I'm going to keep at the records for a while yet, in case there's something better. But, yes, this is encouraging."

The Howler turned out to be something less than a drinking establishment where local people vied for the affection of tourists who might have the interest and capital necessary to carry them offworld. It was, in fact, a dive. Its dim lights concealed the fact that the floors and tables were not cleaned as rigorously as they should be and that the locals offering themselves up for inspection weren't all as appealing as they hoped they were.

The place had flickering holoprojectors on all the walls, cycling between views of Storinal's gorgeous landscapes and cities, but the style of dress of the tourists in those views suggested they'd been recorded when most of the Wraiths were still unborn.

The Howler had one important advantage, however. On an Imperial-controlled world like Storinal, where nonhumans were second-class citizens on the occasions they were allowed any freedom at all, the Howler made no distinction between human and nonhuman clientele. Its operators obviously wanted every cred they could earn.

Falynn and Piggy were already at a back table, shrouded in shadow and occasional gouts of smoke from the establishment's kitchen, when Wedge and Kell arrived. Falynn looked at Wedge's garish costume and burst out in laughter.

"Don't blame me," Wedge said, "it's Face's fault." He laid his hat on the table and sat. "Have you swept?"

Piggy nodded. "All clean." His volume control was turned so low the others could barely make out the mechanical Basic words underneath his grunts.

"This place needs more than a sweeping," Kell said. "Sand-scouring, perhaps. A good laser vaporization of the top five millimeters of every exposed surface."

"I meant, swept for listening devices."

"I know."

Wedge took a last look around, but after Falynn's laughter had ceased drawing eyes, no one seemed to be paying them attention. "All right. Yokel Group has luck to report. First, we got some leads on the sources of the supplies *Hawkbat* carries around; we'll pass that information on to Intelligence. Second, we were thinking of hosting some sort of going-away feast for the *Hawkbat* crew and infecting them there, but we found out that the crew transits back and forth between the ship in two ship's shuttles. If we could put the disease agent on those shuttles, we'll probably infect a third of the crew. I think it would be easiest if it were some sort of airborne agent. We could put it in the air supply."

"Airborne." Kell frowned, concentrating, then pulled out his datapad. "I don't remember if Phanan said this Bee Ess Dee stuff is airborne . . . Ah. Yes, it is."

Falynn grimaced. "Bunkurd Sewer Disorder?"

Wedge said, "You've seen it?"

"I've *had* it. The few parts of Mos Eisley that actually have a sewer recycler use a Bunkurd Reclamation System. An old one. An old, broken-down, and occasionally leaky one. I was sick as a womp rat for a week." She shuddered.

Wedge said, "All of which means Plague Group has a contender."

Kell nodded. "We really want Grinder for the intrusion, though. I was hoping to be able to take him back to Scohar with me."

"It shouldn't be a problem," Wedge said. "Your landing

pad is officially cleared, correct? If you go there to do a little mechanical work today and leave in the company of a Bothan tourist . . ."

"Assuming we can both get back through security."

"Grinder will find a way. It's a matter of professional pride with him. Joyride Group?"

Falynn straightened. "Well, first, I know where your *Hawkbat* shuttles are. Bunker Twenty-two Aleph. I marked their location in case Kell wanted to blow them up or something."

"I don't *have* to blow up everything I see. I just like to."

"And there are TIE fighters all over. But if you want a site where you can count on TIEs being, and being hot, ready to fly, the spaceport keeps four in instant readiness, with pilots waiting in a standby room. These aren't the TIEs they use to escort incoming ships; I think they're for potential threats. The problem is, the little bunker where they're kept is one of the best guarded on the port."

Wedge asked, "How well guarded?"

"The bunker has at least two security doors I can see. I don't mean two outside doors. One outside door with a security station there, and an intermediary chamber, with a second security door inside. Maybe more."

"How do the TIE fighters exit?"

"A roof door retracts. Large enough to let two punch out at a time."

"How about security on top of that roof?"

She shrugged. "I haven't been up there yet. I'd want to wait for nightfall."

"Do it tonight. But first, have Donos retrieve his laser rifle from the smuggling compartment. I want him on station covering you. If you trigger an alarm—"

"Thanks."

"—he can give you the cover you need to escape." Wedge thought over his options. "All right. Here's the preliminary plan. Tonight, Plague Group, with Grinder, goes in and acquires the biological agents. Meanwhile, Falynn and Donos will do the preliminary test of the TIE bunker's security. If all goes well and the bunker looks like we can crack it, we do the rest tomorrow night.

"Tomorrow . . ." He counted off on his fingers to make sure he accounted for everyone. "Janson, Kell, Tyria, Phanan, Piggy, and Grinder will get into the *Hawkbat*'s shuttles and infect them. Janson will command that unit. It would also be good if you can find something to do to make it look like some other sort of mission if your presence is detected—some sort of theft, perhaps."

Kell nodded. "Got it."

"Myn will find a good, high station from which to provide sniper support to either unit. And Atril, Falynn, Face, and I will enter the TIE bunker and steal all four TIE fighters."

Falynn looked surprised. "All four?"

"Yes. Unless you can guarantee that the two we steal will both make it intact offworld."

She shook her head. "Guarantees are not my business. How do we get in?"

"Through the doors on top—when the TIE fighter leaves. We'll grab it when it returns."

"And how do we make sure a TIE fighter will leave when we want it to?"

Wedge smiled. "I communicate with Runt and ask him to strafe the spaceport."

Kell nodded. He turned it into Face's head bob. Falynn and Piggy joined him.

"Stop it," Wedge said.

Wedge left first, then Kell a couple of minutes later, to help minimize the number of people who would see the Wraiths together.

"Ready?" Piggy said.

Falynn nodded.

Then the music stopped and a spotlight pinned the two of them. Falynn rose and half drew her blaster. Piggy grabbed her hand, stopping her from completing the motion, dragging her back into her seat.

An amplified voice said, "The management of the Howler would like to congratulate Master and Mistress Wallowlot on the occasion of their fifth wedding marker!"

Patrons of the Howler offered scattered applause and a fair amount of laughter. A server swept up to deposit a pair of drinks. Falynn peered around the core of the spotlight beam to spot the man on the lighting board, controlling the beam, and Kell standing beside him. Kell offered her a big grin and a thumbs-up, then headed off for the door.

Then the beam was cut off and the bar patrons' attention returned to their respective drinks and pursuits.

Falynn glowered at the door through which Kell had fled. "That wasn't funny."

Piggy kept his translator voice low. "Why not?"

"Well . . . well . . . he might have compromised our identities."

"These aren't identities. We leave here in two minutes. You lose your wig and I resume my guard clothes and we're done with them."

"It still isn't funny."

"I think it is. Though we must have revenge on Kell, of course." But Falynn looked so unhappy he felt compelled to ask, "Why does this bother you so?"

"People will think I'm, I'm . . ." She stopped short and looked stricken. She didn't meet Piggy's eyes.

"That you're wed to a Gamorrean?"

"Honest, Piggy, it's not like that."

"I think it is." He kept his tone reasonable, insofar as his translator could express vocal tones and undercurrents. "Tell me the truth. Would this joke have been funny if you had been with, say, Face?"

"Piggy . . ."

"Please answer."

She took a deep breath. "I suppose it might have."

"So the difference is that it bothers you to have people think you might stray outside your species?"

"No . . ."

"Stoop so low as to become the mate of a Gamorrean?"

She winced, and he knew he had his answer. "I've offended you," she said.

"Not in the way you think, perhaps. But I can't help thinking that the reason you react with revulsion to the suggestion that we are wed is because of Gamorrean . . . lowness."

Finally she met his eyes. "I don't know what to say. I'm sorry."

"That's good enough for now." He drank his celebratory drink in a single long pull. "Ready to leave?"

"Yes."

"Since we are young marrieds, shall we hold hands?"

She grinned. "All right."

Once again in the black getup of her bodyguard identity, Falynn crouched in the nighttime shadow of a powered-down landskimmer. In the distance was the near wall of the TIE fighter ready bunker. Between her and that wall were forty long meters of empty duracrete, poorly lit but featureless enough to show clearly the passage of a human, even one dressed as she was. So far as she knew, pressure sensors could be planted under every meter of the open space around the bunker. But she'd manage to cross it if she had to crawl there across a span of four hours.

She was surprised at the determination she felt. It wasn't just a desire to complete this mission successfully. It was a need to stop being number two at everything.

With her talent for bypassing simple security systems, such as those that attempted to prevent theft of ground vehicles, she was the Wraiths' number-two security expert. She was number-two TIE pilot behind Wedge . . . and if Atril was the hot stick with a TIE that everyone said she was, Falynn was probably about to become number three. Her girlhood sneaking around Mos Eisley, making a living on whatever she could successfully steal, made her the number-two scout behind Tyria. Even Donos hadn't listened to Falynn, to her protests that he needed to live, until he'd heard the same facts from Tyria and others.

Never number one, not at anything. But maybe if she accomplished a few more things no Wraith had ever done, such as dragging those TIE fighters under her stolen skiff the other week, people would stop dismissing her as a second-rater.

She waited there half an hour, seeing one landskimmer arrive at the TIE ready bunker but dismissing the idea of trying to intercept it and jump aboard—the pilot of the small craft would certainly feel it bob when her weight came down on it.

But then, a few minutes later, a bulbous repulsorlift vehicle the size of a multiple-passenger tourist craft cruised in a leisurely fashion toward the bunker. Letters on the side read THOLAN'S COMESTIBLES, and it appeared as though the side panel swung up to become a metal awning.

A mobile restaurant of some sort. She'd seen them, not on Tatooine, but at the New Republic Academy. Late-night garrisons like the men of the TIE ready bunker needed to eat, too . . .

She gathered herself up as the silvery craft neared its closest approach to her. She took off into a fast sprint, catching up to the vehicle's squared-off rear, and found nothing there to hang on to but the rear door's hinges. She leaped up to grab the right top hinge with both hands; her feet swung free. But it wasn't far, and she wasn't stepping across sensor-laden duracrete.

As the repulsorlift food carrier approached the front of the bunker, it slowed, swung to starboard, and continued in sideways, its pilot evidently planning to present the side panel to the bunker's front door. Falynn pulled herself up, scrambling, her boots sliding off the rear panel as she struggled to gain purchase, and managed to pull herself atop the vehicle. When it settled to the ground just a meter from the front door, she stepped off it onto the near part of the bunker roof, then flattened herself on the bunker surface.

So far, so good. What if there were pressure sensors on top? She'd wait to find out. She froze where she was.

She heard the bunker's only exterior door hiss open. Metal swung into position with a clank. There was laughter among men working the late-night shift. Hissing of liquids, clanking of coins. Then, finally, the door and panel closed and the flying foodseller maneuvered away from the bunker.

And no one had come out to investigate an anomalous pressure reading on the roof. Excellent.

She clicked her comlink. A double-click answered her. She repeated the click to assure Donos that he hadn't responded to random garbage from someone else's sending unit.

Then, slowly, carefully, she inched herself up the bunker roof to the point where it graduated from duracrete to segmented metal, then slid leftward until she reached the bottom of one of the huge TIE fighter access doors; better to be at the bottom and less likely to be seen when the doors opened.

If they opened.

Please, she asked no one in particular, *let them have some sort of emergency. Don't let me wait here all night for nothing.*

"Tyria, look up," Grinder said into the mouthpiece of his headset. He sat at the desk in the Wraiths' suite in Scohar, and the picture on the portable terminal in front of him was the jittery view being broadcast from the camera in Tyria's cap. It currently showed the dressed stone rear wall of the Scohar Xenohealth Institute. The view rose along the wall and then became relatively still, now showing the awning and safety light above one of the windowless metal doors on that wall.

Phanan and Kell leaned over his shoulders to watch. Either of them could have executed the image-gathering march around the Institute, but Grinder pronounced them too memorable: Phanan was too mechanical, Kell too tall. Tyria, with her face dirtied, her hair combed out until it was frowsy, got barely a side look from any of the better-dressed late-night tourists on the Scohar streets.

Grinder cycled the picture through a variety of different sensory inputs. The picture on screen polarized, became a negative, and finally returned to a more normal view.

"There's definitely a viewer in the overhang, just like the others. Come on in; I've pegged our intrusion point, and we've got to acquire some materials before we go in."

Her voice, muted, came over the terminal's speaker. "Which is our intrusion point?"

"The only one without a viewer on it. The only one without a lock permitting exterior entry."

"The waste vent," she said.

"That's the one."

A persistent whine made Falynn open her eyes. Another annoying alarm. She reached out to swat it and encountered only metal.

That snapped her eyes open. She'd fallen asleep! She checked her chrono, determined that a couple of hours had passed, and realized that the whining noise was the sound of the metal doors powering up. She took a deep breath and readied herself.

With a jolt, the seam at the join of the two doors widened and the doors retracted in fitful jerks. Falynn looked scornfully at the door's edge as it retreated toward her. Servicing the motors and lubricating the rails would make the process smoother and quieter; she hoped the TIE fighters were kept up better than their hangar.

The door slid into place and locked with a distinctive clang of metal. She grabbed the edge and pulled herself partway up, just enough to see over the metal lip.

Below, a repair and hangar bay. She saw carts full of tools, grease-spattered duracrete flooring, four painted blue circles some eight meters in diameter on the floor with TIE fighters parked upon them. Two of the fighters had men beside them, a crew chief and a mechanic from the look of them. As she watched, the men hurriedly withdrew and the TIE fighters rose slowly, with the rumble of repulsorlift engines, into the air. Their smooth ascent brought them to Falynn's altitude and beyond; when they were a dozen meters above the bunker, they kicked in their twin ion engines and went screaming off into the night sky.

She shook her head. She wasn't here to watch them. She returned her attention to the remaining TIEs, to the men in the hangar. Those men only watched until the starfighters were out of sight; then one moved to a door on the east wall and another went to a wall-mounted control panel and flipped a switch there.

Abruptly the door jerked and began closing.

Falynn kept her grip on the door edge, letting the metal segment drag her upward while she kept her attention on the hangar. One of the mechanics approached a door on the south wall and waved his hand twice, very precisely, across the doorjamb above his head; the door slid open for him.

Then the door Falynn was holding on to was a mere half meter from closing against its counterpart. She let go, rather than have the closing doors crush her fingers, and tried to hold on by sheer friction.

It didn't work. When the door edges crashed into place, the jolt shook Falynn free and she began sliding. She grabbed around frantically for purchase, couldn't find it.

She rolled down the door, then down the roof of the bunker, then off the roof.

It was three long meters to the duracrete ground.

23

Kell, Tyria, and Phanan waited in the shadow of a metal sculpture that depicted, in abstract form, a dance of spirits in Storinal's mythological past. A block away, Grinder, dressed in black, huddled at the base of the Institute wall just by the hatch leading into the waste-disposal flue.

"Is he actually any good at this?" Phanan asked. "I've never seen his record. Never heard of him before joining the Wraiths."

Kell shrugged, realized no one could see it in the gloom. "I don't know. But he was good enough for Commander Antilles to pick him."

Phanan snorted. "Well, if he's as good a code-slicer and intrusion expert as he is a pilot, he's, well, mediocre. Sort of warms your heart, doesn't it? To know our lives are in the hands of a mediocre slicer?"

"I think," Tyria said, "that you left the profession of medicine because it's your nature to make everyone feel worse about everything."

"Ooh." Phanan's tone was admiring. "I've been skewered. I will now take seventeen hours to reevaluate my life."

The comlink popped, and Grinder's voice came across it: "Flue open. Come on in."

It was an unpleasant entryway.

The flue opened a full two meters above the sidewalk. In opening it, Grinder had spilled out a dozen blocks of compressed garbage, each a meter on a side and smelling of rotted organic material. By the time the other Wraiths arrived, Grinder had stacked them into crude steps leading up to the flue opening.

The flue itself smelled like the blocks, only worse. More concentrated. The Wraiths put on their air-filter masks, spattered with perfume by a thoughtful Tyria, before proceeding.

Phanan was first up the steeply angled metal shaft, not because he was at home with intrusion, but because he was in charge of the powerful spray with which he coated every visible surface of the flue. The spray was not antibacterial, antiviral, or antianything; it was a powerful and fast-setting sealant that he believed would prevent the transmission of any disease agents that might be clinging to the flue's surfaces.

They gave the stuff a mere minute to set, then began climbing. Once all four were in, they closed the door behind them. Grinder reset the latch, showing the other Wraiths how to unlatch it, and Phanan continued upward, spraying down the sides of the flue.

This shaft took them first into the hard-sided chamber that acted as a trash compressor. A single ill-timed command to the building computer would cause the sides to come together, squeezing the Wraiths into new cubes of garbage, but no such command came. The hatch out of the top of the chamber led to a larger vertical shaft into which trash apparently poured from every floor of the Institute. "See all the ash?" Phanan said. "Most of the accesses into this shaft are through incinerators. So dangerous wastes will be nice safe ash when they're dropped for disposal."

One floor up, a hatch gave them access into a small mess featuring a table for six and a food-delivery wall unit.

By agreement, Tyria took point; she was to stop whenever she reached a portal or change in flooring so Grinder could check it for sensors. Grinder was second, with Phanan following and Kell bringing up the rear.

The mess gave way to a hallway. The third door down opened into a terminal room, and Grinder insisted that they crowd into the small chamber so he could try to slice into the building records.

Despite Phanan's earlier assertions of his mediocrity, the task only took Grinder a few minutes. "Level A-Four," said Grinder, "that's Aboveground Four for those of you who haven't been paying attention to Storinal nomenclature, is where all test subjects and experiments are kept. A sort of tiered security system. Outermost of three tiers is basically a warehouse of animal subjects, animals not especially dangerous. The middle circle holds more dangerous creatures, like toxic reptiles and ex-doctors from Rudrig."

Phanan muttered, "Much the same thing, really."

"The inner chamber is where they store what we want. Kell, you'll be interested to learn that there's a plasma bomb array there. The sensors detect a leak and it may trigger—the Institute's way of keeping the world safe from plagues."

Kell said, "Can any of your intrusion efforts trigger the bomb?"

"Sure. If I'm sloppy."

"Wonderful."

Grinder stood. "Let's go. There's no time like the dark of night."

Getting up two floors by a back stairwell was not difficult. Slightly less easy was penetrating the security door from that stairwell into the secure outer circle, but this took Grinder no more time than getting through the trash hatch.

The outer-tier warehouse was a large area occupying most of the fourth floor. Some areas of it were well lit, thick with cages holding live, alert animals from all over the galaxy; their noise level increased as they became aware of the Wraiths moving in the chamber, but the human guard assigned to the floor did no more than approach them and shush them. The Wraiths stayed low, then moved away, deeper into the chamber's more shadowy regions.

Pausing against a stack of plastic-sheathed boxes, Grinder was startled to feel something scratching—actively scratching—at the other side of the surface he was leaning against. Peering down, he saw that he was propping himself up against a stack of small containers labeled STORINI GLASS PROWLER. The picture on the container showed a translucent arthropod that walked upon two legs and apparently seized its prey with the other two in a nearly humanoid fashion. Whatever was inside one of those containers was trying to claw its way out, hence the scratching sensation.

He allowed a slow smile to spread across his features. An exotic insect from a faraway world—he could use such a thing. Glancing around to make sure none of his companions was watching, he used a fine set of scissors to cut through the plastic netting holding the cartons together, then slipped the carton with the active inhabitant into his tool bag.

"So," Falynn said, "I got about four hours of sleep. Two just snoozing on top of the bunker, and two lying in a heap along the south wall."

Janson whistled. "And no one spotted you."

"I assume not. I'm not in prison." She shrugged, then winced at the pain the maneuver caused her.

Atril scowled at her. "Be still." She returned to painting a healing agent onto the largest of the cuts on Faly's forehead.

Janson continued, "How did you get out?"

"When I woke up, it was still a couple of hours before dawn. The little garrison's personal vehicles were all lined up on the north wall, and I figured that they wouldn't put pressure sensors along the wall where all their own people would move all the time, just out in the open area around. So I just walked around, picked the biggest of the groundskimmers, and picked the lock to its storage compartment. Got a little more rest there, too, under a blanket and some boxes before his shift ended and he came out. He stopped in at some place to eat and I crawled out there, the glorious image you see before you." Falynn's hair was plastered to her head by sweat, she had scrapes on her forehead, and she walked, when they let her, like a woman who'd avoided a fall's worth of broken bones but stocked up on bruises and muscle pulls by way of compensation.

Janson said, "I'll get your information to Wedge. And you get some real sleep." He rose.

Atril rose and added, "The painkillers should start firing off pretty soon. You'd better be horizontal when they do." She shrugged. "Sorry I can't do more. I wish Dr. Phanan were here."

"It's fine," Falynn said.

Janson and Atril left her quarters, but Donos lingered, kneeling beside her chair. "You're sure you're all right?"

"I'm going to stab the next person who asks me that." But she kept her tone light and there was no sting in her words.

"You scared me to death. Falling and not moving. I was getting a retrieval team in position when you reached me via comlink."

"I'm sorry." She reached out to stroke his chin, felt the harsh stubble of a day's worth of beard there. And she began to laugh.

"What's funny?"

"That mustache. You look like a complete idiot."

"Oyah." He bobbed his head in an exaggerated nod and kissed her on the third bob. Then he rose. "Like they said, sleep. We've got more planned tonight."

"Someone else gets to climb." A wave of tiredness washed across her. She half rose, unwilling to straighten completely up and suffer the muscle pulls such a motion entailed, and crawled onto her bed. "G'night."

Plague Group returned from Scohar tired but triumphant. They met with the mustachioed idiots of Yokel Group in Wedge's hostel quarters.

"Effortless, as I predicted," Grinder said. He clapped his

hands and rubbed them together. "My companions, inspired by my sheer versatility and competence, themselves showed acceptable performance—"

Kell glared at him and he shut up. "We got in," Kell said, "we got out with the goods, and the only thing we did that would indicate someone was there was spray a sealant all over the inside of a trash flue. I even reconnected the plasma bomb."

Wedge came upright. "The what?"

"They had a high-temperature device set to trigger if any of the disease agents breached their security seal and threatened to escape the complex. The thing would have instantly incinerated the Institute and a few city blocks around it— which I assume they consider an appropriate measure to keep some of those diseases in check." Kell shrugged. "I bet that little safety feature is a secret to their neighbors. Anyway, I disabled the array so Grinder could foul up if he liked—"

"Never happen," Grinder said, his voice a growl.

"And then, once he was very, very sure everything was safe, reconnected it."

"Where's the plague?" Wedge asked.

Phanan held up two plastic cylinders, each no larger than a standard comlink.

"Will those . . . containers . . . hold?"

The doctor nodded. "Yes. But to be safe, I'll be inoculating all of us and the rest of the *Night Caller* crew against these little bugs. Kell is going to help me mount these containers in little detonation units, nothing explosive, they'll puncture the sides with a needle. All we have to do is get them into the shuttles' air-circulation gear."

"Good." Wedge leaned back and tried to relax. "We go tonight, then. The sooner we're offworld, the sooner we can get out of these mustaches."

Tyria quirked a smile. "Not to mention the lavender short pants."

"*Not* to mention them, Flight Officer Sarkin." Wedge pulled his wide-brimmed hat down over his eyes. "Or else."

.   .   .   .

They drove at a slow pace toward Bunker 22-Aleph—slow so Piggy, pacing them on foot, could keep up. Not that the Storinal-made refueling and maintenance skimmer was a particularly speedy craft, but it could still outrun a fully armed and armored Gamorrean.

The two human guards and one leather-clad Gamorrean at the bunker's main entrance came on attention as they neared. In the skimmer's cab, Kell fingered his blaster to make sure it was still snug in its holster. Beside him, Tyria gave him an amused look and refrained from doing the same. Back in the skimmer's main bed, hidden among the refueling hoses and swing-out platforms containing diagnostic gear, Janson, Phanan, and Grinder would be making sure the blankets and covers over them were still tied down tight . . . and making sure their blasters were charged to full.

Kell kept a bored expression on his face and brought the skimmer to a stop about a meter from the point at which he was sure the guards would bring their weapons to bear.

The senior human guard stepped forward. "Orders."

Kell handed him his forged datacard. "That's *work* orders, not orders. We don't take orders. Not like spaceport security boys." He gave Tyria a grin he knew to be irritating and cocksure.

"These shuttles aren't due to be serviced until the morning," the guard said. "They depart tomorrow afternoon."

"It's a slack period," Kell said. It was true; otherwise they wouldn't have been able to find and temporarily steal a maintenance skimmer. There had been others lined up, unused. "Control wants us to get a little ahead before the work piles up tomorrow."

The guard gave him a sour look and stepped back to slip the card into the door reader.

Now, their first test. It would have been far too much work to forge a proper set of work orders allowing them to work on the *Hawkbat*'s shuttles—a set that would get proper authorization from the spaceport's main computer. It would have been a mission all by itself to get through that computer's defenses; security on that system was extremely tight to keep malicious code-slicers from doing things like rerouting cargo craft to pirates' landing zones or causing craft to crash.

So Grinder had tried to run completely around the wall of defenses. Just after nightfall this evening, he had climbed to the hangar's roof and sliced into the little retransmitter there. Now, the module he'd planted in that comm device would be intercepting the request for authorization of Kell's codes, waiting an appropriate amount of time, and sending back the authorization . . . all without bothering the spaceport computer. The Wraiths had no plans to retrieve the module; it would interfere with no other requests and would let the retransmitter operate normally. It would probably not be found until the next time the transmitter was serviced, whether days, weeks, or months from now.

The guard returned. "You're clear to work. Under the eye of a spaceport guard."

Kell gestured toward Piggy. "I thought that was what Smiley there was for."

"Right." The guard waved at the two remaining at the hangar doors, and a moment later those doors were rolling open. Maintaining his air of boredom, Kell moved the skimmer through and Piggy paced them in. The Gamorrean guard said something in its own language as they passed and Piggy grunted a reply.

As the doors shut behind them, Kell maneuvered the skimmer to be directly beside the cockpit of one of the shuttles. When it was in place, he lowered the landing struts and shut off the repulsors. Now, the craft would be braced for its mechanical duties. He and Tyria clambered out of the cab and into the aft machinery, Kell swinging a diagnostic module up against the hull of the *Hawkbat's Perch*.

The others didn't emerge from hiding, but Grinder's voice did. "I'm reading one visual-only scanner, up somewhere in the northwest corner."

Kell resisted the urge to look. "Can you disable it?"

"From here? Don't be stupid. Wait a second. Unless I miss my guess . . ."

Kell and Tyria chimed in together, "Which never happens . . ."

"Shut up. Unless I miss my guess, it's piping its data straight through that same retransmitter . . . Yes! Give me a second. Everybody hold still. I'm recording a few seconds of its transmission . . . looping it . . . blending the seam. Now all I have to do is transmit it constantly to my module on the retransmitter and have the module hold the real feed . . . Done!" Grinder emerged, looking sweaty but triumphant.

Janson and Phanan came out from beneath their respective hiding places. Janson gestured to the side of *Hawkbat's Perch*. "Why isn't that panel open yet?"

"Because we don't actually have authorization, remember?" Kell felt, once more, the faint surprise that came when Janson's sudden arrival failed to cause him to tense up. "I need Grinder to run a bypass on it."

"And on the ramp control."

Kell shook his head. "It occurred to me as we were driving over here that we can just put the stuff in the air intake scoop. They'll be running on real air for the first few thousand meters, until they can't ram it fast enough in to supply adequate air pressure. That's when they switch to canned air." He smiled. "We don't even have to break in."

Phanan cocked his head to listen. "We read, *Joyride*." With his built-in equipment, he didn't have to hear the buzzing of his comlink and bring the thing on-line; he was always receiving. "Good news, *Joyride*. Plague out." He looked at the others. "Runt is counting down for his run from the moon. If everything goes well, he'll finish his terrain-following run and be here in about an hour."

"That's our time limit," Kell said. "Don't forget, we actually have to service these shuttles."

Joyride Group couldn't rely on the help of a passing vendor's skimmer. With four people needing transport and a narrow time frame, they had to make something happen.

Of all the vehicles crowding Revos's spaceport, none were as prevalent as cargo-hauling skimmers, used for transporting everything from standard bulk containers weighing several tons to piles of passengers' personal bags. It wasn't difficult to find one unattended, wasn't even difficult to get it running and move it off a few dozen meters into the deeper shadow thrown by an unoccupied hangar. But what they were planning next would be tricky.

"How's it coming?" Wedge asked. He and Face were guards on this operation, keeping blasters at the ready and attention on their surroundings; they didn't often look back at what Falynn was doing.

"How do you think? Slow!"

Wedge heard an electronic crackle and a curse from her. "The trick," she continued, "is to fry the circuits controlling braking without wiping out everything else on the same board. Then I've got to do the vehicle programming you want. Tricky stuff. The jump at the end, the self-erasure, and the data you want left behind—well, I wish Grinder were here."

Wedge managed a smile. If Grinder knew how much his particular skills were appreciated and needed right now, he'd be insufferable. He managed to ride pretty close to insufferable most of the time.

Atril spoke up. "I handle ship's programming all the time, particularly navigation. Let me do a rough cut on the program and you can fix it up in less time than it would take you to do it from scratch."

"Please."

Wedge's comlink beeped. He held it up to his ear, heard the message, said, "Thanks, Six." He turned back to the others. "Thirty minutes and counting."

"We have a problem," Phanan said.

Kell lowered the side panel on *Hawkbat's Vigil*. "Not much of one. We're done." He was covered with sweat and, after only half an hour's work, tired. On a job like this, there were usually two to four trained mechanics and half an hour to an hour per vehicle serviced; he'd done it in half the usual time with a crew of willing but inexperienced hands.

"Nine says there's a maintenance skimmer coming this way," Phanan said.

Janson cursed. "Let's move out. We'll bluff them, and if that doesn't work, we'll tear out of here like Falynn in a skiff."

Kell paused as he was entering the cockpit. Lashed to the bed in back were three plastic containers, each about the size of an R2 unit, that hadn't been there before. "What are those?"

Tyria grinned. "Our reason for being here. Remember? We're stealing something? Those are recreational holos someone had piled up for loading onto the shuttles. They'll figure we're black marketeers or something."

"I forgot."

"You had plenty to do."

Janson's voice came from underneath his blanket. "Would you two stop smooching up and get us out of here?"

Kell positioned his skimmer to exit. The argument had already started outside, with some words drifting in around the edges of the steel doors: ". . . tell you, you're already in there." ". . . obviously not, since we just got here."

Kell nodded to Piggy, who slapped the wall control. The doors ground their way open. The two nearly identical maintenance skimmers faced each other a mere four meters apart.

The lead guard pointed to Kell's skimmer. "As I told you."

The driver of the other skimmer leaned out of his cockpit. "Hey! Who are you?"

"I'm Botkins." Kell glanced again at the name stenciled on the gloves lying in the cockpit. "I'm standing in for Laramont."

"Laramont's in the cafeteria, waiting to start his shift!"

"Dammit! They told me he was sick. So he's going to be servicing the shuttles?"

"No, I am!"

"Wrong. I just did."

"Listen, scab, I'm not going to let you cost me my piece-work for the night." The mechanic clambered out of his cockpit. He was nearly as tall as Kell and had as much muscle, though a fair amount of it was swathed in fat. Tools swung on his belt as he straightened up.

Kell waited until the man reached the window of his cockpit. "Hey," he said, "let's do this like gentlemen. You know, I might not have done such a good job of gauging the hydraulics."

The mechanic scowled at him. "So?"

"So, you scrub my work as not up to spec. You get credit for the whole job but only have to redo the work you don't like. But you don't formally log the complaint, so my record stays clean. That way, you get your pay and I still log the time, so I can keep working toward getting a permanent post here. What do you say?"

The mechanic considered it. "No. I'm just going to scrub your work as not up to spec . . . and report it that way. Right now."

Kell glanced at Tyria. A call like that to Central would probably alert the spaceport operators to the unauthorized maintenance job they'd just done. He returned his attention to the mechanic and said, in an overly reasonable tone, "Well, now. That's my job vaporized. My career at Revos Spaceport. If you're going to take that from me, I think I ought to have something from you."

The mechanic twisted his lip in an approximation of a contemptuous smile. "Such as what?"

"Such as about fifteen square centimeters of your skin, a liter of your blood, and whatever you have left of a reputation." Kell threw open his cockpit door, catching the mechanic off guard and hurling him to the duracrete.

Kell stepped out over him, took a couple of steps to the side, and stretched. He caught the chief guard's eye. "I say I break three of his bones before he gives up."

24

The cargo skimmer swung around to the north of the TIE ready bunker, then angled in straight toward the building. It did not build up speed; it maintained a rate just over a walking pace.

Wedge, Atril, Falynn, and Face clustered at the bow of the thing, braced for the mild collision to come. "I forgot to ask," Wedge said. "Have you ever done anything like this before? The surge at the end?"

Falynn grinned. "Sure. Tried it with a canyon jump back home."

"How'd it turn out?"

"Broken collarbone."

"Just checking."

By now, the sensors in the TIE bunker would show the oncoming vehicle. Guards might even be leaving by the south entrance to come around and see what was happening. The timing had to be perfect.

They were thirty meters away, twenty, ten—then they hit the bunker wall, a bump that merely caused them to sway forward, momentarily off balance.

Falynn counted, "Three, two, one—"

The skimmer's engines whined as they overrevved, and suddenly the craft bounced an extra two meters into the air.

The four jumped forward as they felt the skimmer drop from under them. They landed, awkward, on the bunker roof. Atril immediately twisted and started to fall back into the skimmer, but Wedge and Face caught her flailing arms and tugged her toward them.

Already there were the sounds of oncoming feet. The four flattened themselves as quietly as they could and hugged the roof.

Then there were voices: "You there! What do you think you're doing?"

"Wait a second. There's nobody in it."

"Check under it."

Laughter. "That'd be funny. Someone being squashed under a skimmer."

The other voice became resentful. "You just think it's funny because it's never happened to *you*."

"That's right. Never has, never will. Smell that? It's like an engine bearing has burned out." The man's voice changed. "Control Aleph-One, it's a cargo skimmer. It's unoccupied. It may be a drifter. Jotay's checking out the autopilot."

"I am?"

"You are."

The other man sighed.

They were silent for a couple more minutes, then Jotay said, "It looks like it was slaved to another skimmer, part of a cargo convoy, and its memory was not correctly purged. It would have shot off as soon as it was activated. Maybe even still be receiving signals from the convoy master."

"Well, flush the program and take it back where it belongs."

"Why me?"

"Privilege of rank, sonny. I was hired three days before you."

Wedge heard the skimmer power up and go gliding off, its driver still complaining. The other man wandered back toward the bunker's south face, chuckling and muttering to himself.

Falynn chuckled, too. She whispered, "He's going to have a fine time parking that thing with the brakes not working."

Kell's opponent stood, his face red, twisted with anger.

"I really ought to stop you," the guard said.

"Well, you can do that, or you can get your bets down." Then Kell twisted to avoid the mechanic's charge. He swatted the man's outstretched hand away, continued the twist into a full twirl, and gave the man a slap to the back of his head as he passed. The mechanic staggered, off balance from the extra momentum, and went to his knees.

The mechanic came up with a belt hydrospanner in his hand. This wasn't a small, around-the-house tool, but a heavy metal implement two-thirds the length of a man's arm.

Kell dropped his pose of aggressive amiability and assumed a proper fighting posture, left foot forward, hands up, weight balanced. He'd hoped that potentially deadly weapons wouldn't enter the mix. He'd obviously hoped in vain.

The mechanic charged again, but something in his body language told Kell he was changing tactics. Instead of sidestepping, Kell held his pose, ready to stop-thrust or body-check the man. It was the mechanic, though, who stopped short, swinging the hydrospanner in a horizontal arc that would have connected solidly with Kell's rib cage if he'd duplicated his earlier move.

Kell twisted aside—and the head of the spanner hit him a glancing blow, an impact that kicked the breath out of him and sent him staggering back. He thought he felt a rib give way.

The mechanic, confident now, followed up instantly with another swing.

Kell didn't try to dodge this one. Despite the pain in his left side, he twisted, adding energy to the punch that connected with the mechanic's wrist. Kell felt and heard something break in the wrist. The hydrospanner flew free, clanking into the side of Kell's maintenance skimmer.

Kell followed through with a left that rocked the mechanic's head, then spun around in a kick. He tried to make it look more awkward than it had to, but gave it full force when it connected against the mechanic's jaw. The man uttered a grunt and fell hard to the duracrete.

Kell turned to the guard. "Call this in. He just assaulted me with intent to kill. My career here may be shot, but I'm taking his with me. Get me Central." He suddenly felt drained and was having a hard time breathing.

The guard shrugged and moved to comply. Tyria took a breath, preparing to jump in with an objection, but the mechanic's partner, who'd exited his skimmer during the fight, spoke up first. "Wait. Please."

The guard paused.

Kell said, "Why?" He tried to bring his labored breathing under control. It wasn't working. Still, that added to his act, made it easy for him to simulate fury.

"He's a good man. Just tense. Let him sleep this off, I'll redo the servicing on the shuttles, nobody will report anything, you keep your job, he keeps his job—what do you say?"

Kell took a couple of breaths, as deep as he could bear, and turned to Tyria.

She shrugged. He could read worry for him in her eyes, but her tone was light. "Might as well. Fewer reports."

The guard in charge said, "Fewer reports." He made it sound like a goal of considerable merit.

Kell gave a reluctant nod. "Fewer reports. Sounds good." He moved back to his cockpit door. "I'm doing him a favor, you know that?"

The mechanic's partner, already struggling to pull the unconscious man upright, said, "Yeah, sure." He could not have sounded less interested.

A moment later Plague Group's maintenance skimmer was once again in motion.

Tyria asked, "Are you all right?"

"I want Phanan to tape me up as soon as possible. But I don't think it's anything serious. As long as I don't do too much bending."

"Well, you bought us the time we needed."

Kell checked his chrono. *Just give us thirty minutes,* he thought. *Then, it won't matter how many reports they call in.*

Runt's attack came with such swiftness that even the Wraiths, who'd timed his arrival nearly to the last second, were caught off guard by it.

His X-wing was suddenly over the spaceport, its engines screaming like some mythical demon, its laser cannons blasting at unoccupied portions of duracrete. Men and women on the field ran in the direction of any cover. Some ran to dive into the shadow of refueling tanks. Wedge shook his head as he watched them.

A moment later the shrill keen of an Imperial air-raid alert filled the air. Bunkers all over the spaceport went dark as their occupants or central computers obeyed emergency blackout procedures.

Runt passed over the field, then turned around for another run. His lasers targeted a luggage skimmer and ignited its fuel cell, blowing bags and cases over a fifty-meter radius.

Wedge dimly heard a grinding alarm noise from below. Then the bunker's top door motors whined and the doors began to retract.

He peered through the crack between them. He could see tiny lights below him: green, red, yellow, white, the myriad glows associated with computer gear. But the little TIE fighter hangar was otherwise dark, its occupants also observing normal blackout procedures.

As he'd expected. As he'd counted on.

He moved with the leading edge of the door. As soon as the doors were locked open, he placed his grappling hook where the door edge met the duracrete roof. A few meters over, Falynn would be doing the same at the other door.

With a chilling engine roar Wedge would always associate with the Empire, two of the TIE fighters below lit up their engines, silhouetting themselves with ionic engine wash, and then leaped up into the sky, not bothering with repulsorlifts for initial takeoff.

Wedge gripped the rope attached to his hook and rolled over into the darkness.

Before Runt could make his third pass over the spaceport, a circular slab of duracrete sixty meters from the *Narra* rose from the ground. Beneath it was a ball-shaped gun emplacement, an open-air metal framework with a gunner's chair and a hemispherical durasteel shield from which protruded four linked laser cannons. The rig rose on a metal column, ten meters into the air, fifteen meters, then rotated to track Runt's X-wing.

Kell, at the pilot's seat of the *Narra*, swore and hit his comm. "Six, we have a ground emplacement setting up for your return. Leader reports the roof opening; you're about to have company." He flipped the switch to light up the shuttle's engines and guns.

"We copy, Five." Runt's X-wing heeled over and headed west.

"If you do that," Janson said, "we're going to have to scramble out of here without our TIE fighter support."

"What do you recommend? We sit back and watch them flame Runt?" All the shuttle's occupants heard the roar of the TIE fighters leaving their bunker. "Since that emplacement is taller than the trees, Runt's going to be within its line of sight for a couple of klicks at least—"

Janson shook his head. "Trust your squadmates, Kell."

As if to punctuate his words, a brilliant needle of laser energy leaped from the top of the spaceport's main terminal building and hit the gun emplacement. Kell saw the laser burn through the chair, through the gunner's body. The gunner slumped and the emplacement continued its rotation, no longer tracking a target.

"Donos," Kell said. "Sorry. I forgot."

Two TIE fighters emerged from the target bunker and headed west in pursuit of Runt.

Tyria said, "I'm going out to cover Donos's arrival."

Janson nodded. "Be careful."

Kell added, "Do what the man says."

* * *

The bunker's doors clanged down into place. The crew chief on duty called out, "Back to normal," and switched on the light.

Two black-clad commandos, a man and a woman, their faces covered in dark masks, stood in the hangar, covering the mechanics with blaster pistols. Another two were already going through the door into the office portion of the bunker—somehow they knew the gesture that told the movement sensor to open the door.

The male commando said, "Not *exactly* normal. Don't make a move."

Face entered the bunker's command center, his pistol out and at the ready, Atril just behind him.

The officer on duty was turning away from a security monitor and drawing his blaster as they entered. Face snapped off a shot and missed. Atril's shot was accurate— gruesomely accurate; it caught the man full in the face before he had a chance to fire. He dropped to the polished and waxed duracrete floor, his hair on fire.

Face gestured to the other person in the room, a gray-haired uniformed woman who was already raising her hands. "Put that out before it sets off the fire alarms." He was annoyed to hear his voice try to crack.

Silent, she complied, taking a jacket from the back of a chair and using it to smother the smoky fire.

Face managed to put a little more authority into his voice. "Now. What's the standard recall code for the TIE fighters who just left?"

The woman, her task complete, rose to her feet and put her hands up again. "I don't know."

Face glanced over his shoulder at Atril. "Kill her." He saw her eyes widen and gave her the tiniest shake of his head.

The bunker officer said, "Sakira. S-A-K-I-R-A." Her lip turned downward. "It's his daughter's name."

Face moved to the main control board. Its primary monitor showed the red blip of Runt's X-wing outbound, two blue blips of the TIE fighters closing rapidly upon it. He typed SAKIRA into the keypad and sent the code.

Almost immediately a man's voice came over the comm speaker: "Sun Leader to Base, please confirm last transmission."

Face waved the surviving bunker operator to the panel. She approached, stiff-legged, but her face twitched and she did not use the comm. "If I confirm the code, they'll know it's wrong," she said, her tone sullen.

Face sighed, then keyed the comm. He kept his voice low, making it as bland as possible. "Confirm recall Sakira," he said.

"Base, copy. Returning home. He had him, Base. Why the change?"

"New orders. Come on in."

"Base, will comply."

Face discovered he was sweating. Comm distortion would help a bit, but this was Imperial equipment; its distortion was less severe than New Republic comm gear. If that pilot had any suspicions, he could be calling the spaceport's control center or another fighter base even now . . .

But the image on the sensor screen showed the TIE fighter blips looping around and returning.

Face keyed his comlink. "Six, they're breaking off. Go to terrain-following mode and ease your way back."

"Eight, we copy."

Atril led the female officer back into the hangar. Face sat at the main control board. For the few minutes, it was a waiting game.

Alarms sounded all over the spaceport. A detachment of guards reached the gun emplacement and used a remote to bring it down to ground level. They dragged the gunner's remains out of the chair's remains and another trooper took his place. Kell hurriedly powered down the *Narra*'s systems so a sensor sweep would not detect them.

More troopers were running around on the duracrete near the spaceport's main terminal bunker. Looking for Donos, Kell knew. If the sniper was on top of his game, he'd have rappelled down the side of the bunker moments after killing the gunner. Tyria would know where he was, but he dared not use his comlink to reach her; he might interrupt her at a critical time.

Feet clattered up the shuttle's ramp and abruptly Tyria and Donos were peering into the barrels of Janson's and Kell's ready weapons. "All clear," Tyria said.

Kell sheathed his blaster and raised the ramp. "Anything from Joyride Group?"

Janson, in the copilot's seat, shook his head.

The TIE fighters were slowing to hover over the open doors of the bunker when the comm board sounded again. "Control Aleph-One, this is Central. Why did you break off pursuit of Target X-3085?"

Face grimaced and activated his microphone. "Central, the target's escape profile suggested an ambush. It was not in an escape posture. This indicated to me that it was leading our fighters toward a superior force."

"You decided that on your own initiative, Aleph-One?"

"That's correct, sir."

"Interesting choice, Aleph-One. You know it's subject to review."

"Yes, sir. I stand by it, sir."

"Very well. Your men coming in safe?"

"Two eyeballs incoming hot and normal."

"Two what?"

Face shut off his mike and swore to himself. Then he switched it back on. "Uh, *eyeballs,* sir. That's Rebel talk. I thought you'd be amused."

"Aleph-One, recite your day code."

Face switched the mike off and yanked it free of its housing, then keyed his comlink. "Leader, we've been made."

.   .   .

The two TIE fighters descended to a smooth landing. Wedge kept his cockpit dark, though his engines were hot, and waited.

The TIEs' access hatches did not open. A moment later their engines lit up again and they roared skyward.

"Three, fire!" Wedge had a confirmed lock on his targeting computer as soon as the port-side TIE fighter rose over him. He triggered his lasers. The blast shook his grounded vehicle but hit the ascending starfighter dead-on, hulling it. The TIE fighter continued upward only another twenty or thirty meters, slowing, then stalled and dropped.

Falynn, in her TIE fighter, fired twice. Her second shot hit her target where its spherical body met its starboard wing pylon. The blast didn't sever the pylon, but chopped halfway through it. The vehicle's next maneuver, a dizzying spin to the side, did the rest, tearing the pylon completely free. The fighter spun out of sight.

Wedge's target came straight down back into the bay. Wedge instictively leaned away from the descending, burning mess. It smashed down right next to his vehicle, showering his TIE fighter with half-melted debris. His starfighter shook from the impact. "Gray Eight, Gray Thirteen, I'm afraid you're on foot; your rides are vaped."

"Acknowledged. *Narra,* can you swing by for a quick pickup?"

Wedge heard Kell's voice: "We're already in motion."

"Three, Leader. We're airborne." Wedge nudged his control yoke and was suddenly roaring skyward.

The replacement gunner swung around to try to track the rogue TIE fighters from Bunker Aleph-One. Then Central was back in his headphones: "There's a *Lambda*-class shuttle moving sixty meters west of your position. We think they're part of the same crew. Target and fire."

The gunner almost had the lead TIE in his brackets, but the pilot was good, very good, constantly juking around, then dropping nearly to ground level to roar along behind a bunker or bulk cruiser. "I'm a little busy here," he said. "You're sure the shuttle is the primary target?"

"They're not going to have their most important people on the starfighters, idiot. Do as you're told."

The gunner sighed, then rotated his cupola around to cover the shuttle, which was moving on repulsorlifts more or less toward the TIE ready bunker.

Toward two dark-clad figures running toward it. The shuttle's boarding ramp was opening.

He bracketed the shuttle's midsection—then heard the oncoming roar of a TIE fighter. A glance over his shoulder showed the starfighter swooping at him, lining up for a shot—

He leaped clear. He leaped out over fifteen meters of fall above a hard duracrete landing, and before he was halfway down he saw the cupola explode under brilliantly accurate laser fire from the TIE fighter.

Then he hit, and disobedient shuttles and starfighters were no longer his problem.

Though a squadron of TIE fighters left the city of Scohar and followed them to the outer planet where *Night Caller* waited, their lead was such that they were able to dock all four craft, orient themselves out-system, and go to hyperspace before their pursuit reached them.

They gathered in the lounge for drinks and congratulations, Atril still, for the moment, a fellow commando instead of a member of the bridge crew.

"Here's to everyone making it off that rock," Kell said, and everyone joined him in a "Hear, hear." "Though Falynn and I managed to get slightly busted up, mostly through our own dumbness."

Falynn said, "Hear, hear."

Wedge noticed Janson's expression; the man seemed pensive. "What is it, Wes?"

"Well, I was just thinking. We've really set ourselves on a new mission and have a long way to go."

"What mission?"

"We've now stolen a Corellian corvette and two TIE fighters. That's good, but it's not enough. I think we should steal at least one of every type of ship in use by the Imperial Navy or the warlords."

Wedge smiled. "Ending with a certain Super Star Destroyer called *Iron Fist?*"

"That would round out the collection, don't you think?"

25

Night Caller and *Hawkbat* made rendezvous at the appointed date, in a system whose dim orange sun sustained no life on any of its seven planets. *Hawkbat*'s captain, Bock Nabyl, apologized for not being able to meet with Captain Darillian face-to-face, and explained that an unseemly illness was spreading through the crew. Quarantine measures were in force. Captain Darillian claimed to understand fully.

So representatives of both crews, working in vacuum suits, transferred a set of stealth satellites from *Hawkbat*'s main cargo hold to *Night Caller*'s belly hold, then both ships went their separate ways, their crewmen never having seen one another in the flesh.

A day later *Night Caller* put in at the Todirium system, whose bleak third planet was home to a colony mining iron and refining durasteel. The corporate computer system coordinating activities worldwide was not easy prey for Grinder's skills at slicing, but the corporate chief, speaking to Face's Captain Darillian, asked whether *Night Caller* wanted to pick up the latest load of refined alloys. Since previous stops had not indicated that the corvette had taken on such loads, Face told the man that Zsinj would send a cargo hauler for the alloys . . . but he insisted on sending "Lieutenant Narol" down to examine the cargo. Face reported back hours later with the precise location of Zsinj's warehouses.

"This will be a standard stoop-and-shoot mission," Wedge told his pilots. "With one difference. We know we're going to be recorded. We know because we're setting out the spy satellites ourselves. So as long as we'll be giving Zsinj information, we want it to be the worst information possible.

"Cubber, I want you to repaint all the X-wings with Rogue Squadron's colors."

The mechanic looked unhappy. "If there's anything I hate worse than redoing a bad job—"

"It's redoing a good one. I know. And it gets worse, because immediately after the mission, you'll have to strip all that paint and reapply the Wraith Squadron colors." Wedge shrugged. "Or we can let Grinder do the repainting and put you in his cockpit for the mission."

"No, thanks. I'll paint."

Wedge continued, "So, we unload and situate the satellites. Piggy, I want you and Grinder to calculate the most likely point where an X-wing squadron would enter the system and what their most likely avenue of attack against the planet would be. We'll set up the satellites along that path and get the best possible images for Zsinj and Trigit. Since we'll be doing so much work in vacuum suits, I want Face and Phanan in X-wings flying cover, just in case of trouble. Phanan, you can use mine. As long as you treat it well."

"I'll try not to spill my lomin-ale all over it."

"How professional of you. Then, we load up the X-wings, activate the satellites, and jump out of system. The next day, we come back in the X-wings and perform our ground strike.

"So, spend some time today and tomorrow getting used to calling one another by Rogue call signs. And, Face, when addressing me, don't forget to call me Tycho once or twice. We'll be broadcasting in the clear, like most snubfighter units, instead of using Wraith Squadron's encryption."

Face nodded.

"After the strike, we'll jump to rejoin *Night Caller*. Simple, in theory. Questions?"

There were none.

"Let's do it, then. We'll begin deploying the satellites in two hours. Grinder, Piggy, get us some locations by then."

Grinder was the first one out of the door, Wedge noticed. Eager to begin processing data for his extra assignment?

Grinder literally ran to the locker room adjacent to the Deck Three forward lounge. He took a look around to make sure no one was on hand to observe him, then he keyed in his locker combination. A moment later he palmed the small box he'd taken from the Scohar Xenohealth Institute. Its occupant began scratching at the pressboard sides of the box.

Grinder, increasingly nervous and watchful, headed forward the few steps it took him to reach the upper door into the bow hold. He peered into the hold, was reassured to note the absence of mechanics or pilots.

He pulled out his datapad and keyed in a code for it to transmit. Now, and for about five minutes, the cameras overlooking the hold would show a still image.

He descended to floor level and keyed in another command. When this one was transmitted, the canopy of one of the X-wings on the middle row hissed and opened.

Face's snubfighter. Grinder smiled. It had taken him considerable effort to acquire the passwords and other special keys that gave him access to the fighters, lockers, and quarters of all the personnel aboard *Night Caller,* but it was worth it. It gave him lots of opportunities to enjoy himself.

He pried open the top of the box containing the insect and upended the box over Face's control seat. Flecks of some nameless substance, perhaps insect food, drifted out. Then something black, not an insect, slid free, and he caught it as it fell.

A small, cheap datapad, the kind that was not programmable, with a memory unit only large enough to contain a little data. Its face read "Storini Glass Prowler, Care and Feeding."

He shook the box again and the translucent insect slid out, dropped wriggling to the seat, and stood upright. It turned to look at Grinder as if evaluating him for a possible meal, then slowly looked around in a circle, analyzing its new surroundings.

Grinder issued another command through his datapad and Face's canopy closed. Now Face would be in for a surprise. Grinder hoped the insect would be in an inobvious place when the pilot climbed aboard for his guard mission. Face should make some interesting noises when he discovered the weird little creature crawling all over him.

They set up the surveillance satellites without incident, and Face reported no insectile intruder when he and Phanan returned from their guard mission.

Surreptitiously, Grinder looked Face over, trying to find some sign that the pilot had accidentally squashed the insect, but there was no spot of fluid or crushed exoskeleton to suggest he had.

On his next opportunity, Grinder returned to the bow hold, opened the canopy of Face's X-wing, and spent the next several minutes searching his cockpit, but the insect was nowhere to be found. He even searched the fighter's small cargo bay, again without luck.

He sighed. A prank opportunity wasted. Ungrateful insect. Next time, he'd find a creature more noisy and aggressive, something sure to make Face want to eject in midmission.

Grinder woke that night sure that he'd heard something scratching at his door.

A dream, he thought. Then he heard it again: *Scritch, scritch, scritch.* The precise noise the Storini Glass Prowler had made in its box.

He rose and padded over to the door of his quarters, but the noise did not repeat itself. He opened the door, but there was nothing on the floor outside, just Phanan pausing outside his own door.

Grinder yawned, then asked, "Did you hear something?"

Phanan gave him a curious look. "Do you always come to your door naked in the middle of the night to ask questions like that?"

"No, really. Did you hear anything odd a moment ago?"

"Well, actually, yes. Some sort of skittering. Like something small running around."

Grinder looked suspiciously up and down the corridor, then carefully shut his door.

Eleven members of Wraith Squadron—all but Tyria, whose X-wing was again assigned to Phanan—dropped out of hyperspace in the Todirium system, as close to the mining planet as the hyperdrives would allow. They screamed down to the planet's surface a hundred kilometers from the colony's warehousing district, then looped around from an east-to-west heading to a north-to-south, flying in terrain-following mode to confound local sensors.

Thirty kilometers from their target, they overflew a small residential compound. They saw someone outside the compound, a humanoid figure in a blue environment suit, look up at them as they roared past.

Wedge said, "That may have cost us our element of surprise. Stay alert, people."

"Twenty kilometers," Janson said.

More roads, most of them still dirt tracks, crisscrossed the brown landscape beneath them.

"Ten kilometers," Janson said.

Wedge said, "Reduce speed," and throttled back. "S-foils to attack position."

They now crossed over some tilled fields, the crops a weird blue-green Wedge would not have thought belonged in nature, and irrigation canals. Some of the roads were paved.

"Five klicks," said Janson.

Gate, Wedge's R5 unit, shrieked a warning as his sensor board lit up with an alert—directional sensors seeking a lock.

"Break off by wings," Wedge said. "Deal with the threat first. Worry about the primary target later."

Four pairs of X-wings rolled away from Wedge, leaving him with his temporary wingman, Donos, in the middle of their new, broader formation.

Moments later the threat came into view. Just above the outskirts of the planet's primary settlement rose a line of repulsorlift craft: short, stubby vehicles half the length of X-wings, powerful-looking blaster cannons protruding from their rear sections, red and yellow paint jobs suggesting danger.

Janson said, "Ultra-Lights."

Wedge frowned. ULAVs, or Ultra-Light Assault Vehicles, were still in use—barely—by the New Republic and on backwater planets like this. Their repulsorlifts should not have been powerful enough to lift them to rooftop level; these vehicles had to have been retrofitted with much more powerful engines. "Five, Six, break left," Wedge said. "Eleven, Twelve, break right. Prepare to do crossing strafing runs on those targets. Everyone else, go evasive and continue on to primary target. Be careful: those rear guns are the real problems."

He heard their acknowledgments as he stood his X-wing up on its port wing, then continued into a rollover, maneuvering like a corkscrew on toward the target. Sensors showed Donos sticking close to his tail.

Lasers lit up the front ends of the ULAVs; two beams stopped dead twenty meters ahead of Wedge's nose, stopped clean by his forward shields.

Then he and Donos were past the line of attackers. The ULAVs were indeed floating ten meters up on what had to be improved repulsorlift engines, and immediately behind them and the buildings shielding them were artillery units, small self-propelled missile racks pointed back toward the Wraiths' direction of approach. The pilots of the artillery units watched the Wraiths fly over, their expressions startled; it looked as though the snubfighters' speed had caught them off guard.

Wedge continued his roll. The blaster cannons on the ULAVs' rears opened up, their emissions lighting up the sky behind him; one gunner was good enough to graze Wedge's rear shields.

He heard Piggy's voice: "Five, recommend you—"

Wedge spoke up fast, "Twelve, no personal comments." He couldn't have Piggy commencing his advisory comments, not if they were to bring off their imitation of Rogue Squadron.

"Yes, sir."

Face's voice: "Oh, lighten up, Tycho."

"Same order to you, Eight." Wedge grinned. Face had chosen a good point to insert his "mistake" of identifying his mission leader by name.

"Yes, sir."

"Leader, Eleven. Commencing strafing run."

Behind Wedge and Donos, the two wings of snubfighters crisscrossed above the line of ULAVs and missile artillery pieces, their lasers flashing down from the skies like red shears. The sky lit up again as one of the missile units detonated.

Wedge's distance-to-range was down to a klick. Ahead, he saw the tan warehouse Face had identified in his briefing recording. He targeted the building, saw his brackets go red almost instantly, and fired.

The proton torpedo flashed to the target faster than his eye could follow. The torpedo hit an upper-story window and was inside when it went off, blowing the roof from the building in an uncountable cloud of pieces. Moments later, torpedoes fired by the five Wraiths trailing him homed in on the disintegrating target. As Wedge pulled up, the warehouse became a cloud of smoke and bright light, one that swelled so fast that even his evasive course carried him partway through it.

He saw red glowing light, heard thumps as debris from the detonation rattled against his X-wing's skin, and then he was through the cloud, climbing. A quick check of his diagnostics told him the extinguisher system of one of his engines was reporting failure—which meant that shrapnel had penetrated the engine and might cause more trouble to come.

"All units, report in," he said.

"Nine is fine. But you've got some new vents, Leader."

"Let me know if anything comes pouring out, Nine."

"Tych, this is Eleven. Their defensive line is gone. The missile units committed fratricide."

Wedge winced. That meant the missiles on one artillery unit had detonated, igniting the missiles on adjacent units, and so on up the line—probably taking the ULAVs with them, since they were so close. That defensive line was a bad, sloppy tactic, probably chosen in haste because of the speed of the Wraiths' approach.

"Four is in the green."

"This is Three. I've lost a laser cannon and picked up some drag."

"Twelve is intact. Leader, the primary target is a crater."

The rest of the acknowledgments rolled in, reports of minor damage, no injuries. Wedge said, "Good work, Rogues. Let's get out of here."

Falynn looked as though she'd just bitten into sour fruit. Her body language, as she kept her elbows on the conference-room table and propped her chin on her hands, also suggested irritation. "I thought I wouldn't mind. But it bothers me."

Wedge guessed that it wasn't too deep a grievance. "That Rogue Squadron gets credit for the raid on Todirium?"

"That's it."

"Well, they don't in the official report. And that will be declassified as soon as our current mission is done."

"Well, I have a complaint," Kell said. "I hit my artillery unit dead on and by the time I came around for a second pass, all the ULAVs were gone."

Wedge gave him a skeptical look. "That's hardly grounds for complaint."

"I still don't have an aerial kill! Three strike missions and a score of zero!"

The others laughed at him.

Face's comlink beeped. He activated it. "Yes?"

"Loran, this is the bridge. You have a HoloNet communication for Captain Darillian. It's Admiral Trigit."

"Night Caller," the admiral said, "will join the corvette *Constrictor* and the frigate *Provocateur* as our forward close support line. As soon as we drop out of hyperspace into the Morobe system, launch your TIE fighters to join theirs; they'll serve as our escort force."

"I understand," Face said. "And your own TIE fighters will be the primary attack force?"

"Correct." The hologram of Admiral Trigit leaned forward and his tone became more confidential. "Now, I have something further to ask. How might I persuade you to give me the details of your, shall we say, *unrecorded* adventures at each of your stops?"

Face froze. The admiral had guessed—

No. Trigit had only learned something about Captain Darillian's private negotiations on behalf of Warlord Zsinj. If he had suspected the true identity of *Night Caller*'s crew, he would never have given Face the plan of attack for Talasea.

Face swallowed. "Sir . . . You can't."

"I could make it well worth your while."

"Sir, let me explain." Face tried to compose himself, to make his lines authentic. "First, if I sold you my honor, I could never buy it back. Second, I realize I may be displeasing you . . . but I want you to understand that I'll keep faith with the warlord until I die. People look at me, and see my little habits, and think I am a shallow man, but I am an honorable officer, and will not break faith with my commander." He gave Trigit his most intent stare, abandoning all of Darillian's florid mannerisms. "It may be, sir, that I will leave Zsinj's employ sometime in the future. It may be that I will enter yours. If I do, you will know from this encounter that I will always keep faith with *you.*"

Trigit drew back. He did not seem to be angered. "Point taken, Captain."

"Thank you, sir. And may I say, I would be pleased to serve under you in any formal capacity. But until I do . . ."

"Until you do, let us make no more assaults, no matter how well intended, upon your honor." Trigit gave him a faint smile. "You surprise me, Captain Darillian."

"I intend to do so again, sir."

"Very well." Trigit gave him an uncommonly gracious half bow. "I'll see you at the rendezvous."

"I look forward to it."

Trigit winked out.

Face swiveled toward the comm center doorway, where Wedge stood waiting.

"We have him," Wedge said.

Scritch, scritch, scritch.

Grinder awoke with a start. There was the sound again, no dream, no hallucination, but an intermittent scratching.

Scritch, scritch, scritch.

He opened the door to the hall. There was nothing beyond it.

Scritch, scritch, scritch.

No, the sound was coming from up in the ceiling, just above his bed, beyond plates of durasteel. After another few moments, it stopped.

Grinder tore through his pile of personal possessions until he found the datapad that had come with the Storini Glass Prowler. He scrolled his way through the information. What to feed the creature. How many hours of light and dark it should endure each day. What its preferred temperature ranges were. How to tell male from female.

Nothing about how it could find its way out of an X-wing cockpit and come to a chamber it had never visited to find the man who had taken it from its homeworld.

He switched on the chamber's terminal to the ship's computer. It was not likely that the computer would contain information about the creature, but it was possible . . .

And the index popped up the name Storini Glass Prowler.

He brought the data up on his monitor.

Nothing much that he hadn't seen on the instructional

datapad, except for a sophisticated hologram showing the creature's exterior; on-screen controls allowed Grinder to move his point of view into the creature's insides and look at its physical structure at a variety of magnifications.

But at the bottom of the entry was a link labeled, "See also Storini Crystal Deceiver." He activated it.

And read, in growing dismay, the description.

Often mistaken for its nearest relative, the Glass Prowler, the Storini Crystal Deceiver is far less common and far more dangerous.

He skipped down past the description of the creature's natural habitat.

The Crystal Deceiver's jaws secrete a poison that is dangerous both to the native life-forms of Storinal and to mammals from other worlds. The creature feeds on creatures that prey on the Glass Prowler. It simulates the Glass Prowler's movements, luring predators to it; only when they strike does it revert to its natural speed and ferocity, eluding all attacks and ferociously biting its attacker. Its poison is a powerful paralytic that keeps its enemies helpless while it literally eats them alive.

Crystal Deceivers are a particular danger to mammalian life-forms because of their unusual olfactory-based memory retention. A Crystal Deceiver encountering the scent of a mammal will remember it for the rest of its life and follow it whenever it encounters the scent. This unfortunate trait has led to many instances of Crystal Deceivers following wilderness observers from the wild into communities and attacking them in their residences.

The poison of these creatures is not dangerous to healthy individuals. The life of a victim of a Crystal Deceiver assault can be saved by medical treatment if the creature has not devoured an irreparable quantity of the victim's body mass.

No. Grinder shook his head. The box had said Glass Prowler. Surely the corporation that had captured the insect for resale would not have made a mistake and boxed up a Crystal Deceiver instead.

Rattled, he switched off the terminal, then the overhead light, and returned to bed.

Scritch, scritch, scritch.

He switched the light back on. This time, the noise had come from the bulkhead beside his bed.

He took a close look at the wall. Were there any gaps in the bulkhead, any apertures through which a medium-sized insect could enter?

Yes. Power access ports. Slight gaps in durasteel panel welds. Above, poor fits around lighting fixtures. *Night Caller* was not a new ship; there would inevitably be ways for the thing to get in.

Ton Phanan answered on Grinder's third knock, sliding open the panel to his quarters and glaring with his one eye. "What?"

"Do you still have that spray sealant from Storinal?" Grinder asked.

"I see you remembered to wrap a towel around yourself this time."

"Never mind that. Do you?"

"Yes."

"Can I have it?"

"You have a middle-of-the-night plastic sealant emergency?"

"That's right."

Phanan sighed. "All right. Hold on." He returned to the door a minute later with the spray bottle.

"Thanks, Ton. I owe you."

"You owe me about an hour's sleep."

"I'll stand a watch for you sometime."

Grinder returned to his room and spent the next hour methodically plugging every gap, no matter how tiny, in his ceiling, walls, and floor—except for the air vent. He ran a power cable to the vent so that any creature touching it would be electrocuted. He heard no scratching in the meantime. Perhaps the creature had wandered off.

He switched off his lights.

This time there was no noise.

It took him another hour, but finally he dropped off to sleep.

Scritch, scritch, scritch.

For a moment he was too groggy to understand his own sense of alarm—too groggy, really, to remember his own name. Then he remembered both.

Scritch, scritch, scritch.

The noise was louder this time. Unmuffled. As if—

As if the creature was within his room.

Cold fear gripped him. While he was out getting the sealant from Ton Phanan, the Crystal Deceiver had slipped into his room.

Now it was trapped here, with him. It couldn't escape if it wanted to.

And it wouldn't want to. It would crawl on him and bite him and make a meal of his paralyzed body—

With a moan, he reached out to turn on his side-table lamp.

It clicked, but didn't come on.

He peered around the room, but there wasn't even the faint green glow from his terminal power key.

Power was out to his quarters. Had the creature chewed through power cables to get in at him? No—it would have been electrocuted.

Was it smart enough to— No. Couldn't be.

Maybe it was a dream.

Scritch, scritch, scritch.

The creature was under his bed.

He shrieked and leaped up. He charged blindly across his quarters, slammed into the door before he realized he was upon it, and slapped the door switch.

Nothing.

He grabbed the door where it slid into the wall. He tugged at it, trying to accomplish with friction and finger pressure what it normally took servomotors to accomplish, and dragged it open—a fraction of an inch. Beyond was empty corridor.

Scritch, scritch, scritch. Behind him. Still under the bed? Or coming for him, tottering on its glassy legs, with jaws distended?

He got his fingers into the door gap and heaved, slamming the doorway fully open.

A glassy, chittering mass swung into his face from ahead and above.

He screamed and fell backward. He felt himself hit the hard floor of his quarters.

Then darkness claimed him.

26

"He suffered some sort of fit, I think. Tests may tell us more."

It was Ton Phanan's voice, and Grinder could see light through his closed eyelids. Cautiously, he opened them.

A ceiling, like the one in his quarters, but this was *Night Caller*'s sick bay. He turned his head to see Phanan, standing by the door, talking to Wedge and Face, who were just inside the door, and Kell and Janson, who were just outside. All looked concerned.

Kell reacted to Grinder's motion and the others looked. "Ah," said Phanan. "He's awake. I won't have to amputate."

Grinder half rose in alarm. "Amputate what?"

"Well, it's your head that seems to be malfunctioning."

Grinder cautiously felt his face to make sure there was nothing remaining of the insect. "Don't joke. I was attacked."

Wedge asked, "By what?"

"A Storini Crystal Deceiver. It's an insect. Something like a Glass Prowler, but a lot deadlier."

The other pilots looked at one another dubiously. Grinder felt irritation rise within him. "You can look it up on the ship's computer. And unless I killed the thing, it's somewhere in the ship. Maybe behind the bulkheads."

Phanan moved to the terminal and tapped his way through a series of menus. "I don't find anything about a Crystal Deceiver."

"It's a link from the entry for the Glass Prowler."

"I don't find an entry for the Glass Prowler."

Grinder stood unsteadily and stared over the doctor's shoulder.

Phanan was right; there was no entry in the ship's encyclopedia for any life-form from Storinal.

"I suggest," Phanan said, "that it was a dream. Something stress-induced, perhaps. But I think I'd like to keep you under observation tonight."

"I'm fine," Grinder snapped.

"Do as he says," Wedge said. "Grinder, your scream woke up half the ship. You cooperate with Phanan or I'll have him certify you unfit to fly until you do."

"Sir, that bug is a killer. It bites you and paralyzes you and you lie there while it eats you. If you don't hunt it down and kill it right now, it'll make *Night Caller* its own banquet hall."

Wedge glanced at Phanan, who shook his head. "You have your orders," Wedge said. "Get some sleep." He gestured for the other pilots to accompany him, and left.

Janson followed, but Face lingered and shut the door.

"Face, I've got to make *you* believe me—"

"Sit."

Grinder flopped down on his sick-bay cot. "Please—"

"Let me show you something." From his jumpsuit pocket, Face pulled a crude assembly of small mechanical parts. Grinder recognized a standard speaker from New Republic–issue datapads, a tiny battery, trailing wires.

Face touched the bare ends of two wires together.

The speaker said, "*Scritch, scritch, scritch.*"

Grinder was suddenly standing. He didn't remember rising, but now he was advancing on Face. "*You—*"

Phanan seized his shoulders, dragged him back down

onto the cot. Grinder struggled and glared up at Phanan. "What the hell is going on?"

"Payback," Face said. "Do you deny that you put that bug in my cockpit?"

"I— What? What bug? I don't know—" Grinder saw the implacable expression Face wore and gave up the pretense. "All right. I did. So what?"

"So you also did all that other stuff. The dummy in Falynn's closet. The leaping tubes and wires in Kell's locker. Plenty of other tricks. All the while sneering at the idea of pranks."

"I did not."

"No one else could have done it without leaving a trace on the ship's computer. You cracked passwords right and left to do it."

Grinder set his jaw and didn't answer.

Face shrugged. "So, payback. My way of saying I don't appreciate it. My way of saying stop. Because this is about the lowest setting of payback I know."

"How'd you do it?" Grinder asked.

"Which part?"

"All of it."

Face finally grinned. "To start with, when that Glass Prowler crawled out from under my seat and onto me—"

"Right, why didn't you react?"

"Well, I thought it was Phanan's."

Grinder turned to the doctor.

Phanan shrugged. "You remember when we were sneaking back out of the Scohar Xenohealth Institute? We passed by a pallet full of little boxes holding these things. The sheeting covering the pile was ripped, so I just took one of the boxes. I've always been intrigued by insects, ever since, as a boy, I learned they can make some girls jump. I kept the little thing in a cage in my room. Face, since he's my wingman, comes in from time to time. He's familiar with the thing."

Face said, "Like I told you, I thought it was Phanan's. I turned my comm transmissions way down and told him. We smuggled it back to his quarters so Wedge wouldn't see. And we found his bug still in its cage, so we knew it was another prank. And how had the prankster gotten my cockpit open without leaving a trace? It was someone who knew the pass code . . . and after I cleared Cubber and Kell, that left only someone with the skills of a code-slicer."

Grinder grimaced. "A case of being too perfect. What about the scratching noise?"

Face tapped the pocket where he'd put away the speaker. "Kell worked the little gadgets up. He was tired of the pranks, too. He put some in your room. He also got up into the ductwork and lowered a couple with comlink controls down into the gaps between bulkheads. We could have made it sound like the creature was crawling all around outside or inside your room if we'd wanted. Kell also built the sensor that told us when you switched your lights on and the little mechanism that swung down into your face when you came out of your room, and he killed the power to your quarters. Which he restored right after you screamed, by the way.

"The encyclopedia entry was something I did, just entering it with my comm center access. If you'd sliced into the entry records, you'd have seen those items were recent additions to the encyclopedia. I got the real data off the datapad that came with Phanan's creature. Phanan did a medical scan on his insect for the graphic. We made up all the text on the Crystal Deceiver; there is no such thing."

Grinder sighed. "Well, maybe that does make us even." He glared at Phanan. "But that doesn't mean you can drug me, knock me out. That goes over the line."

The doctor smiled. It was a sinister expression. "I didn't."

"Who did?"

"No one. Or, in a sense, you did. Grinder—you fainted."

"No."

Phanan nodded. "Brave Wraith Squadron pilot fainted dead away. Now, can we consider your career as a prankster at an end . . . or shall we tell everyone how you faint when bugs come at you? That'll be an interesting topic of discussion among Bothan females in the New Republic armed forces, I bet."

"You—you—"

"You bet? You have a deal? Just what are you trying to say?"

Grinder slumped, defeated. "You have a deal."

"Well, then. I imagine that when you wake up in the morning I'll be able to certify you fit to fly." The doctor rose and stretched. "In the meantime, I'm going to get some sleep in the hours we have remaining."

"Mynock."

"Stop muttering, Grinder. It's bad for your mental health." Grinning in a fashion Grinder found completely irritating, Phanan led Face from the sick bay and switched out the lights.

Scritch, scritch, scritch.

"Face! Come back here and pick up your little toy!"

It was the most elaborate deception they'd attempted to date.

Captain Hrakness was in the command seat of *Night Caller*'s bridge, but he was dressed in one of Darillian's uniforms, his hair dyed to match Darillian's. This was so that if one of the other ships in Admiral Trigit's fleet pointed a visual sensor at *Night Caller*'s bridge, it would see something matching Darillian's description—something matching the hologram the ship broadcast whenever in communication with the others.

Face was on station in the comm center, acting out Darillian's part whenever communication was necessary. His broadcast was replayed on the bridge's main monitor, and the increasingly irritable Captain Hrakness tried, whenever possible, to ape Face's motions.

At ten minutes until departure from hyperspace, the pilots were in their cockpits, going through start-up checklists. Wedge, Falynn, Janson, and Atril were in the TIE fighters, with the rest in the X-wings.

They emerged from hyperspace a hundred light-years from the Morobe system, into a system with a white dwarf for a sun.

Night Caller was the last ship on station. Already in formation were the Imperial Star Destroyer *Implacable*, the Imperial escort frigate *Provocateur*, and the Corellian corvette *Constrictor*. *Provocateur* was stationed well ahead of the Star Destroyer; *Constrictor* was some distance to the port of and slightly behind *Provocateur*. Without waiting for confirmation from Admiral Trigit, Captain Hrakness headed to the mirroring position starboard and behind *Provocateur*.

Admiral Trigit's hologram sprang into life before Face a minute later. "Captain Darillian! Your profile has changed since the last time we met face-to-face, so to speak."

Face turned his head to display his profile. "I think it's the same. Regal, yet unbearably handsome. Or perhaps you mean *Night Caller*'s profile?"

"That *is* what I meant. You've picked up a shuttle and made some other modifications, I see."

Face turned forward again and gave the admiral a conspiratorial smile. "The shuttle we took from a pirate. And the outer escape pods on either side are actually my TIE fighters, Admiral. A notion of mine. Instead of taking a minute to deploy all four, it now takes me one *second*. If you like, I'll have my mechanics dig up the modification specifications. I can transmit them to you and *Constrictor*."

"Please do."

"Speaking of modifications, have there been any made to our mission profile?"

"No. We can jump as soon as you're in position."

"Which will be in one and a half minutes. We'll be awaiting your signal."

Trigit disappeared.

The New Republic forces could have attacked Trigit's fleet here, in this unnamed system . . . but since, in theory, only the ship's captains knew where they were making rendezvous, that would have been a giveaway that one of them was a traitor. This would not matter if Trigit's fleet were entirely wiped out or captured, but would have cost the Wraiths their false identity if one or more of the ships got away. By attacking in the Morobe system, they could blame all "treachery" on the "Rebels" should they need to.

Face's comlink cracked. "Coming on station." It was Hrakness.

He sighed. He wanted desperately to be in the cockpit of his X-wing, but he had to play out his role if Trigit communicated again. For once he regretted his theatrical skill.

Face saw elements of the comm board light up as *Night Caller* received a data transmission from *Implacable*. Moments later the corvette's engine pitch changed. All four ships would be matching speeds and courses.

A minute later they were in hyperspace.

Five minutes from *Implacable*'s arrival in the Morobe system, Lieutenant Gara Petothel presented herself to the admiral—unusual, since protocol called for her to speak to him from her console in the crew pit below or to use the intercom. "We have a problem, sir."

"Something we need to deal with before this assault?"

"If I'm right, this assault will destroy us."

He blinked. "Make it fast."

"I've been running the data from the Morrt Project. The data that told us that Talasea, in the Morobe system, was the probable site of the Folor relocation."

"And?"

"Nobody had correlated the data of systems being profiled with the parasite units providing the data. Sir, eighty percent of the statistical hits pointing to Talasea come from the same twenty-two units. For this to happen, those units would have to be attached to ships that jumped back and forth between Talasea and neighboring systems. And when the units changed ships, they would have to have changed to ships doing exactly the same thing."

Trigit kept his features still but felt cold run through him. "The Morrt Project has reached the end of its useful life span," he said.

"I'm afraid so, sir."

The admiral turned to *Implacable*'s commander. "Captain! Drop us out of hyperspace immediately."

The captain, a dull-looking fellow from Coruscant whose appearance belied his reliability and intelligence, didn't ask any stupid questions. He looked up, gauged the seriousness of the admiral's expression, and nodded to his chief pilot.

A moment later the view in the forward window of hyperspace turned into the end-of-jump vista of stars stretching to infinity. Those stars snapped from lines into sharp, unblinking points, with *Implacable* still light-years from the Morobe system.

The captain cleared his throat. "What about our fleet, sir?"

"Have Communications prepare an alert. It should tell them that Talasea is a trap; their orders are to exit the system immediately and signal us when they're sure they have eluded pursuit. Begin broadcasting that over the HoloNet now and continue for twenty minutes."

"Yes, sir."

Trigit settled back into his seat. "Good work, Petothel. You've probably saved us a considerable pounding."

The lieutenant gave him a cool smile and returned to her station.

He followed her with his gaze. He'd decided that she was very nearly the perfect woman. Intelligent, talented, and beautiful . . . and somewhat distant, the way he preferred things. Perhaps she'd be amenable to a liaison. If she was, he doubted she'd be the sort to become too attached, too intertwined in his life. An ideal package.

He'd think about it.

The other three ships of the fleet arrived from hyperspace within a second of one another. The planet of Talasea was close before them; they'd used its mass shadow, rather than a timer, to drag them out of hyperspace. Instantly, all three vessels launched their TIE fighters: *Night Caller*'s four from her former escape pod ports, *Constrictor*'s four from her bow hold, and *Provocateur*'s two dozen from her hangar bays.

Implacable failed to appear behind them.

Face saw the HoloNet indicator light up, but allowed the ship's communications officer to handle initial reception; Face might foul up the process. A moment later Captain

Hrakness's voice came across the ship's intercom. "Attention, all crew. *Implacable* has figured out the trap and held back. The other ships are turning to escape Talasea's mass shadow. We'll fire on them as we maneuver. All bow guns, prepare to fire on *Provocateur*'s engines and communications gear. Turret cannons, prepare to fire on *Constrictor*'s engines. We've got to hold them here for the Alliance forces. Do not, repeat, *do not* target until I give the command; we can't have them bringing their shields up." Face could feel the faintest lateral movement as the captain spoke.

He turned on the chamber's main monitor and split it between a forward visual view and sensor view.

In the starfield before the corvette, he saw the enemy frigate begin to come into range of the arc of *Night Caller*'s bow guns. The sensor showed that all three ships were turning to port, preparing to come around in a 180-degree maneuver that would end with the corvettes still flanking the frigate.

Face swore. The corvette's turret guns might cripple the *Constrictor* even at this range, but her forward paired turbolaser cannons couldn't be counted on to crack the engines of an Imperial frigate. He hit the intercom button for the bridge. "Captain, this is Face. Recommend you emergency vent atmosphere from the bow hold and open the hold door as you bear. That'll give you fourteen, maybe sixteen proton torps to fire at *Provocateur* on your first pass."

"Thanks, Loran. Good thinking."

Face headed out of the comm center at a full run, risking broken legs as he charged down the stairs. If he was fast enough, he could get into the hold, get into his cockpit before they vented the atmosphere . . .

But when he slapped the door control to the bow hold access hatch, it failed to open. The light above the door glowed red. The captain had already vented the hold atmosphere. Frustrated, Face slammed his hand into the door.

In the darkness, Kell waited. Before him, blackness turned into a thin vertical strip of stars; as he watched, it widened, and the frigate *Provocateur* drifted into position from the left, its stern toward them. That meant *Night Caller* was taking a hard maneuver to port. Beyond *Provocateur* was the other corvette, executing the same turn at the same rate.

"Stand by," Kell said. Captain Hrakness had said all bow guns would go on his command, and he had to wait until all seven pilots in the bow hold had a clear field of fire.

Despite his best efforts, his breathing quickened, became harsh. It sounded like gasping in his ears.

The other day, the assault on Todirium hadn't affected him like this. Of course, Todirium's defenders were underpowered. Underprepared. *These enemies, on the other hand, can shoot back.*

Kell shook his head, trying to send that invidious mental voice away.

You're about to stare down the cannons of an Imperial frigate. You're going to be vaped. That's the end of Kell Tainer.

"Shut up."

"What's that, Five?"

"Nothing, Nine."

The frigate was almost centered in the exit from the hold. Kell grabbed his control yoke, gripped it hard to quell the shaking of his hand. "Get ready . . . get ready . . . Target and fire!" Kell activated his targeting computer, swung the brackets over the frigate's stern, and saw them immediately go red; the computer whined with the tone of a good lock. He fired both torpedoes and saw them streak off toward the *Provocateur*.

A dozen torpedoes joined them in the near-instantaneous crossing to the frigate. The stern end of the capital ship lit up in a ball-shaped, glowing explosion.

Kell said, "Five away," and shot out of *Night Caller*'s bow. Even as he emerged he saw *Night Caller*'s forward lasers lance in on the frigate's engines, adding their formidable damage to that done by the torpedoes.

"Four away!"

The sensors showed *Night Caller* turning away from the frigate. As on the Blood Nest moon, for the X-wings to

launch, the corvette had to keep its bow shields down . . .
and to maneuver so neither enemy ship could get a clear shot
at its bow.

"Six away!"

The center column of X-wings was clear. Kell switched
over to lasers, linked them for quad firing, and brought up his
visual sensors. *Provocateur,* until a moment ago in the process of gathering up its TIE fighters, was deploying them
again, a fire drill of confusion. He fired as he raced in toward
the frigate's screen of starfighters, shooting as fast as his shaking hands would let him.

Wedge hovered near his TIE fighter's landing port as if preparing to dock.

The instant the bow vista lit up with the emissions of
proton torpedoes and laser cannons, he announced, "Grays,
form up!" He goosed the engines and moved out in an arc
that would carry them well around the *Provocateur* on a
course toward the corvette *Constrictor.* As soon as his range
meter read two klicks he began firing lasers.

Night Caller's turret guns had already struck home, he
saw. The corvette's engines were awash in energy, their insu-
lating sheaths glowing from absorbed energy; a brilliant ribbon of fire from the portmost topside engine was clear sign of
a sheared fuel conduit. *Night Caller* continued fire against the
other corvette's stern. Wedge also directed his fire toward the
engines, trusting Falynn to do the same, and said, "Gray
Three, Gray Four, take the communications systems. You
know where."

Indeed they did. Different Corellian corvettes had set up
their communications chambers at different points, but all
had the majority of their comm and sensor hardware at the
same position: starboard, in the central portion of the ship,
deck two. Atril and Janson swept far to starboard, then angled back in and began firing continuously against the corvette's far side.

Constrictor finally began returning fire. The stern gun

and top turret opened up on *Night Caller*; the side guns sprayed fire against Wedge and the other TIE pilots.

Face was in the stairwell up to deck two when *Night Caller* was jarred by a powerful blow; it knocked him from his feet and he rolled across the bone-bruising steps down to the deck three landing. He made it painfully to his feet and hobbled up to deck two a moment later.

Lights in the corridor leading to the bridge flickered and smoke drifted through the corridor. Face limped forward. The blast door to the bridge was bowed in toward him. Paint had peeled and burned from its surface, yielding the smoke Face saw, and the metal of the door was glowing red from heat. The door made a hissing noise like a reptile preparing to strike.

He gulped and hit his comlink. "Captain Hrakness? Any bridge crew? Come in."

There was no answer.

Kell tore past the *Provocateur*. His jittery laser fire had missed the first screen of TIE fighters, but his second set of torpedoes had detonated on the frigate's shields. He grimaced; this was going to be a pounding match.

"Five, Seven."

"I hear you, Seven."

"We've lost the bridge."

"What?"

"She took a direct hit from the frigate's stern battery, Five. The bridge is *gone*."

Kell swore and began to swing around for his next pass. Runt was now on his tail. "Was anyone still in the hold?"

"Face's fighter. He wasn't in it. I think *Night Caller* is drifting." Indeed, the corvette seemed to be locked in the starboard turn that was supposed to bring its bow away from its enemies. In a minute, the maneuver would bring the bow toward the other two ships again.

Kell activated his comm unit and personal comlink simultaneously. *"Night Caller,* this is Wraith Five. Does anybody read me?"

Wedge and Falynn roared past the *Constrictor's* bow, reversed, and fired almost before they looked.

The enemy corvette's bow hold was opening and her bow shields were down to allow her TIE fighters to emerge. The Wraiths' linked laser fire went straight down the throat of the enemy ship. As they dove, losing relative altitude rather than follow their shots in, they saw energy spill right back out of the hold at them, evidence that something had lit off in the hold—probably the ion engines of one of the TIE fighters preparing to launch.

The corvette's belly turret swung after them, firing as they passed, but then the guns froze in position, their last blast being half the intensity of a standard barrage.

Wedge checked his sensors. This close, the corvette's shields would have lit up the sensor board, but the only thing doing that was the increasing brightness from the corvette's engines. He swung around to bring the corvette into his firing brackets and switched his comm unit to broad-spectrum Imperial frequencies. *"Constrictor,* this is the New Republic. You are helpless under our guns. I'll give you ten seconds to surrender. If you don't, I'm going to blow a hole through your bridge and fly through it for fun."

It was only a moment before a strangled voice replied: *"Constrictor* to Rebel forces. We surrender. Please bring up rescue craft. Our engines are on fire. And please don't fire on our escape pods." Two of the escape craft ejected from the corvette's center section and began a slow drift toward Talasea.

"Acknowledged, *Constrictor."*

Janson's voice cut in. "Wedge, *Night Caller's* in trouble."

At a dead run, Face worked his way down to deck four and to the combined security hold and auxiliary bridge situated just forward of the engines. The door opened to his voice but the chamber beyond was dark, unoccupied.

He slid into the command chair and hit his comlink. "Grinder! You still among the living?"

"I'm here."

"I'm in the backup bridge. What do I do to bring it up?"

"Why does everyone think that I—"

"Grinder."

"Type in command *wormturns*, W-O-R-M-T-U-R-N-S, then ID yourself by voice and issue the vocal password 'Agamar Rules the Galaxy.' "

Face did as he was told and a moment later the auxiliary bridge sprang to life. He redirected all officers' stations to his command console and immediately stopped the ship's portward spin.

On the main sensor monitor, *Constrictor* was reading green—safe, pacified. *Provocateur* was still red. The board showed a variety of blue dots already in the fight and more onrushing from Talasea and her moons.

First things first. He activated the bow hold door and closed it, then brought bow shields up to full power. "Cubber."

"Here."

"Get a crew up to the deck two bridge door. The bridge is gone and the door is losing integrity. Weld it down or something before it blows out completely and takes half the crew with it."

"We're on it."

As fast as he could process the information, Face flipped between the screens for each of the bridge positions he now commanded. *I used to think bridge officer was such an easy post.*

Provocateur was outbound at full speed, again gathering up the last of her TIE fighters, taking advantage of *Night Caller*'s momentary lack of responsiveness and the Wraiths' inability to do her harm.

"Wraiths, form up," Kell said. "We're not getting

through their shields alone. I want a torpedo barrage. I'll transmit targeting data; have your torps follow it in. Everyone fire on my mark, except Seven and Nine—you fire exactly one second later."

He counted off their acknowledgments until he was sure all were accounted for. Tyria and Piggy had finally emerged from the topside hold, and that gave them a total of seven X-wings, fourteen torpedoes, to fire in this barrage.

He finished his arc and swung into position at the head of the X-wing formation. Runt settled in beside him. "*Night Caller,* come in."

"*Night Caller* here."

"Face?"

"Never mind. What do you want?"

"Sensor data on *Provocateur*. Where are her shields weakest?"

"Uh, wait a second. Uh—"

"Face, hurry." The frigate's guns were beginning to converge on the X-wing formation. A graze from one of *Provocateur*'s stern laser cannons missed Kell's X-wing but came close enough to blow through its bow shields, dropping them to zero power. Kell swore and redirected power from aft shields and acceleration to bring them back on-line and shore them up.

"If I'm reading this right, topside, just astern of the short-range communications array."

Kell gained altitude relative to the frigate, saw the Wraiths following him smoothly through the maneuver, and dove toward the frigate's topside. His targeting brackets went red as soon as they passed over the frigate, but he carefully positioned them over the antenna rig. "Wraiths, three, two, one—*mark.*"

He watched the reddish trails of ten proton torpedoes leap away from the X-wings and slam into the frigate's topside. The next four torpedoes were away before the detonation and debris cloud began to clear; he saw their trails enter the expanding ball and disappear within. The ball continued to swell as the X-wings pulled up and arced away.

"Five, this is Eight. Sensors show shield failure and four

hull hits. I—wait a second, something's wrong, I'm reading two *Provocateurs*—" Dead silence for a moment. Then: "Five, Eight. The frigate has separated amidships. She's in two pieces. Her threat index is zero. Do you read?"

"We read you, Eight, and thanks." Kell tried to wipe away the sweat stinging his eyes, but his hand encountered the eye shield of his helmet. He banged the shield up and mopped at his eyes.

His hands wouldn't stop shaking.

27

"Foolish of us," General Crespin said, "to bring along Rogue Squadron, all those A-wings, *Home One,* and a pair of frigates when all it takes is Wraith Squadron and a battered corvette to deal with the enemy."

They were in the inflatable dome that served the temporary Talasea camp as an officers' mess, unwinding over beer and brandy that tasted something like ship's fuel. The general's words were sarcastic, but his tone was more regretful than anything.

Wedge said, "If *Implacable* had come through, we'd have been dead without those extra forces. As it is, we had the element of surprise—a couple of different ways—going for us. Even so, we lost a good, experienced bridge crew."

Crespin nodded. "I didn't mean to be facetious. I was just itching to give Trigit back some of what he gave us on Folor."

"You may yet." Wedge took another pull from his petrochemical-flavored brandy. "We hit their communications systems hard and fast. They never got off a reply to Trigit. As soon as we're able, *Night Caller* is going back out . . . and we'll tell Zsinj a story of survival against terrible odds. I'm going to do whatever it takes for us to sidle up next to Zsinj or Trigit and stick a vibroblade in his kidneys."

The general smiled. "If you have any opportunity to set up a real engagement—"

"Yours and Rogue Squadron will be the first units I call on, sir."

The general took a look around as though to make sure no one was listening. He leaned close. "By the way, Antilles, about your pilot, Face Loran . . ."

"Yes?"

"You're about to receive some news pertaining to him. Now, I've had my problems with him, but I've also been keeping track of his progress. So, when you receive that news, keep in mind that I had nothing to do with it—one way or the other."

"Very well." Wedge gave the general a quizzical look, but the older man merely rose and departed.

Wedge took a look around. The table where Lieutenants Wes Janson and Hobbie Klivan had been swapping stories was empty. Wedge would track down the Rogues again later to catch up on their news. For now, it was time to check up on *Night Caller*'s progress. He headed out into Talasea's fog-muted sunlight.

The New Republic encampment was a creeper-overgrown field surrounded by trees. The field was now dotted with inflatable domes and various forms of fighter craft and fighting vessels. All were dimmed by the near-permanent haze that shrouded the planet.

In the middle of the field were the two corvettes, *Night Caller* and *Constrictor,* both ships showing considerable damage.

Night Caller's bridge had been cored, leaving behind a blackened hole with peeling edges. Work crews were hard at work welding armor plates and a single transparisteel sheet across the gap. Wedge had insisted that the repairs look sloppy, unsophisticated; they were supposed to be all his crew had been able to throw together in a few hours.

Constrictor's bow hold doors were gone. In fact, the hold

itself was gone, its hemispherical outer hull torn away by explosions from within; the bow now looked eerily like a skull whose lower jaw had been lost. The ship also had scoring damage along its sides.

Provocateur had been unrecoverable. Internal explosions and venting atmosphere had claimed the lives of any crewman surviving the torpedo attack. The frigate was a drifting tomb well before New Republic rescue forces could reach her.

"Commander Antilles."

Wedge turned toward the source of that familiar, gravelly voice. "Admiral." He saluted.

Admiral Ackbar, accompanied by a major, approached. He returned the salute. "My crews tell me you are almost ready for space. Are you sure you want to go back after Trigit so soon?"

"The more time he has to think, the greater the chance he'll see through our disguise."

"I'll leave that decision to your initiative, then." The Mon Calamari lowered his voice. "I did want to thank you for your kind words regarding my niece."

"You're very welcome, sir. I wish—" The extent to which Wedge wished stopped him short. *I wish we could have saved her. I wish I could have found words to help your family hurt less. I wish a bad-smelling pocket of womp rats shaped like men hadn't been there to endanger her. I wish every legacy of the Empire were wiped clean from the galaxy.* He gave the admiral a regretful look. "I wish."

"I understand." Ackbar looked around, at the people moving between vehicles and vessels, at the areas where inflatable domes were already being brought down. "I, myself, wish I could find the pilot who went to such efforts to save her life. I would like to offer him my thanks."

"I'll make sure Flight Officer Tainer wanders across your path."

Ackbar held out his hand to the major, who placed a large case upon it. This Ackbar handed to Wedge. "It has taken some time for the New Republic bureaucracy to catch up to Wraith Squadron's exploits. Even this morning I had to modify the contents of this package. I thought it most appropriate for you to issue these items."

Wedge opened the case and whistled at what he saw.

Wedge had the Wraiths and Lieutenant Atril Tabanne line up in *Night Caller*'s forward lounge. From their faces, it was evident that no one felt much like celebrating; some of them were somber, others looked more than ready to head spaceward and get back into their fighter cockpits.

"Your sins have caught up with you, Wraiths," Wedge said. "And just as significantly, High Command has not managed to lose my reports on our mission progress, and appears actually to have read them. Flight Officer Tyria Sarkin."

She straightened, became impassive.

"I have only a little to offer you, Sarkin. *Home One* has delivered us a pair of X-wings to bring us back to full operational capacity. And that, plus the fact that your behavior has in recent weeks been exemplary, means I'm restoring you to full operations and to your own snubfighter."

She smiled. "That's plenty to offer me, sir."

Wedge took a step to the side. "Flight Officer Garik Loran."

Face looked startled, came to attention.

"In our tour of duty since being made operational, you have consistently shown fine piloting skills and an exceptional aptitude for leadership, both in planning and in the field. For this reason, it is my pleasure to convey to you your promotion to the rank of lieutenant in the New Republic's Starfighter Command. Congratulations, Face." Wedge handed Face his new rank insignia and saluted.

Face, looking surprised, returned the salute. "Thank you, sir."

"Flight Officer Kell Tainer."

Kell came to attention, looking uneasy.

"Likewise, you have shown fine piloting skills and a facility for battlefield tactics that benefit the group. In fact, we have noted on several occasions your pursuit of unusual strategies that cost you the opportunity for personal gain but kept your fellows, and those you are charged with protecting, alive. So I'm happy to convey to you also a promotion to the rank of lieutenant." He handed Kell his rank insignia and saluted. "Congratulations, Kell."

Kell returned the salute. "Thank you, sir." Wedge was surprised to see that the pilot was as pale and stiff as he had ever been when confronting Wes Janson.

Wedge chose not to notice and took another step to the side. "Lieutenant Atril Tabanne."

The sole surviving member of *Night Caller*'s officer corps came to attention.

"It is unusual for an officer of Starfighter Command to be able to offer commendation to an officer of Fleet Command—even rarer for one to want to, given the history of rivalry between our services." That drew smiles from Atril and the pilots. "But our circumstances are exceptional ones. Your record, since joining the Navy, has been one of loyalty and service, and our only regret is that attrition is a part of the speed with which you receive this much-deserved promotion." He handed Atril her new insignia of rank and saluted. "Congratulations, Captain Tabanne. On your new rank, and on command of *Night Caller*."

She returned the salute and looked as though she wanted to say something, but words choked up in her.

"And finally, an award as well deserved as all these promotions. Lieutenant Tainer."

Kell came to attention again. If anything, he looked more worried than before.

"Recently, you were placed in the unenviable position of attempting to save a pilot who had suffered catastrophic damage. I'm not certain that you've ever resigned yourself to the truth that her death does not constitute failure on your part. As a matter of fact, a review of the recordings of the incident by Starfighter Command confirms the fact that your effort demonstrated both unusual courage and enviable piloting skills—a lesser pilot would have crashed in such an attempt. Therefore, I am pleased to be able to present you with a first for Wraith Squadron: the Kalidor Crescent."

The assembled pilots *ooh*ed and broke rank to applaud. The Crescent, always granted for bravery and piloting skill used in unison, was a mark of prestige throughout the armed forces.

Kell gulped a couple of times, did not lower his eyes to meet Wedge's gaze, and grew even paler.

"Kell, lean down."

Kell did so, and Wedge looped the ceremonial silk ribbon over his head, letting the award settle around his neck. The medal itself, showing the Kalidor bird of prey in inverted flight, its forward-curving wings bracketing a gleaming amber-hued gemstone, settled against his sternum as Kell straightened.

"Congratulations, Kell." Wedge saluted.

Kell managed to throw his return salute. He still did not meet Wedge's eyes, and his voice was hoarse. "Thank you, sir."

Wedge stepped back and addressed them all. "Ladies, gentlemen, we return to space in an hour. I know that doesn't leave much time for celebration, but pack in as much as you care to. Not too much for you, Captain Tabanne. We'll see what sorts of decorative hardware the rest of you can earn when we're standing on top of the ruined hulk of Admiral Trigit and *Implacable*." He turned away and let their cheers follow him out of the lounge.

Janson fell in step beside him.

"Wes, what in the name of the Sith is wrong with Tainer?"

"I wish I knew."

"It's a citation for bravery. He's just made up for the mistake his father made. The day I picked up the Crescent, I could have flown without thrusters and knocked out TIE Interceptors just by spitting at them. But he looked like he was going to throw up."

"He still confuses me, too. I say we just kill him," Janson deadpanned.

Wedge snorted.

. . .

Kell endured their well wishes and backslaps as long as he could, until a member of *Night Caller*'s replacement bridge crew rolled out a keg of lomin-ale and glass tankards. While the others were distracted by the prospect of alcohol, he drifted to the back of the gathering and then escaped to his quarters.

He sat shaking on his bed. When the knock came at his door, he ignored it.

The door chirped acceptance of Kell's pass code and slid open. Tyria entered and closed it behind her.

"How'd you do that?" he asked.

"I got on the comlink and asked Grinder."

"Damn him."

She sat on the edge of the bed, her expression worried. "Kell, what's wrong?"

He took a deep breath. "Look, you'll be better off if you just forget about me—"

She leaned in close, almost menacingly, cutting off his words. "Do *not* continue that thought. Do *not* give me some line about how I'm better off without you. You do that, I'll make you wish you'd never been born, and I *still* won't leave, so you'll have soaked up a lot of hurt for nothing." She pinned him with her stare. "Do you think we stopped being friends when we became involved with each other?"

"No, but—"

"No, nothing. Kell, do you really want me to stop being your friend? Don't give me an answer based on what you think is good for *me*. Give me the truth. Set Honesty to On."

Kell rocked as though in the grip of a wrestler as big as he was. Finally he slumped, defeated. "Honesty to On. No, I don't."

Her expression softened. "Then tell me what just happened in there. You look as though Commander Antilles had called you the scum of the galaxy."

"I *am* the scum of the galaxy. Because I accepted this, this—" He gestured at the medal, then pulled it off him and threw it across the room. "This lie."

She looked at the medal where it lay, then turned back to

him. "It's for superior flying skills and bravery. What part is the lie?"

"Both."

"You're not a good pilot?"

"If I were that good, Jesmin would still be alive."

"Oh, I wish I could just beat some brains into your head. If Commander Antilles was impressed with your flying that day, who are you to tell him he's wrong?"

He looked away and didn't answer.

"And you don't think your action was a brave one? I mean, no false modesty here, Kell. You don't see anything courageous in risking your life to save Jesmin's? Going through what amounted to a series of midair collisions, risking a crash with every one, getting half your fighter's systems shorted out, in trying to keep her alive?"

"Maybe. Maybe just that one day. But every other time . . ." He rubbed his eyes. "Tyria, I'm my father's son. I'm scared to death all the time. And it's getting worse, not better. One of these days we'll be in an engagement, and I'll lose all pretense at self-control and run off for the stars, and Janson or Commander Antilles will shoot me down, and that'll be it. Or I'll be dragged back for court-martial and I'll have ruined our family name. The second name in two generations."

She was silent. He hazarded a look. She was without expression, taking what he was saying as input, offering nothing back.

"When I was a kid," he said, "I thought it was a lie. I thought maybe Dad was a spy or something. He received orders at the last minute and had to rush off and carry them out. No one understood, and they shot him down. Or he was drugged, hallucinating. Or it was someone else in that cockpit and my real father was out there somewhere, alive. Then, when I went through pilot training, I found a couple of survivors of the original Tierfon Yellow Aces who'd talk about it, not knowing I was his son.

"Some of them were scornful. Some of them were regretful. But they'd heard his comm traffic. It was him, he'd lost control, he'd left his honor behind in his thruster wash, and he died. And I've inherited whatever he had." He shrugged. "I don't want to get you or any of the Wraiths killed. I'm going to resign my commission."

Tyria was a long time in answering. Finally she spoke, her voice low, serious. "Do you trust me, Kell?"

"Sure."

"With your life?"

"Yes. Absolutely."

"Will you trust me with something bigger than your life?"

"What?"

"I want you to trust me that you are wrong and I am right."

"No."

"Then you don't rank my opinion as equal to your own. My insights. My intelligence."

"Sure I do. But I know myself better than you do."

She shook her head. "No, you don't, and that's the problem. You've told me twice now that for years you've based your life on ideas that were just plain wrong. That your father didn't do what he did. That Lieutenant Janson was a cold-blooded killer. You were wrong about them. You've had the courage to admit it. You also had the courage to admit that you weren't really in love with me before, that you were wrong about that, too."

He didn't answer.

"I want you to have the courage to trust my opinion more than your own. Kell, maybe it's because part of you wants to get out of every fight, but you're always thinking your way around the current situation, and that's a good thing. Everyone who was on the *Borleias* will agree with me on that. And that's why I know I'm safer with you flying with us."

He didn't answer.

"Kell, please."

He sighed and closed his eyes, cutting off her loving, merciless stare. "All right."

·   ·   ·

They dropped out of hyperspace in the system that was Admiral Trigit's original rendezvous point. As they expected, *Implacable* was not there. From that system, they broadcast to Zsinj Captain Darillian's report of the New Republic ambush, of Trigit's "treachery" in abandoning them, of the set of brilliant maneuvers that brought them out of the ambush zone battered but alive.

Their next jump was to the Obinipor system, deeper in the Outer Rim but still in the path of the New Republic's gradual expansion. Obinipor, the next stop on *Night Caller*'s circuit, was a free colony with an admirable mix of natural resources: metals suited to the fabrication of power generators, and active vulcanism providing the colonists with ready power of their own. Their orders were to take two TIE fighters and buzz the largest set of corporate headquarters, much as they had on the world of Viamarr.

As soon as they made their initial drop to normal space they queried Obinipor with a coded transmission on New Republic frequencies and soon received the compressed, encrypted data package from the Intelligence team already in place.

Before they had a chance to decompress and study it, *Night Caller* received a transmission on the HoloNet.

Face took his seat in the comm center and punched up onto the main monitor the new view of himself. With the modifications Grinder had made, it now showed him seated at a much less ostentatious command chair in the ship's auxiliary bridge. He glanced at Wedge waiting in the doorway. "I'm betting Zsinj."

Wedge shook his head. "It's Trigit. Zsinj will have contacted the admiral for his side of the story before getting back in touch with us."

"Ten credits?"

"You're on."

Face shrugged, then activated the link.

Admiral Trigit's hologram swam into coherence.

Face half rose from his chair. "You! I cannot believe you have the sheer, poisonous gall to contact me after that, that *betrayal*—"

Trigit held up a hand. "Please, Captain. As soon as we realized it was a trap, we had to choose from among several tactics, none of which could please everyone."

"Please everyone? Admiral, you salted us and hung us out to dry! If I hadn't been in the comm center, receiving your rather redundant message telling us it was a trap, I'd be as dead as my bridge crew. My bridge is a burned hole. I'm thinking of turning it into a garden." Face let his voice turn from sarcasm to bitterness. "I have to rely on relief officers, untrained officers, prematurely promoted officers—"

Trigit nodded throughout his tirade. "I know. I don't contest your right to complaint. Tell me, though, what would you have done if you were in command of *Implacable*?"

"Follow my fleet in and try to lead them back out again as fast as possible."

"You're certain? You're sure you'd have no other agendas from the warlord that might limit your choices?"

Face glared at him. "No, of course I'm not privy to any special instructions you received from him."

"You may not trust me that I have such orders, but I can perhaps do something to convince you. Stand by for a new transmission."

Face glanced down at the comm board, waiting for the telltale indicators that Trigit was sending data . . . but, instead, a second hologram materialized before him.

Warlord Zsinj.

Kell froze. If this was a separate transmission—and the fact that it resolved itself separately from Trigit's, rather than the warlord's image stepping out of blank space next to Trigit's, suggested this was the case—then *Night Caller*'s computer was suddenly having to do almost double the work it was before. Two HoloNet links with different points of view meant two sets of Captain Darillian images being generated and transmitted. Neither the ship computer's graphical processors nor Grinder's hastily compiled code was set up for such a drain.

If the Captain Darillian image suddenly broke down, lost resolution . . .

Face gulped and leaned back very slowly. "My lord."

Zsinj gave him a close look. "Zurel. It seems you're upset with the admiral."

Face kept his body absolutely rigid. Perhaps, if the system only had to update his face, it might keep pace with the demands being put on it. "I think any commander would be, if he'd just gone through what I did."

The warlord smiled. "I think you're correct. But you have much to be pleased about. I read your report. You did a fine job of getting your ship out of danger."

"The Rebels probably did not appreciate my use of their own Ackbar Slash against them." The desperation maneuver, developed first in modern times by Admiral Ackbar, involved sending one's fleet between lines of opposing ships, causing them to fire upon one another if they missed their primary target. It made up a large part of the fiction of *Night Caller*'s escape from Talasea.

"Yes, but I appreciated it. Further—think about this. With Captain Joshi dead and *Provocateur* destroyed, whom do you suppose is next in line for command of *Implacable*?"

One of the comm boards went completely dark. System failure, or a shutdown by the comm officer in the auxiliary bridge? Face sweated and tried not to think about it.

Especially in light of the question Zsinj had just asked. Why was Trigit smiling instead of protesting the loss of his ship?

Zsinj must have promised him something better. Command of the *Iron Fist*, perhaps, as Zsinj's personal captain? Face said, thoughtfully, "I actually hadn't considered that before."

"You've been busy. And you're too busy now. Because I want you to join the admiral for one last mission. Then finish up your circuit and I'll send you rendezvous instructions to rejoin me. Understood?"

"Yes, sir."

"We have analyzed the data from the spy satellites you left behind," Trigit said. "Do you know who's been following you?"

"No."

"Rogue Squadron."

"Really." Face smiled. "I take it this mission the warlord mentioned involves them?"

Trigit nodded. "We're going to destroy them, Darillian. Annihilate them even more thoroughly than I destroyed Talon Squadron."

Face heard a noise, a muffled grunt, from the hallway outside the comm center. Sithspit, was Donos out there? He didn't dare look to find out. "I will gladly join you for such an operation."

Trigit didn't appear to have heard the noise from the hallway. "Good. I'll rush to a position a few light-years from Obinipor. You just conclude your duties there . . . whatever they may be."

Zsinj smiled.

"Then," the admiral continued, "you'll jump to join me, and we'll reenter the system and position ourselves behind the planet's largest moon. When Rogue Squadron comes in to perform their usual escapade, we'll finish them."

Face took a deep breath. "A good plan, sir . . . but it lacks a little, I think, in ambition."

Trigit smiled. "What do you mean?"

"Between *Implacable* and *Night Caller,* between your TIE fighters and mine, we can destroy more than just one twelve-fighter squadron. If we had a bigger, better target, one for which the Rebels would bring in additional fighters, we could destroy several squadrons."

Trigit shook his head. "Let's keep things simple. The destruction of Rogue Squadron will have a much bigger effect than just the loss of twelve fighters and pilots. Their reputation, their legend, will also be destroyed."

But Warlord Zsinj looked thoughtful. "What sort of target do you mean, Zurel?"

"The Rebels are fairly consistent in the matériel they allocate to various types of missions. If we wish to destroy three squadrons instead of one, we choose the type of site they'd use three squadrons to destroy." Face resisted the urge to shrug, though he felt his shoulder muscles growing tight from his rigid posture. "A rich target. One they figure is worth some risk in assaulting because of what it would cost you."

Trigit's voice rose in protest. "Warlord, we don't even know exactly how the Rogues are tracking *Night Caller*. We can't be sure they will follow Darillian if we vary the corvette's routine. We have no indication that they followed *Night Caller* to Morobe." His holographic image was looking up and to the side, beyond Face rather than at Zsinj's hologram, but Face guessed that on his bridge he was staring straight at the warlord's image.

Zsinj waved his objection away. "We'll make sure *Night Caller* doesn't go through the effort to shake pursuit that she did when she joined you at Morobe. We'll give the corvette enough time to be spotted by Rebel spies. And if even that fails, we'll just try again until we succeed. No, Apwar, I like this plan." He returned his attention to Face. "Zurel, stay in Obinipor system but forget about terrorizing Bonion. We'll worry about inducing his cooperation later. I'll let you know soon where our ambush is to take place."

"Yes—"

Zsinj's image winked out.

"—my lord."

Trigit gave him a rueful look. "You'll make a good Star Destroyer captain, Darillian. If your ambitions don't get you killed first."

Face smiled. "Yes—"

Trigit disappeared.

"—sir."

Face turned.

Wedge stood in the doorway, giving him a piercing look. Behind him were a stone-faced Donos and a jubilant-looking Janson.

Face shrugged. "So I improvised."

Wedge said, "That's all right." His voice became a dead-on mockery of Trigit's precise tones. "You'll make a good lieutenant, Face. If your ambitions don't get you killed first."

"Yes—"

Wedge walked out.

"—sir."

28

Zsinj said, "It will be Ession."

Face nodded sagely as though he had any idea of what the warlord was talking about. Then his main monitor lit up and words appeared on it—one at a time, as fast as *Night Caller*'s new communications officer could speak them.

Ession, Lucaya system, fourth planet (Corporate Sector). Settled four thousand years ago. Major center for industrial manufacture. Nonaligned. Night Caller's *last visit was eighteen months ago. No record of Zsinj-related contacts at that time.*

"The Rebels will see that site as a rich prize," Face said. He carefully pitched his voice so that his words could be interpreted as sarcastic if, in fact, that world was not Zsinj's intended ambush target.

"Which is why you must make sure the site does not suffer too much damage. It would be a costly loss."

"Whom will I coordinate with on the ground?"

"Raffin, of course, for general details. But he's too nervous for the real planning. Work with Paskalian, his security director. She'll set up the site's own defenses, throw another couple of dozen TIE fighters into the mix, and all without

Raffin's shrill complaints. I really think Raffin is due to retire and Paskalian is due to replace him."

"Shall I see to that while I'm there?"

Zsinj laughed. "I meant an actual retirement, Zurel. He goes away to live in a cottage somewhere and writes his memoirs."

"Sorry."

"You're just being your usual efficient self, I know." Zsinj sobered. His hands moved outside the range of the sensor on him. "I'm transmitting your instructions. Do try to get along with Apwar."

"I'm over my initial anger, my lord. And anxious to strike back at those who actually deserve it."

"Good. Until later." The warlord faded from view.

By the time Face made his way back to the auxiliary bridge, the comm officer had accessed New Republic records via the HoloNet and had the data they needed. Members of the bridge crew and Wraith pilots were clustered around him as the man spoke. "Pakkerd Light Transport," he said. "Before the death of the Emperor, it was a division of Sienar Fleet Systems that built TIE fighters and Interceptors. After the Emperor died, Sienar sold it off and now it builds a 'complete line of repulsorlift utility vehicles.' "

Face snorted. "Who wants to bet there are still assembly lines for fighters?"

He had no takers. Wedge said, "If Zsinj thinks the plant can throw a couple of squadrons of fighters at us, we ought to have a little help on the ground to keep it from happening. Like Lieutenant Page's commandos."

"I'll second that," Face said.

The comm officer continued. "Owner, Oan Pakkerd. Probably another false Zsinj identity. Chief officer, Vanter Raffin. Head of security, Hola Paskalian. I'd say that makes it a match."

Wedge stepped away from the gathered officers. "Our orders from Zsinj are to break off our mission here on Obinipor and head with all due speed—but by an extremely simple and easy-to-follow route—to Ession. Can you handle that, Captain Tabanne?"

She gave him a look made up of amusement and scorn. "I hope that was a rhetorical question, Commander."

"We have broadcast codes that will get us past Ession system's security forces. *Implacable* will join us on Ession's primary moon for the ambush." Wedge smiled grimly. "Then we drop the heavy end of the hammer on them."

Donos, who had been studying the screenful of data on Pakkerd Light Transport, straightened and turned toward Wedge. Face was startled by the deadly intensity in the pilot's eyes. "This time he doesn't get away," Donos said. "Even if I have to fly my snubfighter up and down his corridors looking for him."

Two days later Donos merely needed to look out a viewport to see the ship of the man he wanted to kill.

Night Caller rested on the surface of Ession's largest satellite, a silvery rock covered in impact craters and dust.

Floating a few hundred meters directly above them, sustained by tireless repulsorlift engines, was the *Imperial*-class Star Destroyer *Implacable*.

Not far away, a communications relay dish was set up atop a mountain. This was a permanent array, a commercial dish designed to relay transmissions and sensors from the planet's surface to ships behind the moon. But Kell had come up with an idea and Face, playing Captain Darillian, had convinced Admiral Trigit of its virtue—the idea that the dish was the key to their ability to hide from Rogue Squadron and yet remain instantly responsive.

"What we do," Face had said, "is rig the dish to throw off emissions like a failing transponder. Emissions strong enough to conceal the standard engine emissions from our two ships. The planetary communications can issue routine apologies for the problem along with a promise that it will be repaired soon. We can be right here, ready to launch, and Rogue Squadron will be unaware of us—unless they come in close for a visual sensor look at us."

"At which point we have them anyway," Trigit had agreed. "A good plan."

So they had implemented it by the simple expedient of telling the Pakkerd Light Transport head Vanter Raffin to make it so. A short negotiation and a bribe of a planetary government official later, the two ships had their electronic concealment in place.

Face slouched, bored, in his chair in the comm center. Every so often, Admiral Trigit wanted to chat and Face had to be here for it.

The comm officer's voice came over the ship intercom. "The shuttle *Yellow Rover* has just announced its arrival to system ship control."

Face straightened. *Yellow Rover*'s innocuous arrival was the signal that the New Republic attack was half an hour away.

Minutes later the comm officer announced a transmission from *Implacable*. Face brought up Trigit's image.

The admiral looked irritable. "Darillian, are you sure you blazed a clear enough trail for Rogue Squadron to follow?"

Face nodded. "I couldn't make it too obvious, Admiral. If I operated outside our normal procedures, their Intelligence people might note it and realize we were allowing them to follow. I simply made sure that *Night Caller* was within range of Obinipor's planetary sensors, spent the maximum appropriate time on course before jumping, and made sure to jump through a couple of inhabited systems where our presence would be noted by Rebel spies. They know where we are."

"A simple game of follow best."

The phrase didn't ring a bell with Face. He simply nodded. No hint showed up on his main monitor to help him.

The admiral frowned. "Follow best," he repeated.

Face smiled. "I'm sorry, sir. I'm still being distracted by our battle plan. In fact, I was wondering, since my few TIE fighters don't constitute a significant improvement to the strength of your squadrons, if they might have the honor of escorting *Implacable* once the battle starts."

"Don't change the subject, Darillian. You follow best."

Finally words sprang up on the main monitor. Face glanced over them, tried to look relaxed. "You follow best by following from in front. Thus your prey never knows that he's not actually the predator. Standard Imperial Intelligence doctrine."

"You're rather slow with a catchphrase that is practically a reflex among former Intel officers from Coruscant."

Face began to sweat. He hoped Grinder's visual translation program would not pass that particular imagery along. He made his tone a sad one. "Do you know how long it has been since I saw my home, sir?"

"Two years, seven months." Trigit glanced off to the side. "And six days. Thank you, Lieutenant." He returned his attention to Face. "Why is it that you don't know something that should be second nature to Captain Zurel Darillian?"

"Because I'm not Captain Darillian," Face said. At Trigit's expression of surprise, he continued, "Not the Darillian who left home two years, seven months, and six days ago. Everything changed after I left the last time." Data began spilling across his monitor, pertinent facts about the real Captain Darillian, as *Night Caller*'s bridge crew tried to keep Face ahead of Trigit's prying questions. "I'm not the Darillian I was before the *Lusankya* fled Coruscant and my wife died in the disaster that followed. I'm certainly not the compressed set of data in your memory that *you* think is Captain Darillian."

"You're evading the question—"

Face continued as if he hadn't heard the interruption. He glanced away from Trigit's face, tried to inject even more gloom into his tone. "An irony to that, of course. That one woman I adored killed the other woman I adored. I'm sure someone finds it funny."

"You're—what did you say?"

Face returned his attention to Trigit. "When Ysanne Isard launched the Super Star Destroyer *Lusankya* from its berth on Coruscant, the building in which my wife and I made our home was among those destroyed."

"I know that. It's a matter of Imperial record. What was that you were saying about one woman you adored?"

Face could have cheered. He'd finally pulled Trigit off the tracks of his interrogation. "Oh, there's no use hiding the truth anymore. It can no longer hurt anyone. I loved my wife, Admiral, but Ysanne Isard was a goddess to me."

"You're joking."

"Did you ever meet her?"

"Of course. Several times."

"I, too. And I was dumbstruck each time. By her intelligence, by her power, by the sense that she had destiny wrapped around her like a cloak. I would have given up everything for her—my family, my honor, my command, my name." He shook his head ruefully. "It could never have been, of course. I was an insect under her eyes. I think everyone but the Emperor was. But I could dream." He took a deep breath, straining the seams of his uniform, and let his eyes drift as his memory ranged back through time. "Just the smell of her. As clean as if she were as meticulous and uncompromising in hygiene as she was in every other area of her life. And a touch of perfume, something with spice but lacking any sweetness whatsoever—"

The admiral nodded, his expression fascinated. "Leatherwood. A scent few women can carry off."

"That was it." Face managed a sad smile. "And now both my loves are dead. One more reason to wipe the stain of the Rebellion from the galaxy. My reason, anyway."

"I understand." Trigit's tone was solemn, soothing. "Yes, of course your TIE fighters may escort *Implacable*. I'll leave you to your preparations, Captain."

"Thank you, sir."

Trigit's hologram vanished. A moment later the comm system popped. The noise that came across it was not a voice, but the applause and cheering of many crewmen.

The smile that sprang to Face's lips was not Darillian's but his own. "Thank you, thank you. Performances every hour, on the hour. Imperial madmen a speciality."

The communications officer announced, "Cargo carrier *Red Feathers* is passing through Ession's outer security belt."

Captain Atril Tabanne nodded. "That's our contact.

Patch it through to all stations and all fighters. And put it up on the monitor. I want to see what she is."

A moment later the auxiliary bridge's main monitor glowed with the image of a decrepit, ancient container ship approaching one of Ession's warehousing space stations.

Atril hissed. "I know that ship."

"That's not *Red Feathers*," Janson said. His tone was one of amazement. "That's *Blood Nest*."

Indeed, the container ship approaching Ession was the pathetic Super Transport Mark VI that had served the pirates of M2398-3 as a base.

"I can't believe they got it flying," Wedge said.

"You'd better get to your fighters," Atril said. "But first, I've had a bad thought."

"You shouldn't do that," Janson said.

"My current orders are to get clear as soon as the Wraiths are away. The sensor jamming from that relay dish should make it hard for *Implacable* to target me."

Wedge nodded. "Correct."

"What if they're smart enough to blast the dish a few seconds into the engagement? We'll be an easy target."

"I hadn't considered that." Now Wedge did. "Well, there's a maneuver you can perform that will also foul up both their sensors and visual targeting systems." He described it to her.

Atril glanced at her chief pilot, who shook his head. "Sir," she said, "I'm not confident we can do something that sophisticated. We haven't had enough time with this class of ship."

"Atril, you're the most experienced pilot of Corellian craft aboard."

"Excuse me, sir, but I'm not. There is one who's a lot more experienced."

Falynn, dressed in her TIE fighter piloting gear, waited beside the escape pod access hatch to her starfighter.

She heard booted feet coming at a run, expected to see Commander Antilles race past her to his own starfighter access—was surprised when the black-clad pilot turned out to be Atril Tabanne.

"Captain? What happened to the commander?"

Atril skidded to a halt beside her hatch and pulled her helmet on. "We traded. I'm Gray One now."

"Another last-minute foul-up?"

"No, I think we averted one." Atril disappeared into her hatch. Falynn followed suit.

Kell flipped switches, announced, "Five here. Four engines lit and showing green. Weapon systems at full power. All systems nominal."

He heard similar reports from the pilots around him, nestled in the metal brackets in *Night Caller*'s bow hold. Grinder, Runt, Phanan, Donos, and Tyria reported go conditions. Face would join them for initial launch if feasible, or launch subsequently if not. Wedge, Falynn, Janson, and Piggy were supposed to be readying themselves in the four TIE fighters for their own surprise assault on the Star Destroyer.

His breathing was already accelerating, and they were still minutes from launch. He tried to calm himself.

He looked rightward and down. In the next row over, in the bottom rack, Tyria was going through her own start-up and checklist. She glanced his way, saw he was looking, blew him a kiss.

He forced a smile for her, turned away as he felt it turn shaky.

Lieutenant Gara Petothel looked up from her station in the crew pit and caught Admiral Trigit's eye. "I think the old container ship is their delivery mechanism, sir."

"Why is that?"

"It's reporting structural damage from planetary gravity. Possible breakup. I say it loses structural integrity, breaks up . . . and when it blows, it rains X-wings."

Trigit chuckled. "Not a bad tactic. Whether or not you're right about this assault, I'll have to remember that."

She smiled and turned away.

"Communications, put up on our speaker any transmissions you receive to or from the container ship *Red Feathers*. Sensors, give us a visual lock on that cargo hauler."

"Switching to speaker, sir."

"Yes, sir."

Almost immediately a voice came over the bridge's main speaker: "Negative, Ession Control. We're showing failure all along the keel. Fissures widening. Hold atmosphere venting. That's making it worse. We can't hold together until you get rescue craft up here." The voice sounded pained.

"*Red Feathers,* do you anticipate debris entering our atmosphere?"

"I'm afraid that's an affirmative, Ession. We'll do what we can to limit it. We're going to set our self-destruct for five minutes and eject in an escape pod."

"What about the mass of your hull and containers—"

"Hull won't be a problem. Our self-destruct will reduce it so everything will burn up on reentry. Containers, too. I've transmitted our manifest. We're not exactly hauling hundred-ton durasteel ingots up here. You're mostly going to get a rain of manure."

"Planetary communications protocols don't allow me to answer that statement properly, *Red Feathers.*"

Admiral Trigit looked down at his navigator. "Plot their course. Report where they will be at the end of their five-minute countdown."

"Yes, sir." The navigator worked at his control panel for a minute. "Grid seventeen thirteen."

"I mean, in relation to the Pakkerd Light Transport plant."

"Oh." The navigator sounded abashed. "Laterally, within fifty kilometers, plus or minus another fifty. At an altitude of a few hundred klicks."

The admiral settled back, satisfied. "Lieutenant Petothel, award yourself a three-day pass."

"At once, sir."

"All pilots to their fighters."

·   ·   ·

On *Night Caller*'s main monitor, and piped to secondary monitors in all the fighters and common areas, the ancient container ship called *Red Feathers* tumbled helplessly, its hull already deforming, as it reached the outer edges of Ession's atmosphere.

An escape pod ejected and drifted away from the planet.

A minute later the first explosion rocked the cargo ship's surface. Portions of the hull gave way. As the ship continued to rotate, tiny rectangles, standardized cargo containers each capable of holding a hundred tons of raw goods, tumbled free. With them were smaller, more irregular shapes.

Wedge activated the ship's intercom. "Rogue, Green, and Blue Squadrons are emerging." Green Squadron was a unit of Y-wing bombers from General Salm on the world of Borleias; Blue Squadron was a unit of A-wings commanded by General Crespin. Between them and the X-wings of Rogue Squadron, this mission was being handled by a versatile set of attack craft. "Gray Flight, stand by for the command from *Implacable*. Wraith Squadron, are you ready?"

Kell's voice: "R-ready, sir."

"You all right, Lieutenant Tainer?"

"Fine, sir. Something caught in my throat."

The containers that had been ejected first began to glow from friction with the atmosphere.

Wedge's comm officer turned toward him. "Transmission from *Implacable*. 'Launch all TIE fighters.' "

"Acknowledge."

"Yes, sir."

Wedge hit the intercom. "Launch Gray Flight."

Atril, Falynn, and Janson launched smoothly. Piggy was a little slower, more tentative. He brought up the rear, acting as Janson's wing, but seemed to handle his TIE fighter competently.

Above, *Implacable*'s belly hangar was disgorging flight after flight of TIE fighters, Interceptors, bombers. Atril led her group in a climb that carried them far to the side of the emerging streams of fighters, past the starboard leading edge of the Star Destroyer, and over the bow until they came to a halt fifty meters ahead of and above the point of *Implacable*'s prow. "Gray Flight on station," she transmitted, and was very pleased to note that there was no quake in her voice.

She sat in a laser-armed foil can and waited for her chance to destroy one of the most powerful vessels ever created.

Wedge watched the sensors as seventy-two TIE fighters sped along the half-million klicks that separated Ession from her largest moon.

Meanwhile, more explosions, blasts that looked to Wedge's eyes like carefully placed munitions rather than a self-destruct array, broke *Red Feathers*'s hull into huge sheets that began to tumble, burning, into the atmosphere. The entire cargo of containment units and smaller pieces of wreckage also descended.

All those pieces ignited as they fell, but only someone looking as closely as Wedge was, with equipment as sophisticated, would see that thirty-six of those pieces ignited only at one end—their sterns—and descended in a controlled fashion that matched the fall rate of the debris.

The TIE fighters were nearly to the original site of *Red Feathers*'s destruction. Wedge activated the comm system. "Face, mount up. Wraiths, prepare to execute the Loran Spitball." He stood and moved to the chief pilot's seat; the officer yielded it to him and moved to the secondary weapons console. Wedge asked him, "Ready for tractor duty?"

The young man cracked his knuckles and grinned. "It'll be the biggest thing I've ever tried to tractor in."

Face galloped down the narrow metal stairs into the bow hold and down to floor level. The other pilots, already sealed in, stared at him from their X-wing cockpits.

His fighter's canopy was already open, but mounted as it

was in the holding brackets, it couldn't open all the way. He bounded up the ladder someone had left for him, squeezed into the cockpit like a snake seeking safety, and twisted until he was in position to close the canopy and start the engines. "Wraith Eight lighting up. We have four good starts." Outside, Cubber emerged from the shadow of Runt's wing, grabbed up the ladder, saluted, and ran to the hold exit.

Wedge's voice came back immediately. "Preparing bow hold for departure." The lights went out; only a glow from the open doorway out of the hold lit the edges of the X-wings. As soon as it shut behind Cubber, the hold went dark.

Face's canopy suddenly creaked as air pressure changed outside it.

"Wraiths, this is Five. Remember, do not activate targeting computers until ordered. Use my targeting data for torp launch."

Face silently ran through his checklist as fast as each item came up in the green.

"Wraiths, this is Leader. Wishing you good luck. Be strong in the Force. Even you, Wraith Ten. Thirty seconds to Loran Spitball . . . Twenty-five . . . Twenty . . . Fifteen . . ."

A thin vertical line of light appeared before the Wraiths and widened into a narrow view of the lunar vista. Face felt a slight sense of motion as that view swung upward. Within moments, he could see the world of Ession a half-million klicks away, then the stern of the *Implacable* above them. The view broadened as the bow hold continued to open. "Ten . . . Five . . ."

"Admiral, *Night Caller* is maneuvering. Bow elevating. It looks like she's preparing to head toward Ession."

"Damned glory hound. Instruct them to stay on station. Transmit a routine query about their intentions."

"Yes, sir."

      •   •   •

"Transmit 'Talon Strike,'" Wedge told the comm officer. He hit the intercom again precisely on cue. "Zero."

Then he held his breath.

Atril heard "Talon Strike" and responded.

She inverted her TIE fighter, rolling over backward as though she were in a dogfighting loop, but moving not one meter. A moment later the *Implacable* was before her, above her, upside down.

She brought up her targeting sensor, zoomed it in on the *Implacable*'s bridge a klick and a half away, and fired.

Kell activated his targeting computer, bracketed *Implacable*'s hull halfway between her solar ionization reactor and her stern. He shouted, "Fire fire fire!" and triggered his proton torpedoes.

The sensors officer in the crew pit waved to get the admiral's attention. "Sir, we have multiple weapons locks below—"

Another shouted, "Admiral, we have laser painting on our bridge—"

Admiral Trigit shouted down to them, "All shields on full!"

The weapons officer reached for his shielding controls.

The main bow viewport made a noise as though a rancor's fist had hit it. It darkened to near-complete opacity as its phototropic shielding held the first laser blast at bay. A split second later a second blast hit it.

The viewport blew in, raining shards of transparisteel among them, shards that reversed direction and immediately fled into space as the bridge atmosphere vented over Ession's moon.

29

The air screamed from the bridge, flooding into the vacuum. An alarm klaxon sounded, muted by the roar of the wind.

Admiral Trigit turned and tried to force himself against the wind toward the security foyer due aft of the bridge. He saw one of the foyer's stormtroopers, buffeted by the flow of air, stagger forward and fall headlong into the crew pit.

Ahead, the blast doors separating bridge from security foyer began to close. Trigit gave up all pretense at dignity and dropped flat, elbow crawling with the speed of a much younger man. He scrambled into the foyer moments ahead of the door closing and was helped up by a stormtrooper.

He looked around. The foyer's communications crew was mostly intact, though wild-eyed and windblown. The turbolift doors opened and Gara Petothel and a few other officers who had been stationed in the crew pit emerged, similarly rattled.

Trigit pointed at the chief communications officer. "Get the auxiliary bridge to transfer bridge functions to the consoles here." The deck shuddered faintly under his feet. "Are our shields up?"

"Checking." The officer brought up a diagnostics

readout. He winced. "Sir, they took out the shield generator domes when they hit the bridge."

Trigit hissed in vexation. "Take your positions. We're going to spend some time trading body blows."

"Five away!"

"Four's away!"

"Six are on your tail!"

Wedge listened to the Wraiths' launch announcements, silently begging them to get clear faster. He continued to raise the bow of *Night Caller* until the ship was pointed straight upward. He felt a shudder in the keel as the ship's repulsors were called upon to hold a position they were not designed to assume; only the moon's four-tenths of a standard gravity permitted the maneuver at all.

"Wraith Nine away."

"Ten is clear."

He triggered a switch on the console's underside. Up swung a piloting yoke, a lightweight version of the sort of control found in fighters. *Night Caller* was not supposed to go through the sorts of precise, intricate maneuvers that would normally call for such a control, but Corellian engineers knew it happened sometimes. He powered up the yoke. "Ready on tractors?"

"Ready."

"On zero. Three, two, one, zero!" He hit *Night Caller*'s thrusters.

The corvette jerked and her engines moaned. She rose a few meters more above the moon's surface—then hovered, thrusters blasting away, tethered to the moon by her own tractor beam.

The thrust emission kicked lunar dust and stones up in a billowing cloud all around the corvette. In moments, Wedge lost sight of the Star Destroyer above them. But it was still on sensors, distorted but not completely screened by the distant dish emissions. "Bow guns, fire at will," he said.

"*Narra* is launching." Cubber, in the shuttle, was under

orders to hang well away from the conflict but offer help to pilots if they went extravehicular.

"Wraith Seven gone, and I'm coughing up dust!"

"Wraith Eight launching. Eight clear. Bridge, the hangar is empty."

Gray One and Gray Two fired continuously as they raced back toward the command pylon by the Star Destroyer's stern. Atril saw the communications tower disintegrate under their sustained fire.

She shifted her aim to the innocuous hull plating that protected the auxiliary power for the ship's computers. She doubted the TIE fighter's lasers could penetrate the armor, but perhaps, if she and Falynn were just accurate enough, perhaps . . .

Face rose toward the huge hole in *Implacable*'s underside. Blue energy emissions crackled across the ruined metal surfaces within and made Face's comm unit pop. "Looks like a good landing zone for some more torps, Seven."

"Take it, Eight. I'm your wing."

Face fired. His torpedoes and Phanan's flashed instantly into the gradually growing abscess in *Implacable*'s belly. Their detonation forced its way back out as a glowing ball of energy and debris.

Ever more debris, raining down on the lunar surface. Wraith Seven and Wraith Eight vectored away from the cloud of destructiveness, sideslipping to avoid return fire from the capital ship's guns.

"Recall all TIE squadrons," Trigit said.

His starfighter coordinator was dead, locked in with the vacuum in the bridge. Gara moved to an unoccupied console and issued the order.

Trigit's officers were too well trained to protest that the command left the TIE fighter manufacturing facility on the planet's surface open to the Rebel assault. Some knew that the plant would have a few TIE fighters on hand to reduce the assault's effectiveness.

But the plant only mattered to Trigit in the long term. For now, he had to keep *Implacable* in one piece. And that meant throwing as many resources at the treacherous Captain Darillian as he could.

If it *was* Darillian. Trigit cursed silently. He'd allowed himself to be convinced by that man's persuasive knowledge of Ysanne Isard. He should have followed his original instincts.

"Sir, maneuvers?" That was from the man who'd replaced the slain chief pilot.

Trigit gave him a frosty little smile. "Do you see a need for it? When our shields are equally down on all facings and every other craft on the battlefield is faster and more maneuverable than we are?"

"Uh, no, sir."

The admiral turned to the main weapons board. "Weapons, is *Night Caller* destroyed?"

"No, sir. We're suffering sensor malfunction."

"Target her visually, you idiot! We're close enough."

"There's a problem. We can't see her."

"All right, Lieutenant, we're going to try some lateral drift." Wedge saw the lieutenant gulp and nod.

He eased the yoke sideways, just a touch. *Night Caller* jerked as she strained in a new direction against the tractor, then jumped as the officer released it and immediately reestablished it farther to port. Wedge boosted the repulsors to compensate for the maneuver's clumsiness, but the corvette slid to port, kicking up an entirely new cloud of dust and debris as she did so.

"Think we can do that a little more smoothly next time?"

"Yes, sir. This time, I'll lay down a second beam, minimum power, and then transfer power at a smooth rate from one to the other."

"Good." He turned to the weapons officer. "Transfer control of one of the bow guns to my station, Lieutenant. I'm not here just to drive."

The weapons officer grinned. A moment later the thumb trigger on Wedge's yoke lit up.

Kell and Runt cleared the *Implacable*'s bow, spiraling and juking to throw off the aim of the vessel's gunners, and raced back toward the stern, a duplicate of the attack run of Gray One and Gray Two. In fact, those two TIE fighters were just vectoring off from a second strafing run; the damage they'd done to the ship's hull below the bridge was evident.

"That's our target, Six. Stay evasive until we reach half a klick, then fire and vector away."

"We're ready, Five."

They stayed close to the *Implacable*'s hull, making it all but impossible for any gunnery emplacement to have them in sight for more than a split second.

It was tricky flying. *Implacable*'s hull rose in steep angles like the sides of a ziggurat. The instant they cleared the final rise before the command pylon, Kell aimed and fired. His proton torpedoes hit just as Runt fired; the two X-wings vectored away before they could assess the damage they'd done.

"Wraith Five, Six, this is Gray Two. We're going in for another run. Looks like you two penetrated."

"Finish the job up for us, would you?"

"Oh, sure. Afterward, can we do your laundry, too?"

Wedge waited until Donos and Tyria finished their pass before firing.

That first proton torpedo barrage from *Night Caller*'s bow hold, the maneuver they'd nicknamed the Loran Spitball, had targeted the heavy durasteel hull protecting the Star Destroyer's huge array of power cells. Fourteen proton torpedoes had slammed into the unshielded hull, chewing it to pieces but not destroying it completely. Subsequent runs had widened individual holes.

Wedge fired, pouring a linked turbolaser cannon's destructiveness against the *Implacable*'s hull.

He couldn't see what sort of damage he'd done; he was nearly as blind, visually and by sensor, as the Star Destroyer. But his sensors could pick out the larger craft's silhouette and give him accurate aiming against specific points on the underside.

The dust cloud immediately to starboard of *Night Caller* lit up, became a brilliant column of whiteness as return fire from the Star Destroyer superheated and atomized Wedge's protective cloud. He resisted the urge to flinch. "Cease firing," he said. The larger ship's gunners were doubtless aiming at the source of the turbolaser barrages. "Lieutenant, we're going backward, relative ascent. We'll keep movement constant but unpredictable—and keep up our random firing. No constant fire. Understood?"

He got confirmations from the bridge officers and set *Night Caller* in motion again. The corvette's nose tipped backward, threatening a fall, until he brought the repulsorlifts up to compensate; then they were drifting backward.

Much smoother. The officer on the tractor beam was starting to get it.

"Leader, Four. That last shot hit just ahead of the largest hole in the hull. If you can drop back a few meters astern and to starboard, you'll pop right into the hole."

"Four, you can't just hover out there and do my spotting for me."

"I'm not hovering, sir. I'm dancing. Besides, these guys can't hit the side of a bantha. Whoa! Close one."

Wedge sighed. Grinder was trying to get himself killed. On the other hand, accurate damage to the Star Destroyer's fuel cells meant more than any damage Grinder's X-wing was likely to inflict now. "Sensors, plot my shots against a holo of the *Implacable*'s silhouette. We need that to adjust for Grinder's directions." He positioned his thumb over the firing button. "Resuming fire."

. . .

"We're getting reports from the manufacturing plant," Gara said.

"Wait," Trigit said. "Estimated time of arrival on our TIE fighters?"

"One minute."

"All right. Go ahead."

"The Pakkerd TIE fighters never made it off the ground."

"What?"

"The Rebels apparently had commando forces on the ground. The launch tubes were destroyed. They have two squads of TIE fighters sitting around uselessly in the hangars . . . and a squadron of Rebel Y-wing bombers blowing the whole facility to pieces. The other two squadrons are pursuing our TIEs back here."

Trigit hissed in vexation. "This is not good. Zsinj will be furious. Lieutenant, this time tomorrow, *Implacable* may be running as an independent instead of as part of the warlord's fleet."

"That's actually a fine alternative, compared to some."

"True."

"Five, Six. We have incoming fighters."

Kell glanced at his sensors . . . and froze.

Red dots were approaching from the direction of Ession. Countless dots.

"Right, Six. Let's, uh . . ."

His back locked up in a painful knot. He tried to maneuver, to aim toward the incoming TIE fighters, but his flight stick resisted him, jerking uncontrollably.

"Five, what?"

"Let's get them . . ." Kell strained against the flight stick, but it would not cooperate, would not bring his X-wing's nose around toward the attackers.

He glanced at his sensor screen again. There had to be a thousand of them coming.

"Waiting for your turn, Five."

"I'm experiencing a control malfunction, Six. Give me a visual check, would you?"

"You've got some new debris scarring. We don't see anything wrong. What do your diagnostics say?"

"I don't know."

"Five?"

"Let's get them, Six." Kell's X-wing continued on its course out of the line of fire.

Atril felt the blow, saw the lunar landscape and the starfield above begin spinning, saw her diagnostics board light up in the red. "Gray Two, this is One. I'm hit." Sparks shot up from her control board, defying her to do anything but hold on to her control yoke and pray.

"One, your starboard wing is gone, repeat, completely gone. Punch out!"

"No ejection seat, Two." Atril felt a deep sense of regret—compounded by sudden nausea. Her inertial compensator must have failed, leaving her at the mercy of her ruined fighter's spinning motion. "Get clear."

"Leader, Four. Traverse due astern five meters."

Grinder snap-rolled and dove, anticipating the fire from a turbolaser battery that seemed to be tracking him, then rose and rolled up on his starboard wing to watch as a new column of deadly light shot up from the billowing dust cloud beneath *Implacable*. This beam fired straight into the hole in the capital ship's keel, filling it with light. Glowing debris, tons of it, began pouring from the hole. "Right there! Fix on that spot and keep hitting it."

Kell ignored Runt's persistent, annoying inquiries and continued to wrestle with his stick.

Finally it cooperated. He regained control, saw open starfield in front of him, and relaxed.

His sensor monitor showed those millions of red dots

closing on the position of *Implacable* and *Night Caller*. Behind him. Increasingly behind him as he headed toward open space.

His breathing began to slow. That was better. Always bad to be in a starfighter when the controls failed. He was lucky he'd survived it so many times.

"Leader, *Narra* has tractored Gray One," Janson reported.

"Good to hear, Gray Three. Gray Two, your usual wingman is underneath *Implacable*'s keel. He could use some help."

"I'm already there, sir. Sir, I see an opportunity to do some real harm to *Implacable*. Request permission to enter through the hole we've made in her keel."

"Gray Two, negative, repeat, negative. Too much loose material in there, and we have *Implacable*'s TIE fighters returning. Set up for them."

"There's not that much material. You've slagged so much of it. I think you're hitting internal bulkheads now, though. If I can get in there, I can direct fire laterally, hit machinery at an angle you can't match."

"That's still a negative, Gray Two."

"Leader, I'm not reading you. My comm unit—" Crackling and buzzing followed.

Wedge made a noise of exasperation. She was rubbing her gloves together over the mike, just as he'd done a dozen times during his career. "Wraith Four, can you prevent her?"

Wraith Four responded with crackling and buzzing.

Kell's R2 unit shrieked as his sensor display lit up with a new threat: a torpedo lock on his stern.

Kell read the information, puzzled. "Wraith Six, is that you?"

"We are."

"Are you going to shoot me?"

"No, Five. We're just trying to get your attention. To get

the attention of Kell. Not of the bad mind." Runt's voice was slow and sad, even across comm distortion.

"What do you want?"

"We just wanted you to know we're leaving you. We're returning to the fight."

"Don't do that. It's nasty back there."

"Good-bye, Kell." Wraith Six vectored away, looping around to head back toward the *Implacable*.

Kell felt a keen sense of loss at his friend's departure.

Well, at least Runt hadn't vaped him.

Of course, somebody would be along soon to do that.

Probably Janson.

Janson was in a TIE fighter. He could catch up to Kell's X-wing. Kell checked his sensor board and saw no sign that any craft was pursuing him. With his lead, he could be in hyperspace before anyone caught up to him. He breathed a sigh of relief.

He was safe for now. Pursuit would come some other day.

Maybe it would be Face. Or Phanan. Or Tyria—

The shock of that idea hit him like a snap-kick to the chest. What if Tyria had to come shoot him down?

What would it do to her, knowing she had sent her own lover to oblivion? She had lost everyone she loved on Toprawa and would now lose him, too. It would be Kell's own fault, Kell's signature on the scars she would carry—

As though he were rising to the surface after a deep dive, his mind came free of the thoughts in which it had been submerged. *Tyria*. He was klicks away from her and the distance was growing every second. TIE fighters were now reaching the fight.

He looped around and put all his vehicle's discretionary energy toward acceleration.

Falynn rose smoothly toward the largest hole the Wraiths' series of attacks had made in *Implacable*'s keel. It was broad enough to accommodate her TIE fighter, even broad enough to allow the passage of Grinder's X-wing behind her.

Falling debris bounced off her bow viewport. Some of it came at her from an angle, clattering off her solar wing arrays.

She eased through the gap into the darkness beyond. Above would be the giant array of power cells that enabled *Implacable* to move. Without them, the mighty Star Destroyer would be a gigantic mass of worthless junk.

No one, so far as she knew, had ever done this. Flown into an enemy Star Destroyer and reamed it out from the inside. She would be the first. Number one, for all time.

Carefully, she rotated so that she was pointing to the side and upward.

She fired.

Seventy-two TIEs—four squadrons of fighters, one of Interceptors, and one of bombers—swept into the engagement zone, firing as they came.

Face looped and dove, trying to keep clear of the incoming fire from both the cloud of TIEs and the still-mighty Star Destroyer. He rolled out a few hundred meters below and arced up again, got an immediate green flash on his targeting brackets, and fired. His target, a fast-moving Interceptor, took the blast as a graze across its top viewport and kept coming, still in control. He saw Phanan's lasers pass above him, hitting the next Interceptor at the juncture of its fuselage and its wing pylon, separating them. The squint rolled, out of control, and began its dive toward the moon's surface. "Nice shooting, Seven."

Janson and Piggy roared down on the nearest TIE squadron, looping in from behind and opening fire before the squad had a chance to break and engage individual targets.

Janson's first shot entered his target's port ion engine, vaping the eyeball in a spectacular explosion. Piggy's first blast missed his target below, but he continued to fire, tracking up and left, until a burst hit the vehicle's port wing. The

TIE spun out of control and Piggy's next shot hulled its cockpit.

Janson heard confused chatter on the Imperial comm channel. "Let's go right down the middle, Twelve," he said, and accelerated until he was in the midst of the breaking squadron formation. *The Ackbar Slash, starfighter style. Let them fire now,* he thought.

They did.

Donos gritted his teeth and abandoned his attack run on *Implacable*. On the murderer of Talon Squadron. He veered toward the oncoming TIEs. A full squadron of eyeballs was coming in at him and Tyria. "Ten, we are in trouble."

Tyria was firing already. She didn't answer.

Suddenly there were new blue dots among the red on the sensor board, friendlies overtaking the TIE fighters from the rear. Wedge said, "Blue Squadron, is that you?"

"Good to hear you're among the living, Wraith Leader." These were clipped, precise tones, the voice of General Crespin. "We thought we'd show you the virtues of A-wing speed."

"For once I don't mind. But I'm transmitting you our sensor profiles. Four, correction, three TIE fighters are *our people.* Fire only when you confirm they're red."

"Acknowledged."

Wedge saw the communications officer jump to the task of transmitting the proper blue and red designations to the incoming force. Wedge concentrated on sending a different kind of message, a series of turbolaser blasts against *Implacable*'s weapon batteries.

The hair stood up on his head and arms and all monitors flickered as an ion beam struck within forty meters of *Night Caller*'s position.

Another near miss. Another charge against the credcard where he banked his luck.

·   ·   ·

The A-wings flashed through the screen of TIE fighters, shooting continuously as they came, snap-shots not a detriment in the target-rich field of battle. Kell saw them both on screen and through his canopy as he approached.

He got laser lock at maximum range on an Interceptor, fired his quad-linked lasers, saw his shot carve away the upper half of a solar wing. The Interceptor, damaged but still in control, arced away from him.

"Who's that? Five? Is that you?"

"That's right, Eight. How're you doing?"

"It's unpleasant as a Hutt's butt in here! Where were you?"

"It's my sister's birthday. I had to take her a present. Hold tight." Kell aimed at the thickest concentration of TIEs and dove in, firing as fast as his lasers would cycle.

30

"Admiral, we're going to lose *Implacable*."

Trigit fixed Gara with a cold stare. "With the TIE fighters now chewing the attackers to pieces? I don't believe it."

"Something is in the power cell section. Methodically destroying every cell. We've already lost computer backup power. In ten minutes, maybe less, we're going to lose all main power, and that's the end of *Implacable*, even if every one of those Rebel pilots dies."

He brushed past her and looked at the damage report.

She was right.

He felt faint for a moment. All these years of loyal service, the skill he'd shown Ysanne Isard and then the warlord, were suddenly worth precisely nothing. Destiny was balancing accounts and he was coming up short. He was about to lose his ship. His true love.

"Do we surrender, sir?"

Still dizzied by his sense of loss, he shook his head. "Don't be ridiculous. We've lost . . . but we're not going to give those Rebel scum another operational Star Destroyer they can repair and use for their own purposes. *Implacable* will take as many of them with her as she can."

"Sir . . . that will be more than thirty-five thousand people dead."

"And how many dead can we count on if the Rebels repair this ship and turn her guns on the Empire? Really, Lieutenant. Yes, we preserve the lives of those who depend on us . . . but only until their continued existence threatens even more lives."

Her response was a stony silence.

He leaned in close. His voice dropped. "But for those who are most necessary to me, there are ways to survive. Tell me, can you fly an Interceptor?"

Wary, she shook her head. "I always wanted to go through pilot training. I never had an opportunity. They put me in intrusions instead."

"Pity. I have my personal Interceptor standing by. It is equipped with a hyperdrive, as are its two escort Interceptors. I was going to offer one of them to you. Instead, I must recommend you make your way to the launch bay and take out a shuttle. At least you will survive that way."

"Thank you for thinking of me. But, sir . . . the Rebels don't recognize Warlord Zsinj or you as a legitimate government. They won't treat me as an Intelligence operative and trade me back . . . they'll try me as a traitor and execute me." She looked regretful. "I won't let them have that satisfaction. I'll stay here, sir."

"You're a brave woman, Lieutenant." Unwilling to show her the sense of loss he felt, Trigit turned from her. "Attention! I'm moving to the auxiliary bridge to complete our victory there. Don't inform the officers there: I want to see how they're doing as I walk in." His officers nodded.

He gave Gara Petothel one last solemn look, a nod of respect from one officer to another, and then he entered the turbolift.

Kell twisted, dove, sideslipped, all to avoid the mass of TIE fighters and Interceptors in his path. He fired as he came on, paying no attention to sensor readings of his hits or misses—there was no time for anything but firing and dodging.

Suddenly the next vehicle in his sights was an A-wing. Kell rolled into a loop so hard that it exceeded the power of his inertial compensator and pressed him down in his seat. He had to grunt out his next words: "Is that Blue Squadron?"

"Blue Nine here to save your tail, Wraith Five." The A-wing shot through the space Kell had just occupied and fired, vaporizing the TIE Interceptor that had been dogging him.

"You know some of these TIEs are friendlies—"

"We know."

Kell finished his loop lined up once again with the heaviest concentration of TIEs. He dove in again, this time on Blue Nine's tail, using rudder to slew to starboard and port, scattering fire in a cone around the A-wing now breaking trail for him.

Admiral Trigit walked at a fast clip toward the cluster of Interceptors remaining in the now cavernously empty TIE hangar. He spoke into his comlink. "Main computer. Verify identity by voiceprint. Code omega-one, prepare self-destruct."

"Verify self-destruct."

"Apwar Trigit commands self-destruct."

"Confirmed. Verify timing."

The mechanic on duty opened the access port to Trigit's Interceptor. The admiral climbed in, still talking. "Five minutes from mark. Mark."

"Confirmed. Timer running. Verify resources."

"All remaining power. All weapon systems capacitances. All fuel reserves."

"Confirmed. Self-destruct operational."

The sky brightened behind Face.

He twisted to look. Phanan's X-wing was still tucked in behind and to the starboard of his, but its entire stern was ablaze and burn marks peppered his cockpit. The starfighter that had hulled him, an Interceptor with a set of distinctive horizontal red stripes on the upper and lower portions of its wing arrays, was roaring by at an angle. Now well past Face and Phanan, it began looping around for another pass. "Seven, punch out—"

Phanan did so, firing up and away from his crippled fighter. An instant later, it blew. Face felt debris hammer into his stern. "Wraiths, Seven is EV, repeat, EV. *Narra*, can you pick him up?"

"If he doesn't land in *Night Caller*'s dust cloud, will do."

A TIE fighter dropped into position behind Face. Face saw his sensor board try to light up with a laser lock. He rolled left and dove toward the gigantic cloud of smoke concealing the corvette's position.

His sensors showed a clear laser lock. Then the red dot of his pursuer lost resolution and disappeared. "Who did that?"

"You owe a drink to Rogue Two, son."

"Drink, hell, I'll buy you a distillery!"

The dozen blue dots of Rogue Squadron lit up the sensors, and suddenly the odds against the Wraiths didn't seem quite as deadly.

Lieutenant Gara Petothel, her shoulders set with anger, recorded two quick messages on her comm console, then took the next turbolift up.

She exited at the deck of officers' quarters, picked up a sealed package from her small room, and took another lift to the level where the admiral kept his chambers.

Those doors were unguarded. No surprise; Trigit would have taken his favorite bodyguards to be his escort pilots. Gara told the doors, "Emergency override zero seven nine seven Petothel."

The doors slid open.

She entered, shut them behind her, and quickly peeled out of her uniform and undergarments. *Let Trigit remember me as a willing sacrifice,* she thought. *Let him regret an affair he wanted but never had time for. Let him think whatever he wants. He'll be dead in ten minutes.*

How dare he? Thirty-seven thousand men and women.

Angry, she pulled off her black wig. It was the color her hair used to be, at the length she wore it when she entered service with the New Republic fleet and then joined the *Implacable*'s crew, but now her real hair was much shorter, a downy blond. She threw the wig atop her clothes.

She tugged at the mole on her cheek. It came free. There had once been a mole there, a real one, but she'd had it removed by a Rebel ship's doctor and replaced it with an item of makeup. She tossed it onto the pile.

Now, the container. She opened it to reveal clothes—if you could call them that. Lingerie, sheer stuff made from Loveti moth fiber, the garment would have cost her six months pay had she not stolen it.

She put it on. Beneath it in the case were datacards, her choices for a new identity. Beneath them, a makeup case; she'd use it once she was in the pod.

Beside the makeup case was an injector unit already filled with an illicit substance. She picked it up, hesitated. It was a necessary part of the deception. She just had to make sure she was clearheaded enough, in spite of the drugs, to finish what she was doing here. She jabbed herself with the unit, felt the flow of alien fluids into her vein.

Before the drugs took hold, she spoke aloud, a variation on the code that had given her access to this chamber.

A portion of one wall slid aside. Beyond was the access to Trigit's personal escape pod. The one neither she nor anyone else but Trigit was supposed to know about.

She ignored the feeling that swept through her, the sensation of drifting, long enough to grab up her identicards and makeup case and stagger into the pod.

Had Wedge's vision not been obscured by the dust cloud he was maintaining, he would have seen the tiny flight of three Interceptors leave *Implacable*'s launch bay and angle away from the crippled Star Destroyer.

The Wraiths, Blues, and Rogues battling for their lives against a numerically superior force also paid the flight no attention. Those Interceptors weren't entering the fight. They'd be dealt with later.

Gara Petothel's voice came across *Implacable*'s intercom. "Attention, crew. *Implacable* is losing power and will crash in five minutes or less. Abandon ship."

All over the Star Destroyer, officers and crewmen looked at one another.

Only the ship's commander was authorized to issue such an order. But the chain of command could be breaking down just as the ship's systems were.

Crew members began racing toward the escape pod accesses. Only the most loyal, the most foolhardy, remained behind at gunnery positions.

Kell completed his third pass through the TIEs, alone this time—Blue Nine was off again with her wingman, Blue Ten. There were fewer of the TIEs this time around. Much of that was Rogue Squadron's fault; he'd never seen such coordinated skill, such squadron-wide competence in dogfighting, as the Rogues had demonstrated while eating away at the TIE fighters' numbers. But the odds were still bad and he knew his luck could not continue to hold.

It didn't. He heard Runt's voice, "Five, roll out—"

He snapped up on his starboard wing, but the crossfire from an oncoming TIE Interceptor, a gray craft sporting rakish red stripes on the outer surfaces of its wings, struck him with casual accuracy. The first laser blast battered at his stern shields; the second penetrated, burning its way into his fuselage behind his R2 unit.

His flight stick locked up and his control board went dead. All electronics gone . . . he swore to himself as he began a slow, graceful plunge toward the moon below. The interceptor pilot waggled his wings, then rose toward a distant cluster of A-wings.

Kell opened the panel to his left and hit the button for a cold start. Nothing happened.

By his best guess, he had about thirty seconds until impact. Thirty seconds to get an inoperable X-wing started . . . assuming it could be.

And he couldn't participate in the start-up. Only Thirteen, his R2 unit, could reach the damage.

He switched on his helmet comlink, heard the hiss indicating that the interference from the relay dish was still in effect, heard fuzzy voices of the pilots involved in the fight. With his left heel, he yanked at a small, innocuous tab extending from the cockpit hull by his foot. "Thirteen, can you hear me?"

The astromech responded with a whistle.

"Can you get at the damage? Can you bring us on-line?"

Thirteen's next whistle was a low, mournful one.

Kell's tub popped out a short metallic bar. With his foot, he began pumping it, manually generating the current necessary for an emergency deployment of his landing gear. "Are you sure? Not even one engine?"

Thirteen's answer was the same, a sad trill.

Kell heard the landing gear pop open and into place. But there was no power-up of the repulsorlift landing engine, not even its emergency backup power. "Repulsorlifts?"

Again, the low tones of a negative answer.

"Wraith Five to *Narra*. Can you get me? Repeat, Five going down. Can you grab me?"

No answer. Kell's helmet comlink didn't have the range of his fighter's comm unit, didn't have enough power to pierce the interference from the dish.

Kell counted the seconds as the ground came closer and felt a heaviness settle on his chest. He turned to look through his aft viewport at his astromech; the R2 unit regarded him steadily. "I'm going to go now, Thirteen. Thanks for everything."

A trill of good-bye. Then Kell faced forward and yanked the handle for his ejection seat.

The explosive bolts in his canopy blew, sending it up ahead of him, and the thruster under his seat fired off. He felt a blow to his rear as he was launched up and away, momentarily defying the moon's weak gravity. The pressure sensor in his suit registered the sudden drop in atmosphere and activated the small personal magcon field that would protect his body from vacuum exposure.

He watched his fighter speed away ahead, locked in its fatal descent.

He felt almost as though he were losing a fellow pilot. He'd never known, no one seemed to know, just how alive droids were, just how much of their behavior was programming and how much was true personality.

His X-wing hit the far lip of an impact crater and instantly became flattened garbage and flying shrapnel. It did not explode.

Coldness gripped at Kell as his body heat fled his inadequately insulated pilot's suit and the magnetic containment field around it. But for the long moments while he still rose on that rocket thrust, he had an incredible vista of the flaring lasers and bright explosions of the fighter battle before him, of the battle-scarred Star Destroyer beyond.

Wedge's sensors officer said, "*Implacable*'s silhouette is expanding."

Wedge gave the officer a puzzled look. "How again?"

"She's falling, sir."

"Sithspit! Tell Wraiths Three and Four to get out of there." Wedge pulled back on the control yoke, leaning *Night Caller* over at a steep backward angle that, if it continued, would result in the corvette's crash. "Cut the tractor, *now.*"

A moment later *Night Caller* lurched upward, accelerating smoothly but slowly at an angle that would carry it out from under the Star Destroyer. "Drop all shields. Put everything into thruster power."

"Yes, sir!"

The corvette's rate of speed increased.

So did *Implacable*'s rate of descent.

Grinder's last proton torpedo vaporized more mass of the Star Destroyer's increasingly widening power center.

The illumination from that blast also showed Falynn something else.

"She's dropping!" Falynn inverted her TIE fighter, goosed the thrusters—but before she could dive something hit her from the rear. Her ion engines fired, but the thrust merely made her swing to starboard, then back again, and to starboard once more.

She swore. Her starboard solar wing array was hung up on something flexible. "Grinder, get out of here."

"Not without you."

"You moron, if you don't get clear of the way out, I can't get out. Go!"

She watched as, dozens of meters below, the silhouette of Grinder's X-wing rotated, then its thrusters lit off, pushing the snubfighter down toward the way out.

She waited until she was lined up again with the hole in the keel, then she brought her engine thrust up to full power.

She swung to starboard, hit a bulkhead hard, and swung back again.

This time, her front viewport was starred with cracks.

As Grinder shot through the hole, his starboard laser cannon clipped a piece of wreckage. His X-wing tumbled, uncontrolled, as it exited.

The Bothan struggled with his stick and brought his fighter back in line.

The instant he was back in control, one of *Implacable*'s turbolaser blasts washed across him, engulfing him cleanly.

When the beam faded, Grinder was gone.

Janson saw *Implacable*'s blast hit Wraith Four.

Janson climbed, firing. His first shot pinged the turbolaser turret. It rotated to target him—

And Piggy's shot punctured it, the Gamorrean's linked blast hulling the turret. The emplacement went still, its lights dead.

Janson sent his X-wing into a tight, irregular circle

around the hole in *Implacable*'s keel. "Gray Two, this is Gray Three. Do you read?"

"I'm here."

"Get out of there. *Implacable* is falling."

"I'm hung up. Get clear."

"I'm coming in."

"You can't do anything. If I see your profile, I'll fire on you, sir. I promise."

"Dammit, Falynn—"

A bracket of laser fire suddenly erupted from the hole in the keel, burning four neat holes in the lunar surface.

Janson bit back a curse and rolled away from *Implacable*'s underside. Piggy followed, mercifully silent.

As *Implacable* descended, throwing off escape pods by the score, she broadcast one last message. The voice was female, but as distorted as if it had come through a New Republic fighter comm system. "Attention, New Republic forces. The pilots of the three Interceptors who launched one minute ago included Admiral Trigit. If you want him, that's where you'll find him."

The Star Destroyer fell at what looked like a leisurely pace—an illusion fostered by its great size and by the moon's four-tenths gravity. The Wraiths not actively engaged in combat kept their desperate attention on the gap in the hull, waiting for one last TIE fighter to emerge.

It didn't.

Night Caller shot from beneath the descending capital ship like a bar of soap squirting from under a foot, its stern engine array missing the Imperial vessel by a few tens of meters.

Implacable hit stern first, its great mass causing the stern to shatter and deform as it settled. Whole bulkheads and sections of keel blew out the sides and top surface of the Star Destroyer as the ship's atmosphere suddenly compressed.

Even before the bow came down, the vessel's stern detonated, her fuel cells all igniting in an instant. *Implacable*'s command pylon leaped up as if it were a separate ship, suddenly separating for a desperate flight to safety. But it, too, disintegrated as it rose and was consumed by the growing fireball beneath it.

The ship broke at its midsection, its bow spinning almost gracefully before it set down on the crater-pocked surface of the moon.

The Wraiths heard a cry over their comm systems. Wedge and Janson had heard it once before, on the tape of Donos's one and only Talon Squadron mission, the sound of Donos's pain as he realized his squadron was gone.

Wedge rolled *Night Caller* upright. "Divert—" His throat shut down over his voice. Grinder, Falynn dead within seconds of one another. "Divert all guns to fire on the TIE fighters. Weapons, resume control of my turbolaser. Communications, give me the enemy's starfighter channel and our channel both."

"You're ready to go, sir."

"Attention, forces of the *Implacable*. This is Commander Wedge Antilles of New Republic Starfighter Command. Recommend you break off hostilities now."

He got an answer instantly. "Antilles, are you demanding surrender?"

"Negative. Here's the deal. You break off hostilities, we do, too. Go wherever you care to. We've won this round. Neither one of us gains from continuing this battle."

"Not correct. You die, we gain. Prepare to eat vacuum."

Then a new voice, words spoken with biting precision. "Captain, accept the commander's offer."

Wedge went cold. He knew that voice.

The captain's voice returned. "You're only an observer here. You don't issue orders to—" Then a scream.

Face's voice: "Sithspit, he's vaped his own man."

The precise voice returned. "I apologize. A slight question of chain of command. Commander, you have a deal. All *Implacable* forces, break off now. Come to heading two-seventy."

Wedge said, "All New Republic forces, break off combat. Form up on *Night Caller*. If you consider yourself in good shape and have sufficient fuel, fly by on downed fighters and escape pods to report their condition." He drew his finger over his throat and the comm officer cut the wide-channel transmission.

Wedge's weapons officer stared wide-eyed. "You looked like you knew him."

"You might say that. That was Baron Soontir Fel."

The officer paled and returned his attention to his weapons board. Baron Fel, since the death of Darth Vader, was accounted the best Imperial pilot living, and his elite 181st Imperial Fighter Group was the most accomplished fighter unit the Empire could field.

What was he doing as an observer on Admiral Trigit's ship?

On the sensor board, most of the dots obeyed the orders of their respective commanders.

Five dots did not. Three reds headed away from Ession's moon on a straight, out-system course. Two blues pursued. The sensors identified the faster one as Blue Leader, the slower as Wraith Nine.

Squeaky drew Kell in through *Narra*'s emergency airlock. "So glad you are among the living, Tainer. Now that I have you trained to proper manners, I would hate to lose you."

Kell shivered uncontrollably and ignored the 3PO unit. Atril, herself swathed in a blanket, threw another one across his shoulders. Phanan was lying on one of the passenger couches, a blanket over him, his face pallid, but he managed a faint smile for Kell. Squeaky returned to Phanan's side.

"We lost Grinder and Falynn," Atril said.

Kell sat beside her. "Tyria?"

"She's not hurt."

Kell relaxed. He tried to sort out his thoughts, his feelings. Relief about Tyria. Sadness for the loss of Falynn, Grinder, and Thirteen. And an odd sort of jubilation at the loss of a part of himself. He knew that something in him had died and he did not miss it.

"Kell."

"Yeah, Cubber."

"*Night Caller* sends you congratulations. They say this combat was like your first simulator run with the Wraiths."

Kell blinked at him, confused. "Runt gets all my points?"

"No, stupid. One mission, five kills, instant ace. Congratulations."

"Oh."

Cubber snorted. "Much more behavior like that and I'm going to doubt your dedication to the mechanic's profession, boy." He turned back toward his controls. "*Narra* lifting. More packages to pick up."

"Leader to Wraith Nine."

Donos sat stiffly, his whole body cold, his hand holding the control stick in a death grip.

"Leader to Wraith Nine."

"Nine here."

"Report your condition."

Falynn is dead. I don't have a condition. "I'm functional." Automatically, Donos checked his fuel reading, his weapons and shield status. All in the green. He had several more minutes worth of dogfighting power available to him.

Three enemies and one ally ahead.

Commander Antilles probably meant his mental condition.

He'd almost gone away again when he heard Falynn die. But he hadn't. He knew the Wraiths wouldn't let him stay gone.

Best just to keep moving and kill the man who'd killed her. The man who'd killed Talon Squad. "I'm in pursuit of three enemies who are not part of the pacified force."

"If they surrender, you're obliged to accept it."

"If." Donos was silent a long moment. "Please instruct that A-wing ahead of me not to vape Trigit. That's my job."

A new voice came over the comm. "Commander Antilles

doesn't instruct a general to do a damned thing, Wraith Nine."

"Recommend you not get between Trigit and my lasers, General."

"On any other day I'd consider that a threat, sonny. For now, I recommend you just shut up. Blue Leader out."

Donos shut up. Nothing the general could do to him worried him. He just didn't feel like spending energy on an argument.

Donos watched the sensors as General Crespin gained on the interceptor flight. They weren't flying as fast as true Interceptors; the personal vehicles of an Imperial admiral and his favorite bodyguards, they were probably loaded down with hyperdrives and even shielding systems, and that weight would count against them. Even Donos's X-wing, slower than a standard Interceptor, was gaining steadily on these three.

A few more minutes and they'd be far enough from Ession's gravity well to enter hyperspace. But maybe the general was canny enough to stop them.

When the sensor screen showed three klicks distance between the A-wing and the interceptors, Donos's comm board lit up with a cross-frequency transmission. "Blue Leader to outbound interceptors. This is General Edor Crespin. I'm giving you this opportunity to surrender."

The reply came in a dry voice: "Thank you, Blue Leader. I notice a certain disparity in our numbers, though. Perhaps you'd better go home."

Donos heard no reply from Crespin. That exchange had been enough for both leaders.

Moments later, when the range meter showed two kilometers between the Interceptors and General Crespin, Donos saw the Interceptor group change formation. The starboard TIE dropped back and fell into position immediately behind the center one. The port TIE rolled out and turned back toward the A-wing.

Why? Then Donos knew what had happened. General

Crespin had gotten a laser lock on Trigit's craft. One Interceptor had moved in the way of the general's lasers. The other was going back to destroy the A-wing . . . or die trying.

For once, Donos prayed for the success of an A-wing pilot. "Gadget, can we put anything else on acceleration?"

NO.

Donos began rocking in his seat, forward and back, as though the action would coax just a little more acceleration out of the X-wing.

On screen, the rearmost red dot and the blue closed on a head-to-head course.

Donos frowned over the maneuver. *What was General Crespin doing, playing head-to-head with a pilot who was doubtless willing to give up his life to buy the admiral a little extra time?*

They were far from the mass shadows of Ession or her biggest moon. In moments, the Interceptors would be able to jump to hyperspace.

Donos calmed himself. *The general isn't an idiot. He has a plan. If I can figure out what it is, maybe I can figure out what he's going to do to Admiral Trigit—what direction he'll make the admiral jump.*

If he, Donos, were in an A-wing closing with an Interceptor while two other, more important Interceptors were headed away at a slight angle, what would he do?

The A-wings had laser cannons that traversed up and down, giving them a generous arc of fire—something else the drivers of those tiny speed machines were always bragging about. In Crespin's place, Donos could keep his current course but rotate ninety degrees rightward and elevate his guns, bringing Trigit and the other escort back into his sights.

Donos brought up his visual sensor and saw that the general had indeed rotated—in fact, his rotation was continuous, a spin designed to make the A-wing's narrow profile an even more difficult target, and laser blasts from the Interceptor were streaking harmlessly past him. But Donos saw the general had indeed elevated his guns. He wouldn't be able to use them to fire on the Interceptor. He had to be planning for an angle of attack on the other Interceptors.

Donos almost slapped himself. He had it. In Crespin's place, he'd close until he had barely enough time to maneuver out of the head-to-head death trap, then fire the A-wing's concussion missiles. The other pilot, more likely to be locked into a suicide ramming course, would not be likely to maneuver out of their way. That would eliminate the suicide pilot and immediately give Crespin a clear laser shot at the other two Interceptors.

Which way would they jump? Currently, Trigit was in front, his bodyguard trailing immediately behind, Crespin vectoring away from them at a slight angle to port. As soon as they sensed a laser lock, Trigit would have to go to starboard—because that would keep his bodyguard right behind him and in the path of Crespin's lasers.

Donos almost smiled. He switched to proton torpedoes and aimed visually toward empty space to the Interceptors' starboard. He wasn't in range for a torpedo lock yet . . . but was well within the torpedoes' strike range. If he fired at the correct angle, with the torpedoes set to follow any heat source, and the Interceptors broke across the torpedoes' path . . .

He waited, and rocked in his seat for more speed. *Falynn, are you watching?*

When the Interceptor and A-wing were a quarter klick apart, Crespin angled away, but twin streaks of light continued down his original course. The Interceptor he was jousting with reached the point they'd both been aiming for and exploded, victim of twin concussion missiles and bad tactics. Crespin stopped his A-wing's rotation and had his guns directed at the other two vehicles in a bare second.

Immediately, as Crespin's laser lock found them, Trigit's Interceptor and its pursuit vehicle broke away. To starboard. Donos fired. "One for Falynn. Two for Talon."

Crespin's lasers found the engines of the pursuit Interceptor, stitched them with bright red fire. The Interceptor vanished in a bright ball.

Donos's comm unit popped. Trigit's voice. "Crespin, I'd like to reconsid—"

Donos's first torpedo shot between the slit in the Interceptor's starboard wing and hit the Interceptor where the round forward viewport met the hull. The Interceptor detonated in a brilliant flash. Donos's second torpedo entered the cloud but did not emerge from it.

Then there was nothing but the hiss of static over his comm unit, a single blue dot on his sensors.

The A-wing began a long, lazy arc back toward Ession. "Nice shooting, son."

"Nice flying, sir." Donos brought his own snubfighter around.

In his chest was a coldness to match the vacuum around him. It was the emptiness of his future. But Talon Squad had had its revenge. Now, perhaps, eleven good pilots, one ever-helpful R2 unit, and a Tatooine woman who'd never recognized her own worth would be able to rest easy.

31

Her beaches and seas are almost as beautiful as those on Storinal, Kell reflected. *Maybe more so. They aren't as . . . deliberate. As sculpted.*

The world was called Borleias. Once the site of the bio-medical research facility of an Imperial general, later captured by the New Republic as the first stage of the march on the Imperial throne world, Borleias was now home to a fighter training base.

The New Republic had named a troop transport after the battle for this world, and Kell and Runt had saved that transport on Folor. Kell decided, irrationally, this meant the world welcomed his presence.

He certainly felt welcome. He lounged on a puff-cot large enough to accommodate his generous frame—with plenty of room for Tyria beside him. Uniform of the day was bathing suits that might generously be called minimal, and that was a vacation in itself. Beside them on a blanket were half-finished drinks slowly warming in the sun and a small refrigeration unit from which more drinks would emerge as the day grew later.

Up and down the beach, other Wraiths and crewmen of

Night Caller splashed in the waves, lounged on puff-cots, rode recreational speeder bikes, sat drinking around tables under broad reflective parasols. Donos was at the end of the line of cots, alone with his thoughts, but remaining within reach of the other Wraiths instead of distancing himself from them.

Phanan was in Borleias's military hospital, recovering from the loss of his spleen, which had been perforated by shrapnel as he ejected. When Kell had gone to see him, Phanan had explained, "Yes, I got so angry that I had to vent my spleen."

The Wraiths, Kell's fellow pilots, his friends. There were no recriminations in their eyes. Most of them knew that he'd had . . . some sort of attack back on Ession's moon. They also knew that he'd recovered from it, thrown himself into the worst part of the fight. He'd vaporized more than his share of the enemy and had drawn the fire of even more pilots. *Night Caller*, her sensors overwhelmed by the deliberately faulty emissions of the nearby retransmission dish and the dust cloud she was kicking up, had no record of his temporary vacation from reality. So, like Donos's collapse, it wasn't spoken of. It hadn't happened.

And it wouldn't happen again. All he'd ever have to do is imagine what would become of the people he loved if he abandoned them.

He glanced down at Tyria, a teasing remark on his lips; but she was asleep, her head on his shoulder as though it were a pillow.

A shadow fell across them.

Admiral Ackbar stood above him.

Kell saluted out of reflex. "Sir."

"Don't get up." The admiral moved to sit on the next puff-cot over. He turned toward the water, looking at it, as far as Kell could read his posture, with a longing expression. "I am sorry I was not able to speak to you on Talasea."

"I . . . was avoiding you, sir."

Ackbar turned one eye toward him. "Why?"

"I was ashamed." He wouldn't have been able to say it a

week ago. Now, the words were difficult, but not impossible to utter.

"For not being able to save Jesmin?"

"Yes, sir."

"I came to thank you. When I read what you tried to do for her . . . well, it is cruel to learn one you love has died so far away from the heart of her clan, but at least I knew she was in the midst of good friends. Friends close enough to try such a thing."

"She was, sir."

Ackbar took a last, long look at the water, then rose. "Enjoy your leave, Lieutenant. Come back strong and invigorated. Warlord Zsinj is still out there."

"I have a special greeting ready for him, sir."

Ackbar made a gravelly noise like a chuckle and walked away from the sea.

At the top of the hill, Wedge waited in his skimmer.

The admiral climbed awkwardly in. "You're still fully dressed, Commander. Shouldn't you be wearing a scrap and enjoying the weather and the water as they are?"

Wedge set the skimmer in motion, wheeling it around toward the flat field where the X-wings and shuttles waited. "I'm not really as close to the Wraiths as I am to the Rogues, sir. I think I'd make them uncomfortable."

"So, you are not 'one of the lads'? More like a real officer? As intimidating as a general?"

"Oh, yes, our bet. Actually, I was rather hoping you'd take this opportunity to acknowledge that the Wraiths had 'proven their worth,' as you put it."

"Your three months aren't up, General. You are still in danger."

Wedge smiled. "Admiral, that's the story of my life."

Aaron Allston is an award-winning games designer and author. He has written eight science fiction/fantasy novels, as well as some short fiction. In addition to this, he has contributed adventure scenarios, articles, columns, and reviews to computer game publications such as *Adventurers Club, Computer Gaming World, Different Worlds, Fantasy Gamer* and more. Under his editorship, *Space Gamer Magazine* won the H. G. Wells Award for Best Role-Playing Magazine in 1982 and *The Savage Empire* won *Game Player* magazine's Best PC Fantasy Role-Playing Game award in 1990. Texas born Allston has been nominated for the Origins Awards' Hall of Fame category.

He lives in Roundrock, Texas, and is working on the next X-wing book.

The World of
STAR WARS Novels

In May 1991, *Star Wars* caused a sensation in the publishing industry with the Bantam Spectra release of Timothy Zahn's novel *Heir to the Empire*. For the first time, Lucasfilm Ltd. had authorized new novels that *continued* the famous story told in George Lucas's three block-buster motion pictures: *Star Wars*, *The Empire Strikes Back*, and *Return of the Jedi*. Reader reaction was immediate and tumultuous: *Heir* reached #1 on the *New York Times* bestseller list and demonstrated that *Star Wars* lovers were eager for exciting new stories set in this universe, written by leading science fiction authors who shared their passion. Since then, each Bantam *Star Wars* novel has been an instant national bestseller.

Lucasfilm and Bantam decided that future novels in the series would be interconnected: That is, events in one novel would have consequences in the others. You might say that each Bantam *Star Wars* novel, enjoyable on its own, is also part of a much larger tale.

Here is a special look at Bantam's *Star Wars* books, along with excerpts from the more recent novels. Each one is available now wherever Bantam Books are sold.

The Han Solo Trilogy:
THE PARADISE SNARE
THE HUTT GAMBIT
and coming soon,
REBEL DAWN
by A. C. Crispin
Setting: before *Star Wars: A New Hope*

What was Han Solo like before we met him in the first STAR WARS movie? This trilogy answers that tantalizing question, filling in lots of historical lore about our favorite swashbuckling hero and thrilling us with adventures of the brash young pilot that we never knew he'd experienced. As the trilogy begins, the young Han makes a life-changing decision: to escape from the clutches of Garris Shrike, head of the trading "clan" who has brutalized Han while taking advantage of his piloting abilities. Here's a tense early scene from The Paradise Snare *featuring Han, Shrike, and Dewlanna, a Wookiee who is Han's only friend in this horrible situation:*

"I've had it with you, Solo. I've been lenient with you so far, because you're a blasted good swoop pilot and all that prize money came in handy, but my patience is ended." Shrike ceremoniously pushed up the sleeves of his bedizened uniform, then balled his hands into fists. The galley's artificial lighting made the blood-jewel ring glitter dull silver. "Let's see what a few days of fighting off Devaronian blood-poisoning does for your attitude—along with maybe a few broken bones. I'm doing this for your own good, boy. Someday you'll thank me."

Han gulped with terror as Shrike started toward him. He'd lashed out at the trader captain once before, two years ago, when he'd been feeling cocky after winning the gladiatorial Free-For-All on Jubilar— and had been instantly sorry. The speed and strength of Garris's returning blow had snapped his head back and split both lips so thoroughly that Dewlanna had had to feed him mush for a week until they healed.

With a snarl, Dewlanna stepped forward. Shrike's hand dropped to his blaster. "You stay out of this, old Wookiee," he snapped in a voice nearly as harsh as Dewlanna's. "Your cooking isn't *that* good."

Han had already grabbed his friend's furry arm and was forcibly holding her back. "Dewlanna, no!"

She shook off his hold as easily as she would have waved off an annoying insect and roared at Shrike. The captain drew his blaster, and chaos erupted.

"Noooo!" Han screamed, and leaped forward, his foot lashing out in an old street-fighting technique. His instep impacted solidly with Shrike's breastbone. The captain's breath went out in a great *houf!* and he went over backward. Han hit the deck and rolled. A tingler bolt sizzled past his ear.

"Larrad!" wheezed the captain as Dewlanna started toward him.

Shrike's brother drew his blaster and pointed it at the Wookiee. "Stop, Dewlanna!"

His words had no more effect than Han's. Dewlanna's blood was up—she was in full Wookiee battle rage. With a roar that deafened the combatants, she grabbed Larrad's wrist and yanked, spinning him around and snapping him in a terrible parody of a child's "snap the whip" game. Han heard a *crunch,* mixed with several *pops* as tendons and ligaments gave way. Larrad Shrike shrieked, a high, shrill noise that carried such pain that the Corellian youth's arm ached in sympathy.

Grabbing the blaster from his belt, Han snapped off a shot at the Elomin who was leaping forward, tingler ready and aimed at Dewlanna's midsection. Brafid howled, dropping his weapon. Han was amazed that he'd managed to hit him, but he didn't have long to wonder about the accuracy of his aim.

Shrike was staggering to his feet, blaster in hand, aimed squarely at Han's head. "Larrad?" he yelled at the writhing heap of agony that was his brother. Larrad did not reply.

Shrike cocked the blaster and stepped even closer to Han. "Stop it, Dewlanna!" the captain snarled at the Wookiee. "Or your buddy Solo dies!"

Han dropped his blaster and put his hands up in a gesture of surrender.

Dewlanna stopped in her tracks, growling softly.

Shrike leveled the blaster, and his finger tightened on the trigger. Pure malevolent hatred was etched upon his features, and then he smiled, pale blue eyes glittering with ruthless joy. "For insubordination and striking your captain," he announced, "I sentence you to death, Solo. May you rot in all the hells there ever were."

SHADOWS OF THE EMPIRE
by Steve Perry
Setting: Between *The Empire Strikes Back* and *Return of the Jedi*

Here is a very special STAR WARS story dealing with Black Sun, a galaxy-spanning criminal organization that is masterminded by one of the most interesting villains in the STAR WARS universe: Xizor, dark prince of the Falleen. Xizor's chief rival for the favor of Emperor Palpatine is none other than Darth Vader himself—alive and well, and a major character in this story, since it is set during the events of the STAR WARS film trilogy.

In the opening prologue, we revisit a familiar scene from The Empire Strikes Back, *and are introduced to our marvelous new bad guy:*

He looks like a walking corpse, Xizor thought. *Like a mummified body dead a thousand years. Amazing he is still alive, much less the most powerful man in the galaxy. He isn't even that old; it is more as if something is slowly eating him.*

Xizor stood four meters away from the Emperor, watching as the man who had long ago been Senator Palpatine moved to stand in the holocam field. He imagined he could smell the decay in the Emperor's worn body. Likely that was just some trick of the recycled air, run through dozens of filters to ensure that there was no chance of any poison gas being introduced into it. Filtered the life out of it, perhaps, giving it that dead smell.

The viewer on the other end of the holo-link would see a close-up of the Emperor's head and shoulders, of an age-ravaged face shrouded in the cowl of his dark zeyd-cloth robe. The man on the other end of the transmission, light-years away, would not see Xizor, though Xizor would be able to see him. It was a measure of the Emperor's trust that Xizor was allowed to be here while the conversation took place.

The man on the other end of the transmission—if he could still be called that—

The air swirled inside the Imperial chamber in front of the Emperor, coalesced, and blossomed into the image of a figure down on one knee. A caped humanoid biped dressed in jet black, face hidden under a full helmet and breathing mask:

Darth Vader.

Vader spoke: "What is thy bidding, my master?"

If Xizor could have hurled a power bolt through time and space to strike Vader dead, he would have done it without blinking. Wishful thinking: Vader was too powerful to attack directly.

"There is a great disturbance in the Force," the Emperor said.

"I have felt it," Vader said.

"We have a new enemy. Luke Skywalker."

Skywalker? That had been Vader's name, a long time ago. Who was this person with the same name, someone so powerful as to be worth a conversation between the Emperor and his most loathsome creation? More importantly, why had Xizor's agents not uncovered this before now? Xizor's ire was instant—but cold. No sign of his surprise or anger would show on his imperturbable features. The Falleen did not allow their emotions to burst forth as did many of the inferior species; no, the Falleen ancestry was not fur but scales, not mammalian but reptilian. Not wild but coolly calculating. Such was much better. Much safer.

"Yes, my master," Vader continued.

"He could destroy us," the Emperor said.

Xizor's attention was riveted upon the Emperor and the holographic image of Vader kneeling on the deck of a ship far away. Here was interesting news indeed. Something the Emperor perceived as a danger to himself? Something the Emperor feared?

"He's just a boy," Vader said. "Obi-Wan can no longer help him."

Obi-Wan. That name Xizor knew. He was among the last of the Jedi Knights, a general. But he'd been dead for decades, hadn't he?

Apparently Xizor's information was wrong if Obi-Wan had been helping someone who was still a boy. His agents were going to be sorry.

Even as Xizor took in the distant image of Vader and the nearness of the Emperor, even as he was aware of the luxury of the Emperor's private and protected chamber at the core of the giant pyramidal palace, he was also able to make a mental note to himself: Somebody's head would roll for the failure to make him aware of all this. Knowledge was power; lack of knowledge was weakness. This was something he could not permit.

The Emperor continued. "The Force is strong with him. The son of Skywalker must not become a Jedi."

Son of Skywalker?

Vader's son! Amazing!

"If he could be turned he would become a powerful ally," Vader said.

There was something in Vader's voice when he said this, something Xizor could not quite put his finger on. Longing? Worry? Hope?

"Yes . . . yes. He would be a great asset," the Emperor said. "Can it be done?"

There was the briefest of pauses. "He will join us or die, master."

Xizor felt the smile, though he did not allow it to show any more than he had allowed his anger play. Ah. Vader wanted Skywalker alive, *that* was what had been in his tone. Yes, he had said that the boy would join them or die, but this latter part was obviously meant only to placate the Emperor. Vader had no intention of killing Skywalker, his own son; that was obvious to one as skilled in reading voices as was Xizor. He had not gotten to be the Dark Prince, Underlord of Black Sun, the largest criminal organization in the galaxy, merely on his formidable good looks. Xizor didn't truly understand the Force that sustained the Emperor and made him and Vader so powerful, save to know that it certainly worked somehow. But he did know that it was something the extinct Jedi had supposedly mastered. And now, apparently, this new player had tapped into it. Vader wanted Skywalker alive, had practically promised the Emperor that he would deliver him alive—and converted.

This was most interesting.

Most interesting indeed.

The Emperor finished his communication and turned back to face him. "Now, where were we, Prince Xizor?"

The Dark Prince smiled. He would attend to the business at hand, but he would not forget the name of Luke Skywalker.

THE TRUCE AT BAKURA
by Kathy Tyers
Setting: Immediately after *Return of the Jedi*

The day after his climactic battle with Emperor Palpatine and the sacrifice of his father, Darth Vader, who died saving his life, Luke Skywalker helps recover an Imperial drone ship bearing a startling message intended for the Emperor. It is a distress signal from the far-off Imperial outpost of Bakura, which is under attack by an alien invasion force, the Ssi-ruuk. Leia sees a rescue mission as an opportunity to achieve a diplomatic victory for the Rebel Alliance, even if it means fighting alongside former Imperials. But Luke receives a vision from Obi-Wan Kenobi revealing that the stakes are even higher: the invasion at Bakura threatens everything the Rebels have won at such great cost.

STAR WARS: X-WING
by Michael A. Stackpole
ROGUE SQUADRON
WEDGE'S GAMBLE
THE KRYTOS TRAP
THE BACTA WAR
Setting: Three years after *Return of the Jedi*

Inspired by X-wing, *the bestselling computer game from LucasArts Entertainment Co., this exciting series chronicles the further adventures of the most feared and fearless fighting force in the galaxy. A new generation of X-wing pilots, led by Commander Wedge Antilles, is combating the remnants of the Empire still left after the events of the STAR WARS movies. Here are novels full of explosive space action, nonstop adventure, and the special brand of wonder known as STAR WARS.*

In this very early scene, young Corellian pilot Corran Horn faces a tough challenge fast enough to get his heart pounding—and this is only a simulation! [P.S.: "Whistler" is Corran's R2 astromech droid]:

The Corellian brought his proton torpedo targeting program up and locked on to the TIE. It tried to break the lock, but turbolaser fire from the *Korolev* boxed it in. Corran's heads-up display went red and he triggered the torpedo. "Scratch one eyeball."

The missile shot straight in at the fighter, but the pilot broke hard to port and away, causing the missile to overshoot the target. *Nice flying!* Corran brought his X-wing over and started down to loop in behind the TIE, but as he did so, the TIE vanished from his forward screen and reappeared in his aft arc. Yanking the stick hard to the right and pulling it back, Corran wrestled the X-wing up and to starboard, then inverted and rolled out to the left.

A laser shot jolted a tremor through the simulator's couch. *Lucky thing I had all shields aft!* Corran reinforced them with energy from his lasers, then evened them out fore and aft. Jinking the fighter right and left, he avoided laser shots coming in from behind, but they all came in far closer than he liked.

He knew Jace had been in the bomber, and Jace was the only pilot in the unit who could have stayed with him. *Except for our leader.* Corran smiled broadly. *Coming to see how good I really am, Commander Antilles? Let me give you a clinic.* "Make sure you're in there solid, Whistler, because we're going for a little ride."

Corran refused to let the R2's moan slow him down. A snap-roll brought the X-wing up on its port wing. Pulling back on the stick yanked the fighter's nose up away from the original line of flight. The TIE stayed with him, then tightened up on the arc to close distance. Corran then rolled another ninety degrees and continued the turn into a dive. Throttling back, Corran hung in the dive for three seconds, then hauled back hard on the stick and cruised up into the TIE fighter's aft.

The X-wing's laser fire missed wide to the right as the TIE cut to the left. Corran kicked his speed up to full and broke with the TIE. He let the X-wing rise above the plane of the break, then put the fighter through a twisting roll that ate up enough time to bring him again into the TIE's rear. The TIE snapped to the right and Corran looped out left.

He watched the tracking display as the distance between them grew to be a kilometer and a half, then slowed. *Fine, you want to go nose to nose? I've got shields and you don't.* If Commander Antilles wanted to commit virtual suicide, Corran was happy to oblige him. He tugged the stick back to his sternum and rolled out in an inversion loop. *Coming at you!*

The two starfighters closed swiftly. Corran centered his foe in the crosshairs and waited for a dead shot. Without shields the TIE fighter would die with one burst, and Corran wanted the kill to be clean. His HUD flicked green as the TIE juked in and out of the center, then locked green as they closed.

The TIE started firing at maximum range and scored hits. At that distance the lasers did no real damage against the shields, prompting

Corran to wonder why Wedge was wasting the energy. Then, as the HUD's green color started to flicker, realization dawned. *The bright bursts on the shields are a distraction to my targeting! I better kill him now!*

Corran tightened down on the trigger button, sending red laser needles stabbing out at the closing TIE fighter. He couldn't tell if he had hit anything. Lights flashed in the cockpit and Whistler started screeching furiously. Corran's main monitor went black, his shields were down, and his weapons controls were dead.

The pilot looked left and right. "Where is he, Whistler?"

The monitor in front of him flickered to life and a diagnostic report began to scroll by. Bloodred bordered the damage reports. "Scanners, out; lasers, out; shields, out; engine, out! I'm a wallowing Hutt just hanging here in space."

THE COURTSHIP OF PRINCESS LEIA
by Dave Wolverton
Setting: Four years after *Return of the Jedi*

One of the most interesting developments in Bantam's STAR WARS novels is that in their storyline, Han Solo and Princess Leia start a family. This tale reveals how the couple originally got together. Wishing to strengthen the fledgling New Republic by bringing in powerful allies, Leia opens talks with the Hapes consortium of more than sixty worlds. But the consortium is ruled by the Queen Mother, who, to Han's dismay, wants Leia to marry her son, Prince Isolder. Before this action-packed story is over, Luke will join forces with Isolder against a group of Force-trained "witches" and face a deadly foe.

HEIR TO THE EMPIRE
DARK FORCE RISING
THE LAST COMMAND
by Timothy Zahn
Setting: Five years after *Return of the Jedi*

This #1 bestselling trilogy introduces two legendary forces of evil into the STAR WARS literary pantheon. Grand Admiral Thrawn has taken control of the Imperial fleet in the years since the destruction of the Death Star, and the mysterious Joruus C'baoth is a fearsome Jedi Master who has been seduced by the dark side. Han and Leia have now been married for about a year, and as the story begins, she is pregnant with twins. Thrawn's plan is to crush the Rebellion and resurrect the Empire's New Order with C'baoth's help—and in return, the Dark Master will get Han and Leia's Jedi children to mold as he wishes. For as readers of this magnificent trilogy will see, Luke Skywalker is not the last of the old Jedi. He is the first of the new.

The Jedi Academy Trilogy:
JEDI SEARCH
DARK APPRENTICE
CHAMPIONS OF THE FORCE
by Kevin J. Anderson
Setting: Seven years after *Return of the Jedi*

In order to assure the continuation of the Jedi Knights, Luke Skywalker has decided to start a training facility: a Jedi Academy. He will gather Force-sensitive students who show potential as prospective Jedi and serve as their mentor, as Jedi Masters Obi-Wan Kenobi and Yoda did for him. Han and Leia's twins are now toddlers, and there is a third Jedi child: the infant Anakin, named after Luke and Leia's father. In this trilogy, we discover the existence of a powerful Imperial doomsday weapon, the horrifying Sun Crusher—which will soon become the centerpiece of a titanic struggle between Luke Skywalker and his most brilliant Jedi Academy student, who is delving dangerously into the dark side.

The Hand of Thrawn
SPECTER OF THE PAST
and coming soon,
VISION OF THE FUTURE
by Timothy Zahn

The new, two-book series by the undisputed master of the STAR WARS novel. Once the supreme master of countless star systems, the Empire is tottering on the brink of total collapse. Day by day, neutral systems are rushing to join the New Republic coalition. But with the end of the war in sight, the New Republic has fallen victim to it own success. An unwieldy alliance of races and traditions, the confederation now finds itself riven by age-old animosities. Princess Leia struggles against all odds to hold the New Republic together. But she has powerful enemies. An ambitious Moff Disra leads a conspiracy to divide the uneasy coalition with an ingenious plot to blame the Bothans for a heinous crime that could lead to genocide and civil war. At the same time,

Luke Skywalker, along with Lando Calrissian and Talon Karrde, pursues a mysterious group of pirate ships whose crew consists of clones. And then comes the worst news of all: the most cunning and ruthless warlord in Imperial history has returned to lead the Empire to triumph. Here's an exciting scene from Timothy Zahn's spectacular new STAR WARS novel:

"I don't think you fully understand the political situation the New Republic finds itself in these days. A flash point like Caamas—especially with Bothan involvement—will bring the whole thing to a boil. Particularly if we can give it the proper nudge."

"The situation among the Rebels is not the issue," Tierce countered coldly. "It's the state of the Empire *you* don't seem to understand. Simply tearing the Rebellion apart is not going to rebuild the Emperor's New Order. We need a focal point, a leader around whom the Imperial forces can rally.

Disra said. "Suppose I could provide such a leader. Would you be willing to join us?"

Tierce eyed him. "Who is this 'us' you refer to?"

"If you join, there would be three of us," Disra said. "Three who would share the secret I'm prepared to offer you. A secret that will bring the entire Fleet onto our side."

Tierce smiled cynically. "You'll forgive me, Your Excellency, if I suggest you couldn't inspire blind loyalty in a drugged bantha."

Disra felt a flash of anger. How dare this common soldier—?

"No," he agreed, practically choking out the word from between clenched teeth. Tierce was hardly a common soldier, after all. More importantly, Disra desperately needed a man of his skills and training. "I would merely be the political power behind the throne. Plus the supplier of military men and matériel, of course."

"From the Braxant Sector Fleet?"

"And other sources," Disra said. "You, should you choose to join us, would serve as the architect of our overall strategy."

"I see." If Tierce was bothered by the word 'serve,' he didn't show it. "And the third person?"

"Are you with us?"

Tierce studied him. "First tell me more."

"I'll do better than tell you." Disra pushed his chair back and stood up. "I'll show you."

Disra led the way down the rightmost corridor. It ended in a dusty metal door with a wheel set into its center. Gripping the edges of the wheel, Disra turned; and with a creak that echoed eerily in the confined space the door swung open.

The previous owner would hardly have recognized his onetime torture chamber. The instruments of pain and terror had been taken out, the walls and floor cleaned and carpet-insulated, and the furnishings of a fully functional modern apartment installed.

But for the moment Disra had no interest in the chamber itself. All his attention was on Tierce as the former Guardsman stepped into the room.

Stepped into the room . . . and caught sight of the room's single occupant, seated in the center in a duplicate of a Star Destroyer's captain's chair.

Tierce froze, his eyes widening with shock, his entire body stiffening as if a power current had jolted through him. His eyes darted to Disra, back to the captain's chair, flicked around the room as if seeking evidence of a trap or hallucination or perhaps his own insanity, back again to the chair. Disra held his breath . . .

CHILDREN OF THE JEDI
by Barbara Hambly
Setting: Eight years after *Return of the Jedi*

The STAR WARS characters face a menace from the glory days of the Empire when a thirty-year-old automated Imperial Dreadnaught comes to life and begins its grim mission: to gather forces and annihilate a long-forgotten stronghold of Jedi children. When Luke is whisked onboard, he begins to communicate with the brave Jedi Knight who paralyzed the ship decades ago, and gave her life in the process. Now she is part of the vessel, existing in its artificial intelligence core, and guiding Luke through one of the most unusual adventures he has ever had.

DARKSABER by Kevin J. Anderson
Setting: Immediately thereafter

Not long after Children of the Jedi, *Luke and Han learn that evil Hutts are building a reconstruction of the original Death Star—and that the Empire is still alive, in the form of Daala, who has joined forces with Pellaeon, former second in command to the feared Grand Admiral Thrawn.*

PLANET OF TWILIGHT
by Barbara Hambly
Setting: Nine years after *Return of the Jedi*

Concluding the epic tale begun in her own novel Children of the Jedi
and continued by Kevin Anderson in Darksaber, *Barbara Hambly tells
the story of a ruthless enemy of the New Republic operating out of a
backwater world with vast mineral deposits. The first step in his cam-
paign is to kidnap Princess Leia. Meanwhile, as Luke Skywalker
searches the planet for his long-lost love Callista, the planet begins to
reveal its unspeakable secret—a secret that threatens the New Republic, the Empire and the entire galaxy.*

The first to die was a midshipman named Koth Barak. One of his
fellow crewmembers on the New Republic escort cruiser *Adamantine*
found him slumped across the table in the deck-nine break room
where he'd repaired half an hour previously for a cup of coffeine.
Twenty minutes after Barak should have been back to post, Gunnery
Sergeant Gallie Wover went looking for him.

When she entered the deck-nine break room, Sergeant Wover's first
sight was of the palely flickering blue on blue of the infolog screen.
"Blast it, Koth, I told you . . ."

Then she saw the young man stretched unmoving on the far side of
the screen, head on the break table, eyes shut. Even at a distance of
three meters Wover didn't like the way he was breathing.

"Koth!" She rounded the table in two strides, sending the other
chairs clattering into a corner. She thought his eyelids moved a little
when she yelled his name. "Koth!"

Wover hit the emergency call almost without conscious decision. In
the few minutes before the med droids arrived she sniffed the coffeine
in the gray plastene cup a few minutes from his limp fingers. It wasn't
even cold.

Behind her the break room door *swoshed* open. She glanced over
her shoulder to see a couple of Two-Onebees enter with a table, which
was already unfurling scanners and life-support lines like a monster in
a bad holovid. They shifted Barak onto the table and hooked him up.
Every line of the readouts plunged, and soft, tinny alarms began to
sound.

Barak's face had gone a waxen gray. The table was already pumping stimulants and antishock into the boy's veins. Wover could see the
initial diagnostic lines on the screen that ringed the antigrav personnel
transport unit's sides.

No virus. No bacteria. No Poison.

No foreign material in Koth Barak's body at all.
The lines dipped steadily towards zero, then went flat.

THE CRYSTAL STAR
by Vonda N. McIntyre
Setting: Ten years after *Return of the Jedi*

*Leia's three children have been kidnapped. That horrible fact is made
worse by Leia's realization that she can no longer sense her children
through the Force! While she, Artoo-Detoo, and Chewbacca trail the
kidnappers, Luke and Han discover a planet that is suffering strange
quantum effects from a nearby star. Slowly freezing into a perfect
crystal and disrupting the Force, the star is blunting Luke's power and
crippling the Millennium Falcon. These strands converge in an apoca-
lyptic threat not only to the fate of the New Republic, but to the
universe itself.*

The Black Fleet Crisis
BEFORE THE STORM
SHIELD OF LIES
TYRANT'S TEST
by Michael P. Kube-McDowell
Setting: Twelve years after *Return of the Jedi*

*Long after setting up the hard-won New Republic, yesterday's Rebels
have become today's administrators and diplomats. But the peace is
not to last for long. A restless Luke must journey to his mother's
homeworld in a desperate quest to find her people; Lando seizes a
mysterious spacecraft with unimaginable weapons of destruction; and
waiting in the wings is a horrific battle fleet under the control of a
ruthless leader bent on a genocidal war.*

Here is an opening scene from Before the Storm:

In the pristine silence of space, the Fifth Battle Group of the New
Republic Defense Fleet blossomed over the planet Bessimir like a
beautiful, deadly flower.

The formation of capital ships sprang into view with startling sud-
denness, trailing fire-white wakes of twisted space and bristling with
weapons. Angular Star Destroyers guarded fat-hulled fleet carriers,
while the assault cruisers, their mirror finishes gleaming, took the
point.

A halo of smaller ships appeared at the same time. The fighters among them quickly deployed in a spherical defensive screen. As the Star Destroyers firmed up their formation, their flight decks quickly spawned scores of additional fighters.

At the same time, the carriers and cruisers began to disgorge the bombers, transports, and gunboats they had ferried to the battle. There was no reason to risk the loss of one fully loaded—a lesson the Republic had learned in pain. At Orinda, the commander of the fleet carrier *Endurance* had kept his pilots waiting in the launch bays, to protect the smaller craft from Imperial fire as long as possible. They were still there when *Endurance* took the brunt of a Super Star Destroyer attack and vanished in a ball of metal fire.

Before long more than two hundred warships, large and small, were bearing down on Bessimir and its twin moons. But the terrible, restless power of the armada could be heard and felt only by the ships' crews. The silence of the approach was broken only on the fleet comm channels, which had crackled to life in the first moments with encoded bursts of noise and cryptic ship-to-ship chatter.

At the center of the formation of great vessels was the flagship of the Fifth Battle Group, the fleet carrier *Intrepid*. She was so new from the yards at Hakassi that her corridors still reeked of sealing compound and cleaning solvent. Her huge realspace thruster engines still sang with the high-pitched squeal that the engine crews called "the baby's cry."

It would take more than a year for the mingled scents of the crew to displace the chemical smells from the first impressions of visitors. But after a hundred more hours under way, her engines' vibrations would drop two octaves, to the reassuring thrum of a seasoned thruster bank.

On *Intrepid*'s bridge, a tall Dornean in general's uniform paced along an arc of command stations equipped with large monitors. His eye-folds were swollen and fanned by an unconscious Dornean defensive reflex, and his leathery face was flushed purple by concern. Before the deployment was even a minute old, Etahn A'baht's first command had been bloodied.

The fleet tender *Ahazi* had overshot its jump, coming out of hyperspace too close to Bessimir and too late for its crew to recover from the error. Etahn A'baht watched the bright flare of light in the upper atmosphere from *Intrepid*'s forward viewstation, knowing that it meant six young men were dead.

THE NEW REBELLION
by Kristine Kathryn Rusch
Setting: Thirteen years after *Return of the Jedi*

Victorious though the New Republic may be, there is still no end to the threats to its continuing existence—this novel explores the price of keeping the peace. First, somewhere in the galaxy, millions suddenly perish in a blinding instant of pain. Then, as Leia prepares to address the Senate on Coruscant, a horrifying event changes the governmental equation in a flash.

Here is that latter calamity, in an early scene from The New Rebellion:

An explosion rocked the Chamber, flinging Leia into the air. She flew backward and slammed onto a desk, her entire body shuddering with the power of her hit. Blood and shrapnel rained around her. Smoke and dust rose, filling the room with a grainy darkness. She could hear nothing. With a shaking hand, she touched the side of her face. Warmth stained her cheeks and her earlobes. The ringing would start soon. The explosion was loud enough to affect her eardrums.

Emergency glow panels seared the gloom. She could feel rather than hear pieces of the crystal ceiling fall to the ground. A guard had landed beside her, his head tilted at an unnatural angle. She grabbed his blaster. She had to get out. She wasn't certain if the attack had come from within or from without. Wherever it had come from, she had to make certain no other bombs would go off.

The force of the explosion had affected her balance. She crawled over bodies, some still moving, as she made her way to the stairs. The slightest movement made her dizzy and nauseous, but she ignored the feelings. She had to.

A face loomed before hers. Streaked with dirt and blood, helmet askew, she recognized him as one of the guards who had been with her since Alderaan. *Your Highness*, he mouthed, and she couldn't read the rest. She shook her head at him, gasping at the increased dizziness, and kept going.

Finally she reached the stairs. She used the remains of a desk to get to her feet. Her gown was soaked in blood, sticky, and clinging to her legs. She held the blaster in front of her, wishing that she could hear. If she could hear, she could defend herself.

A hand reached out of the rubble beside her. She whirled, faced it, watched as Meido pulled himself out. His slender features were covered with dirt, but he appeared unharmed. He saw her blaster and cringed. She nodded once to acknowledge him, and kept moving. The guard was flanking her.

More rubble dropped from the ceiling. She crouched, hands over her head to protect herself. Small pebbles pelted her, and the floor shivered as large chunks of tile fell. Dust rose, choking her. She coughed, feeling it, but not able to hear it. Within an instant, the Hall had gone from a place of ceremonial comfort to a place of death.

The image of the death's-head mask rose in front of her again, this time from memory. She had known this was going to happen. Somewhere, from some part of her Force-sensitive brain, she had seen this. Luke said that Jedi were sometimes able to see the future. But she had never completed her training. She wasn't a Jedi.

But she was close enough.

The Corellian Trilogy:
AMBUSH AT CORELLIA
ASSAULT AT SELONIA
SHOWDOWN AT CENTERPOINT
by Roger MacBride Allen
Setting: Fourteen years after *Return of the Jedi*

This trilogy takes us to Corellia, Han Solo's homeworld, which Han has not visited in quite some time. A trade summit brings Han, Leia, and the children—now developing their own clear personalities and instinctively learning more about their innate skills in the Force—into the middle of a situation that most closely resembles a burning fuse. The Corellian system is on the brink of civil war, there are New Republic intelligence agents on a mysterious mission which even Han does not understand, and worst of all, a fanatical rebel leader has his hands on a superweapon of unimaginable power—and just wait until you find out who that leader is!

JOIN

STAR WARS®

on the INTERNET

Bantam Spectra invites you to visit their Official STAR WARS® Web Site.

You'll find:

< Sneak previews of upcoming STAR WARS® novels.

< Samples from audio editions of the novels.

< Bulletin boards that put you in touch with other fans, with the authors, and with the Spectra editors who bring them to you.

< The latest word from behind the scenes of the STAR WARS® universe.

< Quizzes, games, and contests available only on-line.

< Links to other STAR WARS® licensees' sites on the Internet.

< Look for STAR WARS® on the World Wide Web at:

http://www.bantam/spectra.com

SF 28 8/97